The Scriver Archives
Book One

JACK SERPENT

E. A. FIELD

This book is a work of fiction. Any references to historical events, real people, or real places are used fictitiously. Other names, characters, places, and events are products of the author's imagination, and any resemblance to actual events, places, names, or persons, is entirely coincidental.

Text copyright © 2025 by E.A. Field

All rights reserved. For information regarding reproduction in total or in part contact Rising Action Publishing at http://www.risingactionpublishingco.com

Cover Illustration © **Nat Mack**
Distributed by **Simon & Schuster**
Proofread by **Sally O'Keef**
Map Design by **Chris Davis**

ISBN: 978-1-998076-73-4
Ebook: 978-1-998076-74-1

FIC009070   FICTION / Fantasy / Dark Fantasy
FIC009100   FICTION / Fantasy / Action & Adventure
FIC009120   FICTION / Fantasy / Dragons & Mythical Creatures

#JackSerpent
#TheScriverArchives

Follow Rising Action on our socials!
Instagram: @risingactionpublishingco
Tiktok: @risingactionpublishingco

For the dreamers who dared to ask why and then worked their butts off to make it happen

JACK SERPENT

Chapter One

Out of 123,000 attempts at creating the perfect barrier between monsters and magic, only five people survived the three trials and earned the title of Scriver. Of the five, there remains only one.
~ Scryptus, The Scriver Archives, Tome 1

Like an infected animal it was unusual to see a Stryga out in daylight. She fled across the Dred Plains in a torrent of stench, and Jack followed at a leisurely distance.

Combus ipsa mala. Burn the Stryga.

Iron, feces, and the sour stink of tainted magic filled Jack's nostrils. Most humans could smell a Stryga if she was close, but his trained nose could scent her miles away. She must have sensed the Milytor hunters on her trail. Jack sighed as he broke into a jog. The soldiers who were also tracking the Stryga operated with all the subtly of a charging gorgon.

Though the Milytor was made up of different branches, all the soldiers belonged to the Royal Guard. These two apparently were from the arcane branch since they were pursuing a Stryga in the open. The Milytor didn't always have the best weapons against magic. Fire and bullets didn't always get the job done. Most people liked to burn them, but sometimes a clever Stryga would bind her soul to a familiar and escape the flames.

Jack had hunted lesser Strygan for over a year now, trying to find out what truly killed them now that they were becoming more than the pests of nightmares. It wouldn't have been such a problem if the Strygan weren't also waking up beasts that hadn't been seen in centuries, if ever.

Rumors swirled like thrown daggers all over Asnor—the High Stryga was gathering a force to her. Strygan, *true* Strygan, were rare, because becoming one required stealing a great amount of magic or sacrificing something no human would want to, either a soul or blood to the point of death. Jack had also been told that they could only procreate with warlocks, whom they enslaved if they would not come willingly. *Who would?* Jack thought with a grimace. Strygan were known to kill any offspring that weren't female because only the females had any magical ability. That war loomed on the horizon.

He adjusted the goblin-made transmitter that fit into his ear. Goblins' spindly fingers were the best at crafting advanced weapons like the gem-stone transmitter the Milytor used. Jack had long ago pilfered a few items, before he'd left Asnor. His transmitter was an older model, since he'd been away from Ocrana for almost ten years tracking and recording all the dark magic and beasts he could find, but it should do the job.

Jack tilted his head to make the buzzing go away. He appreciated the goblins making the devices, but they hadn't quite perfected a long-range communication system yet. The goblins used moon-pool stones to capture sound and transmit it using a simple location spell that they'd altered to cast voices. Locator or communication spells utilized various "frequencies" that also depended on what type of transmitter was used. Ruby-infused transmitters could pick up any communication, but cheaper, older morganite could only pick up a few. Jack could spy from a few miles away, but that also depended on what frequency the soldiers used. All Milytor transmitters employed ruby and moon-pool stone because they were like sponges, able to hold magic for a long time. He wasn't concerned that their equipment was out of date. The devices were convenient—one did not have to be able to use magic or make a sacrifice to use them. The spelled stones did that and allowed for transmission of voice.

A hum alerted him to a flyer overhead. People were still getting used to the sight of the flying ships that now allowed for faster transport of goods across the Elgarian sky.

His rumbling stomach almost veered him off mission. How long had it been since he'd walked an actual market with people? Baking bread, fresh fruit, and sugared treats drifted on the air over the slight stench of sewage and animal manure. And pie. Jack took a deep sniff, and his feet betrayed him, straying toward the bakeshop, its windowsill lined with fresh confectionary. Fruit pie, chocolate pie, meat pie—he didn't discriminate as long as the crust was flaky, and the filling was thick. *Focus, Serpent*, he chided himself.

Voices of two soldiers he didn't know spoke over the comms. Ah, the correct frequency on only his third guess. The gods—or god, depending on your region—might be giving him a slight gift. The goblin transmitters couldn't be tracked, so they didn't know he listened in.

"I see her," a young male voice said in his ear.

"She's heading out of Asnor toward the Dred Plains," another male, older, said in a low tone. He had an O'Nym accent, bit of a lilt, from the southernmost continent. O'Nym was one of the languages Jack had enjoyed learning—the rolling of the tongue, the carefully placed consonants.

"Uncle Gunner, do we persist?"

The deeper voice replied, "Go."

Jack recognized the cryptonym of Narim Gunneran and pictured the tall, blond-haired mercenary with steely gray eyes. It hadn't been so long that Jack had forgotten his fellow soldier, and the other man would most definitely remember the scar Jack had given him in their last encounter.

Jack usually picked his own path and tracked alone. It was just happenstance that these soldiers were on the same trail as him. Or perhaps it was no coincidence—General Grimarr was a clever bastard, and the grizzled man had been trying to contact him for months now. It was getting harder and harder to ignore. The general was an old family friend, but Jack didn't like to keep ties that someone could use against him.

He headed to High Staff stables to collect the blue roan stallion that had come to his aid fighting a gorgon five years ago. The horse had simply shown up and distracted the beast, giving Jack time to discover that the gorgon's weakness was toffee. Ever since then, the horse had stayed with him. While Jack liked to think his equestrian skills and animal communication above average, he couldn't take any credit for the companion seeming to understand him even without commands.

Two stable boys were having a heated argument over the Covering and Strygan.

"Me sister's a Stryga, I swear," the stable boy said to his mate with an emphatic tilt of his chin.

"She can't be. Strygan are born, not made." The freckle-faced boy spit into the bushes and picked up a brush.

"Then explain how she disappears within seconds, and why all of the sudden our dog finds gold."

The first one shrugged, and the redhead began brushing a bay horse to a shine. "Maybe she's a sorceress. Might be less frightenin'."

"They don't exist, Seamus. Houses closed up years ago."

The boy named Seamus shrugged with a curled lip. "I've tried a bit of magic meself; doesn't make me a warlock. She could be dabblin' in fool magic as long as she's givin' somethin' up."

Jack hid a smile as he tightened the horse's girth. He led Shertan down the stone path past the boys, and as he passed, he leaned toward Seamus.

"Your friend is correct," he said as he mounted, leather creaking. The boys gaped at him.

"How would you know?" Seamus pointed, and his friend slapped his rude finger down.

"Don't point at him! He'll curse ya, he's a bloody Scriver." The other boy had switched to the local Asnorian tongue instead of the mostly universal Elgarian.

"He's probably not even a real one. They don't exist just like Malecanta don't."

"Scrivers do exist. I'm sure at least *one* does." He rolled his words. "I told ya there was somethin' off about that horse. Bad luck."

"He could have stolen that sigil. Anyone can use it."

Jack raised a brow. The language was one he'd grown up with. "If you're going to accuse someone, you should be sure they don't understand, or it's a good way to get a knife in your chest."

The boys turned to face him outright, eyes wide. A tremble started in the dark-haired one's hand.

"I told ya, Scrivers speak all the languages, feckin' idiot," Seamus muttered.

His friend shrugged.

"I can't claim to speak all the languages, though I suggest learning more Cafferian—better for insults anyway." Jack gave them a dry look.

The Cafferian people were starting to prefer the coastal wealth that Elgar offered—and their rich soil. And it was true, they had more words for curses than any other language he knew.

"Just cuz he knows a few languages don't make him a true Scriver. What is a Scriver, anyway?" He scratched his chin and wiggled his nose.

His friend shrugged again. "Me da says they were experiments the Milytor couldn't control. Me mum says they're to take bad children away if they don't listen or eat properly."

Jack tilted his head at them. "Or maybe there's just one who has the dull task of finding and recording continental histories that mainly get him burned pies and bad company."

Both boys tilted their heads at him.

"I was just a wee lad when the trials were run," Seamus said. "If you is one of them who made it, then it can't be good news for us. Scrivers bring the darkness. Bugger off." He made a protection sign over his chest and motioned for his friend to do the same.

Jack chuckled at the bickering. At least with boys, there was little fear of a knife thrown at his back or a cursed coin tossed his way. He urged the horse into a trot and left the two to wonder.

He was used to people shying away from the Scriver name and sigil. When they'd gained notoriety after the very public trials, there were also several rogue soldiers who claimed the title, giving them a foul reputation he hadn't even been aware of until a few years ago. As far as he knew three had perished and supposedly Cozael was still around. The entire town of Asnor had shut down for the spectacle of the trials like they were the Centaur Games of old. Spectators from all the continents came for food, drink, and entertainment. Other realms tried to copy them, but only Grimarr and Alaric could have come up with the true tests. They utilized magic to be the final judge on who passed, and everyone loved a good spectacle—especially if it involved life and death. The Scriver

JACK SERPENT

Trials were a spectacle that brought in revenue and prestige and served as a demonstration of Asnor's military intelligence and prowess. After they were over, like most things, the Scrivers fell into a shadowed path of twisted men.

What had been vaulted as a highly skilled, hybrid soldier to protect the people became tainted and feared. Most people wanted to believe their way of life was safe and that if they ignored the darkness, it wouldn't hurt them.

It wasn't even that the position paid well, either. Jack had never been after a dragon's hoard of gold, so the little din and san coin that flowed from the fortress monastery was enough to keep him fed and his weapons in good repair. His parents had also left him a significant inheritance, but that was something he wasn't ready to touch.

Shertan bounded into a smooth canter as they made it to open road. His long, wavy mane and tail streamed in the wind. He was a good mountain horse with a broad back and a smooth, steady gait. The blue roan coat appeared almost black sometimes, and he had striking white socks on two forelimb fetlocks, along with a white star on his forehead.

As they left the busy town behind, Jack thought about the boys' conversation. A lot of humans used magic, but they could only use it in small doses, because all magic required sacrifice. Most people were willing to give up modest amounts of blood, nails, teeth, breath, or hair. To truly wield powerful magic, though, one had to be prepared to sacrifice something far greater. Strygan had once been human and inherently had very little magic of their own. They were, however, clever. They made excellent thieves of magic when they didn't want to sacrifice. And they'd become so twisted they couldn't even mate with human males anymore, needing warlocks instead.

Asnor's famed fields rolled by in patches of green, gold, and yellow. Pumpkins, cornfields, soybeans, and barley rose all around him. A crisp breeze sifted through his hair, and he could almost forget what he was on the way to do. The trees were burning orange and red, the fields ready for harvest.

Jack guided the horse up a low hill and into forested land. The pounding of horses' hooves and shouts sounded ahead. He stayed in the cover of the trees, ducking under branches.

Shertan obediently stopped when Jack shifted his weight back and gave a slight pull on the reins. As he chomped at the bit between his teeth, Jack slid down and opened his pack. The Eagle's Claw Phantom long gun wasn't the newest model, but he'd rigged a few parts for his own purposes. All Phantom models had scopes for distance shooting, but hunting down ghouls, demons, and other monsters required different weapons. In this instance, he had a new hex bullet he wanted to try. He crafted his own bullets, but for scattershots, long guns, and even some swords, there was no better smithing than what the dwarves provided.

Jack climbed a tree with spiked handgrips and settled on a branch, about a thousand paces from the hunters. The scent of the Stryga stung his nose. Amid the leaves, he set up the Phantom in a matter of seconds with practiced, precise movements. The hunters had managed to corner the Stryga, but she had a hostage. Jack sighed. Damn Strygan would never learn that it only made their situation worse. The older woman's long, unkempt brown hair wound around the young boy's neck; her knife was poised above his heart. She was speaking, so he turned on the transmitter to listen in.

"Let the boy go!" The lead Milytor, who had brown hair and a scar down his cheek, fidgeted with the pistol he had trained on her. A Winstar 238—ten rounds, light Carbina steel, and an eight-inch barrel was way too underpowered to take a Stryga down. She'd be injured, but Jack would be surprised if the hexed bullets killed her. Strygan were spelled against pistol bullets. Hadn't they read his notes? To be fair, Jack often forgot to record his findings for months in the thin leather book he carried with him. The spelled pages and ink told of all manner of creatures living in Elgar and the other four continents. The young soldiers were just that—young and inexperienced.

The other soldiers aimed Piat scattershots at her. Better.

The Stryga laughed—Jack heard that plainly—and drew blood from the boy's chest. He screamed as the blade ripped a jagged wound that bled through his shirt.

Jack focused the Phantom's scope and searched for an opening. He tapped the stock for good luck and steadied his breath. He calculated the wind speed and trajectory quickly as he aimed, taking into account the fact that she could duck at any moment. He waited for the exact second the Stryga's head was just behind the boy's shoulder. She was using him as a meat shield, but the slightest patch of her forehead could be seen. This would be the steadiest she'd be for the next few seconds. The shot would have to go through the boy to get her.

The Phantom recoiled against Jack's shoulder as the bullet flew.

The boy lurched as the bullet went straight through and exploded into the Stryga's head. She fell backward, releasing the boy, who fell in a bloody mess, clutching his shoulder and screaming.

Jack tried not to be overly pleased that his new hexed bullet had worked so well despite the damage to the boy. A clean shot through flesh and the magic wards the Stryga had on her.

The soldiers cursed and looked around for the shooter. They scrambled to take cover by their horses and cast shield spells. One of the men knelt and picked up the bullet—it had gone straight through both bodies. He held it up to show his partner.

"Who has an Eagle around here? I thought only tier one Milytor had those."

"They could be thousands of strides away. We should report to General Grimarr."

They remained silent for a minute, and when Jack sent no other fire, they must have assumed the shooter was running away. The soldiers crept back out from behind their horses.

"Do we take the body back?"

"Negative, leave the bitch."

"What about the boy?"

The soldier in charge glanced at the shivering mess of a human. He waved his pistol around with indecision.

Jack waited. *Leave him, he's not the target,* he willed the soldier. The man lifted his gun.

This is why no one in Asnor thinks the king will save them. I thought Cozael was staying around Asnor as the resident Scriver, Jack thought. He hadn't gotten close to any of the other combatants, nor did he even pretend he was interested in what happened to them after, but he kept informed through Grimarr.

There were too many reports of soldiers going on the attack, mistaking civilians for monsters. Creatures like Strygan and warlocks were adept at looking and acting human, serving as spies for their kind. Of course, it was no large stretch because at one time they had been human.

Jack had seconds to decide. He raised the Phantom and pulled the trigger. The soldier's pistol exploded out of his hand, most likely taking some skin with it. The man cursed and cradled his hand.

"What the fuck was that?"

In panic, they took shelter again behind their horses.

The second soldier swore heavily, and Jack heard him pull out another pistol. "Maybe she put a protection curse on him."

She wouldn't, Jack thought with a roll of his eyes.

The boy whimpered and curled into himself. Jack's lips thinned as his decision demanded follow-through—he couldn't just disappear now. First, he needed to examine the body and ensure that his bullet had actually killed the Stryga. Second, he wasn't going to leave a boy bleeding on the ground when it was his fault.

Jack pressed the talk button on the transmitter and hoped it was the right frequency. He would be the first in line when the goblins tried dragon stones instead of moon-pool. They foretold of everyone having a transmitter in their homes to communicate with eventually. For now, only the wealthiest or Milytor had them.

The first try was dead air. He clicked the only other button on the transmitter to strengthen the signal.

"Leave the boy. The Stryga is mine," Jack said into the transmitter.

All four soldiers exchanged incredulous looks and then scanned the forest around them as if looking for a ghost. Their faces paled.

"Who in Corvynia's tits is this?"

Jack debated for a moment. He had no desire to remain in Asnor for long, but Grimarr *had* been trying to contact him for a year.

"Tell the general his Scriver has returned home."

The soldiers mounted up with alarmed faces and started back toward Asnor. Judging from the furious movement of their lips, it would soon be all over the Milytor that he was back.

Jack had trouble admitting that being back in Asnor made him feel closer to Alaric, his former mentor. There had been a certain camaraderie he'd enjoyed being part of something that felt bigger than himself—until his illusions were shattered.

He waited until they left, then mounted Shertan and went down to the boy. The child didn't have the strength to run—he just gazed at Jack with pain-ridden eyes.

"You'll live. The bullet passed through, but it'll leave a nice scar, so be sure to make up a good tale for the ladies," Jack said as he dismounted. He took a bottle of arrunroot from his pack and poured the healing elixir over the wound as the boy squirmed. He saved a bit for the boy to swallow. "Keep pressure here."

"You're a soldier?" The boy inched away.

Jack nodded. He was, in a sense.

"You would have killed me if I had been an inch to the left," the boy panted. He applied a clean cloth to his right shoulder.

Jack didn't answer as he dressed the wound. His transmitter chirped with the two soldiers' talk.

"... he's here. Do we bring him in?"

"He'll come in," a new, gruffer voice chimed in. Narim Gunner.

"The Scriver will come on his own? Shouldn't we alert the general?"

"He's listening, you feckin' idiots. Yes, he will." The channel went silent at his pointed words.

The boy shook and attempted a weak scoot away. Jack sighed and put his hands up in an innocent gesture. The wound was wrapped securely.

"You're a Scriver? I didn't think there were any left."

"So I've heard."

"I heard Scrivers don't leave anyone alive." The boy's Adam's apple bobbled violently.

Jack arched a left brow. "Then my shot wouldn't have landed where it did."

The boy gaped at him but didn't have a retort.

Jack lit the Stryga's remains on fire to ensure she didn't come back. Then he remounted and listened to the transmitter again on another frequency. Snatches of conversation flowed in his ear.

Jack would not be coming near the Milytor camp nor the castle grounds unless they dangled a huge-ass carrot in front of him. He'd find a way to speak with Grimarr that did not involve parading in front of soldiers like a Drannit-damned unicorn. A low voice caught his attention just as he was about to change the frequency.

"Jack, Grimarr has been tasked to bring you in. The king requires an audience. Don't make us waste resources tracking you down," Narim said.

Jack pursed his lips. What would make King Thuramond command his general to find him?

"I want a Cafferian bourbon when I get there," Jack said after a minute. The resulting chuckle was all too familiar, and one he didn't trust in the least. "I have to tie up a few things first."

"Affirmed." The transmitter went silent.

As much as Jack detested royalty, he couldn't ignore a summons. And if Grimarr had to waste his time finding Jack, the general would be in a less-than-friendly mood.

Jack nudged Shertan with his heels, and they started back toward Asnor with the Stryga's remains smoldering behind them. The boy could make it back to his home. A heavy pit formed in Jack's stomach. In all his years recording and hunting monsters, Strygan were the most elusive because they were not interested in peace that benefited everyone. They always wanted power.

Chapter Two

There are a number of poisonous snakes and toads that reside in Gretch swamp (in the realm of Vedan). Some have migrated as far east as the Proepucia swamp. If you see any orange stripes with speckling, be sure to tread carefully.
~ Scryptus, The Scriver Archives,
as recounted by Scriver #5 Jack Serpent, Tome 5

Aylla ducked low and kept to the side of the game trail. She held her notched bow in front of her at an angle and swung her braided hair over her shoulder. In her peripheral vision, two wolf shadows darted behind her. Tall trees with long, sweeping leaves swayed in the autumn breeze with their leaves tinged yellow and fluorescent red. The forest was alive with life seen and unseen. Aylla was good at tracking both.

JACK SERPENT

"Ash, Hugo, *varten, vartir*," she whispered in a low tone that was more of a bark. The old language of the Maidens was all but dead. It came in handy when speaking to her charges—no one else could command them.

She had painted a charcoal-gray mud-ink mixture around her eyes like a mask. The paint was spelled for protection as well as letting her communicate with the wolves more effectively. She suspected it wasn't just the magic, but that they read her expressions and understood her bark-like commands. Aylla didn't mess around with magic very much, but the simple huntress spell in the paint allowed her to connect more intimately with the animals.

Ash loped ahead, silvery gray in the light, while Hugo, darker and younger, slowed to stay behind her. Aylla froze. Leaves rustled ahead, and a stick twanged. She pulled back on the string and waited. A boar wandered into sight, snuffling at the ground, its cloven hooves and tusks digging up the underbrush in search of grubs and mushrooms. She aimed carefully.

The boar screamed in alarm, shattering the calm.

Aylla spun in a tight circle, aiming the point of the arrow toward whatever threat the boar had seen. But there was nothing, no movement of a larger predator. The boar shrieked again as a black substance rose from the ground, coating and choking it. The animal fell over, twitching on its side, and let out increasingly painful grunts. Aylla stood from her crouch, slid the arrow back in the quiver, slung the bow on her back, and took out her Winstar 459 pistols. They were loaded with eight rounds each and were a large enough caliber to take out a charging plains cat.

She approached cautiously even though every fiber in her wanted to put the poor creature out of its misery. The black substance covered his eyes and mouth. Low growls came from either side of her. The wolves refused to get closer and were warning her not to either. Aylla held up a finger, holstered one of the Winstars, and replaced it with a long knife. She quickly severed the spine from the brain, and the boar stopped its pitiful whining. The black substance continued to erode the body as if sucking out all the life. White tendrils of smoke-like essence drifted from the boar and vanished.

Aylla wiped the knife clean on a few large Parshaw leaves. It didn't feel tainted, and the substance hadn't gotten on her. She had seen this last month—a doe she'd been tracking had been attacked by the same black menace. *What in the blighted Drannit is going on?* Her curse was a reflex, not reflecting a belief in the sorcerers turned to gods and goddesses. Everyone prayed to different deities. The continents were moving toward commerce and technology rather than seeking ancient magic. Aylla's mother had been a follower of the Maidens, who worshipped the three goddesses. It was the only reason Aylla even gave a half thought to such things.

Ash disappeared into the black trees. Hugo stayed with her but kept his head low and tail down.

"So much for pack loyalty," she said to the retreating tail. Hugo whined. "I wasn't talking about you. Thanks for having my back, Hugo. What is this shyf?"

The dark wolf licked his lips and paced around her. Something was wrong in the forest, but she couldn't place the source. Aylla didn't want to touch the body, so she shoved dirt over the carcass. There went dinner for the next few days. Hopefully the fishing line she'd set out in the stream fared better. Boar meat was so tasty, though. She sighed. The thought of the stew she had simmering ... it wouldn't taste nearly as good with fish. Which reminded her that she needed more line and hooks, new boots, blankets, and the list went on. As much as she hated to admit it, it was time for a supply run.

"Asnor awaits; aren't you as excited as I am?" Aylla asked the wolf. She marked the spot on her map. The doe and the boar were within ten paces of each other. Like wolves, Aylla kept a good perimeter around what she staked as her "normal territory." A mile took about eighteen minutes to walk, nine minutes to run, depending on the terrain. The doe and boar attacks were too close for her comfort.

Ash came trotting back as they neared the log cabin and the water wheel that chugged along in the shallow stream next to it. The wheel gave her the ability to lift grain sacks into the storage shed beside the cabin, and the filter gave her pure water. It wasn't a large home, but it was hers. And would have been her mother's.

Aylla bowed her head for a moment. Hugo put his big snout under her hand, sensing her sadness.

She didn't bother to lock her doors—this far out in Churk Forest, only lost travelers ever stumbled upon her cabin. The fire was down to embers, which was just as well since she was leaving. She doused it with water, and it sizzled like hissing cats.

Aylla packed a light bag, pulled a dark green cloak around her, and tightened her belt. It allowed her to wear all manner of weapons and tools. Her black shirt kept her warm, and the pants under her long, tapered skirt protected her legs from burs and poisonous shrubs. She put the stew on ice, mined in the deep cave a few miles away that was forever frozen, saving it for later, then washed the paint off. She avoided sticking out whenever possible, and black marks around her eyes would certainly make people suspicious. Some people accepted magic, some even supported it outright like the Volg, but others would run her through if they got a chance.

She surveyed the narrow trail and wished she had a horse or donkey. She'd tried to keep a few horses, but the wolves spooked them so much they nearly broke their necks trying to escape. Elgar wolves were not like those on other continents. She'd seen other species of wolves in geographical books. Elgarian wolves grew twice the size, and with that came an intelligence that made them unfit in every way to be tamed pets or even working farm animals. The scars on Aylla's thighs and neck were evidence of her hard-won prizes.

She smiled. The wolf pack didn't bother her anymore—not since the night she'd stolen two of the alpha female's pups. A pang of regret made her glance at the wolves. She'd taken them from their mother, but she'd been more than enough for them, right? That particular female had had two more litters since.

Hugo and Ash whuffed, waiting to go. She'd given them the chance to return to their pack. Neither had left her.

Aylla had about three hours before sunset, and that was more than enough time to get to the outskirts of Asnor. The city was a capital port of the realm of Ocrana, known for its wealth of goods, untapped veins of magic, and broken monarchy. She bade her two companions stay, and they whined in acknowledgement. They didn't like going near the coastal city anyway.

She picked an easy path through the winding trees and overgrown brush. Within the hour, twilight settled over the land as she made it to the Dred Plains. Farmland stretched like a quilt as far as she could see, a patchwork of different crops ready for harvest. The taller buildings of the inner city loomed in the dusky mist. They towered over a gray wall that surrounded the castle on the hill and the outer soldier's quarters. Beyond that lay the brilliant blue oceans—Aylla had never ventured further than those shores. What lands existed out there were only dreams in her head from the books and maps she'd studied.

Aylla nodded in greeting to the few farmers still out and the tradespeople heading home for the night. She entered Asnor without difficulty despite the guards posted around the perimeter. They were mostly there for show; the king sent all his best soldiers in search of "personal" items or to scout further lands to invade. She had just gotten used to the gas-powered, gem-infused carriages that could move without horses. The people driving them, however, still seemed to need to get used to steering. Only the wealthiest had those new boxes, so there weren't too many to dodge on the street.

Tonight, though, people were riled up and torches flared against the dark sky. They gathered around a central bonfire and gallows. To the left, a woman was tied to a wooden stake, kindling scattered around her. Men and women spat insults, and some held up posters with a Stryga's claw marked on it in crimson.

Others, dressed in layered purple robes with silver belts and embroidered hems, tried to calm them down and protect the woman on the stake. The Volg. Aylla shivered as she kept to the fringes of the crowd. She had to pass the center of the city to get to the Brown Shepherd tavern where she felt secure, not to mention they had the best horseberry pies.

"She has done nothing in accordance with Strygan practices!" a Volg woman shouted at a civilian who'd just thrown a rotten cabbage.

"She's a Stryga! Burn the Stryga!" The chant was taken up by the whole crowd, and the woman moaned as she tried to free herself.

"Strygan are the future. They will lead with more competence than we've seen in a century. The High Stryga will ascend, and everyone will be given fair counsel, a chance to live equally," the Volg woman said, though no one would listen. The skin she showed on her arms was covered in old runic symbols, and her straw-blond hair was kept long, as was a Strygan custom.

The Volg were mostly human, along with some half elves and half goblins, who believed the Strygan were divine. They believed Strygan would bless them, and they'd become more than human. Since Asnor was a free capital, they were allowed to live on its fringes and spread their message. They kept their violence to such a minimum and contributed to the economy enough that most people just ignored them.

Aylla wondered who made their robes. She imagined their leader marching into a tailor and demanding dozens of dark robes with the peculiar, Strygan rune with a sickle, saying they were for "costume" use. Yes, costume parties. She laughed to herself. Whoever helped the Volg put themselves in a precarious position.

Most of them were just loud protesters or vocal Strygan supporters. But of late, they were becoming too violent to be allow free reign. Asnorians were demanding that the king ban them, but he did not seem to hear their complaints.

A fight broke out, and Aylla ducked under a fist. The Volg were getting more and more insistent about how Strygan were the only ones able to wield true magic and thus were the best choice to disperse such power. Aylla had no desire to see or hear a woman burned to death. Pretty soon the townspeople would start to add the Volg themselves to the pyre, she feared. The screams would remind her of her mother's as she'd fought for her life, as she'd struggled against Drace van Hyde.

A hand reached for her. Aylla grabbed the wrist, twisted, and slammed the man into a wooden post on a cart.

The Volg shook his head at the rough contact. He raised his hands innocently. "I only wanted to speak with you about supporting our mission. You look like a capable young woman. You could be valuable in helping establish order with the new Maidens," he said with a kind smile. His purple robe bulged around his middle and several Strygan symbols dangled from a chain belt.

"No, thank you." Aylla shrugged him off. She would have burst into a run, but the crowd pressed against her. She fought the urge to hit the bodies around her to get air. The suffocating chaos started a familiar panic that clenched her stomach and traveled up to her throat.

The arguing rose, and a rogue civilian threw a torch on the accused woman's pyre. The Volg tried to put it out, but the crowd pressed harder, throwing torch after torch. Some of the Volg's robes even caught fire.

Aylla froze as the woman's screams escalated to true pain. The fire licked her dress, burning her legs. Aylla was shoved against a hard wall of bodies and fell under their feet in a state of terror.

The screaming brought back all the darkness she kept in a vault in her mind. She scrabbled back as a foot stomped on her hand. Panting, she jumped up onto a market cart with a canvas roof. Her sturdy, Muran-leather boots gripped the smooth wall, but it was still a struggle to get higher. She slumped onto the canvas with her cloak bunched around her.

Aylla turned and buried her head in her hands. The smell of burning flesh was making her sick. She rocked back and forth as the crowd's raucous shouts grew louder.

She forced herself to look. She wasn't a child, unable to do anything in the face of such cruelty. Not that child who had to see her mother forced to wed her dead husband's brother and then beaten by him—a man who'd claimed to love her.

Her fists clenched around her fingerless gloves, and something snapped inside her head.

A strong wind, much like the one that had been her salvation once, tore through the town center. Hay, dirt, debris, and even a few cats were swept up in a maelstrom, which was so strong it put out the fire and scattered the people. Not even embers remained when it passed.

The Volg wasted no time gathering the unconscious, injured woman and carting her away. The crowd looked around suspiciously, but no one spotted Aylla as she cowered in the shadows on the roof of the market stand. Her hands trembled, and her stomach threatened to bring up vomit if she didn't move.

Aylla ignored the roiling feelings and the tingling of her skin. What was that? It wasn't her. She hadn't done that—she wasn't gifted with magic. She'd given nothing up for a spell. All she'd done was want it to stop. Perhaps the gods had answered her, or perhaps a wind had been cast by a Volg member who could wield magic spells.

The point was, it was over. She waited a few minutes until her limbs would move.

Maybe that woman had been a Stryga, or maybe she'd been in the wrong place at the wrong time. She had a chance now to prove herself. Aylla slowly made her way to the Brown Shepherd tavern. Her body was spent, her mind in a spiral of fog. She needed to lie down.

Aylla gritted her teeth. Just a few more streets.

Chapter Three

I appear to be lost and have been for about seven days' time. The trees in this, unknown, unnamed forest, appear to move. Slowly and mostly at night. Their roots lift and branches sweep any trails or markers, making it impossible for travelers to find their way out. I've seen signs of the man reported missing but have yet to find him, much less a way I would return.

*Archivers note: Dismissed a five-page ramble about compasses, moss growth, and general black attitude from Scriver #5. He did in fact find the lost man and a way out—severely malnourished and dehydrated but all was restored. Unusual method of using Flen Hare feces to mark passages and halt the trees, some sort of barrier they respect. Perhaps not wanting to trample the rabbits' nests.

~Scryptus, the Scriver Archives,
as recounted by Scriver #5 Jack Serpent, Tome 6

Churk Forest, on the north side of Asnor, was known for its plentiful game and black, winding trees. They grew in bent angles in some spots that made it nearly impossible to get out. It was named for the famous explorer Churken, who'd figured out that the trees were sentient beings. Their wood could be crafted into toys that never broke, houses that didn't need repair. However, cutting one down brought the entire forest's wrath. Fighting trees was almost always a losing battle. They remembered those who didn't respect their land and helped those who were lost.

Jack was neither, but the trees never bothered him. He figured Churk Forest was fed from a vein of sorcerer magic left over from the Covering. There were spots all over Elgar and other continents with pockets of magic that were covered with trees or mountains. making it difficult for anyone to get to the magic below. Treasure hunters from all over came to Elgar in search of Ardis, a supposedly mythical substance the Malecanta used to use. It was a pearlescent mineral that could enhance all magic to such a powerful extent that only Malecanta could wield it properly. Jack hadn't ever seen such a thing in the forest, but neither was he searching for it.

The transmitter crackled with another voice on the other end. "Dead Eyes?" The language was universal Elgarian.

Jack sighed. He'd earned that nickname from his short time in the Milytor. Why did they insist on pestering him? He understood he wouldn't be leaving Asnor without granting the general and the king an audience. If he tried, he was certain he'd be met with the force of several dozen soldiers. A fight he could win, but he didn't like the cost of killing innocent people.

"What?" He attached the transmitter over his ear to hear better. The rabbit he was cooking sizzled over the fire.

"There's been a riot tonight. Volg are getting bolder." It was Narim Gunneran again. The man's deep voice held no affection. No doubt he still blamed Jack for the incident with his partner.

"Isn't that your area of expertise? I'm tracking another *mala*. I'll be in when I'm done," Jack said, and tore a chunk off the rabbit's hind leg. The meat's toughness was slick with delicious fat. He glanced around the small clearing and the makeshift shelter he'd built for the night. Not many creatures liked to venture into Churk Forest—and certainly not many people either. He'd roamed these woods as a kid when his father had served in the Milytor, and they lived in Asnor.

"Unlike everyone else, I don't fear you or believe the rumors. Don't make Grimarr waste his time."

Jack pursed his lips. "He'll find me when he truly wishes."

"Cozael died seven months ago fighting a Stryga," Narim said in a low, annoyed tone. "I could have put up a better fight against a diseased Korykoa."

Jack shook his head. That was the fourth Scriver then. Dead. The Strygan were either getting stronger, or Scrivers were forgetting their training. He'd fought alongside Cozael and challenged her, but he didn't know her personally. She'd displayed incredible intelligence in the third trial, Literata. The library fortress Karnuhym was itself a construct of ancient magic and used to test them. It was originally a monastery for Numyn but now utilized for storing valuable weapons and knowledge. The Ardis-infused mineral stone of Karnuhym sat on a crossroads. The magic there had been the final test—it had let her pass and put the Scriver mark on her skin.

He hadn't bothered to get to know any of the combatants, given the high probability of death.

Narim took Jack's silence as an opportunity to continue speaking. "Found any new tricks yet?"

The taunt wasn't lost on Jack. For years, Jack had told anyone who would listen that silver harmed werewolves. It wasn't until a bloody massacre in Bahinda that people started to finally believe him.

Jack didn't bother to respond to Narim. He thumbed off the transmitter by touching a rune on the small earpiece. He imagined the man's curse and rolling eyes in response. It was no secret that Narim desired acknowledgement of his skill set, but he was no Scriver. Grimarr was the only person who could find him if he truly wished. He was also the only one who'd let Jack go when he and Alaric decided to leave the Milytor.

Jack finished his dinner as the fire died to embers. He took a few inside the shelter with him and set them in the stone firepit. The kindling he set on top snapped and caught the large logs within minutes. He didn't care about the smoke giving his position away, as spirits that haunted the dark trees appeared like mist or smoke—another reason people stayed out of Churk Forest.

He rummaged through his pack; it was spelled to carry a lot more than it appeared able to. His old mentor Alaric Zayne had taught him the simple charm. Jack pulled out several potion vials that were about as thick as his thumb. Under the tray of potions were several rifles, compact pistols, and an array of machetes, axes, bows, and arrows. The thin leather journal he was supposed to write in, the *Book of Ryquera*, sat accusingly. The book was spelled to another set of books in the Karnuhym monastery fortress, which was also the largest library on all the continents and guarded night and day along the Thura River. He never ran out of paper or ink because the words transcribed themselves into the permanent book in the library. He'd been remiss in recording his last encounter with a rather ornery gryphon.

"Keep it organized. You don't manifest new skills suddenly, but fall back to the highest level of training," he reminded himself in a nod to Alaric's memory. The gruff, broad-shouldered mentor had always said an organized soldier could handle anything. He had valued duty and preparedness above all else. With his naturally smooth hazelnut hair, hooded green eyes, and tall build, he'd fit into society a hell of a lot better than Jack ever had. He'd started out with Grimarr in the Milytor and then branched off into arcane arts and study—a man intent on experimentation and discovery of magic.

Aye, don't go unprepared. There's trouble coming. I didn't imagine all the Scrivers succumbing so soon to beasts. Alaric's whisper filled his mind. Jack carried on these hypothetical conversations way too often, but like it or not, he missed the old bastard. Often, he was convinced that the man's ghost was actually speaking with him.

It had been ongoing for years now. At times Jack thought he was going mad. Did other people have entire conversations with spirits in their heads? He was so used to the older man's voice popping up into his conscience that it was becoming normal—whatever that was. Maybe there was something residual left inside Jack that Alaric had imparted on him when he'd died. The man had possessed many secrets, and Jack wasn't so confident as to think he'd learned everything about him. Either way, he didn't mind the company—most of the time.

Jack ran a hand through his short hair, which was starting to grow out. Stubble coated his chin and cheeks. His clothes needed a wash; he had three pairs of pants in varying shades of black, some gray shirts, and one spelled coat. A belt of Muran leather kept other tools like knives, scythes, pistols, and Kyadem within a second's reach.

Speaking of that missing blade, he needed to make a stop to get her before seeing the king.

Grimm wants to use you as his weapon. He still wants to carry on what we started. Alaric's deep whisper floated in his head. *We handpicked some of those men and women to compete in the trials. It's a disappointment to see such talent gone.*

Alaric had spearheaded the push to make a hybrid soldier, one who could spy and record weaknesses but also fight with every weapon invented and wield magic better than Malecanta. Only a few humans were able to wield magic with any ability at all. However, this soldier would be under full Milytor control.

Jack refused to be.

The realm of Ocrana cannot fall to Stryga rule, but neither do I want my children used as experiments or cannon fodder. Vedan will destroy the entire kingdom should that happen, Alaric's voice said.

The rival realm was not supportive of Strygan, but the younger king had always been looking for a reason to invade Ocrana and take Asnor. The port city was a valuable asset in accessing the other continents and trade routes.

"I thought I was your only child," Jack said with a snarky smile.

You are the only one I need.

"Grim wouldn't kill me unnecessarily." Despite the intense trials he'd put Jack through, Grimarr had been a lot more sympathetic to the harshness of the tests than Alaric. Several thousand men and women had failed at the trials to become a Scriver.

He always did have a soft spot for you, Dark Drannit knows why. You were a stubborn Bogle to train.

Jack smirked. "Too stubborn to die. Isn't that what you said?"

Saving that boy might have been a mistake—it blew your cover. I taught you better than that.

"I can't turn my conscience off like you." Jack snorted. "Besides, I tracked a Stryga here. I didn't come by choice." Memories flooded over him like a tidal wave, but he shoved it all back.

Your new hex worked. But you could have hunted a dozen different Strygan. You liked that this one led back to Asnor. And Lyra.

At the mention of the woman, Jack paused. He hadn't seen the dark-eyed, chocolate-haired woman since he left, since his team of hopeful, trial Scrivers had been massacred. Lyra had been in charge of the spells to contain a coven, but it had backfired on her. Now, she couldn't lace her boots or speak in coherent sentences. Jack never knew what had happened that night, and Alaric had been oddly silent on the matter. Even after he died.

You find out what kills monsters to protect people who are foolish enough to think it won't hurt them. The Strygan are searching for the old magic. The sorcery Houses are not dead.

"I know. And the Volg are only encouraging them." The Volg Republic were an ever-growing group that thought they could all live in peace with demons, Stryga, and the like.

The Volg will have to choose a side someday. War will come between humans and the creatures beyond the veil. Strygan are just the catalysts. Welcome home.

"You ever going to tell me what happened to Lyra?"

Alaric's presence vanished. Jack focused on getting Shertan ready. The big, dark roan horse crunched on the brittle grass that managed to grow there and snorted.

"Ready for the city again?"

Shertan shook his long mane and pawed the ground.

"Me either."

Chapter Four

Only one Scriver appears to have a unique trait of having no scent. His sweat does not produce malodor like most humans. He underwent several trials with Alaric's guidance and his glands no longer produce scent. While this is not a requirement, was this a contributing factor in successfully completing the three trials? Likely not, but a testament to his skill and unequivocal disregard for living.
~ Scryptus, the Scriver Archives,
as recounted by Scriver #5 Jack Serpent, Tome 1

A rush of emotions hit Jack as he headed into the bustling village. Did he want to deal with the fallout from years ago with Narim? Did he want to see Lyra? Did he care that much that his old life, including Alaric, was tangled here like interconnecting roots of trees too close together?

No. He would rather spend nights alone and out in a new land than deal with his past. Of course, it had been so long since he'd been home that the landscape had changed. Generations of people were shifting, and things weren't the same.

He felt he should head to Harcourt to visit Lyra, but he knew the king wouldn't like being kept waiting much longer. Would she even know him now? It wasn't a question he was ready to answer. As much as he wanted to piss off Narim, he wasn't going to make things harder on himself by ignoring a summons.

Asnor bustled with activity as Jack rode up the main road to the first gate of the castle. The imposing, gray stone structure sat on a hill that overlooked the city. The guards there eyed him, likely taking in his attire: long black coat with silver buttons, rugged calf-high boots, slightly stained off-white shirt, and thin leather armor vest. Twin swords crossed his back, pistols sat on his hips, and a quiver with arrows and a bow was attached to the saddle. Jack had exchanged Shertan's saddle pad for a nondescript black one, one without the Scriver sigil: an upside-down anchor-like sign, sword thrust in the middle, with three claw marks. His blades bore the mark, but it was harder to see unless one was looking for it.

The guard held up a hand. Jack halted Shertan, and the horse snorted.

"What's your business?" the guard asked in a bored voice.

"Summons from King Thuramond."

"Papers?"

Jack sighed. "No."

The guard's transmitter crackled with noise, and he put a hand to his ear. His eyes widened and he stepped back, motioning for the others to open the gates. He whispered to the other two guards, and they also gave Jack a wide berth.

Apparently, the stigma for Scrivers was still present in the royal guard as well. They resented the Milytor trying to exert force and considered themselves elite to the king. Most likely, though, they were wondering if he was a true Scriver, since the other four hadn't fared so well dealing with the darkness. Or so Jack had heard through Scryptus from time to time. The young monk would mention how one of the Scriver's journals had sat empty for over a year—presumed dead—and Grimarr would try to retrieve the body or what was left of it.

Shertan's hooves clopped up the stone drive to the front entrance. Word traveled fast. Doors now opened in advance for him, and a uniformed groomsman came to take the horse. Jack dismounted and handed the man the reins. He glanced to the west, where the Milytor barracks lay. As a boy, he'd spent years visiting his father here.

Big double doors with ornate carvings opened to reveal footmen standing at attention. Courtesans and lower royalty milled around the huge receiving rooms and corridors. Jack followed a guard through twisting halls and past several indoor fountains and gray statues of the old gods. Tapestries adorned the thick walls, and the smells changed with every turn they took, from baking bread to excrement, perfume, sweat, sex, iron, and leather. Jack didn't need a potion to enhance those smells. His nose was keen, even for a human.

The private royal chamber was laden with gold decor and the marble floors screamed opulence. The guards motioned for him to hand over his weapons before entering. Jack had learned not to rely on steel alone to feel comfortable, so he had no qualms at giving the swords and pistols up. He didn't even have the one weapon that made him inimitable—it was being repaired.

The king sat on a giant, gold-plated chair surrounded by a dozen men; he didn't glance up. But another man did notice Jack as he hung about the entrance. A blond-haired man with stormcloud eyes stopped his conversation with a duke upon the Scriver's entrance. The man was a few inches shorter than Jack's six-foot two. He was broad-shouldered and built like a bull. A thin, white, lightning-shaped scar adorned the left side of his face near his ear, given by Jack's rapier five years earlier. It may or may not have been accidental. He also bore a few similar tattoos to Jack's.

Narim Gunneran. Years of furious grief still clung to him like the scar on his face. Jack read it in the lines around his eyes, the tension in his hands, and the glare he bestowed upon him.

A court announcer stood straight. The king rolled his eyes at the formality, but the man was determined to do his duty.

"Enter the Scriver!"

Jack's lips thinned. He was good at entering a room without being noticed—except at court.

"About time, Serpent." Narim cocked his head at Jack. "You look like a Midlian goat had his way with you."

Jack smiled blandly. "You'd know."

Narim didn't respond except to rake his gaze over him. In their training days together, that look had often left Jack with a chill. It hadn't been his imagination that Narim had stared at him more often and more intently than the other soldiers. Others had noticed, and as young soldiers do, they pointed at it and made jokes. At the time, Jack thought it was nothing more than jealousy.

Jack kept his back to the door even as he stepped inside. He scanned every detail of the opulent space. Shelves of dark cherrywood held tomes on supernatural lore, gemstones, spells, and mythical creatures. Treaties on lands and a giant map of the five continents hung on the far wall between two windows. Several plush chairs sat around a hearth with a fire licking the stone back. A giant wyvern head adorned the stone above the mantel, with fangs bared and slitted yellow topaz eyes. Two small tables held crystal decanters of a sparkling white liquid.

King James Thuramond the Fifth motioned Jack forward. His resplendent robes of gold and silver rustled as he stood with a flourish.

"Yes, come, come, Mr. Serpent." He smiled under a short, graying beard. The king was fifty-six years young and had recently taken a lovely bride in the hopes she would bear him more children than his concubines had.

"Majesty." Jack bowed at the waist.

The king snapped his fingers, and the court people scattered. The big wooden doors shut with a thunk. Narim sidled up next to Jack and offered a polite smile.

"I hear you're the last to survive of the honor-bound, elite hybrids we made. Disappointing. I heard what's-his-name, Runvir, died of Caladrius poisoning. Which is particularly hard, as you should know, since those birds possess healing magic, right?" The king bowled on with narrowed eyes. "Cozael was supposed to remain in Asnor to spy on the Volg, but her body was found with Strygan stench all over it. Perhaps you'll convince me why we went through all that fracas. Oh yes, to prove to Vedan that we're the superior city." The king said this with a chuckle and a twitch of his ringed fingers. "I suppose you're looking for gratitude for figuring out the vampyre sickness in Havaria that spread here. You weren't even in Asnor then, but your findings proved ... fruitful." The king narrowed his eyes.

"None required." Jack met his gaze.

The king's face sobered after a second. "We have a Strygan problem."

"Excuse me, Highness, but may I inquire why Grimarr Fox is not among us?" Jack glanced around the room, now empty save for a dozen guards. The most trusted Milytor. He made no comment on the king's first statement. The trials had positioned Asnor in the eyes of all the continents as a powerful, intelligent capital that had superior military strength. But Jack refused to defend a title he hadn't even wanted.

"He is on a hunt and should return tomorrow by dusk," Narim said with a sniff. His dark armor, offset with gold studs, glinted in the firelight.

"No matter, boy, now let's sit." The king sat in a crimson-backed chair closer to the hearth with a drink table next to it. Jack took a seat opposite him. Narim took the third chair and crossed his legs. "We've learned of rumors that an attack is imminent upon my wife, the Queen Sonora. She's begun the end stages of her pregnancy, and her safety is my top priority. There's Strygan movement as far out as the Tango woods, and it's come to Asnor. The High Stryga is near."

Jack couldn't help but glance at Narim. The other man's face struggled to remain passive, and the light in his eyes blazed hot. Narim fidgeted with a gold ring on his left hand. The ring his father had given him, Jack knew, and it represented the legacy Narim struggled to live up to. There was nothing the Gunneran family hated more than Strygan, given Narim's father had been killed by one years ago. "Burn the Stryga" was a sentiment beaten into all Milytor soldiers and hunters. It was the only way they knew.

"I thought we had an agreement with the Strygan," Jack said politely. It wasn't common knowledge that the king had an agreement with some High Stryga, but he wanted him to know he was privy to that information. Which High Stryga, he wasn't sure, as the number of actual High Strygan in existence wasn't clear. Alaric had granted him the inside information when Jack had come back with the head of a vampyre. The king had used a few Strygan hexes to gain his seat of power. His cousin, first in line, had suffered a tragic riding accident on a hunt. The boy's parents had taken ill when they accused James of tampering. The Thurmond line had grown incredibly strong in a few short years, never losing their battles. In return, the Strygan got a foothold in his parliament. The king would never be an outright supporter of them, but he let the Volg run rampant. Perhaps it wasn't wise to speak it out loud with so many listening, but Jack wanted to get out of Asnor as quickly as possible.

The king cleared his throat. "I did have an agreement with her. But she's demanding more power and position than I can grant her. Or will grant her. There is no good Stryga, no white magic. It's all black, and they all take from something or someone. The Volg Republic are stirring up rumors and heresy about Strygan despite all the disappearances of babies and children. They think we can exist with them peacefully. I daresay they even want a Stryga on the throne someday."

Jack didn't argue. Some people had the notion that Strygan could practice "white" magic. In his experience, there was no such thing. Magic was simply a force, something that could be bought and sold; it was like a living thing that could be mastered, and not all masters were benevolent. All magic had a price—even the wards the Milytor used had come with a blood sacrifice. Magic could be useful, of course, but he'd found that those who wielded it never deserved the power it brought them. Himself included.

It seemed to Jack the king had gotten himself in over his head, and now he wanted someone to clean it up. He flicked an eyebrow in irritation. This was one of the reasons he'd left the Milytor and hadn't wanted to compete in the Scriver Trials. He didn't want to take orders from a man dictating on a throne. While the king had done his fair share of investigating problems, there was little he'd done against crimes like child slavery, starving lower class, or regulating of magic. Grimarr and Alaric's brainchild had been a hybrid soldier: someone who could wield magic like the old sorcerers, sneak like an assassin, and spy like the gryphon riders of old, but be under the Milytor's control. Jack had long ago disagreed, and Alaric hadn't stopped him from leaving. Grimarr must've seen the futility of fighting both of them.

Narim spoke. "We can deal with the Volg, but our main goal needs to be the High Stryga. There hasn't been a true one in a century, but we've had sightings. I have information that leads me to believe they're attempting to find the power left from the Covering. They're searching for Ardis, and if that's true, then Sorcery Houses could return, and we all remember the last time Strygan and sorcerers fought." He paused to let it sink in.

The Dranakar Wars had ended so long ago that people were beginning to dismiss history. The continent of Elgar was said to have been a unique place where magic gathered, where the gods blessed the lands. The sorcerers and sorceresses paved the way for others to live and commune with the magic and its creatures in Elgar. Some even elevated the sorcerers to gods.

One powerful sorcerer, Dranakar, had taken a wife, Corvynia. She convinced him to search for deep magic, and together they let magic into the world. They found Ardis caches and hoarded them. Centuries later, it became a war when a traitor sorceress revealed their use of Ardis to enhance their power. All races wanted the chance at such magic. Dranakar and Corvynia used such deep magic, perhaps they had become gods—their bodies were never found, and little signs of them had remained in the world for people to speculate on or pray to. But the damage was done. The magic they'd unleashed let all the races, including humans, began to twist it, to form unnatural creatures.

Narim continued, "Ocrana could fall under Strygan dominance if we don't act now. With Volg supporting the Strygan, we're not exactly evenly matched."

"We have poured many resources into your ... existence," said the king. "I've let you roam freely, recording what you like, but it's time to be the useful weapon I was promised. You've killed how many Strygan?" His gaze bore into Jack, who shifted in his seat.

"I only kill when it's necessary." It was the most diplomatic answer he could give. Jack knew the king was hinting at Ravenhell. How many Strygan had he killed there? Over a dozen. In the beginning, he'd been that soldier who killed on command, who did as he was told and recorded weaknesses, outposts, weapons. He'd fought the monsters that followed him out of the dark.

Narim sighed. "If you don't want the task, I have plenty of other candidates. Eager, young things ready to prove they're better than the infamous Razer of Ravenhell. A Scriver is glorified bait, really."

The king cocked his head at Jack. This couldn't be the first time Narim's venom had reached his ears. How much did the king know about their past? Narim had been first in line for the trials before Alaric chose Jack. The blond soldier had survived quite a bit—and might have lived to secure the title as well if not for the last trial.

Thuramond had let the realm slip into discord while he feasted in safety and comfort. He relied on Grimarr's superior force to keep their enemies like Vedan at bay. It wouldn't be long before the other continents began to sense weakness, though. Jack suspected something else was going in the king's head. The logs on the fire cracked and sparked. Jack's reputation always preceded him, but very few people knew the truth. Perhaps it had nothing to do with Narim, and if so, he had Alaric to thank for that.

"I need a little more information. I'm not a diviner." Jack arched a brow, ignoring Narim.

The king chuckled and motioned to Narim, who held out a book to Jack. "Give him the details. I need you and your team ready in forty-eight hours or less on Task Geist."

Jack paused as he opened the thin leather-bound ledger. "Team?"

Narim laughed outright this time. He grinned like a wolf over a fresh kill. "I'm heading the team as controller, but your 'expertise' will lead us." His sarcasm wasn't lost on Jack. When Jack had decided to leave the Milytor, there was no shortage of hard feelings.

"I work alone," Jack said, ignoring Narim and addressing the king. There was no way he could hunt a High Stryga with other people's lives at stake, including Narim's.

"Now you don't. Previous spies have been unsuccessful." The king motioned for his serving man to fetch him a drink. The clink of ice shards and splash of liqueur didn't cut the silence well enough. Jack assumed the other "spies" were feeding worms in the ground now.

"You want this High Stryga alive or dead?" Jack leveled them both with a stare.

The king sipped his white bourbon and sighed. "Does not matter. I am aware Grimarr has a special fondness for you. If you refuse, I will see that you truly are the last Scriver. I also believe you have a *friend* in an asylum in Harcourt." The threat was implied.

Jack bit his tongue. All his training and instincts screamed that this was wrong, but he knew when he was cornered. In most fights, he refused to back down, but this was one where it might not be worth the trouble. He supposed he could benefit from learning more about a High Stryga and report it. It was all part of his position, right? He might not serve the Milytor as a soldier, but he remained dedicated to his purpose: finding secrets to keep others safe from what lurked in the dark. He turned to Narim. The other man smiled insincerely, and the scar near his left ear puckered. No doubt he'd been feeding the king sensitive information—like what Lyra meant to him. A heart for a heart.

"I won't promise the team will return." Jack pursed his lips. "And you do realize I don't know how to destroy a High Stryga." The king didn't seem to understand that the situation required more than merely tracking a Stryga, but also figuring out her talents, what she drew her power from, and why she was striking now.

"The soldiers understand the perils. I trust you're good at improvising—isn't that the Scriver method? Grimarr made a strong case for you, so I imagine you'll get it done. Doesn't matter how." King Thuramond fixed him with a look as if trying to read him. Jack kept his face neutral.

Narim added with a sneer, "I trust you'll see they fare better than Jethen did."

The name was like a needle in his arm, but Jack had been prepared for it. He leveled Narim with a steady gaze. The loss of a life he should have been able to save bothered him, but he refused to let the other soldier see that. Jethen had put himself in danger without a thought for anyone else. At the time, Jack had only suspected the two soldiers were more than friends.

"Fine, I'll meet the team. But I need to know her name—the Stryga's name. Without it, this data is essentially useless." Jack closed the folder.

The king wrung his hands and tugged on the hem of his jacket. "We don't know."

Jack sighed.

That earned a frown from Thuramond. "Why is it important? You'll know the Stryga when you encounter her, won't you?"

"Strygan are like demons—if you know their name, you can use that against them. Even possibly to kill," Jack said, with more patience than he felt inside. Every second they wasted here, the trail was going cold. The Stryga before the last one he'd hunted had been heading toward the Proepucia Swamp. It was not a place he wanted to be in for any length of time.

"We don't know her name. Always female, right?" the king asked in a rare display of curiosity.

"Their male equivalent are warlocks, sir," Narim answered. "There are rumors the Strygan need warlocks to procreate, and they kill any male born to them. Supposedly only females possess magic."

Jack could confirm that that was true, as could Alaric's voice in his head.

"Sir," a guard interrupted with a pained expression. He tilted his head to listen to the transmitter in his ear. The king stood in alarm. "The queen is under attack!" the guard exclaimed. More guards swiftly ushered the king out of the room, and Narim escorted Jack to the back exit.

Narim pointed at him. "We meet tomorrow at dawn at the Brown Shepherd tavern."

Jack threw the file into the fire. It was of more use as kindling than information. There were things he wasn't being told, and he trusted Narim as much as a venomous spotted Gnarl snake. He'd spent five years in Milytor training with the man before deciding it wasn't for him. Narim had never let him forget that, still called him a failure for it. Then Alaric had stepped in and taken him to train for the Scriver Trials. There were potions to learn how to craft, spells to bind to his body, and physical training that had Jack blacking out and wishing for death several times. All in preparation to see what the darkness hid.

There wasn't time to dwell on the past, though. The queen's life hung between them like a gossamer spider web; once a strand broke, events would wheel into motion that couldn't be stopped. The deal the king had struck with the High Stryga was precarious at best. Perhaps they sensed his weakness was his wife, and they would use it against him now. If they attacked the queen, it was a sure sign they were up to something more than their usual terrors. As much as Jack wanted to stay out of royal politics, this attack might mean a declaration of war.

He raced in the opposite direction, already figuring out the fastest route to the castle.

Chapter Five

The Dolfar elven clan reside mainly in the northern Dolraine mountains on Elgar and even into uncharted islands in the Penware Sea. We assume they originated amongst these islands and migrated to Elgar. They're a colorful people—hair ranging in all tones of red, blonde, and orange. Skin quite pale with freckles being desirable. Their elected head of clans, Trysand, has helped General Grimarr and Alaric Zayne in their plans for the Scriver Trials. Trysand has come up with interesting, if not impossible, tests.
~ Scryptus, the Scriver Archives,
as recounted by Scriver #5 Jack Serpent, Tome 5

Jack grabbed his weapons from the guards and ran. He touched a pointer finger to one of the tattoos on his wrist, and the spell for lightness washed over him. Taking a breath, he leaped from the balcony to another about fifty feet away. The magic balanced him, made him so light he almost floated, and his shins didn't split when he landed. The rune tattoos bound magic to him so he could access it quickly. He'd already given up bits of hair, bone, blood, and one year of his life, to get them.

He was familiar with the castle layout. It had been years, though. The king would be heading toward the queen's chambers, but it might be too late. Jack guessed the dimly lit balcony with flowing golden curtains might be the queen's. He took another running leap and landed softly on the terrace. The stone railing was chipped, as if claws had ripped at it. He sniffed.

The air was rank with iron, sulfur, and decayed flesh. The guards inside the queen's chambers shouted and cursed. Her handmaids scurried around like drowning rats, their hands flailing at shadows and tears streaking their cheeks. Jack dodged a maid who ran past him. He reached out to grab her before she threw herself over the balcony edge. Her eyes were wild, with no sense behind them.

"Hold her," he said, and tossed her to a guard. The maid shrieked as if a demon had appeared before her.

Jack had seen every reaction to a Stryga's magic, from worship, to manic lust, to suicide. The beautiful room with rich, cherrywood furniture could hide all sorts of creatures, but he sensed nothing else here. The Stryga had come and gone. He kept to a slow walk and canvassed the entire area, then swallowed hard when he saw the body on the floor of the chamber.

The queen lay glassy-eyed, mouth frozen wide in terror, abdomen slashed open. Blood soaked into the thick rug under her.

King Thuramond burst into the room with his guards. His screams of grief echoed through the stone halls.

JACK SERPENT

Jack crept closer to inspect the queen. Her dress lay in strips of fabric as if a beast had clawed it open. Her once pregnant belly exposed an empty womb. Jack's mind flashed to his parents' deaths and the mutilations he'd witnessed when the goblins dragged them out in a ritual harvest for Strygan. Organs, fluids, bones. His fists clenched.

"She was ... I can't ... where is the baby?" the king shouted through his sobs. The maidens who waited on the queen bawled.

The women loved their queen. She'd been known for her kind manner and smile. Why had the Stryga cut her unborn child from her? Jack had seen a lot of torturous, unexplainable things in his thirty-four years, but this was different. Not since elves had revolted against the Malecanta had there been such a blatant attack on the monarchy. Had Thuramond given too much to the Strygan in exchange for his seat of power?

This was no elf attack either. The elves were born with magic, but like Strygan, they often stole more. They had created some of the worst creatures that still roamed Elgar today. Jack was sure this wasn't a beast attack either—something with sentience had cut out the fetus.

The Strygan scent assaulted Jack's nose, and his nerves tingled in proximity to the black magic residue. It left a charged odor in the air that he was more than used to smelling.

"I need everyone back." An authoritative male voice broke through the noise in the room, and everyone couldn't help but notice, falling into a hush. General Grimarr Fox, standing inches taller than most men and wearing a dirty uniform, strode through the guards. He always carried a silver, fox-headed cane that housed a rapier inside. The guards parted like a knife through wet paper. His steel-blue eyes met Jack's, and he nodded slowly, as if reassuring himself that Jack was truly there and not a mirage. The lines around Grimarr's eyes tightened as he surveyed the signs of black magic.

"Your Highness, I see you've taken my counsel. I'm glad to see the Scriver here. There's no doubt who's done this," Fox said, laying a soft hand on the king's shoulder.

Thuramond stood with difficulty and swiped at the tears on his cheeks. He took several deep breaths, then collapsed back on the plush chair and wailed. They all waited a moment for him to collect his wits.

"Do whatever you must. I will have satisfaction for this." The king's voice was hollow with grief and raw with rage. He stared at his wife as if punishing himself for not protecting her. As if he could will her back to life.

Jack understood the feeling all too well. He couldn't bring his parents back to life no matter how many times he'd woken from nightmares. What was dead should stay dead. *Could the baby still be alive?* His thoughts were probably echoed all around, but no one wanted to give them voice. *Highly unlikely, given it wasn't supposed to be born for another month.*

Gas lanterns flickered, and a fire crackled in the hearth. Over the next hour, Milytor interviewed the guards on watch, Queen Sonora's handmaidens were taken to another room, and hounds were brought in. The huge black and brindle wolf dogs sniffed the queen's garments and then were led out on the palace grounds to see if they could find a scent that matched hers.

Jack itched to touch the rune tattoo on his wrist that would give him a heightened sense of smell, much like the hounds. He had a vial of a potion that gave him similar senses, but the stuff wasn't reliable, as it wasn't made with blood magic. Grimarr interrupted him before he could. The older man ushered him out onto the balcony and into the early dawn. Strips of pink glowed along the horizon on a city that already bustled with activity. Beyond the city to the west lay a patchwork of farmlands, forests, and indigo mountains crowned with white snow. To the east lay the crest of ocean from where they traded with the other continents and from which hundreds of rivers flowed.

"I must admit I wasn't sure if you'd come," Grimarr said with a soft smile. His eyes were tired, and he'd grayed more since the last time Jack saw him. The general's dark uniform, with brass buttons, high boots, and light armor, suited his build. His silver-streaked hair was tied back and braided on the left side of his head. Scars crossed his left cheek and ran over his knuckles. He was ever commanding, a pillar of strength, reminding Jack of his father.

"Is that Haka blood on you?" Jack sniffed. The notoriously nocturnal fanged beasts with six legs hunted all over Elgar. They normally took cattle and sheep. "What were you doing chasing something like that?"

Grimarr sighed. "I was set up, pointed in one direction when I should have been here. As luck of the hare would have it, I trusted my gut and returned early." He gazed out at the faintly star-studded sky with a sliver of moon. "I assume Narim has informed you of your task. I do not assume you've accepted." He eyed Jack expectantly.

"Does the High Stryga have a name?" Cutting right to the information he needed was his signal to Grimarr that he'd accepted under duress. Now it was even more imperative that they begin the hunt. Jack couldn't go into a situation blind—he needed all the information he could get and would form a plan from there. With every second that passed, the Stryga furthered her own plans or escape.

"None that we know," Grimarr confirmed.

The gravity of the unknown weighed on Jack. Still, they fell into easy conversation. It didn't matter that he hadn't seen Grimarr in almost six years—it was as if Alaric stood right beside him. As if time hadn't mattered much at all.

"I tracked a coven all the way up to Jounder Mountain but lost the trail. I've got new soldiers to train and old ones to remind of their place. I can't be in all places at once." Grimarr sighed. "I need your help. Ocrana needs your help."

"Even though I left, and I don't plan on staying." Jack let the sentence hang. Grim had always hoped Jack would become the next general in the king's Milytor.

"Alaric would roll in his grave to hear me say this, but he pointed you down the exact path you needed. You've made quite a legend out of yourself already, Razer." Grimarr cocked his head and Jack grunted.

"A thing I never intended." Jack didn't care if his exploits and violent history gave him a better image or not.

"I have confirmation that Modon's remains were found—and what we presume is Halyth. Her signet ring, on a very decayed corpse, was recovered in the den of a clan of warlocks." Grimarr's frown lines deepened as he spoke of the other two Scrivers. "She never made it a secret she thought the warlocks were planning something bigger than the Strygan problem. I suppose she would have known since she was Dolfar."

Jack nodded. He couldn't help but remember the red-haired spitfire of a girl who had competed as a human, giving up her elven gifts for a time, and when she won, her clan had come to reveal her secret. The Dolfar may have helped craft the trials with Alaric and Grimarr, but they weren't pleased that one of their own wanted to compete with humans. They considered themselves superior—no need to prove it. Her title had been disqualified in the eyes of the humans and elves, but the ancient stones gave her the mark.

Ah, the sunset to your darkness. Alaric's voice chimed in. *She almost beat you in the Survyvo trial.*

Jack could still feel the icy cold that had paralyzed his limbs as he struggled to survive a snowstorm with minimal protection and little knowledge of spells. The second trial had tested survival skills both elemental and magic. Halyth had remained in that numbing cold far longer than anyone else, and Jack suspected she'd been the one to help him light a fire.

Never confirmed that one. Alaric snorted softly. *She proved herself—even I'll admit that.*

Jack ignored the specter in his mind.

"They were worthy of the title," was all he could think to say. Grim knew he'd never wanted it. But a young man with no future and a talent for magic and violence took what he was handed.

"When do you leave? I know how well you work with Narim." Grimarr's brows knit together with his sarcasm. "It wasn't my idea for him to lead this particular task, but you know his history with Strygan. He seemed impassioned last I spoke with him."

"I'll play for now until this becomes a suicide mission. We leave at dawn tomorrow. I wanted more time to make a perimeter, track a lead. Apparently, we're going to walk blindly into a swamp or forest without knowing what we're hunting."

"I wish I could give you more time." Grimarr paused and thunked his cane lightly on the stone balcony. They both knew acting hurriedly would only hasten their deaths. The Strygan were up to something, and they had to tread carefully. "This is an unfortunate foreshadowing of another realm war, and this time we may not be so lucky to survive. Vedan already eyes our weakening state."

Jack nodded.

"We should have been more prepared," Grimarr muttered as he turned to go. "I should have seen this. Did we not learn from the Dranakar Wars?"

"There was no way to know half of the Malecanta would turn on us back then," Jack said. Everyone knew the faded history carved in stone caves and illustrated in tomes.

Dranakar's wife, Corvynia, had twisted his desire to learn about ancient magic, and they'd taken advantage of human worship that turned themselves into demi-gods. They delved deep into the darkness when the light would not let them pass further. Strange creatures awoke, and the Strygan, already aligned with dark magic, began to aid the first sorceress. Yet the Strygan demanded more and more power until it was too late for the Malecanta to realize they intended to wipe them out.

Grimarr only nodded with a distant gaze to the horizon. "They're getting smarter—and convening together, for once."

Jack knew the lore like the veins in his hands. He had never been a good history student, though; Alaric had had a terrible time getting him to study. In his mind, the lessons learned from the past were only good if they could be applied presently. Why did so many fail at that simple task?

"I will find the High Stryga."

His mind had already started to formulate plans for the current problem: a Stryga hiding out in the Proepucia Swamp. He needed someone who knew the area. He had the thesal tracking potion but only a limited number of vials. It would go faster and smoother if he could find someone who knew the territory and places to hide. If he could find a tracker in time, he'd use them, but it was unlikely.

Grimarr turned to him. There was a tightness around his eyes that Jack read almost as fear. What in the Dranakar darkness would make Grim afraid?

"Beware, Jack, there are monsters unaccounted for and monsters being made new. Things we don't yet know." He switched to old Cafferian for the last words, his deep tone barely above a whisper. Jack didn't have time to respond to the cryptic warning.

Narim walked up to them with a grim face, his lips forming a severe line.

"Timeline still stands. You have twenty-four hours to come up with a way to kill this bitch when we find her," Narim said with a growl. He stalked off.

Grimarr headed inside and conversed with the captain of the king's guard. The commotion whirled back into focus, and the scent of blood still lingered in the air.

Jack turned and slipped out of the palace like a ghost. Already wails of mourning and the frenzy of fear spread among the city like a disease. If the Strygan wanted to create chaos, this was a good way to start. But what bothered him more was the stolen fetus.

There was only one thing Strygan did with babies, and it wasn't raising them to be exemplary members of society. Jack once again forced away the image of his parents hanging from tree branches, a ritual circle in flames around them, their bodies mangled and stripped. He raced against the crowds and against the nightmares of his past. It had been a mistake to come home.

Chapter Six

The owning of people as property dates to ancient times and remains a practice held by some. Slavers are allowed in some towns to use children to mine certain minerals, brothels allow workers for their specialized needs, farmers leverage debtors in the form of unpaid labor. While there are several factions that do not condone this practice, there is equal pushback from those who benefit. Corruption is rampant no matter which continent one inhabits.
~ Scryptus, the Scriver Archives,
as recounted by Scriver #5 Jack Serpent, Tome 8

The Thresher Festival, splendid, Jack thought as he pried an eager, scantily clad older lady off his arm. Two more took her place, younger this time. He moved away, but not before noticing the man who oversaw them. The man who probably took the majority or all of their earnings.

Jack didn't have time to right every injustice in the city.

The owning of people was nothing new, and whether it was called indentured servitude or slavery, he tried not to think about it. Did those women go willingly to earn a wage, or had they been forced as he had been forced as a child when traders came across him? After the murders of his parents, Jack had wandered from town to town until the slavers found him and sold him to Servun Hall, an orphanage.

His time there had taught him that there would always be someone on top, someone who wanted power more than others. Claiming to be a safe home for orphans, they'd instead used children to mine Clarent crystals, as only children were small enough to find them in the deep caves. Jack struggled with enclosed spaces. He still had nightmares about the endless dark hours with only lichen moss to light the way.

Alaric's voice popped up. *You survived. You continue to survive.* He left off as if wanting to say more.

"Yet it doesn't seem to make much of a difference to anyone. And you never cared for helping others." Jack sighed. His training after the orphanage always took precedence.

I helped burn that orphanage, don't you recall? There was a small chuckle. *Although, I don't know if I truly assisted. I think I was simply there to keep you from killing yourself.*

Jack didn't join in the dry mirth. He hated the memory of confronting the couple who owned Servun Hall. They'd shown neither remorse nor fear, even as he threw a torch at their feet.

And that runaway would have met a far worse fate had I not returned him. You couldn't, you still can't, fight a war on slavery until you root out the true evil.

"I'm not fighting any war. I just think some people could use more consequences," he muttered. If he thought too much about other children suffering as he had for years in the slave mines, he might go mad.

He couldn't save everyone. Hell, he'd probably lost his own soul, so what business did he have with anyone else's?

I am still disturbed about your time at Servun. Alaric's voice had an edge now, as if he were holding something back. Jack wondered if he was just echoing his mentor's words from the past or if he was truly speaking with him. It felt real, but he'd learned not to trust emotion alone. And he didn't have time now to decipher it.

"We have more pressing things to focus on," Jack said quietly. The rage and helplessness from his past were best left in a small corner of his mind.

The queen would not have a public funeral given the circumstances—there would be a ceremony and casket for show, but the true burial would happen privately in the castle's cemetery by the sea. The people were adding their own way of honoring her at the festival. King Thuramond had addressed the city briefly, taking no questions and telling them to go about their harvest as usual. The queen's death would be avenged, but it was not a concern of the peasantry.

The people were not satisfied. They exchanged furtive glances and whispers and seemed to jump at loud noises. The tense anxiety was not helped by the Volg, who moved among them like a damp mist. Milytor soldiers could only quell so many at a time. The king had them scattered over various missions, and the prison was full. They had better things to do than fight with humans.

A dozen or so Volg supporters marched through the streets with signs and banners. They wore their signature purple robes and black hats with Strygan runes.

"The time of the Strygan has come! A second war."

"The king betrayed the agreement—the queen is dead because of him."

"The Milytor are useless. They will not protect you."

A young man with bright eyes pushed roughly past him, and Jack stuck his foot out. The man went sprawling as Jack continued on. He didn't often take sides, but the Volg were rude, idealistic dreamers. A Stryga on the throne would enslave humanity. It was an absurd notion. Truly, no one had learned from the Dranakar Wars.

It had been less than twenty-four hours since the queen's death, but rumors spread faster than rats jumping off a burning ship. The murder wasn't going to be covered up, especially given the enormous staff at the castle and the warning bell in the night.

Not everyone agreed with the Volg, and shouts as well as garbage catapulted back at them. The Milytor had not only been put in place to protect royalty but to keep a balance between the night-world creatures and humans. After the Covering, when sorcerer magic was hidden and Strygan were scattered, the peace had seemed as if it would stand.

Some humans still enjoyed working with other species like Dolfar elves, dwarves, and merfolk. Others were so afraid that they shot anything they felt was a threat or that had a tail.

You could try contacting Trysand, Alaric offered.

Jack was tempted, but the message wouldn't reach him in time. He wasn't even certain the Dolfar elf would care even if their kind were responsible for two of the trials Jack had gone through: summoning beasts and speaking to the ancient tomes. They were one of the few races of elves who wanted to communicate with humans. Alaric had been close with their circle of leaders, and Jack had gotten to sit in on several gatherings, not realizing Halyth would put herself into the competition. The Dolfar had agreed that someone should record history and all its mistakes, and who better than a human for the menial task? But that someone should also be tracking the newer threats, not be used only as a weapon.

Nearing the edge of the city limits, Jack took his thesal potion, which allowed him to track and sense supernatural essences. *I used to know this territory but not the swamp.* There weren't any footprints he could see, but traces of glowing mist—spells and wards—wound around shrubs before the wind blew it away. There were a lot of wards around the swamp, and even Shertan hesitated to go close to the edge, where the black trees twisted inward. Sulfuric gas leaked into the clean air, and moss on the branches blocked light.

Alaric's voice piped up as Jack rode back toward Asnor. *You need to get Kyadem and a lot more weapons. This doesn't smell right. You should find Dokoran.*

Jack agreed. There was something in that swamp that might or might not be a Stryga, or Strygan. Who knew what the Proepucia Swamp held? It was the perfect hiding spot.

He left his horse at the livery and moved on down toward the docks. The giant Thura River carried all manner of crops, animals, and trade wares to other cities in Ocrana and Havaria. It was a good place to get lost or hide, as the hub of chaos saw new faces every hour. It was just the place Dokoran would be. Jack checked his map. The red X moved around a lot, but it was stationary now over Bakker Street.

He threaded through people heading into the heart of the city. Whistles pierced the air, hawkers shouted their wares, and children chased each other in the streets. After living in various forests for years, he was startled by how much noise that many people could make.

Jack tapped one of the spelled silver buttons on the left side of his long black coat, and it changed into a shorter brown one. His jacket could be armor, a long duster, simple peasant garb, or the dress of a court official. It made nervous people jumpy if they recognized the ever-present Scriver sigil on his cuffs, but the sigils were wards to keep dark magic from getting into his skin. It also acted as a human deterrent from time to time. Jack was often granted entry or access simply because of the Scriver stigma. But other times, like now, it just made people want to throw torches at him.

Signs on thick parchment flapped on window casements and light posts. Jack peered at the crude drawings of black figures in hoods with daggers for fingernails. Strygan. He recalled a time when the Scriver Trials were all anyone wanted to talk about, how the signs went up overnight. The influx of trade and attention the trials had earned Asnor were still letting the king coast on his mountain of gold.

"Potion to keep the bitches and ghouls away, sir?" A teenaged boy thrust a ruby red vial at him.

"What's in it?" Jack asked.

"Um, hazel wood and Gob toadstools. They keep the Strygan out of your windows, for certain!" The boy smiled. Two of his teeth were missing, and hope filled his eyes.

Jack tilted his head, a shock of hair falling over his eye. "Or it treats warts and fungus. Get to a library; go to school.".

The boy's smile faltered, and he put the vial back into the row of other jewel-toned tonics on the table. "My mum can't afford to send me to school anymore. I don't take you for a fool, sir, pardon."

Jack tossed five san, the gold shimmering, into the collector bowl. "Ginsen root, silver shavings, Jensine talons, and Hawker's salt mixed together and smeared along windows usually works. But not always—be sure to have fire. Burn the Stryga."

The boy nodded and wrote it all down in a notebook. "Thank you, sir!"

Jack paused. "You wouldn't happen to know of any trackers in the area, would you?"

"Can't say as I do, sir. I seen a woman with two wolves once, but she disappeared into the forest."

"Thanks."

Jack hoped the boy would take the gold and go back to school. He wished he'd had the choice. The orphanage had offered meager education at best since it was only a cover for slave mining. Alaric had seen to Jack's schooling, though, catching him up. The Scriver Trials were more than physical feats. He'd been taught speed reading, writing, and over a dozen languages both spoken and ancient. Still, sitting inside a library was not the ideal place for Jack.

He walked down a side street, past the fancy lodging buildings and high-end taverns. Bakker Street loomed like a listing ship—a few shopkeepers but otherwise deserted. A shop with a dark window and a sign that read *Closed* sat to his left. The wooden and steel door was ordinary, and the off-white stone walls showed little wear. Jack went around to the building next to it and scaled the stairs to the roof.

He leaped across and landed on his target building. The roof was clean, with a few chairs on the flat surface and plants growing wild in the southwest corner. Jack spied a colorful rug that was clearly covering the roof's top door. He crouched, moved the rug aside, and tapped on the surface.

A minute passed. The door flung open, and a rifle with a scope on an angled mount greeted him.

Jack put his hands up with a grin.

"I expected you'd show up eventually," the male voice inside said, and the rifle mount retracted inside. Jack followed it down into the house. The second floor was sparse with two rooms, both doors shut. He went down a staircase onto the first floor.

"You wait for me? I'm flattered," Jack said, and cocked his head.

The man paused in his oiling of a silver-etched pistol and cracked a grin. His deep brown, keen, angled eyes crinkled with laugh lines. Tanned skin covered in tattoos, plus his narrow jaw and high nose, gave him a haughtily rugged appearance. His black hair was shaved along one side with the rest caught in a long ponytail. Silver earrings in the shape of ward sigils laced his left ear. He wore his usual plaid shirt with black vest and pants. His style was plain, but the quality was worth more than most people's wages for a month. His boots alone were worth a hundred san.

"Jasyth."

Jack put his pack on the table with a thump and a wry shake of his head. His full name reminded him of a life that was long past, one he didn't share it with many. "Dokoran."

"It's Dean, now. I took after you and shortened it. I hate the formality, and Asnorians like the simplicity." Dean eyed the pack with interest and set the pistol down. "When did you get back?"

"Just now."

"Then, I'm assuming you've just come from the castle," Dean said. He glanced at Jack with a dark, humorless smile. "Tragic. I liked Queen Sonora."

"Stryga hunt starts at dawn tomorrow." Jack grunted. "I'm on a 'team,' and I still need a tracker. All the wards around the Poe Swamp are concerning."

"My stomach's been off, so it's either an Orcyslot of dark magic or it could be the toadstool soup I ate. Wish I could tag along and see you on a team." Dean chuckled. He wiped the pistol once more with a rag and then stood up to put it in a glass display case.

"Not my idea. Grimarr summoned me."

"How is the old salt? I don't see him much. He stopped trying to recruit me." Dean grinned.

"He's convinced this is something Alaric would want me to do."

"Ah, using the old Alaric ploy to get what he wants. What a bloated gibbet." They shook their heads in sync, like two brothers irritated by a father's expectations. "And Gunner still trying to hex you with his lack of skill for magic?"

Jack snorted. "He's trying. This stinks of a plan of his to lure me back and die in a vat of venomous guts. I'd leave if it weren't for Grim's insistence. Something *is* going on, and I doubt Narim planted a High Stryga just for me."

They laughed, but it was tinged with tension. Dean slapped his palms together and shook his head.

"I suppose you're here for Kyadem. Can't really hunt properly without her, eh?" He gave Jack a look of sarcastic teasing. Jack's set of weapons were uniquely put together by his own hand and blood, and he only trusted Dean to forge and repair them.

"I can pay you when it's done. Didn't have time to get the money," Jack said. He spread his hands apart. He also didn't exactly know how much the king would pay him should they be successful. Jack suspected platitudes were about all he was going to walk away with.

However, he also knew Dean, and money wasn't his only objective. As a younger man, he had loved to tinker with weapons of all sorts, magical or not, and rivaled dwarves in his ability to craft them. Dean had been the master pupil of Varen, the master gunsmith dwarf, for ten years. Varen gave him the secrets to crafting unique, priceless weapons, and access to vaults of material that no other human had set foot in. This often made Dean both a popular and unpopular fellow at parties.

Dwarves had crafted the singularly spectacular weapons for centuries and were gaining recognition for their specialty skills. They also owned the mines of Carbina, the light, hard material that made long guns and scattershots so weatherproof and accurate. Fairy lens optics also helped the weapons. Gunsmithing was becoming an art, and Elgar was renowned for its dwarven weapons.

JACK SERPENT

Jack pulled out his cache of weapons from the pack. "I can give you these as collateral." Axes, knives, bow and arrows, a sword, the rifle, five pistols, and a scattershot clattered out. His two main swords, Aetherys and Vyn, he set down, but they didn't need repair.

Dean laughed as he examined them all. "You've worked these to death."

"They weren't good stand-ins for Kya." The nickname for his weapon seemed to sing in the air, as if it knew he was close.

Jack's preferred weapon was a pair of chained blades: a silver-tipped claw on the end of a longer chain with a second shorter chain attached by another silver blade that had a handle. It was useful as both a knife and a sword, as well as a long-range whip. The weapon was also marked with his personal sigils and Scriver runes so that it could only be used by him.

"Aetherys and Vyn look well. Do they speak to you yet?" Dean side-eyed him.

Jack shook his head. "No. Just Carbina and gem-steel-infused blades."

"Hard won." Dean acknowledged with an incline of his head.

Jack nodded slightly. Aetherys had been a gift for winning the Scriver Trials. The long blade kept its sharp edge and shine despite the years of wear. Vyn he'd crafted himself through trial and error. The shorter sword was perfect for close-quarters combat or clearing a room. He hadn't been in the habit of naming his weapons, but magic had a way of telling him what it wanted to be called. The names had floated to his ears like a spectral whisper.

"Ah, Kya's all patched back up. Try not to break her again," Dean said with a grin. He stomped a floorboard, and a trapdoor opened. Jack followed him into the dug-out shelter that was a lot bigger than the trapdoor implied. Spelled torches flared to life when the men entered. The shelter boasted rooms upon rooms of cement-enforced walls, wooden beams, and shelves of supplies.

Dean headed to the room on the right and opened a chest. Jack immediately tensed in the weapon's presence. The hairs on his arms stood up, and whispers assaulted his ears.

"Hearing her again, huh," Dean said with a shake of his head. "I wish she'd talk to me like that."

"You wish women in general would talk to you," Jack replied with a snort.

Some weapons were more than mere tools of destruction. Kyadem was born of ember, bone, and blood. Alaric had given Jack a weapons-binding spell and let him figure it out for a week. What he hadn't told him was that the metal was imbued with natural, raw magic. It was one of the purest metals on all the continents. The deep magic sat within the metal like a soul—it would love and serve whoever was the first to claim it. He'd wrestled with the metal for three days before simply stroking its smooth surface and reliving his deepest memories. Tears woke the metal, it warmed in his palms, and his anguish was taken in exchange for eternal service. Jack should have been back long ago to collect it, but he hated coming home.

He knelt at the chest. The silver chains clinked, the runes on the blades glowed blue, and for a moment it seemed as if his breath had been stolen. He reached out and gently touched the handles of the blades, which were sharpened to perfection. They gleamed like beacons in a fog-covered ocean. More valuable than a Muran pirate's horde. Fixed to perfection after her last encounter with a coven of Strygan. Ravenhell.

"You really must teach me the binding you did with her." Dean cocked his head.

Jack stood, the chains sliding like molten lava over his hands and between his fingers as the blades sighed in the air. It was like a comfortable chair or a well-worn pair of good boots. Kyadem's material made her light like feathers but hit like a ton of boulders.

"I tried." Jack smiled at him.

"We can go again," Dean said with a roll of his eyes.

They went back up to the main level of the house, and the torches extinguished themselves as the trapdoor shut.

"So, you have a plan yet? I'm assuming this isn't just one Stryga you'll have to track." Dean plucked a pair of black pistols out of the pile on the table. "You'll be taking these, I presume."

Jack repressed his smile and nodded. The twin Winstar 459 pistols could hold silver, iron, copper, salt, or gemstone-infused bullets. They'd seen enough action that the springs needed replacing.

"I need to find someone familiar with Poe Swamp. I suspect the High Stryga herself might be hiding there, so close to the city ... she needs the source of life. It couldn't have been a Strix, as the smell left behind was too strong in deep magic, old arcane." Dean was familiar with those half-formed creatures, who desired to be full Strygan but in the process had tainted themselves too much, such that they would only ever be malformed with half power.

"Give me ten minutes with these," Dean said as he took the pistols apart in a matter of seconds. Magazines fell out, slides slid off, and gears bounced into his long-fingered hands. "You don't have a name for this High Stryga yet, I presume?"

Jack was impressed with Dean's knowledge. He often wondered why the other man hadn't tried his hand at being at Scriver. It was probably something to do with his attention span. Dean was many things, but patient and deliberate weren't among them. He was like an air thermal. Or, more likely, it was the unlikely success rate of passing trials, trials that hadn't run since Alaric's death.

"No. And I don't know how to kill her when I find her." Jack eyed Kyadem, and Dean coughed. Aetherys and Vyn were made of a combination of Carbina steel, iron, and infused magic, and they wouldn't be enough either, he wagered.

"I have a lot of faith in you, but I don't know that even Kya is up to that task. I've heard of Strygan surviving iron swords and rune-tipped arrows. Ever since the Covering, they've just unearthed magic that most cannot hope to control. Better bring the usual arsenal. I think you're going to have to get creative," Dean said as he fixed the springs for the pistols.

Jack took a seat and went through his inventory. First were the vials of serum that gave him an advantage when he needed it—night vision, hard skin, fast feet, endurance, and extrasensory ability, among others. They could be given to others as well. For whatever gods cursed or blessed reason, humans were the only species able to adapt and transform magic. Most other races were gifted with innate magic, but humans had learned to take parts from each to make themselves superior. Jack supposed they could thank Corvynia for spreading those secrets across the continents.

The serums were saturated with magic from a tattoo on his calf, which functioned as a multiplier of magic, so he didn't have to keep giving blood, hair, and breath. The tattoos had cost him years of his life in intense pain and recovery time. Some experimental tattoos hadn't worked, and he bore their scars. All was worth it, as it was far faster to simply use the magic in the runes on his body. Jack had only to whisper a word in the tongue of the Old Maidens and the magic sprang to his aid.

He didn't like to rely on them, but he also understood that when going up against creatures that were five times his size with skin harder than dwarven steel, he needed help. Alaric had taught him how to make the serums even though he himself hadn't seemed to need much.

Jack placed everything inside the pack, which was worn in many places with scratches down the leather and patched holes. He took out a cigar case, half-empty, the only thing he had from a father he'd known up until eight years old. The earthy, heavy scent still reminded him of nights around a fire with the other Milytor men, swapping stories. His father, Marken Serpent, had been the hero in many of them as told by other men. Marken was a quiet, steady presence who never boasted of his military career. He'd retired early to open a library that his wife ran for all the children of the village, no matter their status. How a coven of Strygan could take him down haunted Jack.

Dean kept a stash of black-market cigars, and Jack knew exactly where they were. The man barely looked up as Jack opened a humidor and rooted around in it.

"Been to see Lyra?" Dean asked as he clicked the gears, checking the trigger. He cycled a round through the chamber and plucked the bullet out of the air when it ejected. Jack would have ignored anyone else who asked. Dean was always direct and expected the same from any of his friends. He was like fresh mountain air cutting through smoke.

"No." Jack's stomach twisted at the thought of her wandering the halls of an asylum alone. "Is she well?" He couldn't see her now, not before a mission. His head needed to remain clear.

Dean side-eyed him. "What makes you think I check on her for you?" He snorted. "She's calm, quiet. Not herself, still."

Jack nodded. He'd given up trying to figure out what had happened that night with the ward spells when Lyra had lost her mind. Dean knew when to leave a subject. He handed Jack the newly repaired Winstar, and Jack checked the mechanisms by habit.

"Is this going to be worse than Ravenhell?" Dean asked. Jack sensed the man watching him out of the corner of his eye.

He pursed his lips. If anyone would believe the truth, it'd be Dean, but what was the point? The truth was that in the name of vengeance, he'd done things he couldn't atone for and possibly didn't seek any absolution from. His parents hadn't deserved the torture they'd gone through, and he had done everything in his power to erase that memory. Ravenhell had not cured him of nightmares. It was a moment he was not proud of, even if most everyone else spoke about Ravenhell like it was legend.

"And there's those dead eyes that soldiers still talk about. All right, keep your secrets." Dean winked. "It's the only reason people even remember Scrivers."

Jack inclined his head. Of the five, he was the only one who'd done anything remarkable, the kind of thing people didn't soon forget. It hadn't been intentional, but it stuck with him now.

Dean handed him the repaired weapon. Jack smiled his thanks and packed the firearms into his bag. Kyadem followed, folding into a nice compact circle of chain and blade.

He paused. "If you're bored, and I know most of the time you are, how about a flyover once a day with your comms on?"

Dean grinned and tilted his head. "Are you asking for help?" His brows rose.

Jack tsked. "I was actually asking if you still have that flyer that's worth nothing sitting around."

He held out his hand to Dean, who shook it and then opened the front door. Briny air mixed with animal dander and horseless carriages rushed past them. Carriages powered by gem-infused crystals that allowed the driver to move forward and backward. "See, now you want to use her. She's a prize, mate."

They paused at the deep gonging of bells. Death tolls.

Jack didn't wave farewell—the other man wouldn't have wanted the attention. He didn't need any further confirmation to know his friend would circle the area once a day in case something happened. Jack had long ago learned that putting backup plans in place usually increased survival, but it was usual for him to have help as reliable as Dean's.

He walked away from the house using a soft invisibility spell—it was highly complicated magic to disappear entirely, but this one cloaked his presence so no one would notice him leaving. The nondescript building faded behind him like it had never existed.

He headed toward the several rows of semipermanent lodging known as the Inns. He needed sleep despite his mind's whirring. Jack itched to get on the trail of the High Stryga before something worse happened.

Chapter Seven

Why three trials? Seems an arbitrary number of tests and no one has an answer. Vocyre—magic summoning. Salvuros—survival. Literata—intelligence. All combatants are human. Most chosen from the Milytor except for a few. However, they are gifted with certain traits like an affinity to wield magic, high perception and problem solving, physical strength, from certain bloodlines, or other traits. These men and women are to provide service to the Milytor as many things: historians, soldiers, spies, and protectors. Although, like so many great ideas before it, it has become rife with lies, misperceptions, and power mongering.
*Archivers note: modified some text to reflect an academic observance but will leave in Scriver #5's words as much as possible.
~ Scryptus, the Scriver Archives,
as recounted by Scriver #5 Jack Serpent, Tome 2

Aylla stretched, and her back snapped in all the right places. She sighed at the heavenly breakfast laid out in her room: eggs, sausages, tomatoes, and some sort of dark ale, along with a tankard of water. She ate quickly while gazing out the window at the burning colors of the trees that spread out around Asnor. The city teemed with people in the streets already, getting ready for the Thresher Festival.

The Brown Shepherd owners knew her. They were a lovely couple who couldn't have been more mismatched: Dun was a tall, bald-headed giant of a man, while Gladys was a petite, curvy brunette. They had known her mother, Lavynia van Hyde, and welcomed Aylla anytime.

It was one reason to find a place to live in the city, but Aylla would miss her wolves too much—them and the peaceful woods, where there was only the rustle of birds, the songs of the bush creatures, and the hush of the trees. She didn't take the freedom to come and go as she pleased for granted either. She'd lived with a tyrant of an uncle for far too long after her father's death. The black disease that supposedly took her father had never sat well with her. Neither she nor her mother had gotten sick nor shown any symptoms of the cough and fever.

After eating, she bathed hastily with a wet cloth and put on a long, emerald-green tunic dress with slits in the skirt to allow for pants. Aylla had seen other women wear this fashion in other cities, but it wouldn't have mattered if it were a fashion faux pas. She preferred to be able to run, climb, and ride at a moment's notice. The tunic at least resembled a dress. She let her dark hair loose down her back. Wolf hair clung to her pants, and she brushed it off.

Aylla tidied the bed and slung her small pack over one shoulder. She traveled lightly. Gladys met her with a smile and set a mug of ale down on a table.

"Restless night, dear?" Gladys asked with a sympathetic smile.

She frowned. "No, why?"

"Oh, I thought I heard you screaming in your sleep. But after all the chaos that happened last night, it might have been me ears playin' tricks." Gladys lowered her voice. "Did you hear the queen was murdered and her child stolen?"

Aylla let out a breath. "That's horrible. What's to be done?" Her stomach lurched. She'd only ever seen the queen a few times, out walking or standing beside the king as he addressed the people. From all the gossip, Aylla knew Queen Sonora was a kind woman who was going to give the king a dozen children. If she was murdered and her child was missing, Ocrana would be thrown under Milytor control. Life was about to change, and she wasn't sure she wanted to be around for it. It was how she survived—stay low, stay safe.

"The king is decreeing a Stryga hunt." Gladys eyed her pack. "I hope you are prepared to defend yourself. People get crazy when hunting begins. The Volg won't stand for this."

"I won't be staying past this afternoon, but thanks for the warning."

Aylla moved out of the tavern and the sunlight warmed her skin. It seemed to sizzle the bad nightmares of the night away. She did remember waking screaming. Wolves had been chasing her and her mother; then one turned into Drace, her uncle, and he choked the life from her mother before turning his fangs on Aylla's throat.

The Thresher Festival didn't seem deterred despite the tragic news of the night before. If anything, people were more determined to carry on and make mourning into a celebration of life. King Thuramond didn't tend to go out much among the people, nor did he seem to care for their petty problems like high taxes, livestock death—and lately, missing children. All his attention was on how and why some of the other continents were gathering more power and magic than Elgar.

Aylla shivered as she passed the city center. Ash marks were all that lingered of the riot the other night. Her skin didn't tingle anymore, and her body returned to normal. Still, the torrential wind couldn't have had anything to do with her. She was just a forgettable, quiet girl who lived alone with her animals.

"Excuse me," a gruff voice said, and a hand shoved her. The man's hand brushed down her arm, close to her breast.

Aylla caught her balance as a blond man with a scar on his neck glanced her over like a horse at market and smiled. He didn't linger, but his gaze raked her so hard it made her muscles tense like a caught bird. He was flanked by two young men in soldier's uniforms, one of whom carried a long-gun bag over his shoulder. They had packs on their backs and serious expressions.

Aylla didn't make a fuss about the uncomfortable contact, because that was how women got targeted. Drawing attention had gotten her in more trouble than it was worth. It was a sad truth.

She'd never had many women as friends and much preferred men's company. They were less complicated—especially Milytor soldiers like these young men. Most of them only wanted a warm body, and Aylla didn't mind playing into it if it let her leave unscathed. More than once she'd flirted them down an alley or into a room and slipped out as soon as they thought they were getting what they wanted. It let her fool herself into thinking she'd never be in a position like her mother had been in with Drace. She moved away from the soldiers but remained within earshot, and soon she heard the Volg mentioned.

"The Volg could be anyone," one of the soldiers said to his friend.

"They usually smell of crazy."

They both chuckled.

"Wait for me at the Brown Shepherd; ask for Dun to open the back room," the man with the scar said and walked away.

The two other soldiers shrugged and turned left. Aylla's curiosity was piqued at the mention of the innkeeper. Were they hunting for whatever had killed the queen? There were several rooms at the inn that could pass for "back rooms." Dun seemed to be getting into shady business if he was allowing secret soldier meetings.

She trailed the men, buying a few supplies along the way: rope, wire, new boots, and a knife. She didn't want Dun and Gladys to have trouble with the soldiers. The Milytor weren't known for their acts of kindness.

Aylla snuck around the back of the inn as the two soldiers asked Dun for the room and he obliged. He took a golden key and marched to the back of the tavern. Aylla peered in through the windows. She'd never been in the kitchen area, but she crept there now. Past the huge hearths baking bread, the griddles frying meat, and an ice room, there lay a door without windows. Dun unlocked it, and the two men stepped inside. He handed them the key.

Aylla frowned at Dun's almost terrified expression. His hands shook as he ran them over his bald head. The soldiers hadn't threatened him or treated him badly. What was he so afraid of? She slipped around the window.

For the second time that day, a hand grabbed her. This time it was more than a brush, forcibly pulling her back. Aylla spun into a kick, but the man on the receiving end caught her ankle and twisted. She fell but rightened herself quickly and was back on her feet in a second. The man's face was in shadow, and a hood covered his head. His eyes flared purple, and Aylla reached for the knife in her bag.

"You should wear that instead of sticking it uselessly in a bag," he said. His voice was deep and husky, but it had a lyrical lilt like water running over rocks. The accent wasn't exactly local, though it seemed it was almost as if he were trying to make it sound that way.

Aylla quirked a brow. "Says the man grabbing women he doesn't know."

"You were about to step on a thetera." The man pointed to the left, and Aylla glanced down. The tail of a black snake slithered into the bushes. They were venomous, so she supposed he was waiting for a thank you. Aylla looked at him fully now. Perhaps not. His face was blank, as if he didn't expect a damn thing from her.

He wore a long black coat with silver buckles over a leather, armor-like vest and a gray shirt and dark boots. The hood slanted shadows over sharp cheekbones and a razor-edged jaw. His shoulders were broad, and he was tall enough that she had to tilt her head up to look at him. Two swords with black pommels and a small sigil in the circle on the hilt adorned his back, and she glimpsed the butts of pistols in holsters at his sides under the coat. Aylla stepped closer to see the symbols on the hilts of the sword, and her breath stilled. They were of a sword thrust down into a crescent moon, three lines like claw marks slashed below the crescent with a half-triangle shape. She knew that sigil.

"And I was curious why you were spying on two of the King's Milytor," he said with a smile that didn't reach his dark, almost black eyes. They stared with an intensity to rival a raven's, a curious mix of emotionless shadow with flecks of gold.

By the blights of Oreman, she cursed inwardly. *He's a Scriver? A real one?*

Chapter Eight

The Namazu catfish has three hearts and retracting spikes on the pectoral fins. Beware the fins when catching them. To kill the fish, whether in self-defense or for consumption be sure to decapitate but also cut lengthwise to slice through the hearts or it will continue to thrash, in which case a jab from the spikes is inevitable. Also tastes bitter, almost thought it poisoned.
Would not recommend eating.
~ Scryptus, the Scriver Archives,
as recounted by Scriver #5 Jack Serpent, Tome 12

Aylla composed her face quickly. But it was too late; he had caught her, and she refused to admit he intimidated her. If he was a real Scriver, she couldn't be sure how he would react. Likely he wasn't and was just trying to play her for something. The only time she'd ever met a so-called Scriver was at her father's funeral. Apparently, the priest had sent word for the Scriver to come make sure Sebastian van Hyde was truly dead and not cursed, waiting to return. Being only six at the time, Aylla hadn't thought much about it, or why his death was deemed slightly unusual.

A healthy farmer didn't simply keel over in his field and then contract a disease that made him cough up his lungs. The medicus said his heart might have been weak and open to maladies. Some seed pods could release toxins if stepped upon. Aylla and her mother didn't believe that. His older brother Drace had taken them in, even though his attentions and money weren't wanted. He took more than advantage of their situation, and Aylla was always suspicious that he'd somehow created it in the first place.

"I wasn't," she said in answer to the Scriver's last statement. Aylla smoothed her tunic and made to step away. Best to play along if he thought he was a Scriver; she didn't want the ire of a stranger, but something about him intrigued her.

He blocked her so swiftly she barely registered he'd moved. The question was in his eyes, and it was clear he wasn't going to go until she answered.

"I overheard them speaking of a room here that I wasn't aware of. I was curious." It was the truth, but she left out the part where she'd overheard them speaking of Strygan.

"You come here often?"

"As needed. I know the owners. I'm sure you have important business that I won't keep you from," she said with a casual smile. *He's just another man—don't engage, and he'll lose interest.*

The Scriver seemed satisfied with the answer, or perhaps he felt she was no threat. "It would be wise in the future to not follow Milytor."

So, he's with the Milytor. Aylla was more certain than ever that he wasn't an actual Scriver. Supposedly there were only one or two in the world anyway. He was just another soldier looking for fun or making sure she wasn't a threat.

"I was concerned for my friends, the owners. I didn't want trouble for them." Aylla shook her head, unable to let him think she was one of the shallow girls who followed soldiers around, thinking they'd make good husbands.

His lips quirked for a moment. He nodded at her and then glanced at her boots. Aylla followed his gaze. Bits of straw, mud, and wolf hair clung to the black leather. The interior was warm wool, but it did make wolf hair stick to the rim. No matter how she tried to get it off, it seemed to cling to her.

"Do you know of a local who's familiar with Poe Swamp?" he asked after a moment.

"No, why? Thinking of building a summer home in there?" Aylla narrowed her eyes. What had he seen that she hadn't? She mistrusted everyone, but he put her at ill ease just by breathing. Maybe it was the dark eyes that flared with such odd light or the relaxed but confident stance that reminded her of an alpha predator. Most likely it was the association with Milytor.

The man didn't laugh, but his eyes alighted in amusement. "I need to speak with someone who's been in there recently or has knowledge of the terrain."

"Why?"

He fixed her with a stark gaze. When he took the hint that she was to be no further help, he nodded in thanks and headed inside the tavern.

"I've been inside the swamp, a week ago," she called. *What are you doing? He was letting you leave.* Aylla didn't know what made her want to continue speaking to him. But if there was a way to know the danger ahead beforehand, it might benefit her. Right?

The man turned in the doorway, and sunlight glinted off his sword hilts. He'd taken down his hood, which made his face less severe. In the brightness, the gold of his eyes took over. Light stubble covered a square jaw. His lips remained in a neutral line.

"Can I buy you a meal?" he asked.

For an entirely inappropriate moment, Aylla's heart leapt. No one had ever bought her anything for years, unless it was a drunken man wanting to get her into a private room. Her stomach rumbled. Breakfast seemed so long ago. Her mistrust weakened at the mention of food. And the inn would be filled with people if anything should go awry.

"They have an excellent venison pie and vegetable stew, if Gladys hasn't changed the menu." Aylla walked past him in search of her friend. She thought she heard him chuckle behind her.

They passed the secret door where the two soldiers waited and sat at a table in a back corner. Aylla took a sip of water and licked her lips. She had noticed the man giving it a glance and realized he'd obviously been tracking them too. Were they his friends, allies, or targets?

"Do I get to know whom I'm conversing with, or is this on a need-to-know basis?" Aylla asked as she introduced herself.

He paused as his eyes swept the room, keeping track of everyone in the tavern. "It doesn't matter. I'd appreciate it if you told me what you know about the swamp." He didn't say it rudely, and Aylla had delt with surlier men than him.

"So, you're not a real Scriver?" she asked, hoping to get something out of him other than the inquisitive stare.

He cleared his throat. The top button of his shirt was unbuttoned, and beneath it the start of a black rune mark poked out. "Does that have any bearing on whether you'll give me information?"

"Can you do magic?" she asked, ignoring his question. She'd heard true Scrivers, if there were any left in the world, could wield magic like the sorcerers. Most humans could handle a few spells, but their bodies gave out or their minds became corrupted.

He sighed. "Not in here."

"Of course not." She fixed him with a slanted stare. "I've only met one Scriver before, and he didn't seem to know an awful lot about monsters or magic. He did know quite a lot of whores." She raised a brow. Not even that made him pause or frown in offense.

He just raised his brows back at her and drank his ale. Aylla smiled. She liked a challenge, especially if it was one she could have a bit of fun with.

"Nothing wrong with making a living, eh?" he asked with a shrug.

Aylla smiled dryly. "Not quite the same as a soldier killing for fun, is it?"

The man stilled the ale traveling to his mouth. "Are you implying that I am a soldier or I kill for fun?"

Aylla hated that her gaze couldn't match his. The man's dark eyes conveyed a preternatural stillness, wary but lethal, and said more than words could. Most men she glared at looked away and never returned. It was as if there were years, decades, of darkness that he could summon behind those eyes, a pain that was shattered like crystal. For a moment, all sound and air were sucked out around them, and she was only aware of him. Her self-preservation broke through to common sense, and she shook her head. Sounds of cutlery, dropped tankards, stomping boots, and chatter assaulted her ears.

"You came to the defense of the Milytor I was following, so one can only assume." Aylla tapped her fork on the table, waiting for food. "You have the look of a 'trained' man."

The man swallowed, but his eyes never left hers. He seemed slightly surprised by her reaction. "If by 'trained' you mean 'could spot a desperate, disagreeable person with not much to lose' then yes, I am." He toasted her with the tankard.

Aylla's eyes narrowed. "You certainly are arrogant enough to be a soldier." *Why can't you stop?* she chided herself. Perhaps it was just latent aggression toward Uncle Drace—if he could even be called an uncle. What sort of brother moved in on his dead brother's wife within a matter of months? Drace had served in the Milytor for a few years before mysteriously coming home with a tale that he'd broken his ankle, and they wouldn't let him serve anymore.

"As good a reason as I'm sure you have for disliking the Milytor, I either need information about Poe Swamp, or I'll need to take my leave," he said.

Aylla's gaze swept around the room for the barmaid to bring their food. None could be found. She should just leave too. Arguing with a soldier was only going to get her into trouble. Her mother always said that was the one thing Aylla was good at. She half stood, knocking a knife off the table.

He caught it deftly and deposited the slender utensil beside her plate with precision. Aylla couldn't help her curiosity now. Her distaste for his company was overridden by it.

"How did you do that?"

The man raised a brow.

"Move that fast. No soldier I've seen has reflexes that rival a parroche." The sea birds that lived on the coasts of Asnor were known for their extraordinary flying tactics and thievery. Their talons were nimbler than ten fingers.

"I've had some training," he responded with a small, ironic smile.

Aylla grunted. Let him keep his secrets, then. She'd never see him again. She stood with a shrug and felt around her pockets for coin for the meal she wanted to eat, though it seemed it was taking years to come.

"I really would be interested in your knowledge." The man's features softened as he gestured to her seat.

Aylla sat reluctantly.

She gave him base information about going through the Dred Plains to get to the swamp—to look out for plains cats, scorpions, and snakes, of course.

The barmaid delivered their pies with a flourish and a lingering gaze at the man across from her. He didn't return it. The venison pie was creamy, with onion chunks and a flaky crust. Aylla savored it—onions would soon be out of season. The man's only comment was about the crust. The flakiness wasn't quite to his liking; the cook should have used more lard and layered the dough. Her interest piqued. Why would he know how pies were made?

"I worked in the Milytor kitchen for a while—don't ask," he said between bites. Aylla sensed there was something underneath the light words. She'd heard from Uncle Drace that punishments in the Milytor included labor in the mines and kitchens, or even on ships of the line.

Quite the connoisseur of everything, wasn't he? Aylla shrugged her thoughts away.

"Any changes in the terrain over the last month? Gas pits, sand swirls, fire insects?" he asked.

"None that I know of." Aylla thought back to the black substance that had killed the boar and a few other animals a while back. It wasn't rampant, so she didn't think it was important. Besides, the swamp changed a lot. She said as much.

"Are you not familiar at all with Asnor's swamps? Your accent sounds like you're from somewhere near here," she said. He was more closed about personal details than the books on her shelves at home, gathering dust.

"I haven't been here in a long time." He scraped the plate with his fork.

"I imagine you'd know about the Darro then?" Aylla asked as she cut a piece of venison. The meat was unsurprisingly tender, the signature of Dun and his cooks. If this soldier was a Scriver then he'd have knowledge of poisons. She'd read all the articles years ago about the elite Milytor soldiers who not only fought like demons but could kill with all the knowledge they possessed about monster weaknesses. Aylla might never run into a monster worse than her uncle, but she certainly understood how to kill a man should the need arise.

"What form—crushed, dried, infused?" the man countered.

Aylla's lips quirked upward. "Dried."

"Deadly." He regarded her with a tilted chin. "Mashed, it makes for a wonderful poultice to treat wounds, so long as they aren't too deep."

"Do you know why the dried form is poisonous?" Aylla wanted to test him, but she didn't know the answer either. Maybe he did.

"Plant self-defense. As it matures, getting closer to spreading more seed and then death, it becomes toxic for most animals and humans, so they leave it alone. Or one would assume—trial and error, after all." He shrugged.

Huh. That makes sense, I suppose. If I had a library of knowledge available, maybe I'd be a lot smarter. Aylla couldn't help but be envious. She'd heard that some soldiers had access to the Karnuhym monastery library, and inside that building was the most knowledge collected since the Malecanta's libraries were burned.

"A book called *Thorns and Pests* is readily available in Asnor's library."

Aylla nodded. She used caution going into that library again after a merchant sailor tried to assault her. The huge stacks of books and isolated corners made good hiding places for people waiting for unsuspecting victims. Books were also good weapons when used properly, she'd found. Aylla simply "borrowed" books from time to time when she snuck in at night. She always returned them ... except the one that Hugo had torn up.

"I'm assuming you read," the man continued, and Aylla stiffened. His boyish smirk made him appear so much younger.

"And just because you *can* read doesn't make you a Scriver." She brushed hair out of her eyes. He focused on the movement. Aylla thought of herself as very observant, but this man noticed everything around them, from the cat licking its paw in the corner to her unconscious motion. His eyes tracked it all.

He asked about other plants in the swamp, and Aylla could match every one he named. She again thought about mentioning the black substance on the animals she'd seen. Their conversation stalled. Aylla wasn't sure why she hesitated. If he wasn't a Scriver, he couldn't help with that, but his knowledge had almost proved to her that he might be telling the truth. Why else would he brazenly display the sigils on his weapons?

"Thank you for the information," he said, and stacked his empty tankard on the plate with the utensils.

"There's one more thing. Might not have any significance," she said, and described the black mystery substance that had coated the animals and killed them. If it harmed animals, she was sure it wasn't friendly to humans either.

His entire demeanor seemed to change now that he had what he wanted. The genial manner and soft smile vanished, in their place a calculated, hard-featured expression, as if he was already planning for something ahead. He thanked her again, and she could see thoughts churning in his head.

He tossed coins on the table, more than enough to cover their meal, and stood. Aylla looked up at him.

"May I ask if there's something coming?" She could feel magic in the air around him, her skin prickling. He radiated an unusual energy that heated her, like getting too close to a fire.

Aylla wanted to be prepared if there was darkness descending on Asnor.

The so-called Scriver paused and considered her. "There's always something coming. I feel you'll fare just fine, though." He smiled, and it softened the lines of his mouth—the façade dropping for an instant. Aylla stared a moment too long for her taste. She chastised herself and turned away.

He disappeared down a corridor toward the secret door. She warred with herself for a full ten minutes. No, she wouldn't follow. She needed to get back home to Ash and Hugo. It didn't matter who he was because she wasn't going to be part of whatever he was involved in. At least she'd gotten a bit of a warning. Something was certainly happening; she'd better not stick around for it.

Aylla stood, grateful for the meal, and her eye caught a blond man coming in. She ducked behind a stone pillar and waited for him to pass. It was the same scarred man who'd groped her in the market.

Aylla thought about throwing the last of her ale in his face but decided against it. *Trouble will find you all on its own, Tideling—don't go making it,* her mother's voice warned in her head. She likened her daughter to the ever-shifting tides, always seeking, always restless.

And then the soldier's words. *Something is always coming.*

"Isn't that the truth," Aylla said aloud, and left the Brown Shepherd tavern. She could be back home by dark if she hurried.

Chapter Nine

Black stains, disturbed earth where no vegetation will grow, or a ring of dead animals is most likely Strygan magic. They cannot sustain their own and must steal it from the living. Strygan alliances are rare, but they are known to collaborate with other species if it suits them.
~ Scryptus, the Scriver Archives,
as recounted by Scriver #5 Jack Serpent, Tome 4

Jack was up with the sun. The black pack sat beside him as he waited for the team to assemble. The tavern was quiet in the early hours. Drunks slept in the corners, cooks prepared breakfast, and bartenders washed their glasses or picked up the leftover ones. He positioned himself near the back door, able to bolt if he needed to or trap anyone who came in.

He didn't have to wait long. A knock, and then the two soldiers entered. One was female, tall, skinny, and young, perhaps in her mid-twenties, with an umber skin tone and short black hair cut in a slant down her cheekbones. The other was male, a few years older. Fair-skinned, he had a thin layer of caramel-blond beard and carried a Phantom long-gun case. They both carried Piat scattershots, swords, and pistols.

"Are you Jack?" the woman asked with the eagerness of youth.

"He's the Scriver," her companion supplied helpfully, but also in warning as if Jack were an eidolon. Jack ignored them both. As far as he was concerned, the only thing interesting about the man was the Phantom case. He wondered how the scope was on it, it looked modified.

"Oh."

They sat down at a table away from Jack, but the darker, younger woman kept her wide eyes on him. Not many women served in the Milytor, but the ones Jack had trained with years ago had performed and challenged each other just as well as any man. This woman's uniform was spotless, her sword polished, boots comfortably broken in but shining. It was hardly the attire Jack would pick for going into a swamp. He'd read their files; he knew more about them than they likely did about him.

This can't be a real team. Narim's up to something. If this is payback for Jethen's death, it's a poor plan. Jack couldn't place his finger on it, but something was off. Once again, though, Narim couldn't have plotted the queen's death. That would be too far even for him. He might be the shyf-stain of a wyvern, but he wasn't a traitor.

Jack examined the two soldiers. He didn't underestimate anyone, no matter their age, but he was also good at reading people. These two might have certain areas of expertise, but they had no idea what they were going after.

The male, stockier, had wavy, caramel-colored hair and dark amber eyes. He glanced at the tables. The woman got up and offered a hand to Jack with a wide smile.

"Benjamina Hynde."

Jack refused to be rude, so he shook the proffered hand. "Jack."

"Most call me Bean."

The male soldier grinned and added, "Because that's the size of her brain."

Bean rolled her eyes and huffed. They had the raillery of soldiers who'd known each other for years.

Jack nodded perfunctorily. He'd had his fill of talking with strangers for a year, but it seemed he was fated to keep doing it. Although, speaking with Aylla hadn't exactly been torture. He just hadn't been in the company of a woman for months. She wasn't deterred by his ill manners, and she'd broken down a soft, simple spell of focus he'd tried on her. That was unusual. Most people couldn't counter that sort of magic, but she'd done it almost subconsciously. Her hatred for the Milytor wasn't unusual, though. Soldiers often took advantage of young women. Perhaps she had a similar story, though Jack told himself he wasn't interested.

"Mykel Beaumont." The other soldier introduced himself. He did not get up to shake hands.

Jack nodded. He knew from the file he had read that Mykel was gaining a reputation for being the best Phantom shot in Ocrana. His bullets could strike a target a mile and a half out, and they never knew it was coming. Jack noted the sheath around a Golden Summit Phantom. It was similar to his Eagle's Claw, but probably more accurate and he'd bet Mykel modified it. Anyone that good would have modified their weapon of choice. Jack certainly did.

Bean studied him so closely Jack thought he might be under interrogation. Her perfume certainly was making his head dizzy. When had

Grimarr unbanned fragrance on the soldiers? Or perhaps because she was away from the barracks, she was indulging in a former life she still wanted.

"So, where have you traveled? I hear you get to all the continents," Bean said, picking at a scone on a plate. "It's why I joined the Milytor, really—I want to travel. And protect the royals, of course."

"We failed at that, didn't we," Mykel said bitterly. "Can't believe a Drana-fucking Stryga got in."

"You *are* the only Scriver left, right?" Bean asked. Jack inclined his head slightly.

"I believe Grim—he said the other four perished." Mykel pursed his lips, but his gaze was probing.

Jack didn't disagree. The door opened, and Narim strode in. His white-blond hair, slicked back in a braided ponytail, made his dark armor, trimmed with silver, more striking. The Milytor uniforms didn't bear the royal sigil, instead discreet and plain. They were still too polished for Jack's liking, but they were functional. The two soldiers stood and saluted, one arm extended down, the other in a serving position across their body, hands into fists. Formally, it was to show respect to a commanding officer, showing they had no weapons and none within easy reach.

"Morning, soldiers." Narim glared at Jack, who did not salute. He wasn't bound by their laws or to respect command.

Jack inclined his head at him as if Narim smelled like goat dung. Grimarr and the king could force him to serve, but he wasn't going to follow this bottom scrubber blindly.

"You've been informed of the king's mission and Asnor's sorrow. Firstly, we need to confirm the High Stryga is in the swamp and second, take her in. Alive, if possible, but eliminating the threat is the bottom line. If our information is incorrect, then we will follow another path," he said, and waited for responses.

"How do we know she's in Poe Swamp?" Mykel asked.

"Thesal potions and our hounds have tracked dark magic there. It's a logical place to start—the Stryga would need a hiding place to recuperate after such an effort. Even for a Stryga, the murder used a huge amount of magic."

The tavern shook violently, and they all leapt up.

Jack bolted from the room ahead of everyone, out into the main tavern. He peered out the windows. The people who were awake at the early hour ran around outside like rats smoked from their home, but there was no obvious malice nearby, just a dark smoke stain against the brightening sky. It pulsed purple and then faded into a shimmer that rained down like lightning.

"A spell," Narim said as if he were the ultimate authority. "She's definitely in the swamp—look where it's hovering."

"It's a ward, a warning. Could be something tried to get in and failed," Jack said, and the two soldiers looked between them.

Jack didn't wait for anyone else. He sprinted outside, leaped onto a seller's bread table, latched on to the lattice on the side of the tavern, and shimmied up to the roof. The Brown Shepherd wasn't the tallest building in Asnor, but it gave him a clear view to the west. In the far distance, past the Dred Plains, the Proepucia Swamp sat like a wart on a toad.

The haze of a spell fastened around that one spot as if beckoning them to come, daring them to come. Narim, Mykel, and Bean stood in the street and looked up at him.

"We'll go in by air lift. I'll have the flyer ready in an hour," Narim called up.

Jack would rather be dumped in a vat of boiling goblin guts than get on a flying ship. It was a tad dramatic, but Shertan was his best, most reliable form of transport. "I'll meet you at the edge of the swamp. Watch out for plains cats."

He jumped to the roof of another building as Narim began cursing.

Chapter Ten

Strygan do not have four breasts, two hearts, or elongated pelvic regions. No idea where those rumors came from but can confirm none of them are true. Hate to break the disillusionment. The blue spotted Gink, however, does have what could be considered four breasts and the female flaunts this in mating season.
*Archivers note: attempted to replicate crude drawing of said Gink. Omitted the Strygan art.
~ Scryptus, the Scriver Archives,
as recounted by Scriver #5 Jack Serpent, Tome 4

Crisp air was so much better than the layered smells of the city. Aylla stoked her fire and sat in a chair she'd made, testing its balance. Ash and Hugo hadn't left her side, excitedly yipping and play bowing. The small cabin was blessedly silent except for the normal sounds of the forest, yet she couldn't shake the man's face from her mind. It wasn't like he'd been particularly impressive, and he was associated with the Milytor. But there was something about him that stuck in her mind like a pinprick. He was nothing like the rumors she'd heard about Scrivers, if he really was one. It certainly wasn't the deep, dark hazel eyes, or were they more brown flecked with gold—she recalled they changed a lot—or the stubbled jaw, or the long-fingered hands with scars and runes on them that kept her thinking about him.

"I think I've been alone too long," she said to the wolves.

Ash nudged her hand as if offended.

"I know, but who's going to put up with you two? Oh well, I never intend to be partnered with anyone anyway. See where that got my mother." Aylla went out the door to collect more firewood and see if the early-autumn mushrooms had popped up yet.

She'd been woken from strange dreams by a distant explosion earlier that morning. Aylla had raced outside but hadn't seen anything immediately threatening her home, just sparks that rained down like starshine to the west near the Poe Swamp line. The wolves had taken off later that morning but came back with nothing unusual.

Still, there was something off. Aylla didn't like living so close to the swamp anymore. A droning buzzed overhead, and she glanced up. Flyers were getting more and more frequent as people learned how to pilot the vessels. They used hot air in the sails to float and a spinning propeller for propulsion. A fair number of magic-infused geodes were necessary to keep it safely flying with the proper spells and monitoring of fires, so not everyone could fly them. That was the simple version she'd been told by a man in the market who wanted to sell her a helmet and parachute, should she be riding on one.

This flyer had the royal crest on the sail and was outfitted with light cannons. A Milytor flyer. Aylla was fairly sure no one could see her home in the midst of the thick trees. But they probably weren't interested in her. It had to do with the explosion that morning. Now her curiosity was piqued even more.

"Come on, boys." Aylla packed a small bag, slung it across her body, and doused the fire. Her split skirts were perfect for hiking, and the new boots needed breaking in. "If there's a Stryga in our woods, we should know about it."

The trees ruffled their leaves in flutters of gold and crimson as they followed the Flyer. It hovered and then disappeared beneath the tree line in an open field in the Dred Plains. Aylla kept to the tree line as they neared the Flyer. Male voices floated to her. Then a female. Aylla remained hidden as the female soldier went over her gear bag. She knew women served in the Milytor—had considered it herself but knew she wasn't suited to a life of being given orders, nor did she have such loyalty to Asnor that she would die for the kingdom.

The heavy thud of hooves made her crouch in the shadows.

A huge blue roan horse charged through tall yellow grass with the Scriver soldier on his back. She was surprised to see him again so soon, and yet it seemed no coincidence from their discussion the other day. *He seems to be in the thick of whatever's happening ... he never confirmed if he was working with or for the Milytor. So what's he doing with them?* The soldier's black coat billowed behind him as he dismounted, and his swords clanked as he slung a pack over his shoulder. He untacked the horse in a matter of moments. The twin butts of two pistols poked out on either side of his open black coat.

"Took you long enough," a soldier called out, and Aylla recognized the blond hair and scar. From the decoration on his uniform, he was more than a foot soldier. A captain, perhaps.

"I said east field, fifteen strides after the giant Yuckta trees," the man in black shot back. He patted the horse on the neck and gave him a whispered command. The horse arched his neck, snorted, and then galloped away. The man tapped a symbol on the saddle and bridle. They shrank to fit into the pack he'd slung on the ground. Aylla's eyes widened. He hadn't used any sacrifice that she could see. Most people had to carefully give something up for magic like that. The two younger soldiers whispered to each other, but the captain did not look impressed.

"We can't get in from the ground—let's go."

The soldier hesitated at the threshold of the flyer. Aylla didn't blame him.

A soft growl from Hugo alerted her to Ash. The silvery-gray wolf trotted toward her with something dark in his mouth.

"Ash," she whispered. "Drop that."

The wolf let a dead black bird the size of his head fall at her feet. It stank of sulfur and iron. Hugo sniffed it and growled again. The bird was covered in a similar black substance to the boar. A flock rose in the air in the distance, their cries sounding like screams. The wolves flicked their ears back and lashed their tails.

Ash shook his head violently as the black substance started to crawl all over his muzzle like a living thing. He whined and pawed at his face.

"Shyf," she cursed. Aylla dug out a salve and cloth. She grabbed his head and furiously wiped at his face, but the black substance wouldn't come off. It was like touching warm sludge, and it felt as if it were alive. The salve was made of Cumberbane and sunflower oil—it usually got anything off everything. It was very useful in cleaning wounds as well.

"Halt—who's hiding there?" the female soldier shouted.

Aylla turned to see the Milytor soldiers heading her way. "Goddesses boil me." She rose and held up a hand. Hugo stood in front of her with his teeth bared, hackles up.

"Stop, please. I'm not eavesdropping. I live here, and my wolf got into a bit of trouble," Aylla shouted. "We'll be away soon."

The two young soldiers paused at the sight of Hugo and the thrashing Ash. Aylla desperately scrubbed and scraped at the wolf's head. She couldn't quell the panic rising in her chest. What if she couldn't get it off? He'd end up like the boar. His whines became increasingly more painful.

"Ma'am, we need the area clear ..." The woman shifted on her feet uncertainly.

"Do you know what this black shyf is and how to get it off?" She hated the fevered pitch in her voice and didn't care if she'd just insulted the revered goddess Shyf.

Ash lay down with a glazed look in his eyes. Hugo went to lick him, and she shoved him back. The wolf snapped at her in warning. As much as she'd trained them, they were still wild animals with centuries-old instincts.

The blond Milytor captain pushed past them and leveled his pistol at her wolves. Aylla commanded Hugo to retreat, and he reluctantly ran a few steps back into the trees. She crouched in front of Ash.

"He won't survive this. If you live here, then you've seen it for months now. The black disease doesn't have a cure," the captain said. His armor creaked as he motioned for her to move.

Aylla fought back tears as she glared at them. Perhaps a bullet to the brain or a knife at the base of his spinal cord would be a merciful death. She'd done it to rabbits and deer, but her hand hesitated.

"It's Black Insidian." The man who claimed to be a Scriver moved past them, holding a silver knife, a cloth that glittered the same color, and a brush.

Aylla held Ash's head as he knelt beside her. She didn't care if he was working with the soldiers or if he was a true Scriver, she just wanted his knowledge now. He hadn't even paused to consider that Ash could have bitten his throat out. Then again, he looked like he was prepared for it, with his gloves and leather armor. She barely registered that his jacket had changed into more of an armor covering than the long black coat he'd had on before. Thick straps held his sword scabbards, pauldrons covered his shoulders, and the torso plate was etched with jade sigils.

"Hold him." The man scraped the edge of the silver knife into the black substance, and it hissed. Black smoke rose like a scream. It disappeared so the wolf's left eye was clear again, and he panted heavily in her arms.

The man rubbed the cloth over the remaining spots until the fur was clean.

"Thank you," she said, and let out a breath. "What is that stuff?"

He put the tools back in his pack and stood. Ash sniffed his boots and Hugo licked his lips, still behind her.

"It's a life-leeching curse that gives Strygan power the more life it takes. It's been feeding in the forest and swamp," he said, still holding the brush. Just a normal, stiff-haired brush.

"What's the brush for?" Aylla asked, standing as well.

He smiled. "For the hair." He swept it down over his pants to get the wolf hair off it. "It's best to be as neutral smelling as possible."

Aylla laughed. She didn't know what she'd expected, but the warm thrill that went through her wasn't unpleasant. Still, she didn't let any of that warmth penetrate her mistrust. Her doubt about him being an actual Scriver dissipated. His confident knowledge and the acceptance of the soldiers told her all she needed to know about his title. But her sense of self-preservation told her to get far away from all of them. She'd not survived long by trusting many people.

"What can I give you to repay the debt?" she asked tentatively. Aylla had a chest full of coins and items of trade value in her cabin. She didn't want to offer up anything until he named a sum.

"Hate to interrupt, but we don't have time for this," the Milytor captain said. His eyes roved over her as they'd done at the market. Aylla wasn't sure if it was because he recognized her or he was attracted to her. Either made her lip curl like she was one of her wolves.

The Scriver tilted his head at her, ignoring the soldier. "I don't require any payment, Aylla."

He remembered her name, he remembered her ... Aylla's gaze dropped from his.

"You know this woman?" the blond man demanded. He turned to her with a calculating glance. "Do you know this area?"

Aylla nodded.

"Good, you're hired." He turned at the Scriver's disgruntled grunt. "You said we needed a tracker."

"I spoke with one, and that was enough," he replied, his dark eyes narrowing.

The captain shrugged and kept his intensely gray eyes on her. "You can repay your debt by helping us traverse Poe Swamp. We will do our best to see that you come to no harm, but we cannot promise."

"That sounds like a raw deal for me." Aylla crossed her arms, and the two wolves behind her sensed her discomfort. They sniffed and licked the air.

"It is the price."

"She's not coming." The man stepped close to the soldier, and the heat between them threatened to ignite the air. "I will not be responsible for more lives on this ridiculous mission."

"Oh? You're calling your king's grief trivial and the realm's safety less important than your own?" The captain jabbed his finger in the man's shoulder. He didn't move, and his fingers twitched like he wanted to hit back.

"I'll go," Aylla interrupted them. She didn't know the history between these men, but she didn't want to watch a fight either. There was something else too. The smoldering in the blond captain's eyes was far more than hate—it was as if he wanted to quarrel. As if he wanted the man to hit him, to touch him.

"Do you have any abilities?" the female soldier asked. Aylla turned to her in surprise. The captain glanced at her with a raised brow and then back at Aylla, waiting.

"No, why?" Aylla tried to read their expressions. Like all children in Elgar and most of the other continents, her blood had been tested when she'd reached eight years. Most humans, if they had any gift or affinity for Malecanta magic, showed it by then. She distinctly recalled the coppery smell in the air, the nervous shuffling of the other children, the pretentious man who'd pricked her finger. They were always looking for Malecanta.

"Just ..." The soldier trailed off as if unsure what she wanted to say. "Just that we don't know what we're walking into. You could be hurt if we come up against dark magic."

The captain sniffed. "Then you can be the gentlewoman and share your portions with her." He gave a hard glare at the Scriver, who sighed and shook his head as he stepped back.

Then the captain grinned and turned to Aylla with a curt nod. "Your ride awaits, my lady. We're jumping from the flyer into the swamp. It's the only way in."

Aylla swallowed hard. "Jumping?"

"I'll show you the harness." His eyes raked over her body. Aylla refused to let him see her disgust. She deliberately did nothing to cover her shoulder, bared from when her sleeve had fallen. There was nothing to apologize for on her part.

She gave Ash and Hugo the command for home. The wolves whined in protest, but she said it again with a hiss and they slunk away.

"Stryga wards are notorious for having weak spots in the air," said the man. "The harness is easy to figure out on your own." He pursed his lips at the captain, and his glare seemed to keep him away. He turned to her with a less lethal glare, but he was clearly not pleased. Maybe she shouldn't have insulted him so much at the tavern. Aylla shrugged to herself. How was she to know she'd run into him again? He didn't seem to be exactly in league with the Milytor.

"I'll take your word, Scriver," she said with a small smile to hide her anxiety.

"Jack," the man called over his shoulder as they boarded the flyer.

Chapter Eleven

Malecanta were hunted nearly to extinction in the war after the Covering. They split, with some loyal to humans and others playing with whoever would worship them most, like fickle gods. Their powers appear more powerful than any other race but ultimately each Malecanta faces limitations in their magic. Most Malecanta are gifted with only one source of magic such as Elemental, Transfiguration, or Raw magic—or so was recorded in an old journal found in a deceased sorcerer's den.
~ Scryptus, the Scriver Archives,
as recounted by Scriver #5 Jack Serpent, Tome 6

Jack glanced at Aylla, who clutched the railing of the air ship. The huge balloon overhead inflated with a fire generated by a spell to keep it stoked without the use of coal, wood, or peat, and an extra set of sails and rotating propeller moved them forward. It was like a galleon with a helm and deck, but it traveled much faster, a sleeker design. The sails were billows of a silky fabric that was tough enough to withstand sun, rain, and wind. The Milytor navy bought yards of the fabric from Muran, notorious for their privateers and pirates. Ornately carved dark wood adorned the railings and helm. The patchwork of fields and forests with wide streams cutting zig-zag paths flew by as they sailed over top of the swamp.

An entirely unnecessary device, really. Jack didn't understand why people wanted to fly—on dragons, unicorns, wooden ships, or gryphons. Men weren't made to travel in the air.

He would have fought harder to get in from the ground, but time was wasting. Jack could see the spot where they should drop, where the ward was weak. Ravens circled over the spot.

And then there was the newly added problem. Aylla. Narim wanted the tracker here for a reason, and that concerned him. Was she just a distraction? If the captain's aim was to have a warm body at night, Jack was going to correct that immediately.

Not that you wouldn't kick her out of your bed. The thought popped up, and just as quickly Jack squashed it. Still, he couldn't help but feel like there was another motive for Narim to want her here. He just had to wait. Normally, Jack was good at being patient, but this foray into the swamp was not the time, especially after the queen's murder.

Jack didn't doubt Aylla's knowledge of the swamp, but he didn't want another life in his hands. It was going to be hard enough keeping the two young soldiers alive.

He glanced at Bean, who sat in a corner and didn't take her eyes off the main deck of the blimp. The other soldier, Mykel, stood by the helm, talking to the captain. His long, caramel-colored, wiry hair was pulled back in a tail and he had a lithe, muscled frame. He looked like he came from Shay-ela, the continent renowned for bowhunting skills and sharp eyes—and also the home of the warlocks, if one believed old history. Narim had explained that they were only taking two Milytor for scouting. Once they discovered the High Stryga's weakness, they'd bring in the full force.

Jack didn't like it. They were too young, too inexperienced. The air was heavy with anticipation, clogging their lungs like bad cigar smoke.

The wind blew his dark hair. Jack liked to keep it shorter than most men—he'd had an unfortunate incident with a hydra and fire when it was longer. It could be gathered into a short tail to keep it out of his eyes, but it didn't flow over his shoulders. He checked his gear as they neared the circling birds. He kept his coat transformed into light armor. The black studded pauldrons, comfortable dark pants, and boots moved with him like a second skin. The torso plates transformed into a dark gray shirt, a lot lighter for the heat of a swamp yet still impenetrable to bullets and some spells. He'd only wanted the plates in case the wolf jumped on his stomach. He was familiar with the flying suits from his service in the Milytor but had only ever jumped once. Truly, men did not belong in the air.

He slid into the protective jump suit with a parachute attached to the back.

"So, you're from Asnor?" Bean asked Aylla like they were chatting in a tavern and not about to jump into a lethal swamp.

Aylla shrugged and more or less nodded. She tossed her long, raven-black hair over her shoulder, half of it braided. The women glanced at each other. Jack noted the whiteness of Aylla's knuckles as she clung to the railing but almost in defiance, she leaned over the edge to look out.

Jack half smiled. He'd never met a woman who used two wolves to hunt. If they'd been in a different situation, it would have been worth his time to find out her story. If she'd give it to him, of course. He laughed at the memory of her thinly veiled insults. Doubtful that she'd trust him enough to tell him anything significant about herself. He hadn't bothered to correct her when she assumed he worked in the Milytor. Grimarr would've been pleased about her assumption.

For some stupid reason, he was glad that at least Bean and Mykel had convinced Aylla that he was a Scriver. He never had the compunction to prove his title. His work spoke for itself, and most people either stayed out of his way or learned a hard lesson. The reality was, she could be dead by tomorrow night. They all could.

"I live near Churk Forest, but my family is from Asnor, yes." She drew the attention of all the men aboard—the soldier steering the ship, the soldier manning the spelled fire, and the soldiers appointed at the guns in case of attack.

You'd think they've never seen a female before. Alaric chuckled. Jack knew his sarcasm was both about men being men and the fact that Jack was irritated with how many people were now on this mission.

Bean didn't draw the same attention because she was part of the crew—a soldier who had proven herself—and it was frowned upon to fraternize among each other while serving. A light rule that almost no one upheld.

The way Aylla spoke and her shifting weight made Jack think she wasn't telling the entire truth. Her mannerisms were familiar enough—she didn't want to reveal where she lived. He didn't blame her. How often had he lied, to the degree that it was just a part of him now?

"You raised those wolves?" Mykel asked with a grin. "The Milytor uses Midlian hounds, but wolves are different. How do get them to obey you?"

"I raised them from pups. We've just learned to communicate, and they respect me. But they don't always follow," she said with a laugh. To Jack's ears, it was tinged with sadness. He could understand her train of thought: she didn't know what she was walking into, but she understood she might not see them again. She didn't deserve this forced servitude. He appreciated that all too well.

It wasn't every day he got to touch an Elgar wolf. They were dying out as farmlands invaded and cut down their forests. He intended to be sure she made it back home, wherever that was, and to her family. There was something odd about her. Jack couldn't place the feeling, but it was like a veil of energy over her, gossamer threads that obscured a quiet strength. She'd interrupted his spell at the tavern—unusual for most people. Had she practiced with magic before?

He forced these questions out of his mind. Distraction was a good way to get killed.

From the way the two soldiers were paying attention to her, it was unlikely Jack would have to do too much for Aylla. The young ones usually liked to prove themselves, and having someone to protect motivated them. He could focus on the task: the High Stryga.

Even Narim started to ask questions about the wolves, and he stood closer to Aylla than was necessary. She kept stepping slightly to the right, and he followed, adjusting his position so he rubbed her arm or leg. Jack was tempted to rescue her, but she'd probably just jam her boot on his foot. Besides, the vortex was close. They had to focus.

"Slow her down," he said to soldier at the helm. The man nodded, and the fire that powered the propellers lowered so that the flyer now hovered.

"Jumping in two," Jack shouted. He zipped the torso up and hooked the pack on his back, securing it with Carbina clips. He placed goggles on his forehead and walked to the aft railing. Gusts of wind brought a foul smell of decay and damp earth up.

Bean and Mykel hopped into their suits.

"Do we just jump into that?" Bean asked Jack.

They glanced to where he pointed. A dozen crows circled in the air like omens of slaughter. The swamp's mossy trees bowed their heads, and a sulfur smell rose, making the humans' noses crinkle.

"That's what we want," Jack said.

"How do you know it's a weak spot?" Mykel asked as he stepped by Jack.

Jack pulled his goggles down.

"Something has to die for such a big spell, and crows love carrion. Whatever's dead down there is fueling the ward elsewhere, not above it."

Jack caught Aylla's eye, standing by the opening of the railing with him. She'd put her suit on—alone—and now peered cautiously down. He pointed to the vortex and the ravens, which were cawing in raucous alarm.

"Try to aim for the middle." He gave her a grim smile.

He jumped up onto the railing to get a better view of the grayish-green treetops. No good place to land, really. *Can't be worse than Kilwany Mountain, eh?* Jack ignored the soldiers behind him, who were trying to form a better plan and explain to Aylla how the parachute worked. He leaped into the air.

Chapter Twelve

It's not the size of the scroll, but how one uses it.
~ Scryptus, the Scriver Archives,
as recounted by Scriver #5 Jack Serpent, Tome 13

Jack's luck ran out as his chute caught an updraft and whisked him about fifty feet from his intended landing. The ward may have been weak, but it was still effective enough to blow him off course. He swept through the circling ravens, and they cawed like banshees. Their eyes flared red. He shielded his face from the vicious flaps of wings, talons, and snapping beaks. They attacked his face, hands, any part they could reach, and their beaks were sharp enough that he felt their jabs through the bulletproof shirt. Jack reached inside his coat and grabbed his knife. He hacked at the giant birds as he fell the last hundred feet to the ground.

He pulled the cord to let the chute go. It didn't budge. Jack curled his legs up as he plunged through several cypress and black barble trees. Their branches cracked; they broke his fall, but they also cut like dull knives. Needles showered over him. The chute caught on thick, twisted branches, and he hung in the air like a bug in a web.

"Fuck a six-titted gorgon." His curse echoed in the vastness of the putrid swamp.

Jack sawed at the straps, and the parachute let him go. He tucked again and fell fifteen feet onto the soggy, moss-covered ground. A rock "cushioned" his fall and jutted into his right thigh. Jack shifted quickly and rolled onto more rocks.

The Milytor needs more funding, he thought with an angry tug at the knots of the harness. The heat rose around him like another skin, and sweat beaded on his forehead. The crows flapping above him turned their attention to something more interesting. Jack glanced up to see Mykel and Bean floating down into the trees, shouting as the crows renewed their attack. They were landing in the right spot, so there was nothing Jack could do but make his way toward them and hope they survived.

He hadn't seen Aylla yet, but he was sure she would be fine. Narim wouldn't let such a pretty face get destroyed so soon. And the two soldiers might be young, but he had to believe they could manage a jump. *Why are you even thinking about them? Their blood is on Narim's hands.* Was that his thought or Alaric's?

Because this is close to suicide. Jack swatted at some bugs that flitted past his face, irritated. No solid plan, no inside information, not even a few days to study the habits of the swamp.

Jack hefted his pack and walked through brush and rocks, avoiding the wet areas. The swamp had several mini rivers that flowed out into the Dred Plains and eventually emptied into the sea. He swatted away flying insects the size of his fist. They didn't have orange stripes, so there was a sixty-forty chance they weren't poisonous.

As he reached the small clearing, shots assaulted his ears. Bean and Mykel were taking up target practice as they fired into the mass of attacking birds. Jack sighed. No sense in a stealthy entrance now. He took both of his pistols from their holsters. The bullets were normal shot—no need to waste warded ammunition on birds. Jack fired into the mass of black fowl, and feathers rained down. Mykel had pulled out his Winstar 238 and let loose a volley. His aim was spot on as he took out the rest of the crows. Bean wiped blood from her cheek and shook her head. Around them huge, dead beasts festered in the heat.

"Those are huge conductors—this swamp is full of spells. I can feel them." Bean stepped carefully around a body, a silver earring in her left ear glinting in the muted light. The giant beast looked like a crocodile had lost a battle with a bison. Horns protruded from a scaly forehead, and teeth the size of arms stuck out like knives.

"There's at least a dozen here," Mykel said, turning in a slow circle. Some of the bodies bore obvious signs of the crows' appetites. Others were sinking into the ground with small creatures running over them, taking what scraps they could.

Jack ignored them both, concentrating on his own investigation.

Stryga used living things to fuel most of their more powerful spells. The Black Insidian, the ward around the swamp, required quite a bit of sacrifice. Narim and Aylla landed in the clearing, but Jack didn't pay them attention. His mind was a whirring machine of finding tracks and listening for sounds that didn't fit in. Only half an ear was even listening to the others.

"All right, let's get the equipment ready," Bean said with the eagerness of a soldier whose only mission had been in a training cornfield. She set her pack on the ground and pulled out a transmitter, a few crystals, and some wires.

"What, we don't get the good gear? Where are the earpieces?" Mykel asked as he handled the old, chunky transmitter. The hunk of moonstone, shaped like an oval, glowed a soft, pale blue. It was nowhere near as easy to use as an ear stone.

Narim cleared his throat and grunted. "The king is waiting to replace all our old transmitters. Didn't want to lose good ones in a swamp. These will do the job."

Jack tuned in slightly more at that. His feeling of something being off kilter intensified. Why would Grimarr send them out with old transmitters?

"We're not splitting up anyway. I don't see the need for transmitters—I bet they won't work well out here," Mykel said with a snort. He got his out and rubbed a circle on the stone to activate it. "Do you hear me?"

Bean gave him a roll of his eyes. "I read you, Sky Fyre."

Mykel laughed. "And I'm proud to hold that title."

"No one else has hit a mark from three thousand strides," Bean said with admiration.

Jack surveyed the territory and sniffed the air. Clear and clean. He whispered a few ward spells to test if anything else crept around them, but the invisible spell bounced back with nothing. Yet. Aylla had moved into his line of sight, so he had no choice but to notice what she was doing. She walked a slow circle, split black skirts flaring out around legs clad in skin-tight pants and calf-high boots, studying the shrubs and plants. She knelt and carefully extracted a pink flower with pointed leaves. After crushing the leaves in her palm, she set them in a small bowl she pulled from her pack and added a few drops of water. Then she applied the light mixture on her arms, legs, and ends of her hair. The tell-tale citrusy vanilla wafted in the air.

"Bainswort?" he asked with a sniff.

Aylla held out the bowl to him. "Bainscot, actually. It's more potent to keep away the poisonous insects."

The soldiers leaned in, and none objected to smearing the substance over their armor and on their boots.

Bean swatted at bugs that buzzed past her ear. "Do you think Ghoul Base will send people after us if the transmitters don't work?"

The Milytor barracks was nicknamed Ghoul Base because it was rumored to be haunted. Too many soldiers and nurses had gone missing or died there. Grimarr refused to move it. He liked the intrigue, or so he'd told Jack.

The blond man smiled. "I'm sure the transmitters will work fine. If we don't return within four days, they'll send more soldiers. Let's move out."

Narim took out a vial of thesal, a tracking potion. After he drank it, a halo of emerald light floated around his being for a moment before disappearing.

"What is that?" Aylla asked.

"I don't doubt your tracking ability, but this lets us track magic." Narim grinned. "I can see a Stryga has been through here, as well as a huge cat, crocodile, and snake."

"Wouldn't that just look like a normal human print?" Aylla cocked her head. The other men stifled smiles.

"Yes, to a point. But there's a trace of magic around the prints that glow green. We go north." Narim started walking, and the other two fell in line behind him.

The wind shifted, and Jack's lip curled. The humid air and the smell of magic hit his nose. He didn't need a potion to tell him a Stryga and a Strix had been in the area. Not even the swamp's decay could cover the putrid smell of black magic. The problem was there hadn't been just one Strix here—there had been at least three. Jack didn't like the thought of that many together. Where there were Strix, there were full-blooded Strygan. Most Strygan operated in small groups or alone until they were called to a convening. The last time had been Ravenhell ... and the memory haunted him like a disease that slowly ate away at his mind. Jack suspected the Strygan were running out of magic to tap, and in a desperate effort to find sorcerer magic, they were pooling resources.

He took the rear and kept his weapons holstered. A knife, pistols, Kyadem ... he could need any one of them, and he didn't want to already have a weapon in his hands that was the wrong one. Kya's thrum was like a protective blanket.

Narim made use of his machete as he slashed a path through old, overgrown brush. Their feet alternately sank and hit hard ground, so they stumbled every minute. Jack didn't want to waste a potion on lightness.

He focused on the hush of the trees and the sounds of the animals, keeping the Stryga scent as long as he could. The others went ahead as he hung back to make sure nothing followed them. How was he going to kill this High Stryga? Situations, spells, makeshift bombs catapulted through his mind. There was nothing like trial and error.

"Get to your left. Off the ground!" Aylla shouted.

Smokey char hit his nose, and Jack stepped to the right instead of left. Spurts of fire exploded from the earth. Ahead of Aylla, Narim cursed and jumped to the left. Mykel and Bean scattered. The bursts of fire didn't stop—they were triggered by weight. Bubbles burst up from the ground and gas rocketed up to burn as white flames, sparking molten hot.

Jack balanced on a moss-covered log with Aylla. His boots kept traction, but hers were slipping off. She didn't grab at him but tried to keep her own balance. Her arms pinwheeled as fire blasted in her face and her pack threatened to topple her. Jack steadied her by taking her left arm. Aylla pulled away and landed on another log behind them.

"I'm fine."

"Apologies," he said with a tilt of his head. He didn't usually feel like he'd overstepped someone's boundaries. He was typically the one being cornered uncomfortably.

Aylla paused as if she were going to say more but then shook her head. *Good, this isn't going to get personal.* Jack moved ahead, hopping logs ahead of her. The fire was just good old swamp gas—it didn't smell like tainted magic.

The soldiers shouted instructions at each other, trying to get away from the fire. Jack jumped onto Aylla's log and motioned to the next one. The ground beneath them roiled with gas bubbles that could erupt at any moment.

They launched from one log to another until the logs ran out. They were standing at the edge of a boggy area filled with sludgy water and water lilies. Bugs with wings that appeared as if they were on fire flitted over the water, leaving trails of orange sparks.

Jack slipped his pack in front and grabbed a rope with a small, weighted grapple. He threw it over the nearest tree branch, tapped a rune on his wrist, and flicked his fingers. The rope flipped the hook so that it held fast. Bean and Mykel tried to do something similar. Narim did the same and propelled himself ahead of them all, swinging from tree to tree across the water as if he were proving he was better than them all and didn't need help. Jack didn't care as long as the other soldier kept moving far away from him. Aylla bent low to grab a rock near the edge of the water. She threw it five feet. It splashed, and they waited a beat.

The fire burst from under the water and birds shrieked in flight. Frogs surfaced out of the muddy liquid and lay on their backs, dead. Jack's jaw tightened. The fire mines were farther out than he'd hoped, and from Aylla's concerned expression, she felt the same.

Jack figured there was one way to find out if the ropes would hold. He swung over the water and landed on another branch. Then he flicked the rope and hook again, but an indignant yell made him turn his head.

"You have to fling it up and to the left," Mykel was telling Bean.

Aylla had already fashioned a harness around herself and was swinging over the algae covered water. She landed on a low branch and started to climb, hopping delicately from limb to limb. In his focused state, Jack still found it jarring to find people around him. He was so used to working alone it was like blinking rainwater from his eyes and finding a specter in front of him.

They crossed the bog branch by branch and avoided a fiery death. Jack's boots soon crashed on solid ground, and the smoke-filled air started to thin.

"Oy, wait up." Bean's soft call cut through his focus. He had been concentrating on where on the solid ground might kill them next. He turned to see Aylla next to him.

"You gonna give her a hand, mate?" Bean asked as she scrambled up a branch.

Jack didn't think the she in question needed help, but manners drilled into him by a mother he couldn't remember made him hold out a hand for Aylla. She shot him an irritated glance. She clasped his hand tightly as she leaped down, then let go the instant she was steady on the ground.

They walked in silence for a while until the chatter of their transmitters burst the awkward bubble. Jack's attention returned to the immediate threats and spells he could use against the High Stryga.

"Scriver, you coming or what?" Narim's voice crackled.

Jack held the transmitter somewhat close to his mouth. "Heading northwest to your location."

"Do you need direction?"

"I can smell your cologne."

Aylla stifled a snort. Bean and Mykel raised their brows at the raillery and failed to hide their smirks but didn't comment.

Focus. It wasn't Alaric's voice but his own that mentally slapped him.

Jack blocked out everyone. He tried to keep scanning and sensing wards or traps. To his left there was a pulse of darkness, like a blind spot, and he turned toward it. Something was sucking energy, its pulsing a warning.

Jack strode past Narim and bent down to inspect an almost hidden composition of leaves, sticks, and other items. Upside-down crosses hanging on bone altars. Scraps of tan lay flattened, with blood drawn runes on them. Jack peered closer, and his brow quirked. Skin. Human skin. The sticks, strung vertically with runes burned on them, were for stealth and speed. The bones were for protection, and there was a faint whiff of some kind of animal urine—either it was part of the spell or again the swamp covering up the Stryga's dirty work. The altar was large enough he wondered if it protected not only the Stryga but the Strix, that lesser being that wanted to be a full-on Stryga but lacked the strength. They were like leeches whose purpose was to suck life.

A chill ran over his arms and neck. Strix loved to serve their idols, the Strygan. If there were three here, then it was a good bet the High Stryga was close. He recalled some lore Alaric had told him—years ago, when he'd first started.

"What do Strygan usually want the most?" Alaric had asked.

Jack shrugged. "Toad eyeballs?"

"Youth and power. Immortality. They acquire this by assimilating other's organs, fluids, and souls to remain young forever."

"That's disgusting."

Alaric smirked and lightly punched him on the shoulder. "That's a Stryga."

Chapter Thirteen

Grimarr Fox is the first general of the Milytor to employ equal training for men and women. His unusual methodology and warfare intelligence must come from a deep place inside him. Not much is known about where he came from, his parentage, or birthplace. He does not share information about himself lightly. What we do know is he respects life in all aspects. His goal in creating the Scriver Trials was to provide an elite soldier to go into the dark corners of the world, to record legends or weaknesses, preserve life of misunderstood species, but also to be the hammers of the realm if needed. They will be like smoke in the night until called upon.
~ Scryptus, the Scriver Archives,
as recounted by Scriver #5 Jack Serpent, Tome 7

Aylla jumped back as two luminous eyes stared back at her. She blinked and they disappeared. The dark underbrush of the swamp swallowed everything, including light. *Maybe I didn't see eyes.* She frowned. She knew reflective pupils when she saw them. They reminded her of Ash and Hugo. Hopefully the boys would be comfortable at home, hunting and playing, until she got back.

If she got back. The thought wasn't far from her mind. She didn't trust any of the Milytor, especially Narim. Bean might share her gender, but the other woman was a trained combatant with her own agenda. Aylla had never been good at making friends given her seclusion—and she hadn't ever minded it. However, she did like the bond between Bean and Mykel. They seemed like brother and sister. She often wondered whether things would've been different if she'd had a sibling.

Then there was Jack. A Scriver so unlike the first one she'd met. A true Scriver, the only remaining one, as she'd learned. Aylla wasn't entirely sure he was working for the Milytor now either. The blond captain, the controller, didn't treat him like part of their group. There was something she was missing.

And Jack didn't seem to care. He was so focused it was almost fascinating to watch. However, it did not bode well for any sort of group cohesion.

Aylla felt as if she had to prove herself every minute. She understood that Jack and probably the other two soldiers didn't want her there for her own safety, but she really couldn't afford to refuse. She couldn't stand the thought of being imprisoned or having to leave her home. While she didn't love Churk Forest, she also didn't want to leave it unless it was of her own accord. Her parents were buried there, and it was the only life she'd known. Her parents had taken her to visit Muran a few times—the beaches of white sand and uniquely blue waters were the only other place Aylla had considered living.

"Did you see something?" Jack asked. His voice startled her back to the present. He held a potion in his hand, ready to imbibe, but paused.

The Milytor soldiers glanced at her as well.

"I thought I saw ... eyes," she answered.

"You probably saw changelings. I saw one an hour ago. They're compelling you to leave our protection and follow," he said.

"Is that fylnoc to enhance vision?" Mykel asked.

"Yes." Jack drank the fylnoc potion. His eyes flared bright green then simmered back to his usual hazel gray.

A faint cry like a baby's wail sounded in the distance. Aylla cringed. Even though she'd sworn she wouldn't have children, the cry tugged at something ancient and undeniable in her core. She was sure the men here would never admit to having any paternal bones in their body, but they tensed, nonetheless.

Narim grunted. He checked his weapons over and pulled a hood over his eyes.

"Get some rest, it won't hurt you," Narim said. "We move in an hour."

"Two." Jack's contradiction got him a glare from the captain. Narim noted the fatigue on their faces and nodded tightly.

The other two agents pulled out thin leaf packs. Bean heated hers with a fire-rock and it became what looked like an oat cake. Mykel just chewed on the leaves, took a swig of water, and a contented smile crossed his face. It must taste good. Aylla had seen spelled food before but never ate it. Her mother always warned of magic mixing with food.

Bean held out a leaf turned oat cake to her. "C-ration?"

Aylla took it with a nod of thanks, despite her mother's warnings in her mind. Her rumbling stomach and headache overrode caution. To her surprise it tasted better than it looked; notes of honey in the oats and packed with nutrients that made her feel better in minutes. The soldiers lay back down with their packs under their heads for pillows. The swamp hummed with life that lulled them all into a stupor. Aylla laid back as well on a blanket and tried to relax. It would be a while before they'd rest again, she wagered.

Aylla couldn't sleep, so she contented herself with watching her back and the surroundings. Bean and Mykel switched shifts every two hours, one keeping watch while the other slept. Narim paced their perimeter and drank occasionally from a flask. She was grateful he didn't suggest they sit together.

That left one person unaccounted for. Jack had disappeared a while ago. Then, as if summoned by her thought, he entered the clearing, checking everything around them. Aylla moved slightly away from the circle as if the shadows beckoned to her. Her legs were impatient to get whatever this was over with. She had never wanted to get back home as much as now. If her mother were still alive, and they lived contentedly in the cabin, she'd never even have been dragged into this.

Not true, Tideling—you would have followed the flyer, and Ash would still have gotten into trouble. Her mother's laugh floated on the air. Aylla didn't deny it. She knew going over the past wouldn't help her get out of the mess she was in now.

Was there a faint hum in the air? She cocked her head. Nothing but insects and rustling leaves. Aylla glanced around. Jack didn't even look her way. He moved like a shadow, silent and dark.

"What are you looking for?" Aylla asked as he passed by. She always liked to be prepared, and as much as she didn't want to speak and draw attention, her sense of self-preservation won out.

Jack glanced up, his expression not quite startled but seemingly surprised that she was talking. He didn't answer her question but instead acknowledged her by whispering, "Still want to be here?"

He drew a rune on a tree trunk with a red stick. Aylla moved a little closer, lifting her skirt over a root.

"Why do you care?"

Jack's eyes narrowed. "Because I don't relish the idea of dragging bodies out of here, and judging by your size, I wouldn't get far—even for a man of my strength."

Aylla wasn't sure if she should burst out laughing or slap him. She peered hard at him. Was he joking, or did he truly despise her presence that much? The amusement in his eyes didn't match the hard set of his square jaw. Aylla was almost relieved, but the feeling was instantly replaced by a raging desire to kick his shins.

"Did you just insult my *size*?" Her eyes widened, and she fingered the dagger hilt at her belt. "If you want to be rid of me there are surely better ways than hollow insults. You keep saying we're all going to die, yet it seems the only one who doesn't have his back watched is you."

"I don't need anyone for that."

"Then why do you stay with them?" Aylla used the dagger to swat at a black bug as it flew past her face.

He didn't answer, just licked his lips and turned away. Always focused.

"Don't tell me it's the first time you've been offended," he said with a flourish of his fingers on the last rune. "I'm offering you one more chance—whatever attacks first, you run. Get out."

"Just what sort of attack do I need to run from?" Aylla shot back.

"The kind you shouldn't have agreed to come along for."

"I didn't exactly volunteer."

"You didn't fight it too hard, either." Jack's tone was distant, almost cold. He seemed to be more interested in something else.

"I can't have Milytor on my trail for the rest of my life," she said with a sneer. "I live here."

"Live somewhere else."

Aylla spun around. "And I suppose you're just here for the coin, right? Or just following orders?"

"I don't get paid to haul dead bodies."

"No, you'll just leave them and go on with life."

Jack turned sharply to her. "I'm sure there's a reason behind this hostility, but whatever it is, I don't have time to find out."

She cut him off. "I met a supposed Scriver years ago, and he lied about how my father died. You don't seem much different from the stories I hear passed through villages." Aylla lowered her voice as she finished, annoyed at herself for giving away so much information.

Jack pursed his lips. "If you're expecting any of them to hold your hand or warm your bedroll, you're going to be sorely disappointed—and possibly injured. They're trained soldiers. They do their duty."

She barked a laugh. "I would expect nothing less of the vaunted Milytor. And I don't need any *warmth*, thank you. I'll get home on my own."

His silence spoke for him; he'd given her a chance to escape, and she'd made the choice.

"I've told you, I don't want to be here, but I'm not useless. Especially if I know what to expect. It seems your skills aren't necessary when every man here has the same knowledge as you—and the same questions," she said in a low, forced tone.

Jack's position relaxed. Aylla wasn't sure what flitted across those dark features, but it wasn't anger. He grunted as he turned back to face her.

"A question I still need answered as well," Jack said. It was as neutral of a response as she'd gotten in the short time she'd known him.

"You don't work for the Milytor, do you?" she asked.

Jack sighed. "No."

"You let me believe you did." Aylla considered him a moment. His hard features didn't reveal much. "So, what are you doing with them?"

"Would it satisfy you if I told you they hired me?" Jack scanned the surrounding swamp.

"Fine." Aylla knew it wasn't the truth, but she didn't care because the mist was thicker now. She paused, biting her lip. "I did appreciate you helping Ash."

Jack inclined his head with a small smile. "I can't say it wasn't a pleasure getting that close to an Elgarian wolf—not many left."

The swamp had changed in the last few minutes. AyllGa sensed it even as the Scriver began making his preparations. He'd clearly felt the threat long before she had. The fog inched toward them. It clung to her clothes like a swarm of leeches and sat heavy there.

That hum again. Did no one else hear it? No, that was beside the point. When the mist got this thick, it was about to rain, and rain in the swamp was far more dangerous than on the plains.

Aylla scolded herself for being too busy to notice the change in the weather earlier.

"It's going to rain, and we need to get to higher ground," she said, snapping her head toward the others. Flicker flooding could kill them in minutes.

Jack didn't comment as his coat once again changed to a light, waterproof jacket and he rushed over to the group. Raindrops splattered on their heads as he relayed her instructions.

Aylla stuck her foot into the loamy ground. It sank. She backed up and waved a hand at him. "Don't step on anything that looks like vomit-green shyf." There was some satisfaction in ordering him to do something crucial—and that he didn't argue with her.

The rest gathered their things quickly, also without argument. Narim made sure he was the one behind her. The rain accumulated fast, and the ground started to give even as they slogged upward.

Narim helped Aylla over a boulder the size of a small pony. From the summit of the rock, she could see the trees thinning and a hill in the distance.

"Let's get to that hill!" Aylla shouted over the rain.

"I want to get my waders on," Bean said as she pulled thin, waterproof pants made of snakeskin. They ballooned out like a float.

"No," Jack said, and waved to get his attention. "The water will pull that whole thing right down—and you with it."

Aylla silently agreed as she slogged through the ever-softening ground. The rain beat down relentlessly.

Bean frowned. "Are you sure? Wet feet means we could get rot, and if I can't walk I'm as good as dead."

"Your choice." Jack continued wading through the rain. Their path was starting to turn into a stream of water.

"Come on, leave the waders." Aylla held out her hand to help Bean up the rock. Mykel jumped down and sank up to his knees in soggy water. He cursed. Narim leapt up the rock and over as well, crashing into the water.

Aylla held up her hand, motioning for them to keep going. Jack nimbly leaped up rocks and fallen logs in an attempt to get to higher ground.

"This isn't Stryga work, just bad luck," Narim said as he kept pace with her, shoulder to shoulder.

"What are those?" Aylla pointed to several gray shapes sliding from the mist behind them. They ran on long legs and looked like disjointed spiders.

"A scorpii legion!" Bean shouted.

Aylla froze as dozens of dog-sized, scorpion-like bodies scuttled toward them. Narim got his pistols out, while the other two wasted precious seconds deciding what to do. Jack, of course, reacted ahead of them all and fired a pistol into the water as warning. The scorpii didn't slow.

The scorpii legions advanced easily through the water. Their beady, black eyes glared from their nightmarish, human-like heads. Curving over their backs, their long, black stingers hung in the air. Milky venom hung in thick, viscous drops from the points. As their armored shells cut through the water, the creatures released high-pitched shrieks. Four knobby, jointed legs propelled them forward with speed.

"Get to the hill and form a death blossom," Jack said, his voice rising above the din of pounding rain and attacking creatures.

"A what?" Bean turned to him.

Jack shot a glare at Narim. Aylla assumed it was a Milytor tactic that the young soldier should have known.

Narim swore and turned to Bean. "Kneel on either side of him and fire until the fuckers stop coming."

Bean shook her head but set her sights forward.

Aylla could barely see two feet in front of her for the mist and rain. It seemed like they wouldn't make the hill. Jack ran out in front, taking point. Mykel veered off to the left and climbed a tree with surprising ease. Aylla caught glimpses of steel points protruding from the toes of his boots, and he'd put on silver spiked knuckles that helped him climb. She wished she could have prepared for this, but all she could do now was hope her survival instincts kicked in. She wiped water from her eyes with a slick hand. The air smelled of gunpowder, tangy blood, and damp earth.

Bean had both her pistols out and slogged behind them with ragged breaths. Jack reached the summit of the hill before any of them. He set his pack down, pulled out a pistol, and aimed at the scorpii. Crack after crack broke through the swamp. Aylla jumped as Mykel and Jack's shots rang out and black blood spewed into the air. She pulled out her Winstar from the pack, and the men gave her half a glance.

"Hold," Narim said as they crested the hill. Jack ceased firing. Narim took up a spot beside him and knelt on his left just as the scorpii raced up the hill, water flying in their wake.

Shots fired in discord. Aylla took careful aim, controlled her breathing, and was gratified to see black blood ooze from a few targets she hit.

"Your left!" Aylla shouted.

Jack fired into one scorpus that ran up. The side of the beast's head slammed black, and the scorpus's body collapsed, slid down the hill, and splashed into the water. Jack turned his gun back on the next target. With intense precision, he picked off the creatures as if they were standing still. Legs flew up into the air and heads exploded in dark gushes. Aylla reloaded quickly, watching him out of the corner of her eye. His movements were fluid, practiced, effortless. He was almost lost in a trance of precision—he didn't seem to notice the men firing on both sides.

Bean and Narim fired round after round. Empty magazines fell into quick-fingered hands as they reloaded in a blur. Aylla spied Mykel in a tree off to the side with his Phantom. He took out the scorpus that raced from under the cover of drowning bushes.

"Where's Kyadem?" Narim asked Jack. Aylla turned her eyes on them.

"If you don't want your arms, I'd be happy to bring her out." Jack's eyes narrowed as he focused on the scorpii.

"Fair point." Narim shrugged and fired.

"Fifteen strides right!" Jack called to Mykel.

Mykel shifted his sights, and Jack looked toward the right side of the hill. Geysers of black water and guts flew up in seven shots. He racked the scattershot and fired into the mass of scorpii that skittered up the hill.

"I'm out!" she shouted. Jack tossed her a heavy bag filled with Winstar bullets. She loaded the eight rounds, and the slide locked shut.

"Contact in one minute," Narim said and reloaded.

Aylla eyed more scorpii legionnaires flooding up from the left, black-tipped stingers poised above their bodies, ready to strike.

Jack threw the scattershot down and plunged his hand into his pack. He came up with a bottle that sloshed with green liquid. He lit the wick on fire from a rune on his finger that ignited at his touch, then lobbed the flaming bottle down the hill. When it hit, an explosion of emerald fire rained over the scorpii. They screamed and scattered up the hill. Bean and Narim kept firing as Jack threw bottle after bottle; a haze of smoke mixed with the rainy mist.

"Hold." Jack's low voice carried across the air.

There was no more scuttling, and the rain washed the blood in rivulets down into the swirling water below them. Barrels smoked, shells rolled down, and a series of clicks sounded as they each reloaded or checked their gear. Rain continued to pour and slick everything in shades of gray-black. Aylla's hands shook, and she took a big breath, steadying herself.

"Don't see anymore." Mykel's voice rang out. "Looks like a shallower river if you go straight down behind. There's another hill twenty meters ahead."

Jack strode in that direction. Aylla spotted a scaly body just inches from him.

"Pathana snake on your left!" she shouted.

Jack froze with his weapons pointed skyward. The snake was at least fifteen feet long and a foot in diameter, with patterns of brown and white scales. Two more snakes followed. A head cruised past him, but he remained still. Aylla swallowed a ball of fear. It was a constrictor, and several dozen more bobbing heads followed the first one.

Narim trained his pistol on the floating heads that dipped up and down in the water. The snakes passed them in the rushing water and continued in search of other prey.

The humans started to move forward again. Mykel jumped down from his perch in the tree and waded towards them. Aylla panted from the adrenaline and fiddled with the pistol in her hands. She'd heard stories of the constrictors in the swamp. If it had been just one, it wouldn't have been a problem, but that much snake weight could drown a herd of cattle, let alone two men—even if one was a soldier and the other a Scriver. Although, Aylla would bet Jack could have escaped should her warning have failed.

The ground started to rise, and the flicker flood river diverted around the hill. Jack shook droplets from his hair, shirt clinging to his chest. His light armor was slick with beading rain as it cascaded down.

As they slogged up the hill, the downpour slackened. Aylla could make out a whole new terrain of water-laden trees. The trunks grew gnarled roots that poked up from the water and slithered across rocks. It was a maze of tiny rivers with who knew what underneath them.

The Scriver started ahead through the brush overflowing with a few inches of water, which was a lot more manageable than the flooding pathways.

"We should stop and wait until the water clears," Mykel said, shaking droplets from his hair. Jack didn't turn around or halt. He seemed to be muttering to himself as he wrung his clothes out and advanced.

Narim called out, "Agreed. Jack, you scout ahead for any more surprises. Mykel, those gesala leaves could be fashioned into foot floats. Bean, keep those grenades handy. Aylla, stay with me."

Jack's figure grew smaller as he disappeared into the gnarled trees.

Aylla tamped down her annoyance at Narim's sudden "authority"—not that Jack had even acknowledged the captain. The misty rain made their figures appear ethereal as they moved. It grew so thick she started to reach out to at least make sure they didn't lose her ... but her hand only caught air. Hadn't Bean been right alongside her? The men's voices faded as she scanned the swamp landscape ahead, looking for a drier place to regroup. She did need to let her socks dry out at least before foot rot caught them—Bean was right about that.

Then the silence struck Aylla. The only sound was the hiss of rain. A low moan bounced off the tree trunks.

"Jack?" Aylla called. "Anyone?"

No one answered, and the swamp swallowed her voice. She clutched her pistol with wet fingers and walked in a small circle. How had she lost them? They'd been right next to her, hadn't they?

Aylla screamed out each of their names in turn, but no one answered. The heavy mist poured around her like a blanket.

Chapter Fourteen

The invention of spelled food is nothing new; however, the cooks in generation Havoc have perfected a meal with which any army could sustain itself for years before the magic ran out. Chena or C-rations are spelled thin, lightweight leaves of any plant that can be changed into protein, oats, and fruit pastes depending on the spell used. Note: the leaves must be spelled before travel as it takes a few minutes for them to fully absorb and compact down into neat squares. One man can carry a few hundred meals with him in a pack. Must be used within a year, however, before the spell wears off.
~ Scryptus, the Scriver Archives,
as recounted by Scriver #5 Jack Serpent, Tome 7

Jack doubled back, his instincts telling him something was wrong. The mist was thicker than horseberry pie, and the shiver of old magic hung in the air. He had been so preoccupied with tracking that he hadn't realized how far behind everyone had gotten. It was like trying to travel with a lame elephant. He gritted his teeth; this was not going according to any plan.

Aylla was gone. The other soldiers had spread out. He lit a torch from his pack, and the rest did as well, each with a different identifying color.

"Aylla!" Bean shouted. Her voice echoed across the pools of water and loamy ground.

Jack's enhanced vision only told him that the animals had gone to ground. His nose told him a Strix was nearby. The smell wasn't quite as potent, so it wasn't a full Stryga. They were trying to divide the group.

"Do you have Runycs?" he asked Narim before the mist swallowed them all.

"Always." Narim pulled out a patch like piece of fabric, muttered, "Ignatia," and slapped it on his right arm. The other two did the same. A Runyc patch allowed Milytor to identify and track each other. At least Jack would have a way to call the group back if they separated. The patch would vibrate and pulse green when searching for others with the same Runyc. The magic would pull them together if they were within a few dozen miles.

Jack closed his eyes and listened.

"Oy, what's he doing?" Mykel whispered.

"How would I know? Let him do it." Bean shushed him, and their voices faded.

Narim's heavy footsteps headed west. Jack picked up the dripping of water off trees. The hush of insects went silent; no birds or animals rustled. Distantly, a woman shouted. Aylla. His eyes snapped open, and he headed south with the soldiers in his wake.

"Mykel, get up in a tree," he called over his shoulder. The Strix was close; the stench of the swamp couldn't mask her sulfuric magic stink.

"Don't order my men, Serpent," Narim growled in his ear as he took the lead.

Jack rolled his eyes. He pulled out his Winstar pistols and whispered the hex word to activate the wards on the bullets.

Aylla's slim form wandered in the mist as she tried to get her bearings. Jack hesitated. On one hand, she was perfect bait. She'd give them the opening he could use to lure the Stryga. On the other, she was terrified and making mistakes. He could smell the heightened sweat, the fear, and she was licking her lips a lot, much like a wolf when stressed. He did observe that she didn't panic—her steps were deliberate, and her eyes scanned constantly.

Well, what she doesn't know won't hurt her. I won't let it. The afterthought was almost like a reflex, and it took Jack by surprise. A muscle clenched in his jaw.

Shadows with tentacle-like arms flowed from between the hanging moss. They splintered into several more arms and moved like a spider toward her. The Strix took shape, her yellow eyes blazing from a hollowed face. Aylla fell back and fired the pistol, and the Strix shrieked. The creature shot straight at her.

The Strix' head snapped back with a crack, and she fell to the swampy ground, letting out a single moan.

Jack had fired and so had someone else. He turned to see Mykel in a tall tree with his Phantom long gun still aimed at the fallen Strix. Jack fired again, and her eye socket blew out. Mykel gave him a smile.

"Did no one hear me?" Aylla stood with her hands on her hips and a frown. She fixed Jack with a stare, and he held up a finger.

He jogged to the fallen Strix and checked to be sure she was dead. Behind him, he heard Mykel sling the Phantom onto his back, leap down, and walk toward them.

"Great shot," Bean said, running up behind Mykel. "Both of you, eh." Her face was pale, though, as if she'd been running for miles and not a few yards.

"You used me." Aylla glared at them all. She'd taken her dagger out, and it shook in her hand.

"Not at first, no," Bean said with a hasty smile to reassure her. She held her hands up. "I swear, one moment you were there and the next you were gone."

"The Strix was dividing us." Jack holstered his pistols and tapped one of the tattoos on his forearm. It warmed, and when he snapped, his fingers fire burst forth. They all backed away a step. "Combus ipsa mala."

Bean and Mykel nodded as they spat on the corpse. "Burn the Stryga—er, Strix," Bean said in explanation to Aylla. "It's supposed to ensure her soul doesn't remain behind."

Aylla sighed. "I know the old tongue." Her sharp features flickered in the firelight as the Strix burned to ash.

Jack turned to her. "I'm glad to see you took that toothpick out of your bag and put it where it's useful."

She huffed. "This toothpick could still kill you."

He stepped to her so fast she didn't have time to blink. He palmed her dagger and flipped it, hilt toward her. Her move. His posture dared her to try to attack.

Aylla's ears went red, and she took up a firm stance, fists raised. Jack read her body signals, readying for a fight. He almost smiled. She was enraged—and she should be. The other soldiers stood with wide eyes, unsure if they were to interfere. She glared at them, too, as if daring them to come at her. Jack could practically hear her thoughts: she was sick and tired of the swamp, fatigued to the point of irritability, all rationality abandoned. She wanted to hit something. Mykel and Bean put their hands up and backed away.

Aylla grabbed for the knife and spun in a circle, probably to see if she could slice at his kidneys. He countered with a smooth sidestep and used her own momentum to shove her forward. Aylla bared her teeth as she turned to spar. He deflected blows with his leather bracers. They sparred for another few minutes until he was sure Aylla understood he was testing her.

When he slammed her into a tree trunk, she kicked at his ankle and then his groin. He blocked both but grunted at the impacts. Jack grabbed her arms and pinned them to her sides. The dagger quivered in her hand.

Their bodies were close. Too close. In an instant, it seemed a fire consumed the air around him, robbing him of focus. This was not acceptable. Once again, he sensed something different about her. Jack didn't move for a heartbeat as his gaze roamed over her face. His hands encased her slim wrists like irons.

"You were in no danger," he said in a low voice. The others pretended not to watch; they went over their weapons and whispered to each other.

"I can haul myself out." Aylla flashed her teeth in a growl to cover what he guessed was embarrassment. Jack figured she'd cool off in a few hours, but he respected her confidence, her anger. She hadn't given in to hers as he had to his a long time ago.

Jack let go of her and stepped back. The lines around his mouth creased.

"If it comes down to my life or yours, don't bother with mine," she said in a low hiss. She sheathed the dagger with dignity even though Jack could tell she was ashamed she'd lost.

You should tell her something encouraging. But he had nothing. Alaric's version of encouragement was "do it again until you bleed." Jack didn't think she wanted to go another round.

Mykel and Bean had crept up around them, and Bean whistled low. "You did well. I wouldn't have tried that."

Aylla pursed her lips and glared at her. "My mother always taught me to try something once—even if you fail, you can learn." Pain flitted across her face.

"Solid advice. You'll survive; don't be embarrassed," Bean said in a hushed tone. Aylla gave her a small, tight smile.

Aylla scowled at Jack, but her rage dissipated at Bean's expression. She let out a long breath as she flicked strands of hair from her face.

"Fine. But don't do that again," she said and reloaded her Winstar.

Jack inclined his head. The other two made promises and tried to assure her she was safe with them. He grunted. While Mykel was an excellent shot, they were far from safe, and Jack felt the weight of keeping them all alive like an anchor around his feet.

He glanced around. Someone was missing.

"Where's Narim?" Jack asked.

"I just saw him ..." Mykel spun in a circle.

They fanned out. The mist had cleared completely with the death of the Strix. Bean held up her transmitter, and they tapped their Runycs to start searching.

"I doubt you'll get through. This was a setup," Jack said. His suspicions were confirmed as the Runycs went back to their pale green glow, not the fluorescence that signified them working. Narim must've taken his off.

He should have refused this mission. Narim's vendetta remained alive and burning. It was more than just Alaric choosing Jack as his apprentice; Jethen stood between them like a pillar of fire. For the thousandth time Alaric's voice echoed in his mind, *Jethen's death was not your doing. Narim's jealousy and love have twisted his ideals. And whatever he felt for you in the past ...*

Jack agreed, but he was sure the captain's feelings were a thing of the past. There was nothing that would make Jack revisit that. It was more likely Narim still harbored hate over the death of his partner.

"Did he just leave?" Mykel asked skeptically. He scratched his chin.

"I wouldn't take bets on him returning," Jack said with a shake of his head. "There are at least two more Strix out there—and the High Stryga." In the back of his mind, he went through several scenarios and matched the weapons he had to each. He still had no idea how to kill or ensnare a High Stryga. Most of his success came from heuristic methods anyway, so he figured this would be no different. The problem was that it could cost other lives—innocent lives. If he were alone and died, well, it wouldn't follow him with guilt into the afterlife. Jack had enough to atone for that he was doing his best not to accumulate more.

"Brought in the best of the best," Bean said with a snort.

"I thought he *was* the best," Mykel said with a quirked brow toward Jack.

Jack grunted. Grimarr had greatly exaggerated his skill set, clearly, or more likely Narim had talked him up so that when he failed it would be catastrophic.

"You sure he's not out there waiting to see what happens to us, then?" Bean asked, scanning the trees.

Jack sighed and rubbed his face. "He probably took a cloaking potion, and he's long gone. I don't know if he's tailing us, but he's definitely using us as bait." Jack slung his pack on, and his lips thinned.

"Doesn't feel good, does it?" Aylla quipped, and the two other Milytor were silent. She glanced at him. His lips quirked up in a barely suppressed grin.

He directed his attention to the two soldiers. "You two, take off your uniforms."

Mykel and Bean's jaws worked as they tried to determine what he was getting at.

"I don't want a show—I want to see your wards," Jack said with a brow twitch. "Bean, keep your undergarments on, and lift the back of your shirt up."

"Coulda just led with that," Bean muttered. She unhooked her vest and gear and slid the black uniform off. She wore a thin black shirt under that and lifted it to show her back. Mykel did the same.

Jack inspected the tattoos etched over their lean muscle. Black ink, occasionally highlighted with color, snaked across their torsos, backs, and biceps. Some were Milytor team symbols, but others were attempts at binding runic magic. Grimarr's work again: he wanted his soldiers to be protected like Scrivers were. But it was difficult to teach everyone how to handle magic and apply it to their bodies. He grunted when he got to their backs.

"This is wrong," he said, and took out a small, thin, sharp object from a pocket on his jacket that had turned into more of an armored shirt, sleeves rolled up, and a harness for all his weapons over it.

"Oy now, watch it." Mykel turned his head to see what Jack was doing.

"Do you want me to go into the history of runic tattoos or simply tell you that you've got a target literally on your back and that in less than twenty-four hours, you'll be dead?" Jack waited for an answer.

"I'm gonna need a little explanation, yeah," Mykel said in a challenge.

"This tattoo is to make a shield around you when attacked, correct?"

The other man nodded.

"It's almost right. The little curled line here and the arrow here shouldn't be here at all, though—it's pointing to your heart. It won't protect you."

"Fine, can you fix it?"

Jack uncorked the sharp quill and fixed the rune tattoo on Mykel's pale back. He turned to Bean next, and the younger woman didn't hesitate. When Jack's fingers skimmed her skin, it was hot. She was sweating more than seemed normal. "Are you feeling all right?"

Bean nodded uncomfortably. "I'm good, just anxious. This is my first mission."

Jack let it go but kept an eye on the soldier.

Mykel cleared his throat. "Well, now that we know we've been set up, should we bother heading back? Aylla, you're free to go. Narim dragged you into this for no reason."

"He has a reason. The Stryga might prefer female sacrifices," Jack muttered.

Bean winced as she stretched her back. The new tattoo rune glowed red for a moment. She put the black uniform back on.

"Are we going to check you?" Bean asked with a raised brow. Jack bestowed her with a withering glare. She gave him a sly grin back and shrugged as if saying "worth a try." Jack noticed Mykel's apprehensive expression hadn't changed, and he'd more than flinched with Jack had touched him.

Bean tapped his friend on the arm. "What's wrong?"

"Did ... did Narim ever have you alone in ... in a room?" Mykel asked in a voice just above a whisper.

Jack turned to him with a sharp stare.

Bean's eyes narrowed. "Yes, but it was to put more runes on me."

Mykel shifted with discomfort and shook his head. "Never mind. Let's get the Drannit out of here."

"Wait. Did he do something to you other than alter runes?" Bean demanded as Mykel stepped away.

Jack didn't stop them. Mykel glanced back at him and Aylla. With a sigh, he threw up his hands. "He wanted me to do more than talk about runes and missions, all right? I refused, and now I'm here." He rolled his eyes.

"I thought the rumors of forced, er, interaction were with women," Bean said. She glanced at Aylla. "I thought I was lucky I never caught that kind of attention. I think I didn't have exactly what he was looking for." She motioned to her small chest without a hint of embarrassment.

"Lucky, indeed. He seems to like both." Mykel licked his lips.

Jack didn't want to speculate on Narim's preferences, especially when he'd already experienced them. He could still hear the young soldiers joking about Narim's attention—always sparring, always like a shadow. It made sense why Mykel was here: he'd embarrassed the captain, which was as good as a death sentence. When Jack had spurned his advances, the captain had seemed to take a personal vendetta against him as well.

Bean spoke in hushed tones with Mykel for a minute. Jack scanned the trees. Mist entwined their branches, but it was otherwise still. So much for solitude to get the mission done. He couldn't ignore the fact he had a "team" now. Jack debated leaving them, hoping the Strix would follow him so they could escape. It wasn't likely, though, and his conscience couldn't handle the not knowing. Better to remain together and find a way out.

"Just answer us this," Mykel said as they walked, picking their way over moss-covered logs and rocks. "Are you the only Scriver left?"

Jack wasn't sure why all three of them compelled him to speak more than he had in an entire year. The soldiers wanted him to be the eidolon he had no interest in being. Normally he'd have set them right, but they needed to survive, so he'd be their flimsy hope if it got them out.

"I am." Jack stared at them all with what he hoped was a neutral face. Aylla didn't make eye contact. She stayed in the shadows while the two soldiers glanced at him fleetingly.

"What do you think happened to the others? Didn't you all survive the same three trials?" Bean ultimately asked. Her tone held no cruelty.

Jack sighed. How to sum up weeks' long trials to win a lifetime of darkness? To be the one that charged into the unknown with half a chance to survive. It seemed not even elven Scrivers like Halyth stood a chance against combined malice like Strygan. He had heard the trials were to be rerun to test more men and women, but so far Grimarr hadn't pushed to revive them. Asnor was prosperous from them still. He supposed when the capital ran out of money, they'd hold another spectacle.

"We were all turned into hybrid weapons," he explained. "Soldiers with the stealth and intelligence of assassins but with the addition of wielding magic better than most. I don't know details about what happened to the other four. Our experimental methods don't leave room for a lot of error."

He left it at that. Of course, their task had also been to transcribe what they found in the dark places of their enemies. Spy on enemy territory, figure out what beasts they were breeding that could be used against the realm. Record monsters and their lairs. But there would always be the most dangerous monsters of all—those that hid under the guise of humans, or those humans who wanted the monsters to take control.

Aylla saved him from further explanation. "So, do you sense Strix or Stryga are close?"

She was very preceptive, and Jack appreciated that about her—even if she was frustratingly out of his control. "I do smell Strix. They have to feed on life forces of the young to stay alive. They aren't cognizant half the time. They've given up too much and deteriorated."

"This is the part where you tell all of us to get out, right?" Aylla smoothed a piece of hair off her cheek.

Jack met her gaze. "Normally. But then I would absolutely use you as bait to flush them out." He smirked when she lifted her fingers in a rude gesture.

Bean and Mykel snorted.

"We feel it's our duty to get you out, miss." Mykel dipped his head. "But we also have a task."

"Although, sometimes more eyes and ears are better." Bean shrugged. She ran a hand through her short, dark hair and adjusted the pistols on her belt. "We have enough rations to last all of us another month if we wanted. But let's hope to Numyn it doesn't take that long."

Aylla snorted. "I won't ask you to get me back home. So, I can either leave and find my way back, or I can help you."

Bean and Mykel glanced at Jack. *Apparently, I'm the newly elected leader of this mission,* he thought with a sigh. *And I guess the mission is still on.*

"You know the territory; you know the risks. It's up to you if you want to stay," he said to her.

Aylla squared her shoulders. "Your tone says I shouldn't."

"My tone says nothing since my inflection hasn't changed. I can't guarantee your survival any more than my own." Jack didn't know why he felt compelled to have her stay now. Perhaps it was because he couldn't know for sure if she would make it out now that the Stryga knew she was there, or perhaps he'd gotten accustomed to her presence. She still had a chance, no matter how slim, to get back to her wolves and live a happy life.

Aylla exchanged looks with the other two soldiers. Their wishes were a lot more transparent. She nodded. "I'll stay. But as soon as it gets hazardous, you don't have to worry about me. The Stryga is the more important task."

Jack turned to her. "Do you want me to put a protection rune on you? I don't have time to teach you how to effectively use it, but it could buy you some time when we're attacked next."

Aylla considered it for a moment, then nodded and turned around, loosening her corset belt so her dress could be pulled up enough to expose her lower back.

Mykel and Bean excused themselves to regroup ahead. Aylla ripped the long skirt so it was shorter, then pulled it up like a shirt. Jack's hand touched her warm back. Despite his best efforts, he couldn't help but think of how long it had been since he'd touched a woman—or at least one who wasn't trying to kill him.

"This will sting for a few hours. It's to keep the Stryga or Strix from sensing us too far ahead. She knows we're here, but she won't know exactly where. I can only put one ward on at a time."

"All right." Aylla flinched. "You said I can't learn how to use it? Doesn't it just work because that ink mixes with my blood?"

"Yes. If you learned how to channel this type of magic and even learn a few words of the other Maiden languages, the rune would work better. It'll do the job though without all that," he said. Aylla ground her teeth as the sharp runing instrument sliced through her skin.

"What makes you think I don't know any other language?" Aylla asked with a challenging smile.

Jack tilted his head. "That's fair. Do you?"

She winced in pain as the quill dug into her skin. "Some Murana."

"Should I stop?"

Aylla shook her head. "No, it's not the pain. I just felt something weird ... like I've felt this rune before or something." She turned her head away, and the flush on her cheeks was not from the heat between them. Jack reached out with his senses, and indeed there was some undercurrent of foreign magic sliding on her skin. He'd been ignoring it to focus on the Stryga, but now that he concentrated, it was back—something about her was off, oddly fascinating. Like a smell he couldn't quite place that conjured up mist-covered cliffs and wild bell-bloom groves. He didn't know what it was. The Scriver part of his mind was insanely curious. Was she not all human? Was she a gifted human who didn't know she possessed an affinity for magic? It reminded him of a time he'd happened upon a cursed princess. The poor thing didn't know she transformed at night and was in tears that something had killed her lover. Jack had broken that news—and the curse—but he'd come away bloody and exhausted.

"How many languages do you know?" Aylla asked, and Jack could tell it was to distract herself from the burning he knew all too well.

"Thirty tongues, give or take a few. And no, I'm not fluent in all of them."

Aylla stepped back, and the connection broke. She tucked her shirt back in and did a twirl. "Well, that's far more than I even figured existed. Do I look better?" she teased. Her spin put her closer to him, and she put a hand out on his arm to steady herself. She tilted her head up to see into his eyes. A few raindrops cascaded down his nose and past his lips. He didn't need a focus spell to see her riveted gaze, or how her breaths came in soft spurts, and her heart pumped faster. Her skin on his ignited small whorls of electricity. Jack ignored the sensation, but the thought crossed his mind of how long it had been since anyone touched him without violence.

Jack blinked. He leaned in toward her and then abruptly stopped. He didn't miss the confused look that crossed her face before she too pulled herself together. It had been a long time since he was drawn to someone's energy so potently.

"What happened between you and Narim? He left us all for dead, so you all must have pissed in his ale or something," she said with a toss of her head.

Jack wasn't sure if he cared to get into it, but the change of subject was welcome. They headed to where Bean and Mykel were waiting.

"It's a long history." When she kept looking at him expectantly, he continued, "Narim has always hated I trained with Alaric—an elite hunter and magician who knew Grimarr. Alaric never was Milytor, but not because he lacked the skills. Narim thought he deserved Alaric's wisdom and training. He tried the Scriver Trials and survived all but one." Jack paused. "Before that, though, I served in the Milytor for a short period. We were on a mission. He had a partner who was kidnapped by dwarves, and I went in solo. His partner wasn't alive when I got there—he'd been tortured to death. Narim always said I left him to die, and that I did so because I knew their secret. Or, at the very least, that I took my time getting there. They were lovers." There was more to it than that, but it was the short version. Jack didn't feel like getting into it after all this time.

Aylla blew out a breath and nodded. "So, Mykel and Bean were right that he's been with both men and women, but he seems to prefer men?"

Jack snorted. "And trolls and goats and elves. The story got convoluted, as happens with gossip, and I left the Milytor to train with Alaric who was setting up the trials with the Dolfar elves at the time." He brushed aside a low-hanging piece of moss for her to pass under.

Bean and Mykel continued ahead over the soggy ground. The rain turned into a mist that coated the swamp like a mask. Frogs bellowed, crickets chirped, and wild cats yowled in the distance.

"Speculation can do a lot of damage." Aylla shrugged and followed him.

Jack paused and turned to her. Before he could answer, a fiery arc blazed from the shadows of the trees. Aylla froze. The ball of fire landed in a splash of flame behind Mykel and Bean, just a few feet in front of her and Jack.

Chapter Fifteen

I have discovered Grimarr's birthplace, born in Fort Wildhorne in the Corvea Mountains. He let it slip over a rare drink while we discussed the goblin issue. I also discovered he likes pickled Alecton gizzards and the color blue.
~ Scryptus, the Scriver Archives,
as recounted by Scriver #5 Jack Serpent, Tome 10

"Get to cover!" Mykel shouted, his voice echoing back to them.

Jack instinctively jumped to the right, Aylla following. The trees weren't much protection, but it was the best choice for now.

Fireballs fell from every direction and lit the trees like they were made of incendiary sap. Within minutes, they were surrounded by flaming pillars. Jack operated on instinct and muscle memory as he dodged the sparks that turned shades of purple and white.

A scream rose above the roar of the fires, and a huge black shape catapulted out of the smoke. Jack grabbed Kyadem off the loop on his belt, and the weapon hummed. The blades gleamed faintly blue, runes lighting up like black lightning, and the chains clanked as he let the long blade fall. Then he whipped it up into a swinging arc and shot it at the Strix that flew towards them. The wraithlike woman materialized from shadow into a solid form as the blades caught her skirts and sliced into her leg underneath. She shrieked and changed direction. Her hair flew in tendrils of filth, her ragged clothing trailing behind her like smoke, eyes blazing white hot.

The Strix flew towards Bean.

"Contact behind!" Jack shouted, and Bean turned just as the Strix swept past her.

Before Bean could react, she was holding the bloody stump of her left hand. Her face went pale, and she fell to her knees in shock, cradling her arm. Mykel leapt over her and unloaded his pistol at the shadow. The Strix laughed, and it made the fires flare brighter. Their flames flickered brilliant orange and whispered like sirens.

"Drannit," Jack muttered, and took off in a sprint towards the two soldiers. Aylla followed on his heels.

"She's baiting you—get down!" Jack shoved Mykel out of the way as the Strix's claw swept past the tall man's head. He ducked just in time, but a few brown curls drifted in the Strix's wake.

Jack ripped off Bean's sleeve and handed it to Aylla. "Tourniquet around her arm."

He shielded the young woman with his body as the Strix flew back and forth. The fire billowed and crackled the wet tree trunks.

Bean's eyes rolled into her head, and she turned chalky white. Jack sensed more than saw the High Stryga in her mind. That was how she'd been spying on them. She was inside Bean's head and using her as her eyes. Bean grabbed her pack, one handed, and threw firebombs at her allies. The torpedoes of fiery death exploded as they hit the ground.

"What are you doing? Corvynia's tits!" Mykel shouted.

"Get back!" Jack didn't have time to deal with Bean. At this point, she was just a pawn in the High Stryga's grasp. If Jack could get the Stryga out of Bean's head, he might be able to save her ...

Jack grabbed Aylla. He pointed toward Mykel, and they ran. Jack lingered a few moments to see if the Strix would come close to him, but her white eyes leered at him from high above.

Come on, bitch.

But he didn't have time. Jack snarled at her and ran as Bean lobbed another fire orb at them. His back warmed uncomfortably as he sprinted away and then dove into an alcove formed by giant roots. Mykel and Aylla were huddled there already. The explosion leveled the trees, and the trunk that sheltered them groaned. Jack pointed ahead and waited as they ran again toward the next smoldering ruin. The tree slid forward, and Jack glanced back as it fell into the alcove they'd been sitting in seconds ago.

The Strix's cackle surrounded them in a cacophony of noise. "You will pay for my sister's death. Come, Razer, let's see if you bleed."

Jack ignored the threat, focusing on Bean. Her movements slowed as her mind was overtaken. She tied a tourniquet around her bleeding stump. The High Stryga glanced at him through Bean's eyes, controlling her now. She controlled both of them—the Strix and the soldier.

"What's a Razer?" Aylla panted. She held her pistol out and pointed at the striga's moving shadow.

Jack wasn't sure if he was relieved or annoyed when Mykel jerked a thumb at Jack. "He is. He's known as the Razer of Ravenhell. Thirteen Strygan died, and the town burned for a week straight." The soldier glanced at him for more detail. "Ever since then, Strygan have had a reason to make themselves scarce."

Jack ignored it. Narim had done a great job spreading his "infamy"; he'd have to thank the bastard when he saw him again. Jack ground his teeth.

Aylla glanced at him for confirmation.

"I don't make up the cognomens." The guilty conscience reared its head every time someone called him the Razer, and the only way Jack knew how to make it stop was to kill something.

He got out Kya again, and the chained blades circled like a halo around him. He waited. When the Strix passed overhead, he let it fly. She yowled as the blades nicked her legs and the trees behind her. They fell in piles of embers that jettisoned hot sparks. He swung the weapon again at a few trees that weren't on fire, and Kyadem got tangled in their branches. Jack tugged hard and they were cleanly cut, falling over the embers and igniting to create a barrier, stopping the fire from jumping toward them.

Bean stood beside them with blank eyes, eyes that appeared larger than normal. Watching.

"What's wrong?" Mykel shouted at her. "You're in league with the Stryga?"

She didn't answer. Then she convulsed, and her eyes cleared. "Wait! Wait!" She panted and thrashed in the burning brush. "Please, she's in my head. Can you—" Her own scream cut off her words.

Mykel started toward her, but Jack held him back. "She's gone."

The soldier shrugged him off. "You're a fucking Scriver, do something." He ran toward Bean with an outstretched hand.

Jack had seen this before, and it wasn't pretty. He could get the Stryga out of Bean's mind, but he didn't have the proper tools in his pack or the time. He hoped the woman had a strong enough will that she could last until he could kill the Strix.

"I can give you something that might help you keep your wits, but you'll have to stay awake," Jack said, and held out a vial to Bean. The soldier gulped it down. The tincture of wormwood, ichitla, giant kelp leaf, and sea viper venom was a concoction he'd experimented with when a siren held him captive for months. Any sort of mind control was the same, so he hoped this would help Bean. To truly get the dark magic out, though, would take more time than they had.

"Can you keep her out of your head, mate? We'll figure something out if you can keep your wits. You'll bleed out if we don't treat that wrist." Mykel grabbed his comrade and steadied her.

Bean nodded and took his hand. "I'll try. I'm sorry." She blubbered on and on about how the High Stryga had been giving her orders and haunting her sleep for months. She'd thought this was the mission where she could kill the Stryga and get the monster out of her head.

Jack stowed Kya on his hip holster as they neared. He leveled Mykel with a look. He'd have to kill the soldier if he defended Bean when she truly was taken over. "You're responsible for her," he told Mykel. "You watch her every second."

Aylla shivered as she went to Bean's side and tried to help her walk. Bean gave her a grateful look. Then Bean caught Jack's eye, and her face froze. The High Stryga saw him through the young woman. Yellow eyes rimmed with silvery gold flickered back; the whisper of a laugh. Jack didn't break eye contact, pondering whether to use a short blast spell, but he didn't want to punish Bean any more than she was already being tortured. She lowered her head. They crashed through underbrush away from the flaming forest.

"The Strix isn't following," Mykel said as he walked, supporting Bean. They left the trees and headed into an expanse of overgrown bushes that twisted up toward a weakening sun. Their branches sported thornlike projections.

Jack debated going after the Strix alone but figured she'd come back anyway. She couldn't let them leave the swamp. Better to conserve energy and wait it out. *And my nagging conscience knows that I can't leave them with Bean ...not with the Stryga in her head. She could attack from all sides.*

"The Strix will attack again, but we will make camp if we find a space and wait for her to come to us." He reached a hand out to Bean, and the soldier flinched. "I need to check your vitals."

Bean nodded and let him check her pulse. Her heart beat erratically, and she was silent from shock. Her clammy skin alerted Jack that her temperature was dropping.

They fast walked through the claustrophobic bushes. Mykel hacked away at branches and kicked rocks out of the way. His chest heaved with exertion, and sweat rolled down his neck. Ahead, the brush opened up a little and Jack paused. There were several rock formations protruding from the bush maze, forming caves. Who knew how deep they were. He directed the group into a medium-sized opening.

Mykel knelt with a heavy sigh and looked around the dark entrance. He threw a pebble into the yawning darkness to test the depth, and it bounced roughly ten feet in. Aylla helped Bean, seemingly unafraid of her. Maybe they didn't realize what a threat she was now. In her weak state, and with the loss of one hand, she certainly did not seem like one.

"Doesn't sound very deep. We should be able to defend from here with stone at our backs," Mykel said, and reached into his pack to get a light. The portable lantern glowed with a gemstone, illuminating the small cave in white. Lichens and glowing crystals clung to the damp walls.

"Spread the canvas out," Jack said as he tied Bean's wrists in front of her. Aylla rushed to make a resting place. Bean lay down, shaking. She clutched the arm where the hand had been severed.

"Is that necessary? She's lost a hand," Mykel asked.

Jack rounded on him with narrowed eyes. He didn't need to justify his actions, and Mykel clearly did not understand the severity of the situation. Mykel held his hands up and let Jack secure Bean. He didn't make the rope tight, but he knew if the High Stryga truly got a hold of her again, there was little rope would do. There was no time to ward the bindings.

"We should cauterize the wound at the least," Aylla said in a small voice. She had stayed back, her expression wary as if she expected him to give her the same glare he'd given Mykel.

Jack didn't debate her use of "we." He didn't expect her to do it.

When he loosened the tourniquet, fresh blood gushed from the wound. He tapped the fire rune tattoo on his wrist. Flames burst forth in his left hand, dancing up his fingers and flickering in hues of orange and white. "Hold her."

Aylla sat on the young soldier's legs, while Mykel grabbed Bean's arms. She visibly braced herself but didn't look away. Jack placed his hand on the severed limb, and flames sizzled the flesh.

Bean screamed and writhed as the wound burned over. The bleeding stopped, and charred flesh invaded the cave's air. Mykel didn't relax his grip until Bean stopped and lay curled on her side, breathing steadily. Jack got out his only medical kit and retrieved a vial of pain numbing serum. There wasn't much he could do about the lost hand, but hopefully the serum would let Bean rest for a few hours. He poured it down her throat, and she coughed.

"My entire pack is gone," Bean croaked.

"We've still got ours, we'll be fine," Mykel said, and put a hand on Bean's shoulder. "That bitch is going to pay for what she took."

Bean smiled half-heartedly. "I don't need aid and don't transmit my location to Ghoul Base. I can finish this—I can keep her out of my head. I gave her my mind willingly before, but I can fight her. I've been fighting for a few months now."

Jack stood. She'd put up a Drannit good fight if the High Stryga had possessed her mind for that long. Most people would have gone mad or left to join her. The woman's eyes tracked him as he put the comm near his lips. Aylla sat back with an unease flickering over her face.

"Ghoul Base, you out there?" Jack didn't expect the Milytor headquarters to answer, but it was worth a try. He had no issues with the sardonic nickname—in fact, he liked to tease Grimarr about it. Static filled his ears. He tried saying the code word to transmit to Grimarr's stone, but nothing went through either. Of course, it hadn't been Grim, but Narim who gave them shoddy equipment. There was no aid coming from the Milytor.

"Ghoul Base, requesting extraction immediately. Mortal wound on a soldier. Needs containment." The shorthand term for a soldier who was compromised wasn't lost on Mykel. The man swore as he paced.

"You can't do anything more?" he asked, running his hands through his brown curls. "I know a few spells."

"Spells on spells won't work for an enslaved mind," Jack said in a low voice. Since Bean had given her mind willingly, the process to unlatch her from the High Stryga was far more complicated than anything Jack could do in the middle of a swamp. "Let me try someone else." This was the reason he'd asked Dean to do a flyover once a day. It might not be the right timing, but he'd bet his friend had his comm on.

Jack pressed his transmitter and changed it to a different color, whispering a different word so that it would light up Dean's.

"Dean, if you're not busy wiping a boar's ass, we need immediate extraction in the Poe Swamp."

Jack waited and scanned the darkening swamp. Insects lit up as they flitted after a meal, and fish jumped to eat them in turn. The transmitter echoed for a moment with a faint voice, then came in clear.

"Confirmed, you helpless git. What's your malfunction?" Dean's voice had never sounded so good to Jack's ears. He exhaled.

"Need immediate extraction but have no idea our location. Soldier needs containment."

"I can do this—I'm not going to die," Bean interjected. Her entire body shook with the effort of talking.

Jack eyed her with narrowed brows.

"Is that all? I thought you'd be able to handle a little Strix wound. Why don't I bring you some Bessy's bulging bacon pasties along the way, shall I?" Dean asked, the irritation plain in his tone. Jack knew he was covering his frustration at not being able to help more. He'd have to search for them for a while, and he'd be lucky if he found them at all.

"That'll do." Jack grunted. "Look for smoke if you leave now—I'm going to set the swamp on fire. Otherwise, get to Ghoul Base and get Grimarr to transmit to me. Something's messing with the transmitters."

"If I had to guess, I'd say Mr. Tightwad isn't with you anymore?" Dean's voice broke up at the end.

"He's abandoned ship. We're losing signal. We can't wait for long."

"Confirmed."

Jack put the transmitter back into his pack, the stone cooling and turning a flat gray. He didn't give much thought to Narim beyond that the bastard had betrayed them. This was probably part of his plan to get Jack killed and see how powerful the High Stryga had become. Such careless use of innocent lives made his jaw clench.

"A Bessy does sound really good," Mykel said, and licked his lips.

Aylla laughed and added, "I had a cherry pastry all the way from Shay-ela. I've always wanted to see that continent."

Mykel nodded in agreement. "I've only been once, and those city folk have tech we only dream about."

"We're stuck for the moment." Jack scratched his head and smoothed back a few hairs that had fallen over his face. "We rotate watches like before. Keep that rifle out."

Mykel pulled out a small music box, spelled to play songs as if a whole orchestra were there. He kept the volume low. Jack would not normally have allowed any noise, but given the situation, the Stryga already knew where they were. Plus, he was going to start a huge-ass fire in a few minutes as a beacon for Dean, so why not let them listen?

The melodies took them away from the hellish situation for a second. Symphonic strains floated around them like a warm blanket. It reminded Jack of ballrooms filled with twirling princesses and duchesses, brought him back to when Alaric made him learn to dance and how to execute court etiquette, to blend in. It reminded him of just how alone and unfitting he was for society. All the people dressed in finery, too many utensils to be considered safe at a table, wine that was worth more than Shertan, and whispered politics that used to unnerve him.

"Who are you?" A young man in dark silk and wearing a half mask came up to Jack, who was trying to merge into the shadows.

Jack cleared his throat. The spiced wine might have been too much, as his collar felt heated and his legs wobbled. Alaric would have him gutting Myri fish for days if he caught him drinking so much. But it was the only way to take the edge off thinking everyone there was about to kill him. Or how differently he'd lived from any of them. He doubted these patrons had been forced to watch their parents be murdered, or ever fight for a piece of bread.

"Invited by Prince Derek," Jack said in hopes the young man would lose interest.

"Oy, personal invite, eh? Kindrik, come have a look here, we've got royalty!"

Another young man with an expensive coat and pants wandered over. A drink spilled in his hand, and he leered at a woman's cleavage as she walked past.

"Who's this?" Kindrik smirked.

Jack felt like he was back in the orphanage. Everyone was looking at him like he was a foreign specimen. Was it that obvious? He wore the same clothes, his hair was in the same style (a low ponytail), and he carried a tasteful but small dagger at his side. He even had a small black mask with ornate silver etching hanging on his belt. Perhaps he should have worn it.

"Newest eligible bachelor." The men snickered together.

"Not with that nose." Kindrik sniffed.

Jack kept his face and posture neutral. Did they really think speaking of his nose would achieve insult?

"I'm Donath. My father is the prince's cousin, since you don't seem to recognize me." The young man blinked as if waiting for Jack's acknowledgement.

Jack did know who he was but made it a point to never let anyone know anything until he wanted them to.

His silence seemed to only taunt them more. They started sniping about the cut of his coat, made off-color remarks about his mother and other insults that compared him to various animal parts. If he started a brawl here, Alaric would lock him in a cave for sure. He started to slip away, but Kindrik sloshed more of his drink on an unsuspecting woman.

"Leave off, Kindrik!" she sputtered, and shook her now-stained skirt. The fabric was light and shimmered pale blue as if made from starlight.

"Bit of fun, Lucy. Come on, let's have a dance to make up for it." Kindrik and Donath turned their unwanted attention on the girl. She sidestepped his hand.

"No, thank you." Yet the auburn-haired girl was too polite to shrug his hand off when he reached a second time. She stood with a perplexed, almost fearful arch of her brows.

Jack stepped forward and knocked Kindrik's hand away. The other man, being as drunk as he was, didn't bother with gentlemanly preamble before his fist was flying at Jack's face. It was easy to dodge, and even simpler to use the other's momentum to send him sprawling on the ground. Jack didn't have to turn fully to deflect Donath's attack. He swept the other man's arm forward in an elbow lock and swung him around. His left foot caught Donath's right, and he grabbed with his right hand to careen the gentleman into a banister.

Lucy shrieked and fled in a floof of ballgown. Jack tried to sidle back into the shadows, but people started to yell for help as the boys on the floor writhed in pain. Alaric's tall form parted them like water as he approached Jack. His face and demeanor were calm, almost curious, instead of the anger Jack had expected.

Later, he'd learned that Alaric had set it up to see what Jack would do in the defense of a "helpless" girl. It hadn't been hard to convince Lucy to play her part, and the two boys had done the rest naturally.

"I wanted to know you still had some emotion, some humanity in you," Alaric said in his crisp Cafferian accent. He'd come from the southern continent but stayed in Elgar for the women—supposedly. Jack suspected it was for the potent magical markers, but it was anyone's guess.

"Am I supposed to thank you?" Jack folded his arms. "Of course I have ... whatever." The tightness in his chest never abated. Alaric didn't talk about emotions, so this was a first. Jack had lived with pain for so long he'd learned to embrace it, challenge it. Maybe it was his willingness to die that Alaric loved. He didn't have anything or anyone holding him back—there was nothing he wanted except to overcome pain in all its forms until it killed him. Perhaps he accepted the physical and mental anguish over having to think about his parents, the years at the orphanage, and what he now knew had been child slaves mining for crystals.

Alaric let out a slow breath. "All your training, spell work, and studying ... I have been wondering if I let you slide too far into the dark." He studied Jack's face with a concentration only a father could understand. "A Scriver doesn't have to operate on mission alone. Your judgment and evaluation could mean the difference between killing a monster or an innocent. I just wanted to be certain you'll know the difference when the time comes."

Jack had let the conversation melt into the recesses of his mind after that. They never spoke of it again. They did, however, speak of how Jack could blend in better and how it wasn't always worth it to reveal his presence unless necessary. A lesson he'd taken to readily—he was proud now of his ability to become like shadow.

The putrid, decaying smell of the swamp swept Jack out of his memories. He shook it off. He might be able to remain unseen, but Ravenhell had put him on so many people's radars it had made Alaric squirm with discomfort. At least in the ten years since, the fervor had died down to rumor and whispers.

"You know, I love Hessia, but I think Mendan was a better composer," Mykel said. He lowered the volume even more but continued to listen for a few more minutes.

"That *is* Mendan," Jack couldn't help pointing out. He didn't like overstuffed rooms with painted people, but he did appreciate a good piece of music.

Mykel and Aylla's eyes bored into him, as if he'd just said he'd mated with a centaur. Apparently, the title description for Scriver didn't include culture. Jack busied himself sorting out the weapons in his pack, even though there was no need.

The soldier chuckled softly. "You're right; this is a piece Menden did before he was famous. Hard to tell over this piece of shyf." Mykel grinned and then shut off the music box. "To better days ahead." He sat down and took out his canteen. He handed out a few more C-rations. The taste of the spelled food brought back memories of training days.

Aylla stood and took a hesitant step toward the black trees. Jack watched but didn't comment. She was staying within their perimeter but obviously needed a moment alone. He'd give her about ten seconds.

Bean had closed her eyes, her breath steady, body still wracked with tremors.

Chapter Sixteen

Sirens travel in pods but can be solitary creatures. Stories would have you believe their song alone lures men and women to their watery deaths. Not entirely true. Some people find their vocal racket quite irritating, myself included. They change tactics to use strong, forceful magic, and I have the scars to prove it. There are ways to ward against their song, runes and spells.
~ Scryptus, the Scriver Archives,
as recounted by Scriver #5 Jack Serpent, Tome 9

Aylla took deep breaths and forced herself to quell the nausea that rolled in her stomach. It had felt like the cave wall and fire were closing in on her. She'd recognized the signs of panic but stepped away to fight it.

More than anything, she wished she were in her cabin, lying by the fire with Ash and Hugo. She should have left well enough alone. But she'd chosen to stay, hadn't she? She didn't think her skills and knowledge of the swamp terrain would help them much, but she did think it was better than nothing. They were good men—even Jack. The enmity between them had fizzled to a survival instinct now. She had never met a Milytor soldier who was as kind as Bean or one who was as sharp as Mykel. From the little Aylla had learned, it had taken Bean longer to prove herself in the Milytor than Mykel. The Milytor boasted of equality, but there were still some men who refused to serve with a woman.

You shouldn't have stayed, she scolded herself. Perhaps it was because it had been far too long since someone wanted her help. She wanted to be needed, if she admitted the truth. She'd always told herself she didn't want children, but deep in the recesses of a broken heart she wanted to be a mother, to have a family. The wolf pups had filled that void for a little while. Aylla could fool herself into thinking she didn't need anyone, but she wanted connection with someone human. She didn't think humans were made to be alone, but she didn't know how to get close to anyone either.

A footstep cracked a branch behind her, and she spun, Winstar out. Jack's silhouette materialized, hands up. He'd deliberately made noise, she realized. She put the pistol back in the holster and composed her face.

"I need you to stay closer. I can't watch everyone at once," he said, mildly annoyed, and Aylla fixed him with a fierce stare. The awkward silence stretched. The chirps of insects and buzz of frogs didn't cover the moment.

Aylla thought she *had* been close. Now that she looked around, maybe she'd strayed slightly farther than she'd thought. The cave was more than a few paces behind them.

"I don't need any 'watching,'" she snapped, more irritably than she'd intended. *He can't do everything? Shocking.*

A muscle ground in Jack's cheek, but he offered no retort. He simply spread his hands with exaggerated patience and a neutral face.

"Just didn't want you thinking I was leaving you out here as bait again." He turned and started back toward the cave.

Aylla sighed. The exhaustion and constant vigilance were making her nerves raw. She probably should have been grateful she was still alive. It wasn't his fault she was stuck here.

"Can I ask you something?" Aylla stepped closer to him.

"No, I didn't choose to be a Scriver, and no, I wouldn't change it," he said with a shrug.

"I guess you get asked that a lot, but that's not what I wanted to know." Aylla snorted. "I wanted to know how many kinds of weapons there are to fight monsters. Which ones do you find the most effective?"

Jack tilted his head, and his eyes found hers. "Really."

"I figure if I survive, it won't hurt in the future. Right?" She plucked the Winstar from the holster. The sensation that pulled at her when she was around Jack was turning into something more than curiosity. The embarrassment from when he'd disarmed her still clung to her, but she wasn't too proud to admit when she could learn something that would help her survive. "My father taught me how to shoot, and my mother always told me to keep it clean."

"You chose well. The Winstar 459 bullets are larger and easier to put hex sigils on than the 238s." Jack clicked the slide back and popped a round out. He held up a silver-encased bullet and twisted it so that she could see the runes.

"How did you learn what hexes work?" she asked.

"Experiments. I study texts, listen to locals, and try something. If it works, I record it and use it later. A Scriver's job is particularly inglorious, and I should have died a long time ago messing with things we don't know much about—just like the others." Jack grunted.

"I wish I'd learned how to smith," Aylla said, tracing a finger over a huge fern leaf.

"You can learn. It's not hard. Everyone modifies their pistol for what they need it for. Scattershots are another story—so many varieties, but in general they're better for long range. Heimmers are similar to Winstars, but I've found they're not made as well currently. They'll shoot through wood and some metals, though."

Aylla couldn't imagine being the first to hunt anything. To go first into a situation no one had been in and try to record it. "You mentioned a mentor or trainer before?"

"Alaric. He was a hunter before. He found me in a slave trade orphanage and thought I'd be a good soldier, but then decided I was fit for trials in his soldier experiment with Grimarr," Jack said, then looked away as if he'd revealed too much. He cleared his throat. "We should get back. I don't trust that the Stryga won't use Bean again soon."

Aylla walked with him back toward the cave. The situation, as she'd feared it would, had turned for the worse. She might not want to work with him, but her life probably depended on it. "Do you think she'll be able to keep her mind shut?"

"No."

Aylla took a beat. "And you really can't do anything for her?"

"It's not as simple as making the right potion or freeing her of a curse. The High Stryga in her head is casting powerful magic that isn't broken lightly. I don't have the time, and most people under this kind of control end up dead."

She let the pang of sadness stab her chest for Bean. It was unlikely they could get out of the swamp fast enough for someone to help her now. All that hard work she'd done to get into the Milytor, and for what? To be controlled by a fucking Stryga. Aylla wondered if there was a potion or something to slow the progression of mind control.

"How do you make potions?" She realized she was asking him questions as if he were on trial, but it kept the anxiety at bay as they waited, and her curiosity was piqued. Jack's life sounded so interesting, so necessary. It made her want to do more than hide away in the forest, to be more than a scared girl who lived alone and would die alone. Jack didn't seem to mind her questions now, answering them patiently and simply. He seemed resigned to the fact he wasn't going to be tracking a threat on his own and had to deal with being part of a group.

"There are spells, blood, gemstones, and sometimes organs involved. For humans, acquiring magic means you must sacrifice something. Malecanta were the only ones who could manipulate magic without sacrifice." Jack didn't expand on that, so Aylla figured it was too complicated. They weren't eating a meal at a tavern, after all—something could attack at any moment.

"Do you think the Malecanta are truly extinct?" Aylla asked.

"I don't think so."

Her hand brushed his arm as they walked, and she immediately shied away. He didn't move. Did that mean he wasn't alarmed by the contact? Or did it mean he hadn't felt it? Either way, her cheeks blossomed with heat, and she turned her head. What was the matter with her? She barely knew this man, yet her blood was racing. *Probably from the stress ... when is this Stryga going to show up?* He'd embarrassed and taunted her the entire time she'd known him. Aylla ground her teeth. The unknown feeling made her stomach roil and her skin heat. She needed to get rid of it immediately.

The image of her mother recoiling at her uncle's touch shimmered in her mind. She'd been such a knowledgeable, powerful woman, and it was still unsettling to have seen her uncertain, almost scared. Lavynia had been a well-regarded healer in their village. Her marriage to Sebastian van Hyde was toasted even a year after.

"Then, the sorcery houses could still be functioning? Training new Malecanta?" Aylla asked in a low voice. Her mother's stories about the three prominent houses of sorcery often popped up in her imaginative dreams. There were tests to get into a house and trials meant to weed out the unworthy

"Houses Elementum, Meta, and Venena were all disbanded years ago but that doesn't mean they executed all the professors." Jack side-eyed her as if wondering what she knew. "Do you believe Malecanta formed the continents or the gods? Or Numyn alone."

Aylla tilted her head. Some races, like the elves, dwarves, and some humans, believed in the one god, Numyn. Others, like Strygan, some sorcerers, centaurs, and fairies believed in the plethora of gods. Her mother had been a believer simply in faith, in magic. She'd opened her arms to anyone no matter their beliefs, and Aylla had fully embraced that philosophy.

"I don't care who formed what. We're all here now, and we need to figure out a way to distribute power evenly," she said with a shrug. It was as banal a statement as possible, but it was true.

"Hmmm." He pushed vines out of their way. The darkness had not lightened, and in the murk, shadows seethed, insects whined, and the trees shivered with a warm wind.

"My mother would tell me tales of the Houses. And some Malecanta could even speak to unicorns and dragons."

"Which haven't been seen in decades," Jack said with a shake of his head. "The old magic is dying out. Maybe it never existed, and the sorcerers were just trying to maintain control, the illusion of power."

Aylla pursed her lips. She didn't want to admit she'd been hoping Jack would confirm the existence of such creatures. Surely, he'd experienced and researched so much that if they existed, he would know. Speaking of that ...

"With all your knowledge, I just thought you'd know how to get a Stryga out of someone's head," Aylla said as they turned back toward the cave. It was a lame insult, and they both knew it.

"Don't let the rumors make me into more than I am. Anything that has a will to live is hard to kill."

Aylla nodded. *The way those soldiers look at him, though, he's either their worst nightmare or their hero.* He moved so quietly too ... and she lived with wolves. But it wasn't a compliment she was going to give him.

"Can your friend on the comms get Bean out of here?"

"It's worth a try," Jack said. He stepped over rocks and roots.

Aylla shut herself up. Enough rambling, despite the anxiety still clawing at her stomach. She hadn't known the soldiers long, but they felt like friends. She'd had precious few of those, but Mykel and Bean actually seemed to care. Primary school had been a blur of being shuffled around—she didn't like to read the books assigned and often corrected other students. Was it her fault she liked to read so much and therefore amassed an unusual amount of information?

Keep your ears open and eyes up, my Tideling. Those who fly the highest never worry about what is above them. So, you must fly higher. Her mother's soft words stayed with her. *You can have it all. You just cannot have it all at once. There is a time for everything.*

They returned to the small cave. Mykel's hand remained on his rifle as he kept watch over Bean. The young woman sat up with a wince. She was covered in sweat and shook like she was sitting on an earthquake. The rings on her fingers of her remaining hand clinked together from shaking, wrists still bound in front of her.

"I can't seem to get warm." Bean's teeth chattered, and she lay back on the stone wall. Lichen glowed around her head in a sickly green.

"The Strix is close—she's watching," Jack said with a curse.

Mykel nodded, clasping his Phantom long gun.

"Anyone have a pipe?" Bean asked with a hoarse laugh. "I brought some Boar leaf for a celebratory smoke when this was all done. It's in my pack. Dalton, get it for me, would you?"

"She's delirious," Mykel said with a shake of his head. "You're right, she'll overtake her mind any second now."

Black, veinlike marks appeared along her arms and up her neck. Jack moved toward the entrance. "Stay here."

No one argued when he left. Jack didn't intend to go far. But he didn't want them all to be in the cave when the Strix attacked again. He leaped up a pile of rocks, took out the red rune stick, and started to draw symbols on the cave rocks. The stick was imbued with some of his own blood. The runes wouldn't keep the Strix from killing them, but it could buy time. Aylla and Mykel's low voices floated up to him. He didn't like eavesdropping, but he couldn't help that they were speaking when they should have remained quiet.

"You live alone in Churk Forest—may I ask why?" Mykel asked.

"Sure." Aylla's light voice held a slight tremor. "My father died, and his brother took over the family, which was just me and my mother. My uncle—formerly in the Milytor, actually—was not exactly a beacon of good will. So, when he killed my mother, I left to make a life on my own. My mother and I had been secretly building a cabin, a place to get away from him."

"Everyone has a tragedy, don't they?" Mykel didn't say it out of pity, and neither was he being sarcastic. Just one person connecting with another. Jack hadn't done that in a long time, and he doubted he would again. Her information made sense though—the way she didn't trust as easily as some people, the challenge in her stare.

"Indeed, we all have something that hurts us." Aylla sighed.

"My sister and I were separated when our parents died at a Volg riot. They were against the Republic and supported the king," Mykel said. His voice cracked, but he steadied himself. "I didn't want the responsibility of her. She was thirteen, and I thought she could handle herself. Just like me. I left her at a pub while I met up with friends. When I came back in the morning, she was gone. I enlisted in the Milytor the next week when I couldn't find her."

Jack's insides tightened. Memories of his own abduction as a boy tried to surface. He shoved them far down. He glanced down at Aylla and Mykel sitting by the small fire.

"Have you given up hope finding her?" Aylla asked.

"No. I'll search for her until I die." Mykel cleared his throat. Jack heard them shifting around in the cave.

Bean moaned and spoke old Malecantan chants. The Strix was on the move.

"You've done more than enough for a doomed mission. I don't think Jack believes we're getting her out," Mykel said, shaking his head. "But I'll wait the night out and see. She deserves to get back home."

"You trust him ... without knowing him. Why?" Aylla asked and took a sip of water from a canteen.

"You ever just get a feeling from someone? Shooting and fighting are what I'm good at. Strygan lore and monsters are just bedtime stories my gran used to tell me. I must admit I was curious about this particular Scriver, the Razer of Ravenhell. Rumor alone gives him respect, even if half of it isn't true. The others recorded a few things of note, but they're only remembered by older Milytor now."

"I've heard of Ravenhell—it was a village, wasn't it?"

Mykel nodded. "It was. A coven of Strygan took over it, and I don't know if Jack was ordered to kill them or he did it on his own. But the entire village burned for a week, and thirteen Strygan were held captive and died over many days. I heard people say that the screams were so bloody bad that even animals won't pass through that village now. People go there just to feel the stain of magic left behind. There hasn't been a gathering of Strygan that large since then. No one knows how he survived. He gave the Scrivers a reputation as being elite for sure. Maybe the other four perished because they tried to gain the same legacy. There are plenty of monsters on this continent that we haven't catalogued. I wouldn't go out for the trials, because I can't wield magic for shyf, but they were discontinued anyway after Alaric's death."

Mykel cleared his throat, and Jack resisted the urge to interrupt. He liked hearing about himself about as much as he liked being flayed by leeches. And it wasn't entirely true—animals did wander in and out of Ravenhell.

"Imagine just a human taking on a vortex of black magic that large. I wouldn't have gone to that village if they paid me."

"Maybe they didn't appreciate his sarcasm and overconfidence," Aylla said.

Jack stifled a snort. He deserved that.

Mykel sputtered and coughed out a laugh. "Cheers to that. I wouldn't want the burden of a Scriver. It's easy to cower under covers or keep the lanterns on—it's harder to face true darkness and find out what makes it that way." He took a sip from his canteen.

This is all so flattering I think I might need my own statue, Jack thought with a grunt. If they knew the truth, they'd probably shoot him on sight. There was no longer a chance he could leave and do the mission alone. The wind shushed through branches, and a faint stench floated on the air. Finally.

Jack took the opportunity to jump down from the ledge, and the two started in surprise. Mykel's Phantom was up and sighted on him. Jack nodded approval at his reaction time.

"Eyes up. It's coming," he said. "I'll try to flank it and drive it back here. There are wards on the cave, but they won't hold for long."

Mykel stood, nodded, and looked through his rifle's scope.

Jack ran as lightly as he could, following his nose. The Strix's scent blew like a dead carcass, which made it easy. A huge shadow emerged from the misty twilight. Jack drew Kyadem, and the blades flashed into the air before the Strix even knew Jack was on her tail.

She screamed as the chained blade whipped at her legs. The Strix raced from tree to tree, trying to escape the man behind her. Branches snapped, and bark flew like sharp rain.

Jack parried, dodged, and thwarted his prey in an elegant dance like lightning, except that he knew where he was striking. There was no hesitation in his moves, just a cold and calculated assault.

He sprinted across the soggy ground, leaped up a trunk, and landed on the Strix's back. She flailed and fell face-first to the ground with Jack's boots on her back. He sliced her head from her shoulders and raced back to the cave, just in time to see Bean's shadowed form looming behind Aylla.

Chapter Seventeen

The Houses of Sorcery: Venena, Elementum, and Meta existed to help young ones come into their magic, learn to use it, and to protect themselves. Not all students, and there were few to begin with, continued this education—whether due to insubordination, lack of talent, or attacks on the schools.
~ Scryptus, The Scriver Archives,
as recounted by Scriver #5 Jack Serpent, Tome 11

Bean's form rose, and Jack shouted at Aylla to get out of the way. She whirled, just as Bean slashed with a knife. It nicked her shoulder, and she threw herself sideways. Mykel threw down the Phantom, picked up his pistol, and aimed. But he couldn't fire.

Jack saw the tremor in his hands and knew the soldier's hesitation was going to cost another life. He fired his Winstar. The soldier jerked back, but she remained standing despite the strike to the heart. The High Stryga's puppet. Jack swore. Bean must've given up bone in order for the Stryga to keep her animated as a corpse.

Bean knelt at Mykel's pack and grabbed the first weapons on top: Heimmer pistols. The soldier's eyes went dark as she aimed at Aylla and Mykel.

"Get out!" Mykel grabbed his Phantom. Aylla was already sprinting from the cave. They dove to the side as bullet hail stormed after them.

Jack whipped Kya into the mouth of the cave and cut off Bean's other hand. The pistol clattered to the stone ground, and the young woman dribbled blood from her mouth as she collapsed.

"The Houses of Sorcery will never rise. Strygan will inherit the continents!" Bean shouted with her last breath.

Jack decapitated her with Kyadem's blade. The body lay still. The High Stryga couldn't hold a corpse for long—but she could send her sister in.

Jack ducked as the Strix charged at him. A shot from Mykel went wide, clipping the creature. Jack whipped Kya up and caught the Strix around the neck. He dragged her down, wrapped another layer of sharp chain around her neck, and jerked. Her head snapped off in a gush of black blood, and her body thrashed under his feet. He backed up so he wouldn't get her filthy blood on his boots. Kyadem folded neatly onto his belt, and Jack took the flint from his pocket.

Mykel was murmuring a prayer over Bean's headless body. Aylla knelt and bowed her head as well. Jack took a deep breath before joining them. He was to blame for Bean's death. It pricked him like fine needles under fingernails.

"She's truly dead?" Mykel asked.

"I had no choice—" Jack started, but Aylla cut him off.

"We know."

"I hesitated too long. Her death is on me, not you," Mykel said in a hoarse voice. Tears glimmered in his eyes. "She was the first person to offer water when everyone else was looking out for themselves."

Jack shook his head. It was no use arguing with the young soldier. The blame didn't matter anyway. A life was gone, and nothing could repair that.

He funneled his rage into the dead Strix. Lighting the flint, he burned her body with no ceremony of respect. The Strix erupted in a pillar of white-hot flames. Dean would have to be a blind fool to not see the beacon. Jack stalked back to his dropped pack. He retrieved a set of cigars in a gold leaf box. The calmness of fury settled over him.

Jack offered cigars to a very confused Mykel and a white-faced Aylla. They both declined. He shrugged and turned back to the flaming pile of shyf. He cut the end of the cigar with his knife and lit it. Smoke puffed around him like spirits of the underworld. Elgarian monks crafted the finest pipes and cigars, some with enchanted properties that kept one in euphoria for days. This was not such a cigar, but it reminded Jack of Alaric and his father, and that in turn kept him serenely, acutely aware of his surroundings and the threats. The old sod had been quiet of late. Perhaps Jack really was mad and hearing dead people's voices.

He scanned the darkening forest, hoping to all the gods the High Stryga was watching.

The full flavor of chocolate and earthy bark mixed with dark Cafferian citrus filled his taste buds and relaxed his senses. Jack leaned against a tree and forced his body to still, to calm itself. It was times like this, stuck and enraged, when he had learned to take a moment before he did something rash. Like burn an entire village to the ground, or torture Strygan to learn their black secrets. Rustles sounded in the brush a few feet away from him. Insects stilled their hum and a black mist rose.

"Um, what are you doing?" Aylla's soft voice called to him.

Jack turned to her with a tight smile that covered the anger, the failure to protect Bean that burned him. He'd been responsible for her, even if Narim had the official title of being the Milytor controller. Jack had told the king the risks, and he couldn't be responsible for the lives of the team, even though he'd known deep down he'd do almost anything to preserve life.

This was Narim's doing. That fucking six-balled, Drannit-damned ogre. Jack hoped he was also watching him. He glanced at Aylla and was grateful she didn't look at him like he was a torturesome monster. From her solemn gaze, he knew she understood.

"Taking a minute before I do something I regret." If he'd been alone, he would have hauled ass out of the swamp and kicked in every palace door until he got answers. Jack stalked back to the cave entrance and knelt by Bean's body. "We will bury her and move out."

Mykel and Aylla looked at him with the obvious question: what do we use as a shovel? Jack opened his pack and plunged his arm inside, pulling out a foldable shovel. The pack's depthless bottom came in handy all the time.

Aylla cocked her head at the bag. Then she gathered Bean's head gently and laid it by her body. She covered the woman with a cloth from her bag, doing her best to make it look neat. They took turns digging out a hole and arranged rocks over the mound. Jack didn't have to state the obvious; they couldn't bring her body back for a proper Milytor burial. Her name would join others on the Infinity Tree where all the lost soldiers were honored.

"... trouble in south ..." the comm chirped to life, and Dean's grainy voice came over it.

"Repeat, Dean."

"Can't get in. Found the smoke, but nowhere to land or drop a ladder down ... warded ..."

Jack sighed. "Can you see anything where the High Stryga would be using as a power source?"

Silence, and then, "I think there's a huge totem to the northwest ... big, lots of bones ... confirm?"

Jack's transmitter turned gray as the signal was lost. "Well, we have a heading. Maybe we can find a place for him to drop in. But we're also going to be heading straight for this High Stryga. She'll keep a power source close to her living quarters, I assume." He leveled them both with a serious stare. Neither balked.

Jack nodded. Mykel disassembled the Phantom and got out his dual pistols, both Heimmers. They were similar to Winstar 459s, and the Milytor used them interchangeably. Jack couldn't help but glance at the Golden Summit Phantom long gun. It was a similar caliber and make to his Eagle's Claw.

The soldier side-eyed him and then wordlessly passed him the weapon. Jack grinned as he held the long gun in his hands. Modifications were slight but effective: fairy optics, barrel was half an inch longer than normal, sights custom for Mykel's eye width. It was light, obsidian black, and held fifteen huge rounds. The bullets were sharply pointed, with runes etched into their sides and a red gem affixed on the tip.

"Blasting tips, nice," Jack said with a grunt. The red gems were mined in the Corvea Mountains and, when used in conjunction with the force of a rifle, made the bullet able to penetrate just about any material on the continents. Iron, rock, wood, walls of water, and supposedly even small hills. Jack returned the Phantom, and Mykel snapped it onto his back.

Then he slung his pack over his shoulders. "We've got three packs with enough C-rations for months, as Bean said. I only have three hundred rounds left for my Heimmers and one hundred for my Golden. Five knives, a machete, and ten grenades. Blessed Water, a few potions for night vision and speed."

Aylla pursed her lips. "I have a knife, my Winstar, and blankets. And a plucky, I-may-not-survive attitude."

Mykel snorted and nodded. Jack gave her an ironic side glance.

He started walking northwest towards the totem. If they were unlucky, the Stryga would find them along the way.

"It'll be enough supply to get us through. Or we improvise." Jack gave them a rundown of his inventory, which was similar to Mykel's with the exception of a lot less rounds. It might be a huge pack, but he hadn't stocked it with everything. He didn't like to travel heavy, and enchanted or not, the pack got weighty when it was at capacity. Each round was etched with runes to kill most monsters, but he bet the High Stryga wouldn't die that easily. Her Strix sisters were just tests.

The swamp did not work to their advantage as the terrain got soppier and soppier. Aylla was helpful, warning them about sinkholes and possible fire mines, but they made progress like a lame horse. Half the time they stepped into calf-high hidden puddles of water. The remainder they tripped over rocks and logs. Insects buzzed in their ears, and sweat seemed to permanently stick on their skin. There was the occasional random cool spot, and in one of those, Jack called a halt to rest for half an hour.

Mykel leaned against a tall cypress tree and chewed on dried fruit. Aylla spread a canvas down to lie on and closed her eyes. Her petite features were pinched, face pale, but she didn't falter or complain. Jack sat two feet from her and drank water.

"I need to know something before I die," Mykel said, looking at him, and Jack knew what was coming. It always did.

"Shoot."

"What truly happened at Ravenhell? I've heard the lore, but I want to know the truth, and odds are I'll take it to my grave."

Jack grunted. "I'm not that old."

"Old enough to become legend, mate," Mykel said with a grin. "Alaric trained you, right?"

"He did." Jack didn't answer the previous question because he didn't really know how to. How could he explain what it was to become the kind of monster you were hunting? How could he describe the scars it left him despite all the praise and esteem? Ravenhell had been his breaking point. He'd taken innocent lives along with the evil that night. He'd tortured every single Stryga to get information. He'd killed civilians because they were under Stryga control, just like Bean. And then he'd learned that there were children that had been hiding ... and they'd burned along with the entire village. In his blind rage, he hadn't checked homes well enough, had thought anyone that wasn't a Stryga would have run. He'd told them to—that anyone not under Strygan control could leave, and the wards he'd placed around the village wouldn't hurt them.

None of it had brought his parents back. Never again.

"Just tell me—that *was* you, right?" Mykel seemed resigned to let it go.

Jack let out a slow breath. "It was."

"Boiling goddess tits. We'll find this High Stryga no problem and be out of here before autumn solstice is over. I can't wait to get out of this fucking heat," Mykel said, and slapped a stinging bug that landed on his cheek.

Jack inclined his head at him. There was no way to tell the boy the truth—it changed every time the story was told. What was the point in defaming his own legend when no one would believe him? He also didn't want to give Mykel false hope. He still wasn't quite sure how to kill her; hexed bullets would be the first try, then runed spells on his body, fire ...

and there were also the spells he'd never tried before. Wasn't his whole life based on experimentation? Maybe he'd get lucky, or maybe he'd get them all killed. They seemed resigned to that possibility, though.

"The Thresher Festival is nearly over." Aylla spoke as if she were lost in bad memories and hadn't been paying attention to their conversation. Jack was glad of the interruption. He glanced at her, and the sleepiness in her eyes confirmed it. She'd been in and out of consciousness. He knew what that kind of sleep was like—unable to truly rest but the brain and body demanded at least a little time to decompress.

"Have you been to it?" Mykel turned to her.

"A few times, when my mother was still alive," she said, and neither man questioned what she meant.

Jack would have taken exception to this uncle had he been alive. He wasn't going to ask further questions based on what he'd overheard—he didn't like to get involved, but for whatever reason, she'd been thrown into his path, and he didn't entirely dislike it. She'd shown bravery, a willingness to learn, and she'd challenged him. Not many people did that. He felt slightly bad for disarming her the way he had. The memory of the shame in her cheeks made his guilt flare up. There would have been better ways to prove his point, but Jack wasn't as adept with words as he was with weapons.

Aylla's long, dark hair twisted in rivulets over her shoulder in a braid, and her large golden eyes held a pain much like his own. For the first time since he'd met Lyra, he wanted to protect someone not out of obligation. For the first time in a long time, she made him curious.

Mykel cleared his throat and changed the subject. "We'll make sure the Milytor knows what Bean did for the team. We can give her family a dignified salute."

Aylla smiled and then pointed with a start. "There it is again. A changeling."

Jack turned. A flash of pale face with sharp teeth, quickly vanishing. He stood, and two more changelings appeared. They were no taller than waist height and appeared like children, but with dark red eyes and mouths full of fangs.

"She sent her children to spy on us," Jack said with a sniff. He unleashed Kyadem from his belt. Chain links clinked like crystal, and the changelings hissed as they scattered. "Mykel, I'm going to need you to flush them toward me."

Mykel took a breath and got up. He ran to the left and fired a few rounds to get the changelings moving. They hid, but Jack drank the fylnoc potion, which enhanced his vision and allowed him to see body heat signals in the dark. Their glowing purple outlines were clear; they thought they'd found a place to hide and keep spying.

Jack threw Kyadem out and the chain looped around a white neck. He pulled and dragged the changeling toward him.

"We only need one," he said as Mykel flushed more out. The white, childlike creatures hopped and scuttled like beetles as they dispersed.

Jack hauled the screaming thing to their camp and tied it with rope. The changeling gnawed at the bonds, but they were infused with night-thorn and didn't fray.

"What are you going to do with it?" Aylla asked as she backed away.

"I need her name," Jack said, pulling out his knife. He knelt to meet the changeling at eye level. "What is the High Stryga's name?"

The changeling spat at him and gnashed its teeth. Black hair lay flung over its face, and its skin chafed raw as it tried to escape. It called out for its siblings to help, but the swamp remained silent. Jack slid the knife over its boney arm, and black blood gushed.

Aylla turned away as the changeling's screams changed to resemble a child's sobbing.

"I'm sorry, I don't know," the thing said with bloody tears running down its face. Jack steeled his nerves. This was not a child, and it would kill him at the first chance if it could.

He stuck the knife in the changeling's thigh and left it there. The creature shrieked and writhed. Mykel handed him another knife, but Jack could see in his eyes that he was breaking. The changeling sensed it and turned its attention to the soldier.

"Sir, please, I am only a servant. She orders us to gather information and food. That is all we can do," it said tearfully.

"And as a servant, you must overhear things," Jack interrupted, and waved the next knife in front of its face. "What is her name?"

The changeling closed its eyes and continued to wail.

Jack slapped the changeling to get it to stop. "I know what she commands you to do. Things you regret, things not in your nature. Give me her name and it'll stop."

The changeling's sobs stopped, and it glared at him with burning eyes. "She does not make us do anything. We take human children so she grows more powerful, and one day we will not have to hide. One day—"

"I don't need a monologue. Name, or this knife goes into another body part." Jack flipped the dagger in his palm and waited.

The changeling didn't move or speak. He sighed and then jammed the knife down—just as the thing screamed for him to stop.

"Franziska! Franziska Strain," the changeling shouted, then convulsed as if it had been shot. The name died on its lips and black blood dribbled down its chin. Its eyes turned glassy and its skin shriveled.

"What just happened?" Mykel asked, peering over Jack's shoulder.

"Betrayal spell, I bet." Jack stood, retrieved his flint, and burned the changeling. He glanced at Aylla, expecting revulsion or fear, but she just stared back with her full lips in a straight line.

"Why do you need her name? Will that lead us to her?" Aylla asked. She twisted the leather pack in her hands.

"Her name gives her power. I don't have materials for a name-tracking spell, but I can use her name against her."

Jack turned to walk closer, but the ground trembled beneath their feet. He leaped to Aylla as mist rose like a wall. The Stryga's wards were at it again. She must have sensed the changeling's betrayal, and now she sought to separate them again.

"Jack? Aylla?" Mykel's voice echoed in the distance. How had he gotten so far away?

Jack clamped down on Aylla's hand as a new voice exploded around them.

"I know *your* names too. Aylla van Hyde," the High Stryga crooned, and her cackle sent a chill into Jack's bones. "And if it isn't the Razer of Ravenhell. The infamous Scriver, Jack Serpent."

The mist thickened. He could barely see Aylla even though he held her hand. She went limp, and he pulled her into him. This magic smelled like ancient pits of fear.

"Oh, yes, hold tightly, dear. She might come back to you," the Stryga said, her voice far away. She sounded as if she weren't even near them but rather in a dream fog, casting her spell from the safety of her home.

Jack cursed her and held Aylla's body close. Her breathing was steady, but her pulse raced as if she were caught in a waking nightmare.

Chapter Eighteen

Sirens or merfolk as some refer to them are a diverse, complex people. At first glance they can appear very human on top of the water but that is their illusion. They have two sets of gills and skin ranging in color from a light green to tan. I was captured by three females (I didn't see a male until much later). The females appeared very interested in my lower half. I spent most of my time fending them off whilst trying different runes to repel and protect myself. Curious creatures who did not seem interested in killing me straight away.
~ Scryptus, The Scriver Archives,
as recounted by Scriver #5 Jack Serpent, Tome 9

Aylla ran through fields of wheat and honeysuckle. The wind blew its sweet scent into her hair, and the sun warmed her golden skin. She laughed as a frog leapt out of her way and splashed into a pond. Nine years had taught her that being alone with animals and trees was the best sort of company. Her mother had taught her all the species and how to recognize tracks. Chockta County burst with enough game and fertile soil to feed hundreds of families for years.

"Aylla!" Her uncle's voice boomed across the meadow, and it seemed as if even the wheat stalks froze.

Aylla slunk toward the big farmhouse. Every step was heavy, as if lead dragged her down, but she knew the consequences if she didn't come. She approached the big wraparound porch and glanced up at her uncle.

"I thought I told you to wash the dishes. Drannit, girl, you're useless. Get in there!" Uncle Drace grabbed her arm and threw her into the house.

Aylla rubbed at her bicep and headed toward the sink, where a pile of dishes sat. She passed a picture of her mother and uncle. Even in the picture, her mother was withdrawn, her eyes haunted. What no one saw were her uncle's marks that colored her black and blue. She hid them with pretty dresses and jewels he gave her as apologies afterward. Even in her grave, she'd been fully dressed—no one had seen the bruises on her skin.

Uncle Drace had started to try to strike Aylla as well if she wasn't quick enough or didn't think of his needs before her own. Yet the blows were never as hard or as frequent as those against her mother. The angrier he got, the less he could strike her, as if an invisible hand swatted his away.

She didn't hate her mother for leaving her alone. Her mother had thrown herself in front of a sharp piece of pottery for Aylla. The cracked plate had lodged into her neck, and she'd bled out before Aylla could stop it. She'd seen the whisper of something terrifying in her mother's eyes before they'd closed forever.

Aylla soaped up the dishes and cranked the pump for water. The window let her get lost in her mind—the wide-open spaces with a few trees dotting the horizon were like a blank canvas. She could imagine whatever she wanted on it. Far in the distance were lands she could escape in and never have to feel a rough hand on her again. She and Mother had secretly started building a cabin in the forest. Even if they'd never live in it now, it had been a safe place to be together sometimes.

Clouds gathered purple and vicious over the blue sky. Aylla inhaled the scent of imminent rain as it blew through the half-open window. Spring storms were common this time of year. Sometimes they popped up within minutes, but the winds were different today. She reached to close the window as the first drops spattered the glass. Something made the hairs on her arms stand up. This storm wasn't normal. Her skin burst with tingles, and something flashed purple before her eyes. It was gone in a second, but her head spun with the impact.

Had that been real magic? Aylla had never touched magic before—perhaps by some miracle, she'd wished the storm into being. She wanted to understand how sorceresses of old could use such power. But there was no talk of magic in her house—they were low-lying folk who minded their own business. Magic was for the rich or schooled. Her uncle had screamed for months at her mother, accusing her of harboring some kind, nonetheless. Lavynia had always denied it, even when her wrist was broken. Aylla didn't quite believe her, because a mere week later the bone was fully healed. Even as young as she was, Aylla understood that the body didn't just mend that quickly. Had her mother been some sort of practitioner?

She refused to call her a Stryga. No one with as good a heart as her mother could be a Stryga.

The wind whipped up clods of golden meadow and flung bushes at the house. Shutters clanked against the casements, and debris floated in the air like deadly fractures of light. Drace yelled for her to close the windows and doors. Aylla walked past the big living room where her uncle lay on the couch, guzzling his cheap Shay-elan beer and listening to the music transmitters.

"I think I left the barn door open," she said.

Uncle Drace grunted. "Go close it then, idiot."

Aylla ran from the house, the front door slamming shut, and she knew it would be the last time she ever went in there. The barn was close, and she slipped inside. Horses whinnied anxiously, smashing their hooves against the wooden walls. Aylla let them out and shooed them from the barn. They'd have a chance of surviving what was coming if they weren't stuck in their stalls. She glimpsed the sky as she closed the barn doors; savage rain pelted the ground, and the wind moaned so loudly she thought it was in pain.

And then she spotted it.

A torrent of black updraft, a roaring zephyr that twirled and danced across the meadow toward her house. The house she'd grown up in, the house that her uncle had taken over just two weeks after her father's death. The house where her mother had died trying to shield Aylla from Drace's drunken rage.

Aylla raced to the back of the barn and opened the cellar door. She got in, latched the door, and ran down the short steps. Canned goods and a few leather parts of a harness surrounded her. The wind screamed and boards groaned under the pressure.

"Dranakar damn you," she whispered.

Boards in the barn shattered. The earsplitting, shrieking wind could have been her parents, or maybe it was her guilt. Aylla shoved a fist into her mouth as she sank to her knees.

"I didn't mean to ..." Aylla whispered as she stirred in her nightmares. "I should have warned him."

A woman, a beautiful woman, with a pale face, luminous blue eyes, and hair the color of ravens spoke to her. She radiated calm and safety. Dimly, from far away, Aylla was aware it was the High Stryga. Franziska.

She looked too much like Aylla's mother. Aylla shuddered and shut her eyes.

"Too soon, I understand. Come, Tideling, look now," the Stryga whispered. She used Aylla's nickname, and it quaked in her core.

Aylla opened her eyes, and the Stryga was an entirely different person. Her dark eyes were offset by sienna-colored skin; waves of ebony locks entwined with gold cascaded like vines. She adjusted the straps of her gown, which glowed like fairy wings, virescent and changing color with the light.

"They deserved it. He would have kept you as a slave or worse. You're stronger than your past," the Stryga whispered.

Aylla hung her head. "I don't know how. I could have protected my mother just as she protected me."

"A child cannot comprehend what a parent will do to keep them safe. You can only use the future she gave to you." Franziska's soothing voice was like a mother's. Her serene face lulled Aylla into that soft feeling of being heard, understood.

"I don't think you intend for any of us to leave alive." Aylla swept her eyes down as if realizing she shouldn't have admitted that.

"I do not waste life." The Stryga paused. "Your company is quite interesting. Watching humans interact is amusing for me. Jack fancies you; I can feel it."

"Funny way of showing it." Aylla hunched her shoulders. "He'll go on with his life when this is over. I don't have much of a life to get on with." She sighed.

"The coven can give you a new purpose. I personally oversee young women who need a place to call home. You could become so powerful no man, elf, troll, or dwarf would ever touch you without permission. You could rule a land with fairness and kindness."

The Stryga reached out and touched Aylla's shoulder, but then she tore her hand back as if she'd been burned.

"What's wrong?" Aylla asked.

She didn't answer, just peered at Aylla with narrowed eyes and a grim smile. Something else pulled at Aylla through the fog, a voice that overrode the Stryga's. Aylla turned with disgust, realizing whom she'd been revealing her darkest secrets to. The Stryga cursed and vanished.

Like the pull of moonlight on tides, his voice lured her back. His presence and solid warmth built a wall around her.

Jack reached Aylla, and she surfaced.

Chapter Nineteen

One of the worst monsters I encountered was a half-mad old man who had been torturing and killing people for over a decade. The truly puzzling and concerning thing was, he had no background of violence, no abusive upbringing. Some people are simply evil.
~ Scryptus, The Scriver Archives,
as recounted by Scriver #5 Jack Serpent, Tome 12

"Aylla." Jack shook her shoulder. "Aylla, can you hear me?"

She opened her eyes. Her body shivered but her skin was burning to the touch. She clutched Jack's hand. He waited for the spasms to stop, knowing coming out from under a spell took time.

"Do you know where you are?"

Aylla let out a shaky breath and sat up.

"Yes."

He steadied her shoulders and let go. To his surprise, she pulled his hand back to hers and rested on his side. She glanced down at her chest. A dried blood rune sat on her open shirt, just above her breasts. Jack held up his right hand, bandaged from the cut he'd used to draw the rune in blood.

"It was the only way to get you out of the mind trap," Jack said, and handed her a damp cloth to wipe his blood off her.

"Thank you. I'm no help," she said with a sigh and lifted herself up. "Guess I made the wrong choice after all." She avoided eye contact and laced up her blouse.

"You're more help than you know."

"Yeah, as bait."

"Not what I meant." Jack gazed at her, wishing for anything to get that fire back in her eyes. A second later, he wished for anything to get him out of the situation, another attack, a viper nest, a sky bomb. He did not want to wade through the torrent of emotions wreaking havoc across her face. It tortured him more than she could know.

"I'm not a good person," she said, and her voice shook like a snow crystal clinging to a leaf on a sunny day.

"Depends on your definition of good."

"I'm going to die here. The Stryga was in my head, and I felt like there was no way out." Aylla shivered and folded her arms across her chest. "If that was anything like what Bean felt ... I don't know how she lived so long like that."

Jack turned to her. "I'll get you out."

Aylla's eyes filled with tears, and she dashed them away angrily. "I'm not worth it. I'm a murderer."

Sitting back, he offered her a canteen of water. "I wish I had something stronger."

As she took a sip, she let out a weak laugh. Mist coated them like a blanket so thick they couldn't see a foot around them. The distant dripping and cawing of birds were the only sounds he could discern. Jack was on the defensive, but he also knew the High Stryga would be somewhat drained from getting into Aylla's mind. They had a slight reprieve.

"You kill monsters. I killed my uncle."

Jack didn't avert his gaze. It seemed all the encouragement she needed to tell him about what the Stryga had made her relieve: the day she'd left her Uncle Drace to be taken by a torrent storm.

"It's part of the reason I live alone. I don't want to feel that way ever again, and if I'm not around people, then I won't." She shrugged.

"Some of the worst monsters I've ever encountered were human," Jack said. He noticed how she was leaning on him again and didn't push her away. Her body curved into his as if she were made to.

"What about your family?" she asked. It was as if the solid mist made her brave, as if nothing could penetrate this small piece of time.

Jack didn't like to divulge anything about himself, but the feeling of wanting a sky bomb to interrupt the moment dissipated slightly.

He half shrugged. A muscle in his jaw jumped when he said, "Strygan murdered them for their flesh and blood. Some sort of ritual for knowledge. My father was a Milytor man, but when he retired, he built libraries in various towns that needed them. My mother taught school, but not just the usual subjects. She taught children how to defend themselves with magic, and not everyone liked that. The night of the attack, they hid me in a warded closet. I got out and found they were dead—hanging, gutted, from our tree. I was picked up by slave traders and worked in mines for Clarent crystals before Alaric found me. I tried training with the Milytor, but turns out I have a problem with authority."

Aylla chuckled half-heartedly. "I'd like to say the usual 'I'm sorry'—and I am—but for that kind of situation there just aren't words that are appropriate. I suppose that's why you did the Scriver Trials." She glanced at him with an open expression.

"I had nothing else to lose. Alaric, my mentor, hated Strygan in particular. He never really told me the entire story why." Jack hadn't thought about that much until now. Alaric had been a staunch human ally even though Jack suspected he wasn't entirely human. How else did someone seem to know things that should have been from before he'd been born? How did Alaric move with a preternatural prowl that Jack still hadn't mastered, and how did he know so much for only being a "simple hunter" as he called himself?

It would also explain why he kept speaking in Jack's mind.

"And what happened in Ravenhell?" Aylla asked sadly, in understanding.

Jack grunted and handed her a biscuit. "What I did in Ravenhell wasn't as selfless as they want it to be." He hesitated, but her expectant look somehow persuaded him to keep talking. It was against his instincts, but in this case, he didn't think his survival mattered in her knowing the truth.

"I tracked the coven that murdered my parents, and I exacted revenge. I didn't know they chose my parents' house for the crossroads—a place of deep magic. I'd like to say I remember what I did, but there was a point where all I heard was the screams and all I wanted to do was keep them in agony," he said in a hoarse voice. Aylla didn't move. "I extracted information. Valuable information, of course, but in my blind rage I didn't know there were a few civilians among the fires I lit. I couldn't differentiate their screams from the Strygan."

Jack couldn't describe the power he'd witnessed those three days and nights. It was like a force greater than himself had propelled him, soaked into his skin. Something had liked what he was channeling and used him to do violent things. Or was it simply his own darkness he couldn't control?

"Ever since, I've never let my emotions get the better of me."

Aylla chewed her lips. "And you've never felt good about the revenge either. It didn't fill the holes the way you thought it would."

Jack nodded.

She looked at him, and it made something tighten in his chest. She truly looked at him for a moment, as if she saw through the attempt at modesty.

"The soldiers only know me because Grimarr flaunts my career like I'm his son. I grew up knowing who he was because of my father's short-term career in the Milytor. Guess it wasn't for either of us," Jack said with a wry shake of his head. "I heard later that Grim searched for years after I was taken."

Aylla nodded. "He sounds like a good man. And his reasoning for wanting you to work for the Milytor makes sense ... if I trusted the Milytor to keep the citizens safe." She swallowed the biscuit with a drink of water. The canteen rattled as she twisted the cap back on.

Jack was silent for a minute. There had been a time he'd believed in the Milytor as well, but it was getting too big for Grimarr to handle alone. He could only imagine how much more divided they were now, with the queen's murder. Those soldiers who wanted to serve the people and those who wanted to be elevated to royalty if the Milytor took control. "Things can change. There's always corruption somewhere."

A faint shout made them both swivel their heads west. Jack activated his Runyc patch, and he guided them toward Mykel. He lit a torch, the fire dispelling the mist, and soon Mykel's form materialized out of the gray.

His face was crusted with dried blood, but it lit up when he saw them.

"Thank the gods the Runycs still work. Did you hear the singing? What the Drannit was that? I'm down to my last tracking potion. Didn't want to waste it on you lot," he said, words spilling like pebbles down a mountainside "You all right?" He addressed the question to both of them but went straight to Aylla and inspected her for wounds.

Jack rolled his eyes. "I'm great." He thought back and realized he hadn't heard any song. That was troubling.

Aylla chuckled. "I'm still in one piece. What happened to you?"

"Mist disoriented me, and I kept hearing a voice I thought was you. Then I was attacked by either changelings or something else in these trees. Rosie plucked them off well enough, but I'm down to fifty rounds." Mykel lifted his Phantom.

"The Phantom's name is Rosie?" Aylla shared a wry grin with him.

"Rosie, after my great-grandmother, who fought off a werewolf and then proceeded to give birth." Mykel kissed the rifle and said a prayer into the air. "No idea how a woman that pregnant could do that, but we give her the credit."

"A worthy name," Aylla said.

Jack took a vial from his pack. "Change of plans. If we get lucky and Dean finds us, great, but since we're stuck here, we might as well try to kill the High Stryga first."

"Oh, is that all the new plan is?" Mykel asked with a droll smile.

"Objections?" He glanced at both of them in turn, and they shrugged. If they were going to die, it wouldn't be without a fight.

The purple liquid sloshed in the glass container, and sparkles of white slipped in and out. Jack downed it in a gulp. His eyes lit up with amethyst flecks around his hazel irises. He spied the closest tree he could climb, scrambled up, and found what he wanted. The totems Dean said marked where Franziska made her home stood above the canopy like lightning rods. He climbed back down and brushed leaves from his jacket.

"Stryga's trail heads northeast. Conserve your ammo. We'll have to make a fire tonight to boil more water, but we should be able to get at least six more hours of trail in," Jack said.

He jumped down and started walking toward the Stryga's lair. Aylla paused to get her bag tied, then stood.

"Mykel, stop!" Aylla warned.

The soldier turned his head, then let out a yelp as he was sucked into a mud trap.

Chapter Twenty

Magic is like working hot metal or glass. It can be molded, shaped, and used, but push it too far and you'll get burned or a bad result. Rush the process of learning magic and it will repel you. It's not exactly a living thing but it certainly has opinions on who it likes to work for. Who it calls to.
~ Scryptus, The Scriver Archives,
as recounted by Scriver #5 Jack Serpent, Tome 6

Jack threw his pack on the ground and got out a length of rope. He jumped across several rocks, making his way toward Mykel, who was still submerged. Bubbles and roiling mud told him the man was desperately fighting for the surface.

"Tie it to a tree," he said, and tossed Aylla the end of the rope.

Fucking Stryga couldn't live on a beach or in the mountains? He plunged a hand, then his whole arm into the mud pit. The watery sludge splashed into his face as he grappled for Mykel. His hand caught a strap and grabbed on. Jack lay on his belly just at the edge of the pit and hauled.

Mykel's head broke the olive-green surface, and he gasped like a fish out of water. Jack grabbed his hand and looped the rope around his wrist. Mykel wiped guck from his eyes and thrashed toward the edge, but the mud sucked him back. Long, translucent-winged insects took flight at the commotion and buzzed around them. Frogs leapt into the murky, deeper water, and turtles snapped as they too retreated.

"Just stay still." Jack backed up as Mykel got a better grip on the rope.

"I can't find my pack," the soldier said with a hoarse groan. "Take Rosie." He thrust the rifle up out of the mud, and Jack took it.

"Don't kick your feet, it'll make it worse." Jack nodded to Aylla, who began to pull in unison with him. Hand over hand, they dragged Mykel out until he stood shakily on solid ground.

"Sorry, I should have been paying attention, I saw it too late," Aylla said as she raced up.

Mykel bent over his knees, catching his breath. "I'm going to kill that ass-licking, rattlecapped, Drannit, child-murdering bitch!" He stood and shook more muck off. "Not your fault, Aylla."

Jack exchanged a look with her and began coiling the rope up. They tromped back to where Aylla had tied it to a tree. Jack tugged at the knots. They didn't budge. He side-eyed her, and she shrugged.

"I learned from my uncle." She smiled sardonically, pain laced in her features. Jack imagined that man using said knots to tie Aylla up, and it burned down his spine. If Drace were still alive, there would be a reckoning that would send his soul into a place where it wouldn't exist anymore.

"Let's keep moving. Tracks and scent go this way," Jack said.

Mykel took up the rear, muttering about cleaning Rosie and with his boots squelching every step. Jack's tracking vision had a few more hours left, as he plainly saw fluorescent green footprints and a hazy trail of scent through the tall, white-barked trees. Half-submerged logs stuck out from the wetlands on either side of their meager trail. More mud pits dotted the path, and Jack skirted them around. A few crocodiles lay basking on the logs or peered at them from the surface of the water, only their eyes floating above it.

The Stryga's tracks wound around rocks and bushes and through water. Even without the potion, Jack could smell her. In a training exercise, Alaric had kept him blindfolded for two days and made him find different scents. Mainly to recognize the smell of tainted magic. The sulfur, copper tang of a Stryga, of dark magic. Most humans couldn't detect it, but it had been seared into his senses when his parents had been slaughtered that night. Jack could always detect that scent, no matter how faint.

He had one tracking potion left, and with Mykel's pack gone that was it. Their food supply wasn't an issue with C-rations, but they had maybe three hundred bullets between them.

You need to get them out of here, Alaric's voice whispered in his head.

Oh, now you want to talk. Jack sloshed through a shallow area of water.

Bean already weighs on your conscious. You'll never forgive yourself if the other two die on your watch.

I don't care for either of them in any capacity that will diminish my ability to finish this hunt. They agreed to fight, and they'll either survive or not.

Alaric's chuckle echoed in his head. Jack pictured the older man in his casual white shirt, black pants, and long, dark robe. Alaric never went anywhere without at least three weapons on him. He could summon magic faster than anyone Jack had ever met. Even without drawing runes, he could cast magic.

So, just like the trials, eh?

Jack sighed. He'd taken no pity on anyone who'd fallen—they'd volunteered for the challenge. Halyth, the auburn-haired elf in human guise, had come to him once with an offer to join her group. He'd refused. She'd soon learned the trials were not a group sport. Runvir, a man from Havaria, had had thoughts toward alliances and eventually won as well ... but alone.

This isn't the trials. Let yourself have some pleasure once in a while, Alaric said in that knowing tone.

Jack ground his teeth. *We're in the middle of a swamp. Please don't say "pleasure" ever again.*

He could picture Alaric's noncommittal shrug. *Physical indulgence isn't the same as true connection.*

Jack clenched his jaw. The other lesson he lived by, which he'd learned by experience and had nothing to do with the trials or Alaric. *Anything that means more to me than my own life can be taken, can be used against me. If these two die it won't be because of my inadequacy—the High Stryga is unexpected and foreign.*

I died for something ... for you to live. Alaric's sad chuckle swirled around him. *I'd do it again—remember that. While I never had true intimacy with another, that doesn't mean you shouldn't.*

Jack didn't answer. His mentor hadn't said it in a guilt-ridden way but in that sometimes-surprising tone when he became more like a father figure.

Not the time, Alaric.

"Jack? You okay?" Aylla's soft voice interrupted his thoughts.

"Yeah." He pointed to a semi-open spot on higher ground. "Let's camp here for the night, and Mykel can wash off in that pond over there."

The soldier was already stomping toward the bigger body of water that connected all the little streams. He cautiously waded in and then submerged himself fully to clean the mud off. Aylla pulled out the canvas and strung it up between two trees with a few big boulders at their backs. It was a good choice for a place to sleep. Jack gathered what little dry wood he found and used the flint to light it. No sense in using up magic reserves with the tattoos on his body when he didn't know how much he'd need before long. Without kindling, it took a few minutes, but it eventually caught. The spell ward he set up with the last vial of sacrificial blood of an albino elk would disguise their smoke and make them all but invisible to a Stryga—he hoped.

Mykel stripped to the waist and hung his clothes over the fire to dry them. Jack took off his boots and socks to dry as well. Aylla removed her black corset belt and untucked the now-stained green shirt. Her tattered dark skirt was flung over a branch, and her long legs in skintight black pants were an unusual sight, as most women exclusively wore gowns with petticoats. She hung her socks to dry and put her feet up by the flames. Even without the belt to give her a shape, she was beautiful.

She trusts you. Even after you humiliated her.

It wasn't Alaric's voice; it was his own. The last time Jack had been in a relationship was with Lyra. And that had ended so well. He recalled that Alaric had vehemently disagreed that Lyra was of any use to their mission. Lyra had neither wanted to be a Scriver nor asked him for his knowledge, but for some reason, Alaric had taken personal offense to her presence. While it was true she distracted Jack from training, he'd never thought it detracted from his purpose. He'd always returned to study and practice with any weapon Alaric threw at him. Now she sat rotting in an asylum because of Jack. But this was not like Lyra ... Jack refused to get sidetracked and get Aylla killed—or worse.

He filled a foldable pot with water and boiled it, then poured it into their canteens. Jack handed out one biscuit, two pieces of dried meat, and a handful of nuts and dried fruit. He'd normally take Chena, but he wanted to use up the perishable food first. Mykel contented himself with a C-ration. There was always game in the swamp; however, Franziska might have poisoned the fish, rabbits, or wild boars in their area. Never underestimate a Stryga. Especially one that liked to use human skin as her canvas and baby's bones on her altars.

A bottomless pack, and you didn't bring a poison detector, he chastised himself.

"So, how close are we?" Mykel asked as he crunched.

"Less than half a day—if the swamp doesn't move. I'd travel at night, but we can't afford another sinkhole accident. We can use fire, but I'd rather not," Jack said with a shake of his head.

"Perhaps fire doesn't frighten all predators here." Aylla raised a brow. "Ash and Hugo don't like it at all. Took me a month to get them to sit around a fire." Her tone implied she missed her companions, and Jack couldn't help but think how no one missed him like that. Not even an animal. Maybe Shertan. But he was probably enjoying the freedom of Asnor's plentiful meadows. He'd probably driven a younger stallion off his mares and was commanding his own herd.

"Should we douse the fire, perhaps?" Mykel raised a brow.

"There are insects in here that are attracted to the light and our scent. So, it depends on whether you want to be warm and dry or stung to death," Aylla said with an impish smile.

Mykel considered both possibilities. Jack went to put dirt over the fire, and Aylla stopped him. "Hold on, I was joking. I see yarba tree pods. Throw a few of those on the fire and it'll be a repellent."

Jack plucked a few seed pods from a nearby tree and threw them into the flames. The fire turned a muted shade of blue, like weak moonlight.

Mykel snorted. "Can't wait for the next thing to attack us."

Aylla laughed in agreement. They started to trade war stories about what creatures they'd encountered around Asnor. It was so easy, so natural that Jack found it irritating. Even with all the etiquette lessons, he still found it hard to speak to other people. Mykel just slipped into a comfortable camaraderie with Aylla that Jack couldn't even pretend to have.

Mykel snorted at something she said and lightly touched her leg. "Sure. Now, let me tell you about my first day as—"

Jack interrupted. "I'm going up to scout the terrain. I'll take first watch." He spied a low-hanging branch of the yarba tree.

"Alright," Mykel said, and continued to clean Rosie and tell his story.

Aylla lay back and closed her eyes, listening. Her lips parted slightly, and long eye lashes caught the shadows of the fire.

The tall yarba had thick branches that were sturdy and not completely covered in moss. Jack reached the top and sat back, breathing in fresh air. This far up, the swamp smell didn't gag him, and more than a patch of sky was visible. Stars winked in the swath of night, and a three-quarter moon rose in the west. Bats winged after insects, and birds flew to their nests. Somewhere up there, he hoped Dean was still trying to get to them. Jack couldn't see the ward over the swamp, and for a second it seemed like the sky wavered. As if he were looking through glass and it shattered.

"You're draining your magic keeping this up. Good," he said to the Stryga.

Was Narim also up there in a Milytor flyer, tracking them, or was he lounging back in the barracks telling tragically heroic stories? Narim would understand now the High Stryga was more of a threat than they'd thought. If she had others working with her, it meant the rumors were true; more Strygan were being born than usual. The covens were convening.

Jack leaned his head back against the trunk and sighed. If there was one thing he envied of the beasts of the world, it was their blissful ignorance of darker events. They went about life existing in the moment. He glanced down at the peaceful, white-blue, muted campfire below and the two bodies lying next to it.

From the shadows, something crept.

Chapter Twenty-One

Enlisting in the Milytor is a lengthy endeavor often filled with injury both physical and emotional. To achieve Scriver status is why the trials were run; since it is akin to demi-god powers, endless glory, purpose, and having your name scribed on the halls of infinity. Scrivers earn a place in the heavenly afterlife if you believe in such a place. Or so we were led to believe by Grimarr, Alaric, and the Dolfar elven leader Trysand. Such promises of gain and glory have fallen quite short—though their oaths were not the reason I went through the trials.
~ Scryptus, The Scriver Archives,
as recounted by Scriver #5 Jack Serpent, Tome 7

Jack started upright and all but leapt down the tree. His gloves protected his palms as he grappled branches to break his fall, just enough so he didn't shatter his kneecaps when he landed. Black, scaled shadows crawled from the water's edge, hissing.

"Mykel, Aylla!" Jack shouted and grabbed Kyadem. They shouldn't have camped so near water, but they needed the fresh source.

The two shot up at his warning. Mykel's head moved back and forth quickly. Then he aimed his rifle at the crocodile that nimbly slithered toward him. Mouth agape and claws scraping on the pebbled ground—it was too close.

"Get up the tree," Jack said as he swept Kyadem out in a silver arc. The blade on the long chain sliced through the croc's mouth, cleaving teeth and severing the upper half of its head. But in death, the joke was on them. A red rune flashed along its hide.

Jack shoved Aylla up on the boulder just as the croc exploded. His back seared with pain as sharp scales hit him hard enough to bruise and a few others got in the cracks of his armor. Another crocodile was on the other's tail, and its jaws snapped at his boots. Jack ignored the wounds on his back as he turned to fight. Pivoting on his right foot, he avoided a snap. He used the short-chained blade in his fist like an extended knife and punched down. The eye socket of the crocodile gushed, and it thrashed like a fish on a line. Soon, it went still. Jack sprinted away as the rune glowed crimson before detonating in a spray of fire and blood.

Jack glanced up at Mykel, who was in a tree with his rifle aimed at more crocs that were clambering out of the pond.

The crack of the gun deafened him, and Aylla winced even as she too fired a quick series at the crocs. The crocs fell one by one and exploded in violent bursts of scales and guts.

Jack led Aylla to higher ground and boosted her up a cypress tree. He threw both their packs up, and she caught them.

"Stay here."

She might have protested, but Jack didn't wait to hear it. He ran back to Mykel's position and vaulted up into the tree.

"I think she's getting the message. They're disappearing," Mykel said as he scanned the ground beneath them. The crocodiles that weren't dead hissed and slid back into the water. Ripples of dark, lily-covered water fanned in their wake.

"Or she's sending something worse," Jack muttered. He forced his vision to widen, his breath to slow, and his muscles to relax. In the moments during an encounter, he found it more beneficial to slow down than react faster. Sometimes an instinctual reaction was just the thing a creature wanted him to do. The swamp sloshed with water, overflowing the edges of the pond; ground animals scurried for cover, and insects droned away from the tumult. The moon's light penetrated weakly and made dappled shadows across fallen logs and slippery, moss-covered stones.

A howl rose a second later, and several more joined it. In the pale moonlight, Jack could make out sleek shapes running between the trunks and leaping over rocks. Splashes and growls echoed.

"Are those jaguars?" Mykel peered out and groaned. They both understood their safety in the tree was gone.

"Familiars."

Mykel looked at him with a frown. Jack heard the worry that coated his tone, but he needed the soldier to be sharp. Familiars were much worse than jaguars. He glimpsed one as it sniffed the air, standing on the remains of a dead croc. Its long limbs and torso were humanlike, but that was where the similarities ended. The familiar's face was elongated like a big cat's with protruding canines, clawed hands and feet, and a lashing tail. Runes glowed a soft white against the slick black fur all over its body. Ropey muscle gathered and bunched as it lifted its head to howl. It turned to Jack, and he met its stare head-on.

Those crimson eyes flared, and the familiar let out a low growl.

"We can't outrun them—or climb high enough. Do you have a blade?" Jack asked as Kya rattled in his palms.

"Yeah." Mykel's eyes were trained on the familiar and then the five more that joined it. "Do you have any tricks you want to use now?"

The familiars yowled. They leapt at the tree trunk, and Jack swiped Kyadem down like a whip. The blades slashed the first familiar's face.

"Incine," Jack said.

Kya purred as she burst into pearly orange phoenix flame. The chains flickered with dancing fire and the blades shimmered in shades of orange and white, blue flickering at the center. The familiars crouched back, hackles on their backs and teeth bared. Phoenix fire was unique; when properly bound, it wouldn't harm him, while remaining lethal to anything else it touched. Jack leaped from his branch and hit the ground. He barely heard Mykel follow as the catlike people attacked.

Jack whirled the chained blades in a frenzy of melee attacks. They sliced and hacked through bone, but the familiars did not stop from loss of limb. A black claw scraped his shoulder, and Jack pivoted. He grabbed the claw, wrenched it down, and whirled with the screaming creature. He jabbed his elbow into its side and got it down to its knees. Jack whipped the flaming chains around its neck and yanked. The head flew off in a geyser of black blood.

He sent a back kick to another on his six. A roundhouse stopped yet another that leaped from the side. Jack grabbed a lean, muscled arm that flew at his face and used the momentum to throw the familiar away from him. He clutched the arm and twisted its wrist, using his left foot to pivot and slam his body into it. The familiar yowled as its wrist snapped and Jack kneed it in the side. Jack let it topple to the ground, then stomped his booted foot into its throat. The jaguar-man gasped and clawed at its neck. With its windpipe crushed, it would still take minutes to die. Minutes Jack couldn't spare to watch.

He back-elbowed a familiar charging behind him. Jack flicked Kyadem into the shorter blade. The familiars were too close for the chain. He punched left, parried right. Jack threw his metal-protected fist into the face of a familiar, and the thing hissed. He charged it and kept punching, backing it up and dodging the long claws that grasped at him. The familiar fell back into the pond water, and Jack followed.

He snap-kicked it in the stomach and pounced on top of it. The familiar's head went under as Jack sliced open its belly with the blade. Viscera oozed out, and the runes went dark.

He had sloshed to the edge of the water when a hard thump hit his back. Jack flew forward and landed face-first in mud.

Pain blossomed in his right side as a claw dug deep through a gap in his armor. Jack rolled to the right, toppling the creature on him, and had to use both hands to grapple with the weight. Kyadem was lost in the scuffle. Jack's fists found hair, and he latched on like a leech. The familiar gnashed his teeth at him, and saliva splattered Jack's neck. He rolled, hoping there was a big rock for him to bash the thing's head with. The familiar's jaws grazed his cheek.

Jack had to get it off before his strength wore out. Familiars didn't feel pain the same way humans did, and they certainly had more stamina. He risked letting go with one hand, keeping the jaws from crushing his face with the other as he reached for the knife in his boot. The blade slid free. Jack rammed it up into the familiar's lower jaw. The black-furred creature yelped and loosened its grip enough that Jack kicked him off. Jack instantly tracked it and charged. He made full-body contact and plunged the knife into its eye socket. Then he withdrew the blade, flipped the familiar over, and jammed the dagger into its heart. Jack sawed the blade down to cut through the runes to disrupt them, and they stopped glowing. The familiar vanished in a puff of black smoke.

Jack panted as he scrambled to find Kyadem—thankfully, the flickering white flames made it easy. In the light, he spied Mykel on his back, swiping at three familiars. He struck one in the calf, and it went down. Mykel rolled on top and drove the knife into the base of its spine and skull. The other familiar roared and leaped onto his back. Mykel screamed as long fangs bit into his left shoulder. He twisted and managed to drive his long knife into its torso.

Jack lashed out with the chained blades, and they whipped around the closest beast's neck. He jerked back hard, decapitating it. The third familiar's jaws dug deep into Mykel's neck, and the copper tang of blood filled the air. Mykel gurgled and clawed at his attacker, falling to the ground.

It charged. Jack gripped Kyadem short blade out and sprinted toward it.

He met the familiar in a collision that jarred his skull. Jack punched the familiar with the blade, slicing down its face. The jaguar-man roared and grabbed the blade, pulling it even as it mangled its hand and threw it feet away. Jack wrapped both his hands around the thing's neck and clamped. The familiar threw its weight against him, but Jack pinned it down with his legs and crashed its head against a rock on the ground. Blood pulsed from the familiar's nose and mouth as it lashed out. The runes went dark, and it disappeared with a pop of black mist. Jack fell forward and wiped blood from his eyes.

He ran to Mykel, but there was already someone there. Three someones—Aylla and two wolves knelt by the soldier. The dark silver and light gray wolves licked and yipped softly at her. It was like a family reunion he shouldn't intrude on. Jack took up a solid, defensive stance as the wolves squared up on him.

Aylla glanced up as her wolves growled. Their hackles rose when Jack approached. How in the Dranakar dark had they found her?

He held up a hand. "Styntalla." He was ready for a blasting spell too. The wolves perked their ears and cocked their heads. Aylla did too.

"Apologies, force of habit, but you said they respond to the Old Maidens' language, right?" He held up his hands innocently. He didn't want to give commands to someone else's charges, but his survival instincts had kicked in. The wolves would not easily tear him apart, but he was tired enough they would probably succeed.

"I did. I don't know how they got here. I don't want them here," she said in a low voice. "I don't know how to send them back either. They won't leave."

Jack scanned the darkness, but the low sounds of the nighttime swamp resumed as if nothing had happened. The stench of blood and sweat lingered like poison. Jack spat out a mouthful of blood. He knelt by Aylla and cursed himself for not being faster. Mykel's cooling body lay at his feet, and the failure coated his throat with acid.

"Just make sure they stay close." It was all he could offer. He had no idea how to operate with wolves. He'd have to trust she did.

Now you're responsible for two wolves, Serpent. Fuck.

"The familiars didn't attack you?" Jack asked, looking her over with a shrewd eye to make sure she hadn't been hurt.

"They tried, but Ash and Hugo's timing was impeccable ..." Aylla's voice faded as if in shock. "But even before then, those things sniffed around, and they didn't try to jump at me."

"That's not good." Jack sighed, but he didn't have the energy to get into why. It just meant that Franziska was testing him further. She was going to use Aylla against him.

"I don't know what to say," Aylla said, and her voice cracked. "I didn't really know Mykel, either, but he ..." She pounded a fist into a tree trunk.

If there was one thing Jack was worse at than conversation, it was comforting someone. He stood and muttered an old Ocrana prayer. It was something his mother always said, and the one thing he could accurately remember of her.

"Birth is life, life is death, and peace under the godswoods."

"I've heard that before. My mother used to say it sometimes."

"My mother said it to me too." Jack's adrenaline wore off, and aches started to set in his wounds and overworked muscles. Fury still simmered in his nerves. Mykel and Bean might have volunteered to be in the Milytor, but their lives were carelessly discarded because of Narim.

Was this any different than the children he'd seen die in the mines at Servun? People pressed into service. People forced to choose a path that they didn't want because someone "owned" them.

Aylla seemed to sense his mood. She put a light hand on his shoulder for a second. "This isn't your fault." She stepped back as if waiting for an explosion from him. He took several breaths before looking into her eyes filled with wary concern.

"Their deaths might seem voluntary, in service to the crown," he said in a low voice. The wolves cocked their ears, as if they understood. "The Milytor make people think they are getting that freedom, the exotic travel, the renown, the respect, but in truth most of them are just cogs and doomed to die. Grimarr knows this, and he doesn't treat his soldiers like most do, but it's just the way of old kings, the way it'll always be done, because someone needs to fight for realms, for protection."

"Hasn't your training demanded you risk your life too? You aren't free either." She raised a brow, but it wasn't accusatory.

Jack was quiet for a moment. "I thought I was, until I was summoned back to Asnor. Back to where it all started."

"And that's also why you were so angry that Narim 'hired' me to help guide in the swamp. You didn't think I had a choice until ... well, you know, I did." Aylla lifted her hands helplessly.

Jack nodded. He had long ago learned to control his anger, but there were some things that demanded a response. They were silent for a moment as they regrouped.

"What do we do now?" Aylla sniffed and looked up at him. The wolves whined and licked her hands.

Jack tried to read if she wanted to be comforted or told the truth. Her hands trembled in her lap as she stared at Mykel. Her usual sarcastic stoicism was faltering.

"We get to a place where I can get a look at these cuts, and you get some rest. The Stryga might send more our way before we have time to recover." Jack jabbed the rune tattoo on his wrist, and fire ignited at his fingertips. "We can't bury him, no time, so we'll give him a pyre."

Aylla stood and backed away as the flames consumed Mykel's body. In the fire's light, Jack noticed how pale she was, but determination lingered in her straight back and now calm hands. Maybe that had to do with the comforting presence of Ash and Hugo. The huge wolves prowled in a circle around her.

"Where's Rosie? I don't want to leave his Phantom," she said, looking around.

Jack spotted it still up in the yarba tree and pointed. He sagged against the thought of climbing and was glad when she offered to. He helped her up, her weight hardly a concern even with his injuries and despite the distasteful joke he'd made before.

Aylla retrieved the long gun. Jack checked the magazine, empty, and the chamber, empty as well. It disassembled easily into small parts, and Aylla put it in her pack.

They walked further into the swamp in silence, the flare of fire still behind them. The darkness enveloped them in a shroud of grief. Jack took them as far as his body would allow, but after an hour, his weeping wounds forced him to stop.

"You should have said something. You look like you're going to pass out," Aylla said. The concern in her voice warmed him more than any tonic, more than he had any right to feel.

"I'm fine. Just need to set up a perimeter, and then I'll need you to pull the scales from my back." Jack limped around a small, enclosed space of huge boulders. Trees blotted out the moonlight here, and the ground was dry. The wolves settled at Aylla's command, though their ears swiveled, constantly scanning.

Aylla spread the canvas on the ground and took out the aid kit. Jack whispered spells Alaric had taught him that required very little energy. Alarm spells, mainly, like invisible fences that would let them know if anything supernatural came close.

"What were you muttering? Spells? Why didn't you use those before?" Aylla sat, ready with bandages and salve.

Jack sat with his back to her and peeled off his spelled coat, which was still armored, and then the shirt under it. A few scales had penetrated the seams around his arms and along his torso.

"I did, but in a lesser capacity. Spell work is tricky and uses up a lot of energy. Mykel and Bean had used a few when we camped before, and if there are too many spells in one place, it conflicts." Jack winced as the air hit his injuries.

"It looks like these have started to clot and heal—how is that possible?"

"Arrunroot. I make it into an elixir, along with a healing spell, and it helps the healing. Magic doesn't solve many problems, but it can aid," he said with a derisive chuckle.

"Some of these are in pretty deep," Aylla warned.

Jack bit down a curse as she plucked scales from under his arms and two from his side, but as soon as they were gone, he felt as if ten-pound weights had been lifted off him. He hoped she enjoyed it as payment for his embarrassing her.

Aylla didn't mention anything of the sort, of course. She dabbed blood that ran down his back and applied the salve. It wouldn't last long, but it would hold him.

"There's a nasty claw mark in your side too. It looks bad." Aylla's gentle hands mopped up the blood and mud.

"It'll be fine as long as it's clean. Thanks." He glimpsed her thin lips and narrowed eyes. She was used to this kind of work.

Don't ask. It's not your business, and you don't care.

"I used to help patch up my mother when the beatings were bad enough." Aylla bit her lip and tossed the dirty rags.

Jack didn't know what to say, so he remained silent.

"Do you have a partner or extended family somewhere?" Aylla asked, looking away from him. She folded her hands together.

"I did, but she doesn't remember me anymore." Jack swallowed hard. "Lyra was just another reason why black magic shouldn't be tampered with." Saying her name out loud seemed to lessen the painful memory.

"I agree. My uncle used to buy illegal magic powders, and they made his drunken rages seem tame." Aylla shivered.

"She's in an asylum." It was all Jack could stand to say, and Aylla didn't press him further, for which he was grateful. Lyra had somehow gotten spells mixed up, and when cast, a hex had rebounded on her, turning her brain to mush. Days later, he'd found her wandering the forest in her shift, her hair in snarled curls. She hadn't recognized him, had tried to run. They'd still managed to capture the goblins, but Alaric hadn't stopped grousing about her distraction and lack of skill.

Jack had been surprised. Lyra didn't often make mistakes, and certainly not on as important a task as subduing bloodthirsty goblins who worked for a coven.

He started a fire and stood, acutely aware of Aylla's gaze on him. Perhaps it should have made him feel guilty about Lyra, but there was no coming back from the hex on her. Not even Alaric had been able to help her.

He caught Aylla's stare, and a jolt hit his chest. She whirled away and busied herself gathering sticks. The wolves followed her, sniffing the area. Jack's smile faltered on his lips.

"Apologies. If I embarrassed you before. With the knife," he said, low and fast.

Aylla turned to him with an arched brow. "Words I never hear from men." She lifted her hands, and a soft smile crested her face. "Thank you."

Jack nodded and busied himself drying their clothes. He was very much aware even with bandages that he was shirtless, and that she was down to her thin shift. But it was a necessity to avoid swamp rot on their skin. Was it his imagination, or did her eyes linger on his chest? Probably just wondering what all the runes were for. Did he even want her to look at him in that way?

He didn't regret the glances he took at her.

They used the long sticks to hang shirts and socks on. Aylla avoided heavy subjects. After a minute, she laughed, a manic release of tension, the overwhelming grief and stress coming out in a natural way. So, he did the only decent thing—he laughed with her. Their mirth defied the swamp's claustrophobic atmosphere and anything that was stalking them. Jack hoped Franziska heard them and started to think hard about what she was going to do.

He anticipated the wolves could protect Aylla when the time came, and they'd be able to escape while he distracted the Stryga. Otherwise, they'd both be dead within twenty-four hours.

Chapter Twenty-Two

Karnuhym is strategically positioned at a crossroads where veins of old magic have pooled and remained for centuries. The monastery fortress is home to the One God Numyn, but all are welcome. It is a shelter for those in need but also a training ground for soldiers and it was the site for the third Scriver Trial. The library is a living thing unto itself.
~ Scryptus, The Scriver Archives,
as recounted by Scriver #5 Jack Serpent, Tome 14

Jack was between sleep and waking when he heard Aylla moving around. She drank from a canteen, ate a biscuit. He was aware of small pigs, frogs, snakes, and fowl that moved in the brush around them. The wolves panted, and soft paws circled them. Nothing was a threat.

"I'm amazed he even needs sleep," she whispered to the wolves. Their quiet panting and licking told him they had lain down next to her.

"I'm not that amazing," Jack said without opening his eyes.

Aylla started, and Jack heard the water slosh in the canteen. He turned to her with alert eyes and a teasing grin. She threw him a biscuit, and he caught it before it whacked him in the face.

"Are you feeling all right?" she asked. Hugo and Ash pricked their ears, and their tails thumped the ground in anticipation of moving on.

Jack sat, stuffed the biscuit in his mouth, and nodded. "Let's get moving. I need to pick up her scent again."

"You can smell a Stryga?"

"I smell tainted magic. Whether it's a Stryga or wizard or sorceress, doesn't matter. But I'm also following the totems—they're hard to miss." He winked at her. "If we had more time, I'd love to study them more." He thought of Scryptus, the monk who organized and expected all his findings in the Book of Ryquera. The younger man was probably waiting for him write something in the book, anything for him to work with while he copied books, prepared food, inventoried weapons, and trained other monks at the monastery fortress and Jack's second home, Karnuhym.

Scryptus would have to wait.

They packed up the meager camp site, slipped on dry boots, and traipsed through the murky woods. Jack brought out his transmitter and turned it on. Static bounced around the air as he tried to raise Dean.

"... copy? Repeat I'm over northeast corner of Poe, come in," Dean's scratchy, distant voice said over the transmitter.

Jack sighed and pushed the talk button. "Confirm."

"Jack? Holy Stryga bits. I saw the light show last night ... hurt?"

Jack closed his eyes for a second and exchanged a glance with Aylla. She carried Rosie like a torch for Mykel.

"Soldiers down. We're not going to make target," Jack said. If he could get Aylla and the wolves out of the swamp, it would be worth whatever price Dean wanted.

"Volg Republic ... Ghoul Base was attacked last ... need to wrap it ..." The line cut out again, and Dean's voice didn't return.

Jack ignored Aylla's groan of frustration. He felt similarly. There were a lot of moving parts, and he wasn't sure how to stop any of them. The swamp surrounded them like a second skin. Jack loosened the top button on his shirt.

"You said it wasn't good that the familiars the other night didn't come after me. It wasn't just because of Ash and Hugo." Aylla stepped over a half-hidden root. The wolves flanked them silently. A frog croaked, and electric-green birds winged through the trees.

"She's been in your head," he said after a lengthy pause. "She'll try to use you sometime." He didn't want her to think that she was too weak to help fight the High Stryga. Jack wasn't sure if she could or not, but sowing doubt was a surefire way to ensure she didn't.

It was possible he was starting to care a lot more about Aylla than he thought best. Jack shook his head. They were too deep in the trap now to lose focus.

"What does this High Stryga want?" Aylla asked with a huff. She swatted bugs that flew around in suffocating clouds. The wolves twitched their ears and lashed their tails.

"I'm starting to wonder that myself. She could send an army of anything—we're just two—but she's waiting. Maybe she has informants on the outside, perhaps even inside the castle. Maybe she has another plan, and this is just a distraction while they get the real prize, Malecanta magic." Jack had a lot of theories, but none of them could be confirmed unless he were face-to-face with the High Stryga or found out what Narim's plan was.

"There's no way out except through her, huh." Aylla bit her lip. "So, is Dean an actual friend or just another cog in the system?"

Ash, the lighter gray wolf, came close to Jack's left side with a sniff. Jack kept a wary eye on the animal, but the wolves seemed to accept him. They hadn't growled or bared their teeth.

"He's my weapons dealer. Has been for almost ten years—he's the closest thing to a friend I have," Jack said, realizing as he said it how true and sad that was. "He's independent but will support a throne if it's a fair one. He's one of the best weapons smiths on all the continents, though you wouldn't know it, and the Volg would love to get their hands on him."

"I haven't run into many Volg Republicans, but the ones I have were very odd."

"That's one word for them." Jack scratched his chin.

"And you're sure Narim isn't a Volg supporter?"

Jack shook his head. "He may be a bastard who uses humans for bait, but he's no Strygan supporter. If a Stryga were to ever gain control of the throne, the first thing she'd do would be kill the Milytor. There's no way she could gain the support of an entire armed force. Narim's job is his life," Jack said with an annoyed grunt. "Warlocks, though, they've been after control of the Milytor for years. Grim allowed a few to join, but they never seemed to work out. They only wanted more position and power after a few months."

"Narim went to an awful lot of trouble to have you killed here." Aylla hopped over a cracked rock.

"Can't argue that." Jack shook his head. "He sees himself as a loyal soldier and wants Grimarr's position someday. He also blames me for his partner Jethen's death several years ago." He picked his way through dense brush.

"What happened?" she asked.

Jack was silent for a moment. "Jethen went into a cave to treat with the dwarves. There was a rumor he'd been dabbling in alchemy—giving soldiers an elixir that made them nearly immortal or impervious to pain. There was an argument, and before I got there, one of the dwarves had run Jeth through with a polearm." He swatted away brush and carefully stepped over some rocks. "Narim had wanted to go on that mission. But Alaric chose me instead."

"That was before the Scriver Trials."

"Yes."

"What are the trials? I've only read a few clippings or heard talk, because when you were going through them, my mother and I were trying to escape my uncle." Aylla peered at him through a shock of hair that had fallen out of her braid. "The influx of people and spectacle actually made it slightly easier to hide what we were building from him. He was distracted by it all."

"Three trials: magic summoning called Vocyre, survival called Salvuros, and literacy called Literata." Jack anticipated her look of skepticism.

"Literacy?"

"Karnuhym library is deadlier than any prison or mountain fortress. You'd be surprised how being able to read and write will save your life," he said with a grunt. "It tested intelligence with riddles and puzzles. Someday I hope to complete a library like that. Where everyone could come study or learn." He had a secret fortress of his own that he hoped one day would become the library his mother would be proud of.

"Considering most of Asnor doesn't know how to read and write, I'd say that's not a far-fetched idea. I was lucky my parents taught me," she said. Aylla didn't press him further about the trials, but her gaze drifted to the Scriver sigil on his swords and Kya's blades. The three claw marks symbolized the trials and the Houses of Sorcery. Alaric had made an alliance with an ancient sorcerer who no longer had a body, but his soul resided in Karnuhym library and protected it. It was a monastery for all—the main monks served the One God, Numyn, but others were welcome to live among them. Magic was key to the Scriver's abilities—one had to be able to wield it as easily as breathing.

"Where would you build such a library?" she asked.

Jack hesitated but figured it wasn't like she was asking to find his safehouse. The half-finished castle fortress was warded and in a remote location that no one knew except him and Grimarr. It was a dream he had put on hold—or the only place he had if things went truly sideways and he needed to lie low.

"I have a safehouse by the sea. Two gargoyles watch it for me. They should be building it, but I doubt there's much work going on." Jack laughed.

"Gargoyles, huh?"

"They're surprisingly trustworthy." He exchanged a small grin with her.

Aylla absently scratched Ash's ears as he trotted beside her. "Narim can't know for sure what happened back then. So why does he blame you?"

She'd brought it back to Narim and yet it didn't bother him. Jack glanced sideways. "I didn't kill the dwarves for killing one of our own. I didn't give Narim the names of the dwarves in that cave. There was a trial, and some of them were executed, but Narim's justice and mine weren't the same."

"I see." Aylla didn't say it like she was judging him. It was just agreeable words. "You said serving in the Milytor was akin to having no true freedom." The question hung in the air; what did Jack know of freedom?

"When I was a boy, I lost my parents ... to Strygan doing a ritualistic sacrifice. My dad hid me in a spelled closet. I remember being let out, but I'm not sure by who or if I got myself out. There was no one left. They'd even killed all our animals." Jack's jaw clenched. "I ran as far as I could until I collapsed. Long story short, I was only about seven at the time, and slave traders found me dehydrated and delirious with hunger. They sold me to an orphanage that used children for labor in the Clarent mines."

Aylla's hands twisted together. "You mentioned that before. Those are the crystals used for navigation aboard ships and compasses?"

"Indeed. Only children are small enough to get into the caves and use silver pickaxes to chip them out," Jack said. "They are also used by the higher-paying gentry to be crushed into powder and put into wine. Then it acts like an aphrodisiac—but it can also lead to heart explosions and uncontrolled bleeding."

"I had a friend once tell me about that," Aylla said with a shudder. "She went to a secret underground gala, and they had to burn the whole mansion afterward because the powder wouldn't dissipate. I didn't know the drug came from child slavery, though."

Jack caught a pitying look before she hid it; he supposed she wouldn't be human if she didn't have some compassion. From her, it didn't irritate him.

"Alaric found me after two years. I don't know if I would have lasted much longer." He didn't want to admit it, but the thought of just jumping down a black hole in the caves had started to seem like a real possibility. Maybe he would hit bottom, so he'd thought, or maybe he'd hit water and be able to swim to freedom.

"I'm glad he did then." Aylla smiled and left it at that. There wasn't anything more to be said about the past, and Jack was happy to leave it that way.

They trudged through trails covered with vine trees and lush overgrowth. Birds chittered and flapped in the bushes.

"That's definitely filled with poison berries and thrash," she said, and Jack stopped. He glanced at her, and her eyes sparkled, her mouth barely containing a laugh.

"Are you trying to prove Scrivers don't know everything? I will readily admit that." He gave her a mock glare and shouldered past. Aylla chortled behind him.

They entered a semi clear opening in the forest of mossy trees, and it was eerily quiet.

"What's that?" Aylla pointed to their right. A faded mauve and yellow fabric lay torn among the reeds and lily pads. Farther out on dry ground, more strips of fabric fluttered, caught on branches and in the moss. A few birds pecked at the scraps but flew off, disinterested.

Jack changed their course and headed toward it, finding a path around the marsh and staying on dry ground. As they neared, he recognized both merchant and Milytor flyer sails. The scraps of fabric turned into whole pieces and even half a wooden hull. There had to be at least a dozen crashed in the swamp, but it was hard to tell from all the clutter and wreckage.

"These aren't terribly recent," Jack said as he poked at an algae-covered piece of wood. The remains were scattered like gravestones marking the final resting places of the people who'd inevitably died when they crashed. Ash and Hugo sniffed curiously at the wreckage. They obeyed Aylla's command to stay closer to her and didn't get their paws wet in the murky water.

"This looks pretty new," Aylla said, pointing at a flashy red blimp sail with a royal seal on it.

"This is how she's getting power."

"What?"

"Strygan get their power from stealing others' energies—body parts, fluids, organs, even souls if they're skilled. Remember the Black Insidian? She probably subsists on swamp animals but needs a larger source. Franziska shoots flyers down because they have more souls on board, more to fuel her black magic." Jack kicked at a board, and his lips thinned into a frown.

"There are no bones," Aylla said. "No footprints, no clothing. It's like they all vanished."

Jack shook his head and rubbed the stubble on his jaw. He wished he could give her an explanation like that the swamp had swallowed them, or crocodiles or some other beast had eaten them, or they were incinerated in the resulting fires from crash landing. But the truth was worse.

"Let's keep moving," he said. Aylla shook herself and even Jack felt the chills through the humidity and warmth of the decaying swamp. He pulled out his compass. It pointed northeast, toward the totems.

The large cypress and yarba trees grew thicker. Trails of water snaked between their huge root systems, and leaves blocked the sunlight trying to get through. Vines crisscrossed their path, and more than once it was a snake, not a branch. Dragon-like insects hovered over muddy water, spiders caught black bugs, and the occasional turtle plopped off a log into the water.

"How to you intend to kill this Stryga should we get to her before Dean can get to us?" Aylla asked as they walked, or rather sloshed, through yet more soggy ground.

"Working on it." Jack kept his head on a swivel, but the shadows were just shadows. His goal was the same: burn the Stryga. But he wanted Aylla and the wolves to get out of the swamp first.

"Care to share?" Aylla swatted at the buzzing flies around her. Her tone wasn't adversarial or skeptical, just slightly fearful.

"Burning is always the first option, but I'm going to guess she won't disappear in a blaze of fire," Jack said as he led the way through brush and weaved between trees. "Hold." He held a hand up, and Aylla almost ran into his back. She stepped back, and the wolves stilled. In his peripheral vision, he saw her peer around him.

A small clearing appeared through the trees, and the water drained into a pond. In the space was a brown log hut with a thatched roof that looked like it could use some repair. A garden sat to the left, and a mini-water wheel rotated in the pond to churn the water.

"I think this is the part in stories where we get eaten," she whispered.

Jack snorted but gave her a grin.

"It's not Franziska's—it's probably one of her sister's. Stay here," Jack said, and glanced at her.

Aylla cocked her head and put her hands on her hips. He didn't see the point in arguing if she was going to sneak behind him anyway.

"At least let me make a round and make sure there are no surprises."

"Okay." Aylla sat on a log and crossed her legs. She patted the wolves on their heads, and they licked at her fingers.

Jack made a circuit, with frogs leaping out of his path and the drone of insects in his ears. The dappled sun made shadows over the hut, but nothing moved inside. No wards on the windows or doors either. They had probably disappeared when she'd died—if this was one of the Strix's huts.

He motioned to Aylla to come to the front door. Jack tried the handle, found it unlocked, and shoved it open with his pistol leading the way. He debated asking Aylla to stay outside, but something told him she wouldn't. Better to have eyes on her anyway to be sure there were no tricks again.

"Stay behind me," Jack said, and then covered his mouth with a free hand.

Aylla scrunched her nose and gagged. Rotten flesh, old blood, and urine assaulted Jack's senses, and she was clearly affected as well. She pulled a piece of her shirt up to cover her mouth and followed him inside. A big, blackened hearth sat on the back wall with a table and chairs to the left. In the room to their right, it looked more like a slaughterhouse than a living space. Aylla barked at the wolves to stay outside—unnecessary, because they'd whined and backed up as soon as the door had opened.

Blood coated the slotted floor that drained into the ground. A table with restraints stood on thick wood legs, and jars of body parts lined the shelves. Wooden vats filled with who knew what stood in the corner. But it was what lay beneath the table that made Jack check on Aylla. She visibly paled and froze.

Children.

Bodies, ranging from fetuses to perhaps six-month-old infants, lay piled on top of each other with blood pooling under them.

Jack didn't tell Aylla to avert her eyes. There was nothing he could say in the face of such carnage of innocents. He checked his own fury and prowled around the hut.

"What was she doing to them?" Aylla whispered as she clutched her stomach.

"Probably trying to make herself younger and more powerful. Children are the only ingredient that works for those kinds of spells," Jack said, the muscle in his left jaw spasming.

"You've seen this before."

"Yes." All of Ravenhell had been full of dark massacre, and the memories threatened to dim his vision, to enrage his senses all over again. Jack reeled his thoughts back to focus on the present.

He tore open the cabinets and threw anything that wasn't of interest on the ground. He scanned a few worn pages. They boasted the Volg Republic's seal, a wand and sickle over a pentagram, stamped on the documents. Some of them were also trade orders for women and children. Children who were older than seven years were to be sent to Muran or other villages in Elgar to mine magic. Other papers dealt with warlock prisoners for procreation only. Those names were out for capture.

He handed them to Aylla when he was done reading. Her breath came in horrified gasps.

"They stole the queen's baby to curse the entire lineage. There will never be a Thuramond who isn't mad if this succeeds. They state that no human will sit on the throne if the curse is completed, and there will be a plague, an unstoppable weapon unleashed, until the Malecanta's magic is found and bound to them. Do you think they've completed the curse?"

"If they have, our mission is futile, since killing the High Stryga won't stop it. If they unleash a plague and resurrect the Sorcery Houses, who knows what creatures they will unveil or create?" Jack paused to think. "We don't know what 'unstoppable weapon' means. We have to assume it's not too late and still try to take out Franziska."

The hut shuddered at the name as if it had a heartbeat. Aylla stepped toward the door.

"I imagine Narim sent us here to flush her out. He probably told Grimarr this was a standard Strix hunt." Jack swore and shook his head. "It's just become a declaration of war. If Strygan take over the lands, humans won't be wiped out, they'll be enslaved."

"Oh." Aylla bit her lip.

Jack frowned. If the realms went to war, there was a good chance half the population wouldn't survive either. If the Strygan dominated the throne, they would control goods trading, magic allotment, prisons, and water supply. They required not only freedom, but to have an endless supply of power, meaning souls they could harvest.

And warlocks to breed with. A slave colony. They need to neutralize the Milytor or persuade those weak minded enough to support their cause against the warlocks. Alaric's voice popped into his head. Jack nodded in agreement. He didn't have vast knowledge of how Strygan reproduced, but he knew they could only have children with warlocks. The power struggle had been ongoing for decades.

Not that he wanted to be involved. In fact, most of his training and purpose was to be invisible and not interfere. He said as much at Aylla's questioning gaze.

"We can't exactly keep this to ourselves, can we?" She wiped at a stray hair and glanced around the cabin. Jack inclined his head.

"I'm assuming these records are copies and that someone in Asnor has the originals. Someone in the royal court or Volg. Either way, let's say the Volg release them to the public. That's a good way to start chaos and get the people thinking about how they can cheat and get the miraculous Malecanta magic. As if getting it makes them able to wield it," Jack said with a grunt. "It's just what the Volg want."

"Some people can use magic more easily than others. It won't be hard for the Volg to convince them Stryga rule will give them freedom with that power," Aylla said, thinking out loud. She wasn't wrong. Jack knew he wielded magic a hell of a lot easier and faster than most humans. Yet he wasn't another race. He often wondered if his bloodline included something other than human, but Alaric had never confirmed that.

Jack folded the papers and shoved them in his pack. Aylla stilled and took a step back inside, away from the front door. "Did you hear that?"

Crying, faint and pathetic, came from somewhere ... up? No, down? Jack tracked the sound with Aylla until it led them to the hearth. It sounded like the noise was coming from under the floor. The rug there was crooked. Jack threw it aside to reveal a board with a metal ring. Aylla yanked the door up and gasped.

Inside the black space was an infant, soiled and thin.

"Oh my Orcystars," she breathed. "Are there clean clothes anywhere?"

For a brief moment, Jack thought the baby might be better in the underworld—Orcys. He opened more cupboards and threw her relatively clean sheets and a blanket. Aylla reached in and plucked the child up. She cradled it gingerly, as if afraid to break it. Her. The naked baby was female. Aylla wiped filth off the infant's cheeks.

"Here." Jack handed Aylla a basin of water. He eyed the baby with the skepticism of experience. He didn't feel malice or spells bouncing off the baby, but he didn't trust that the Stryga would have the Strix leave her here accidentally.

Aylla washed the baby and put her in dry clothes. The girl's wailing stopped for a few minutes but then continued at a high pitch.

"What does she want?" Jack asked, and grimaced. "We can't ..."

He didn't finish the sentence. Aylla stood up, carrying the girl with her as she searched further in the hut.

"The bitch must've been keeping her alive for something, so she must have food. We have to take her with us," Aylla said as she flung open every drawer and cabinet. Soon she found a stash of bottles of white liquid. She sniffed it. "I think this is milk. Spelled because I don't know how fresh it is, but it doesn't smell rotten."

"It's going to get us killed or die anyway." Jack's tone wasn't cold, but he didn't think they could keep a baby alive. They were on the brink themselves, and they'd added two wolves to the list. His job was getting harder and harder. Nowhere in Scriver training did it include mission completion with a baby.

"We have to try. You can leave us behind and come back when you kill the Stryga. Or Dean will come through," Aylla said, and the desperation in her voice made him curse in his head. He couldn't in truth abandon a child, but it was putting his mood in a foul place.

She placed the rubber nipple in the baby's mouth, and the baby sucked so hard it was evident she hadn't been fed in quite some time. Every rib was visible, and her arms and legs were like toothpicks, not the round, chubby softness they should have held.

"We can't rely on that. The swamp is warded, and he might not be able to find a way in," Jack said, glancing at the baby.

"We did." Aylla's feisty attitude returned with a surprising vengeance. Did she not understand the severity of taking a baby with them? It must have shown on his face, because she glared at him.

"I'm not a mother, but I'm not leaving this baby to die of starvation." She stepped toward the door of the hut.

Jack held his hands up in acquiescence. "Fine. We take her, but I can't promise her survival." He didn't want another child's death on his conscience, but it was a risk he would take.

He motioned for them to exit the hut, then grabbed a piece of wood from the hearth. He ignited fire in his fingers and grabbed some dry sticks, and when they caught, he tossed them inside. Wooden chairs, mats, and boards caught the flames.

"You can leave us," Aylla said, seeming to realize the enormity of what she'd taken on. "I'll find a way out of the swamp or wait for Dean." She adjusted the weight of the baby and folded her into her chest. Ash and Hugo came up to investigate, pushing at the baby with rude noses. They laid their ears back but didn't harm her.

Jack couldn't be sure they would have enough food for the baby, or if they were attacked, that he could protect both of them. He'd probably die trying, but then what? The High Stryga won?

"This is why I work alone," Jack muttered.

Aylla's chest caved in, and she hastily turned away.

He sighed, softening. "Just don't name her."

She nodded. "All right."

The baby wiggled in her arms and cooed. He prayed Dean found them before he was forced to leave them. The task was still his priority ... wasn't it?

Chapter Twenty-Three

Male sirens have two reproductive appendages. Makes me wonder why ever the females were so interested in mine.
*Archivers note: Did not include crude drawing. If one would like to read entire diatribe on how sirens attempt to mate see appendix 46.7
~ Scryptus, The Scriver Archives,
as recounted by Scriver #5 Jack Serpent, Tome 9

Jack lay back as Aylla straddled him. Fog swirled around them, and he struggled to center his focus. His pulse raced like lightning across a storm-swept sky, and his arms reached for her instinctively. The sheer muslin gown showed every curve of her body, the elegant arch of her neck and firm breasts that swelled under his touch.

"This isn't real," he rasped, and struggled to get his mind in check. This was a dream, or some sort of conjuring. Aylla rolled over his hips, and he closed his eyes for just one moment. Heat electrified his senses. She guided his hands to her breasts and moaned. His fingers traced her nipples and then the hardened lines of her torso down to her thighs. Rose and vanilla scents floated around him, and Jack opened his eyes. That wasn't Aylla's smell.

He thrust the girl off him and sat up.

Aylla grinned like a banshee. "They sent a Scriver after me. The first one, a pretender, tasted delicious." She cackled.

Jack cursed. Franziska. Aylla transformed into a black-haired, rosy-cheeked young woman with long limbs. Her skin shone like golden sun. Her green eyes sparked mischief as she remained naked.

"How did you get into my mind?" Jack mentally reviewed all the tattoos on his body. There shouldn't have been a way around them.

"You let your guard down thinking about Aylla, *tsk tsk*. A little lullaby and I slipped past your guard. I thought you'd learned your lesson with Alaric."

She knew Alaric? "What would you know about that?"

"Alaric kept many secrets; don't think he let you in on all of them. I heard about Lyra from him ... poor girl. Couldn't even do a boundary spell correctly," she said and licked her lips.

"He'd never tell you something like that." But Jack wasn't sure from the confident smile the Stryga radiated. How else would she know about Lyra? Alaric's death was no secret; he had died in a blasting spell when warlocks and Strygan caught them during a hunt for Jack after Ravenhell.

"Let's agree to disagree. Alaric was one of the best. I wish I'd had time to taste him," she said with a laugh. "All of the Stryga wanted to create with him."

Jack searched for something concrete to hold on to or she'd trap him forever in this dreamland. He spied Kyadem in the corner of the room, not at all where it should be. It was fake. He shook himself. This was his mind, and he would have control. He thought of Aylla and her wolves. If she'd been the thing to let the Stryga in, she'd be the thing that let him get control back. It was something grounded in reality, and it forced him to center.

His heart rate slowed, and he faced the Stryga with a clear mind.

"You can give yourself to me now and I'll let the girl go." Franziska paced across the room and examined things on the shelf as if she didn't have a care in the world. Her long hair cascaded over faultless skin. She now wore a simple, almost sheer sage-green dress that flowed over her curves like poison mist.

"Why would you do that?" Jack wrapped a sheet around his waist and stood.

"Because I'm in a generous mood. Things are looking up for me, and I think you'd be fun to play with for at least a century." She turned her head, lip curled. Fanged teeth glinted at him.

"I'll pass."

"This is my swamp, and soon the entirety of Elgar will be mine too."

"Oh, the five continents will allow Strygan rule, will they?" Jack laughed; it gave him more power back. He imagined his armor back on.

Franziska narrowed her eyes at the ripple of control. "The Volg Republic has more influence than you give them credit for. But I won't waste breath convincing you, because you're not going to get out of my swamp alive." She winked. Her shapely backside waggled as she bent down to pick up a feather quill that had fallen from the shelf.

"There would be a place for Scrivers in my court, but I know I'm wasting my time on you. However, I do need something inside here." She ran a cool finger down his forehead and cheek.

Inside his mind? "There's a lot of landmines in here—I wouldn't." Jack focused on Aylla, and it sucked air back into his lungs, that much more control over the dream. He shoved clothes onto Franziska's appealing form. The Stryga now wore a boxy, flowered dress that an old mansion's wallpaper would envy.

"How are you doing this?" Franziska clapped her lips shut as if she hadn't meant to let it slip.

Jack cocked his head at her. "Get out."

"You have two things now that are very easily taken away. You had a chance. I'm sure I'll be seeing you soon, handsome." She blew him a kiss.

"Goodnight, Franziska."

Jack snapped his fingers. The Stryga's eyes bulged and flared crimson. Her mouth hung open as she was kicked from his mind.

Chapter Twenty-Four

My horse is unusually intelligent. Having spent years studying and recounting other animals across the continents, my conclusion is that the horse is odd. He's free to leave but always comes back. I haven't seen a herd, so I assume he's alone.
~ Scryptus, The Scriver Archives, a
s recounted by Scriver #5 Jack Serpent, Tome 2

Aylla poked the Scriver with a finger. He'd been thrashing for ten minutes in some sort of trapped sleep state. The baby lay in a puddle of blankets on dry moss with Ash sniffing her toes. She cooed and reached for his nose. The wolf snorted and walked away.

Jack's eyes opened and he sat up.

"Are you okay?" Aylla had her knife out. She was sure she'd be done for if the Stryga controlled him, but she wasn't going down without a fight.

"You should have stabbed me to incapacitate as soon as I woke up." Jack's lips quirked up, but respect shone in his eyes.

Aylla's cheeks heated like she had sunstroke. She put the knife away in her boot. "Um, not unless I had to. What happened?" She knew the wolves might have helped defend her if necessary, but then again, they were still only animals. One time, they'd run from a moose she'd hunted when it charged. Aylla didn't blame them; she'd seen prey that large take out an eye or break bones.

"I'm fine. Franziska was in my head, but I don't think that's a trick she'll be trying again." Jack shook his head to clear the fog. "I hate to admit it, but if one were going to amass power, she's done an incredible job."

"Oh?"

"Most people, even with the aid of magic, can't break into minds. I used her name, so that's a surprise we don't have anymore," Jack said with a shrug. "But it can still be used against her. I'll try to contact Dean again." He looked at her with an odd expression, like she'd done something to him. Something not entirely unpleasant? The light in his eyes wasn't lust exactly, but it was heated like molten gold, and its intensity threatened to make her forget where they were. Aylla sat back as he shook his head.

"Do you think he'd take Ash and Hugo too?" She bit her lip.

Jack's face twisted back into his usual scowl. "He'll be more interested in them than us."

Aylla nodded and held up an empty bottle. "We need more food for her soon. I had no idea they ate this much."

"She smells." Jack wrinkled his nose.

Aylla sighed and rolled her eyes. "You can change her, then. I need to clean these cloths anyway." She handed him the baby, and Jack looked like he was trying not to grimace.

Aylla watched him out of the corner of her eye. The small, warm bundle of bones swatted at his thick stubble and sucked on his fingers. Jack jerked his thumb out of her mouth, and she wailed. He put it back in. Aylla chuckled as she washed the dirty cloth diapers in the semi-clear stream that ran past them. Jack set the baby down and peeled away the filthy diaper filled with urine. He tossed it to Aylla, but his throw was short, and it splashed into the reeds next to her. Jack gave her an unapologetic smile.

He wound a clean cloth around the baby, and it seemed to hold when he tied the ends in knots.

"How am I supposed to get that off later?" Aylla asked as she came up next to him.

Jack shrugged and handed the baby back to her. "I'll get us dinner if you take care of her." He lit a fire.

Aylla didn't argue. She was the one who wanted to keep the baby, and it was likely Jack would be the faster hunter. Besides, she needed to find food for the girl first. The wolves circled for a moment and whined. Aylla's brow rose.

"I think they want to go with you. Probably tired of being cooped up next to us so much," Aylla said, and let him decide. If he wanted their help, he knew the Old Maiden commands.

Jack's face lit up, softening his features. "Would they listen to me?"

"I don't see why not."

Aylla told him how to make a slashing gesture that meant "hunt" and hold his hand out for them to drop the prey. "It doesn't always work, so I apologize in advance."

JACK SERPENT

The wolves had been eating game in the swamp for days now, and Aylla assumed the animals weren't poisoned by the Stryga. The Black Insidian hadn't claimed anything lately either, at least that she had seen.

Aylla busied herself finding a food source for the baby. She set the infant down and searched the shoreline of the ponds. She remembered feeding Ash and Hugo when they were pups, with brownish green reed bulbs that when mashed and mixed with water or milk turned into a milk substitute. She came up victorious.

After half an hour and a full bottle later, Jack and the wolves returned. Ash nipped playfully at Jack's jacket, and Hugo loped behind them. Two hares hung over the Scriver's shoulder.

"I'm going to be spoiled now; hunting with them makes it too easy," Jack said with an edge of a grin.

Aylla laughed and reached out to stroke Ash's head. Hugo nudged her in greeting and then settled down by the baby. She was a sleeping ball now.

"I see you found food for her."

"I used it for the wolves when they were pups, and I hope it'll tide her over until we can get her out."

"You never did tell me how these two became your companions," he said as he skinned the hares. The wolves licked their lips, and he glanced at them. "You two caught six; these are ours."

The wolves licked their paws and grinned.

"My mother and I were building a little cabin in the forest for our own retreat to get away from Drace ... my uncle. We were having a late night, since we knew he'd be gone all night in another town. I didn't hear the pack until they were on top of us." Aylla gazed at the two wolves with a shiver. "The alpha female was the smartest one. She stole our dinner, and then her pack tested us to see if we tasted as good. My mother injured one, and we made it to the cabin—waited out the night there. She was upset she'd hurt the wolf."

Aylla smiled at the memory. "That morning, we tracked the pack to their den. She insisted on seeing if the wolf had made it. He had—the bullet had just grazed his leg. That's when I saw the female had a litter. It wasn't until a year later, after my mother's death, that I went back to the same pack, saw she'd had another litter, and stole two of her pups."

Jack put the hares on a spit. The fire licked at the meat. "Your mother sounds like she was a brave woman."

"Not enough to save herself," Aylla said with a sniff. "I always wondered what happened to her when she was faced with Drace. She shrank. Was it because he was my father's brother? Was it because she thought she was saving me?"

"Probably all those," Jack said as he turned the spit.

The baby cried in her sleep, and Aylla put a shushing hand on her. "I wonder who her mother and father were?" She wasn't under any illusion that she could save the baby or herself, but she knew she'd hate it if she didn't try. To someone, this baby had been everything.

"Unlucky." Jack scanned the site with his usual caution.

"You're awfully short today," she said with a frown. She found she liked his company, and that in itself was surprising because there weren't many people she found tolerable. She didn't blame him for being irritable under this much stress.

"I—" Jack stopped and huffed out a breath. "Apologies."

Aylla spoke softly. "It wasn't your fault the soldiers died. You were set up. You're doing a lot more than I thought a human could against monsters."

Jack half smiled. "I'm still at fault."

She understood the guilt that gnawed at him. She turned her attention to the baby, who had woken and now gurgled while kicking her legs. "Do you have any siblings?"

"None that I know of," Jack said as he continued to scan the landscape. He climbed up a tree to get a better view.

The baby continued to make odd noises below, and Aylla laughed.

"There's higher ground—a little more east than north. I'll see if the transmitter will pick up Dean's signal from there." Jack tilted his head, listening to the wind. He jumped back down to the ground in a crunch of leaves.

They ate quickly and began the trek uphill. The hard, drier ground was a welcome relief. Jack tried the transmitter again, and Aylla breathed out when he got a hold of Dean.

"Need a flare if you can manage one. I'm drifting northeast and can't see for shyf down there. Terrain spells work half the time, but the Stryga's warding is still strong," Dean said in a distant, tinny voice.

"Hold." Jack glanced around and pointed at the dry wood. Aylla understood where he was going with this. A signal fire. She started to gather sticks and break larger, dying branches off trees.

"Once this fire starts, we're going to draw major attention," Jack said, addressing his words to both Aylla and Dean. "Do you have anti-ward grenades?"

"When do I not?" Dean replied.

"You'll need them all. I'll cast a hex net and hope that weakens the ward enough for you to get in. Her power can't hold it up forever. And you'll be taking a baby and two Elgar wolves."

Silence, then an amused chuckle.

"I've got extra fuel—I'll get there within ten minutes." The breezy words defied Dean's serious tone.

"Five would be better."

"I'm not a miracle worker, Jack—my legend doesn't precede me."

"Asshat."

"Pillycock."

Jack snorted and put the transmitter in his pocket. He worked on getting a sizeable fire pit started. As he tapped the fire rune on his wrist, flames burst into the air, guided into a fall from his fingers to light the pile. Aylla would never tire of seeing it. Even though she knew it was simple elemental magic, she couldn't imagine being able to do it.

"The tattoos bind magic to you? Can anyone use them?" she asked as she walked around with the baby in her arms. The little girl weighed next to nothing and seemed soothed by the movement.

"It makes it easier to summon magic quickly. Yes, anyone can use them, but not everyone can handle it. Sometimes the runes start to leech a person's soul or take more than they bargained for. You've got to constantly fight the balance," he said with a glance at his wrist.

"Sounds exhausting. How many do you have?"

Jack took off his long jacket and rolled up his sleeves. Tattoos covered both arms and swirled on his chest. He didn't take his shirt off, but she could see the faint outline of dark lines on his chest where the dark shirt laced. She recalled their stop at the swamp when they'd dried their clothes. He'd been entirely shirtless then. She'd tried not to stare too long, but now, when he was offering, she couldn't help gazing at his tapered torso and wondering just how far those runes went.

"Some are useless experiments; some are concealed. You won't see them until they're activated," he said. The fire crackled, and he threw leaves on it to make the smoke black. It billowed high above the trees. Jack got out his rune stick and a handful of marbles that looked like they had cat's eyes in them.

"Another spell?" Aylla peered at the symbols he drew. Then he arranged the marbles in a star pattern.

"It should blast a hole through the ward if we're lucky. If not, the smoke will let Dean know our location, and he can drop a grenade on it." Jack grunted. "And hopefully not on us."

Aylla stood in silence for a minute. Ash and Hugo lay together away from the fire, their tongues lolling. For a moment, she didn't want Dean to find them. She wanted to stay and learn.

"Will..." she stopped herself but plowed on before she lost her nerve. "Will I see you again?" Aylla glanced at the ever-increasing smoke cloud.

He turned to her with the hint of a smile, then dug a small carving out of his pocket. The little rocking horse was crude at best, but it was a gift. Aylla's skin prickled as she took it.

"It's supposed to be a horse." He didn't meet her gaze.

"Thank you." She clenched it in her fist as if she were afraid of him taking it back. She knew she shouldn't be getting attached to him—he worked alone anyway, right? Even if they did survive, they lived very different lives.

"When all of you are safe, we'll see each other again, all right?"

It seemed to be all Jack could offer, and Aylla didn't want to distract him. He'd tossed around a lot of ideas of how to kill a High Stryga but didn't seem overly confident in any of them. He'd explained the heuristic methods, and she wasn't sure she could gamble with her life the way he did. The best thing she could do was get out of his way. He muttered a word in old Elgar and threw one of the marbles high. Cerulean fire blasted in the sky. The ward shimmered as it failed. The smoke curved around the ward and ripped it open.

"All right."

"I don't know what's coming, but shoot anything that isn't me," he said with a lopsided grin. Aylla smirked and pretended to be insulted. Ash and Hugo sniffed her feet and paced. She gave the command for "circle," which meant stay close, and she hoped they'd be able to board the ship without delay.

A high-pitched, siren-like scream rose followed by bellowing roars that shook the air, and they both turned to the source. Down the hill to the west, trees shook as if they were alive. Aylla squinted. No, the trees weren't moving, but something was moving over them. Leaves flew up in puffs of clouds, and brush scattered as something huge shoved them out of the way.

A lot of somethings—black, orange-striped bodies on eight legs—skittered toward them with alarming speed. Jack pulled back the slide of his pistol, and Kyadem dangled from his other hand. Aylla chambered a round and waited.

"Orbvi spiders," Aylla said with a curse, and she felt her face go pale. "I thought we were lucky we hadn't run into them."

Their piercing blue eyes were now visible as they scuttled up the base of the hill. They were so large that two of them had riders: the jaguar-like familiars, who lifted spears in their hands and yowled. Two dozen spiders halted behind them and clicked their chelicerae in an eerie pattern.

"They spit poison from their eyes, but they're large, so aim for them," Aylla said.

The familiars roared, and a spear catapulted toward her and Jack.

Chapter Twenty-Five

The invention of hexed bullets came about from a drunken wager decades ago. Two soldiers were so drunk they couldn't remember whose bullet was whose as they challenged each other to a shooting match. A corporal in the arcane branch etched runes on each one to glow different colors. He was also inebriated and when the first soldier shot, he blew up the target and everything around for fifty yards.
~ Scryptus, The Scriver Archives,
as recounted by Scriver #5 Jack Serpent, Tome 15

Within a blink, Jack shot the spear as it arced toward them. It splintered and veered to the left, missing them widely. The Orbvi spiders crashed through the brush and took down small trees as they charged. He spared a glance for Aylla and saw she used one hand to steady the baby that was snugly lashed against her and the other to aim the pistol. Ash and Hugo growled and snapped at the spiders that got close to them. Whether or not they were intentionally protecting the baby wasn't clear, but at least she was safe for now. The spiders gave the wolves a wide berth, sizing up the nonhuman opponents.

Jack made sure Aylla stayed behind the fire. She had her Winstar and his other pistol.

He fired eight times into the mass of black and orange bodies. Legs flew, eyes popped, and guts flared into the air. But each time a spider went down, another took its place. The familiars growled as they rode on the backs of the creatures. The one on the left got out a bow and nocked it.

Aylla fired. The bullet missed it but sent a spider falling back down the hill. Poison shot at her, and she sidestepped. The baby girl's cries at the noise were drowned out by the growls and clacking legs.

Jack glanced at the sky, hoping to see a flyer propelling toward them.

He gave up reloading because it was too slow and used Kyadem instead. He wielded the chained blades like lightning. The silver weapon flickered from body to body, slicing and hacking. The force of the bladed chains created an incendiary path. He tried to get to the familiars, but they kept their distance, letting the spiders do the work. The arachnids formed a circle around them.

Aylla picked up the end of a long branch with fire dancing on it. She thrust it at the spiders nearest to her. They hissed and batted at it with their long front legs, but the flames burned them, and they backed off.

"Get the purple vial in my pack," Jack said as he fought the swarm. Kya whirled around him like a protective charm.

Aylla plunged her hand into the pack and rummaged around for the vial. She brought it up and held it out to him. He nodded tightly.

"Drink half."

Aylla didn't argue. She downed the potion and handed him the half-empty bottle. Jack didn't have time to warn her what the effects would do, but she seemed to get the hang of it quickly. Her skin became impenetrable and her reflexes faster. She grabbed another stick out of the fire and wielded the pair like swords.

Aylla slashed at the spiders with inhuman speed. The spiders didn't have time to react as their legs burned and they collapsed. She jammed her left stick into an eye, pulled it out, and rammed it into another eye. The poison cloud in the air made Jack's eyes water.

He swallowed the rest of the potion. His eyes flared amber, and then his skin turned to liquid armor. Even at half strength it was effective. He filed that away for later—he'd messed with dosing before, but not half. The spitting poison bounced off him, and fangs couldn't penetrate any exposed skin.

"Incine," he muttered.

Kyadem burst with white-blue fire, the edges ringed with orange, and the spiders scattered before it. He swept it in arcs of destruction and pirouetted among the beasts. The familiars screamed as their horde of spiders diminished.

A hush fell over the hill as if the entire swamp held its breath.

Shyf. Jack forced back a groan. Whatever was coming was about to test his luck.

Aylla stood, brimming with energy from the potion, and her eyes widened as a stag flew toward them, a female rider on its back wearing an elegantly twisted black crown made of poisonous barbs. The white animal had antlers that were fifteen prongs at least, and wings with gold-tinged pinions. He stood as tall as a draft horse. Jack had to admire the beast for a millisecond—he hadn't seen Perytons very often. They were like unicorns, written in myth but with not quite enough evidence to support their existence. This one was utterly real. The stag snorted, and fangs protruded from his delicate mouth. Nope, the legends were correct about the demon stags that ate the hearts out of their prey.

The woman on his back turned her attention on them, and hairs on the back of Jack's arms stood up. Her intensely dark eyes took them in as if they were dinner. The woman's long, black hair flew out in waves around her black headpiece, her golden skin shimmered in the gray light, and a pale blue dress sparkled as if stars were caught in her skirts.

The stag landed in the middle of the Orbvi spiders with a soft thump. The woman gracefully inclined her head, the light glinting crimson off her hair, to the two familiars who bowed their heads.

The High Stryga Franziska.

On the one hand, Jack was curious that she'd been drawn out to face them herself. On the other, he was afraid their chances of survival had dropped quite low. Jack's lips thinned into a severe line.

Franziska sat still on the stag's back and appraised them all. Her arched brows came together, and her eyes glowed white. A pulse of crystalline light exploded from her, and Aylla cried out as it shot into her right arm. She'd bent to grab the baby. The wolves froze with hackles up. Twin growls issued from them. Jack turned just as the second bolt came, and it hit his left arm. Pain exploded, and his vision whited out for a second. He spasmed, his breath coming in ragged gasps.

Breathe. Find the pain, acknowledge it, tell it to fuck off. Alaric's words penetrated through the agony, and Jack's head cleared.

"Run," he whispered.

Aylla shook her head, but then the baby girl kicked at her to loosen her grip. She stood on shaky legs as Jack turned to the Stryga with Kyadem streaming twisting, white fire.

He broke into a sprint, and the Peryton reared. The Stryga let out an ear-piercing shriek, and the stag charged at Jack, wings tucked back, antlers down.

From the corner of his eye, he saw Aylla lob the torch as hard as she could at the Peryton. The beast sidestepped and nearly unseated the Stryga. Ash and Hugo ran in controlled hunting circles, and the Peryton snorted uneasily, slowing to a walk. He flicked his hooves and bared long, slim fangs. Aylla laughed as the Stryga glared at her.

Jack took the distraction and swept out Kya. It caught the stag's cloven-hoofed legs. He pulled, and the stag let out a bellow as it flipped over. Charred fur and flesh filled the air. The Stryga flew in a graceful leap off his back. She landed on her feet in a crouch with her hair draped over her shoulders.

The hum of a flyer caught both of their attention. Jack raised his eyes to the sky. The thrum of the oil and spell-powered engine preceded his view of the muted barn-red sail as it flew toward the smoke signal.

Jack batted at a spider and took another's head off with Kyadem. The black things hissed and spit at them. He noted Aylla's strength wearing off. The baby's cries were in earnest now and it spurred him to get the pair to Dean as fast as he could. The wolves cried out as the Peryton kicked Ash in his side. Ash limped away, and Hugo snapped at the beast, grabbing his leg but letting go before another hoof could inflict damage.

Two loud booms sounded overhead—the grenades.

"About time," Jack muttered.

Aylla ducked at the rumble. The warding over the swamp flashed purple and then disappeared. The Stryga stood regally, surveying the damage. Her dress floated out around her like wings, the iridescent color of ocean waves. A hum on the wind caressed them like a warm blanket. Jack shook his head as it started to get fuzzy. The spiders renewed their attack, apparently having a different effect from the Stryga's song. Jack continued his fight with the remaining spiders, which ran at him like rabid dogs.

"Give me the child and I'll let you fly away, darling," Franziska said. Her voice echoed over the battle, sliding like ice down Jack's neck. Even though she wasn't addressing him, malice invaded his senses. It was highly unusual for a Stryga to have that much power with just her voice ... was it an enhanced spell?

"No." Aylla backed up and clutched the baby, trying to soothe her.

The flyer dropped lower and lower. A ladder rappelled down the side along with two harnesses. They dangled feet from her now, and Jack glanced back at her. They locked gazes for a split second. He silently communicated that he needed a minute, that she should distract the Stryga if she could. The potion he'd taken earlier was helping to stave off the Stryga's siren song. Her hum lessened as Aylla hurled insults.

"Can't have any children of your own to mutilate and murder?" Aylla spat as she stalled for time. Jack knelt on the ground, cut his finger, and drew a rune he hardly ever used in the dirt. The familiars yelled for Franziska's attention, but Aylla held it for a moment longer.

"I can smell that you've chosen the Scriver over my offer. Pathetic. A man ruined your mother, and you'll do the same to yourself," the Stryga said with a smile.

"At least I'm not ruled by fear." Aylla glared at her.

Jack willed the ladder to come just a little closer. Dean's head popped over the side as he assessed the situation. The man frowned, his deep-set eyes narrowing. He threw the ship into hover, and then he leaped from the side of the flyer. He landed silently and flung a rope harness over the nearest wolf. Ash snapped at him. Jack whispered in the Old Maiden language. The wolves went quiet, though they didn't make it easy for him to put the harnesses on.

"Fear does not exist when there is only power." The Stryga eyed the baby with glowing eyes.

Jack's blood ran hot, and his muscles tightened. He recalled the burn marks on the corpses, the bones sticking out in the baby as she starved. He'd seen a lot of torture, endured even more of it, and killed innocents in the name of doing the right thing. He had not saved the other children in the orphanage. But all he could do was move forward. He glanced at Aylla and nodded.

"I think it's quaint you want to save your pets," Franziska said with a pouty smile. "Those wolves will make a nice cape, don't you think?"

Jack muttered ancient Elgarian spell words and completed the Underworld Wheel. A rumble like thunder reverberated through them, and Franziska fell to her knees. Spikes of light seeped from the ground into the air in a circular whorl of magic, holding her in place. Aylla turned to grab at the rope-and-wood ladder.

Dean lobbed another grenade at the familiars, which exploded in sparks of fire. The magic flowed to Jack like a cooling wind around him, drawn to him as easily as breathing. The wheel pulsed and crackled over the spiders. His blood seemed to slow as the magic sucked all the energy he had left like cracking ice. But he channeled energy into the wheel while Aylla hauled herself up, mindful of the baby, and the flyer lifted slightly. Dean dragged the wolves up and then reached to help Aylla over the side railing.

"We have to wait for him!" Aylla yelled, though to Jack it was barely audible.

Hopefully Dean would ignore the plea and leave.

"We might not have a choice," the man replied.

Jack's spell could only be used once. He gave up breath, blood, and parts of his mind as the magic spiraled out. His chest tightened, and muscles strained to their limit.

It had taken out most of the spiders, but Franziska rose with only a cut on her cheek. He sprang from his kneeling position to face her. The

Stryga threw bolts of black lightning at him. Kya cracked them out of the air, but her onslaught was so heavy it started to create a web around Jack.

"Fuck!" Dean's growled shout echoed in Jack's ears as the flyer roared into the air.

He smiled. At least they would escape.

Jack fought the lightning web around him, but his skin burned as his strength started to wane. As easily as magic was drawn to him, his body had a limit. Time to try something else, or he was dead.

Chapter Twenty-Six

There's always another way, another secret, a different way of thinking. There's always a way out. And if this is to be the end perhaps even death is a way.
~ Scryptus, the Scriver Archives,
as recounted by Scriver #5 Jack Serpent, Tome 6

Jack was pinned to the ground as jolts of electric magic shocked his body. An Orbvi spider stuck its fangs into his right leg, and he didn't have the breath to scream. He hoped to all the gods, if there were any gods left, that Dean had gotten them away. His spell had worked for the few minutes they'd needed. It hadn't injured the Stryga as badly as he'd hoped, but it had pissed her off.

He blocked out the pain and searched his mind for options. Alaric would tell him there was always a way if he wasn't dead yet. Jack kicked the spider off him and rolled away. He muttered every healing spell he knew and tapped the runes on his forearm. The poison was fast—he could feel it traveling to his heart already. His wards were faster, though, and stopped it from rendering him unconscious. Black magic tugged him down again, and he thrashed under its power.

Use her name again, Alaric whispered.

Jack ground his teeth. He tried to move his right hand, but it didn't budge. He hadn't wanted to use this spell before, because it would utterly drain him. He focused one finger at a time and inched it up in front of his face. The binding runes on his pointer finger glowed at his command as he whispered her name in the ancient Elgarian dialect. The finger throbbed like it was cut off as the magic surged through him. He resented all the sacrifice for this fight. He'd much rather fight with weapons than magic. He wasn't even quite sure the spell would work given that he was not a Stryga or warlock.

"Franziska *infentessum!*" he shouted with all the breath he had left as the magic crushed his lungs.

The black electricity let up, and he gulped in air. The Stryga's scream pierced his ears as he rolled to his knees.

Franziska doubled over and clawed at her face. Her skin cracked and grayed, hair frizzed to strands of mud brown, and her smooth muscle decayed on sinewy limbs. Her dress blackened as if caught on fire. She shrieked and put the flames out with a flick of her finger, but that left her panting. She flung a hand at him to cast another spell.

Nothing happened. Jack grinned even as his body gave out like a sieve empty of water. His spell had done its work. She was temporarily stripped of her enchantments and power. He didn't know how long she'd be down, so the time to strike was now.

His back, still barely healed, protested as he rose to his feet. His right calf, bitten by the Orbvi spider, caused him to limp. The poison dissipated but left his entire body stinging. He struggled in a fog of exhaustion that slowed his movements, but he fought through it. Jack hustled to where Kyadem lay on the ground, the flames dissipating. He picked her up, and her thrum vibrated through him. Jack spied the Stryga shuffling away and the Peryton cantering up to her. *Drannit.* His wings flicked back, and she grabbed a tuft of his short mane. The right front side of his body was blackened from Kya's damage.

Jack's entire body seemed weighed down by iron as he whipped Kya at the Stryga. The blades nicked her arm as she clambered aboard the Peryton. She called out to the last remaining two familiars, and they rose from their prone positions.

"Bring him to me," she said, and the familiars saluted.

"You can end this now!" Jack shouted.

Franziska arched a brow, and her smile chilled the air. "I *am* ending it. You have no idea the part you're playing in my destiny."

"You're a fool if you think the Malecanta will let you steal their magic."

The stag leaped gracefully off the ground, and his wings caught the wind. The High Stryga waved a graceful, if withered, hand. "I am going to take it, and you're going to help."

"Fuck." Jack staggered, his wounds impairing his mobility. He collapsed to one knee as his injured leg gave out. The jaguar men advanced on him with spears and swords. The one on the right took out his bow and let an arrow fly. Jack didn't have the stamina to dodge or flick it from the air with Kyadem. He could only turn slightly so the arrow pierced just above his already injured leg.

Gritting his teeth, he plucked the arrow out of his leg, then took out his remaining knives, and prepared for close quarter combat.

Two loud bangs sounded out.

The familiars staggered and then puffed into ash. Jack's surprised gaze fell upon the last man he'd expected to save his ass.

Narim Gunneran. He lifted a hand as he holstered his pistols and walked up to Jack. The blond man wore a mostly clean pair of black pants and a loose off-white shirt covered by Milytor armor, which included a vest with extra ammo and knives. His pack was camouflage green and hopefully filled with reinforcements like extra magazines and food.

Jack looked around for his own pack. It lay a few yards away, looking as it always did: grungy but serviceable.

"What the Orcyshells are you doing here?" Jack grunted. He stood despite the pain in his right leg. The underworld seemed close to taking him. His entire body ached.

Narim held up his hands and made an apologetic face. "I suppose I should be glad you're unable to cast another spell. I won't lie, that was an impressive fight." He tilted his head, as if knowing what Jack was thinking. "Yes, I used those soldiers as bait, and no, I didn't think of you as one of them. The tracker was just for fun for me—too bad she wasn't interested. I figured you'd get out of it, and now we know what we were dealing with."

Jack ground his teeth and scowled at him. There was no "we." Narim held out a vial of revival potion, which Jack refused. He had his own; he just had to get to his pack, though it seemed an eternity away at the moment.

"I don't expect a thank you—"

"You didn't save me."

Narim pursed his lips and sighed. "From where I was watching, I think I did. But let's not get into semantics. This is bigger than everyone thought, don't you agree?"

Jack took a deep breath to keep from punching the man. He didn't answer as he turned away to get his pack. It took an irritating amount of time with his injuries. His right arm had gone numb, and his head throbbed. His lip was swelling where he'd bitten it, and he could feel bruises blossoming up and down his torso.

"I'm still your superior while we hunt this Stryga, Jack."

He slung his pack on and faced Narim. His eyes bored into the other man's so hard that Narim had the sense to step back.

"Two soldiers dead under your watch. Two innocents who thought they were doing their kingdom a service," he said in a low voice. "I don't give a fuck what Grimarr told you, but you are not the lead on this any longer."

Narim shrugged. "They *did* perform a service. Because of them, we know the Volg Republic isn't just making up rumors to create chaos. There is a High Stryga powerful enough to call covens together, and that hasn't happened in a century. She's after the Malecanta, and for that she needs more than a normal coven. This is greater than them, than us." He raked a hand through his hair. "I will admit I was surprised the girl survived."

Jack's jaw clenched.

"You risked quite a lot to get her and that baby out of here," the man continued. "And did I see her wolves being hauled up in the flyer? I'll have to have a word with Grimarr about rounding your friend up when we're done. Dean, isn't it? We can't have rogue weapons dealers just running around." Narim sniffed. "You always did like a damsel in distress."

Jack swung at him, but he was off balance and the agent sidestepped. He yanked Jack's right arm into a twisted hold and threw him to the ground. Even though Jack was the one on the ground, Narim panted from the effort.

"I'm going to let that go, but try it again and I'll have you in lockdown in Barassus for a year," he said. The Milytor prison was located on an island off Asnor's shore, notorious for its security—and perhaps the occasional experimentation on prisoners that went awry.

Narim's finger traced Jack's right cheekbone as he struggled. A shiver went through Jack, but he didn't have the energy to shove the other man off him. Narim let him up.

"You really want to lose fingers," he muttered, and glared at the captain.

The man stared at him with hooded eyes. Was that longing that Jack saw? He was used to seeing anger and a kind of haunted need for revenge, but not this. This reminded him of years past. Did he still want something Jack couldn't give?

In a near whisper, Narim said, "I knew you'd survive. I understand why Alaric chose you. In another life, perhaps we would have been ..."

"I don't have time to revisit the past. Decision still stands. I'm not what you want," Jack said in a low voice. There was so much to unpack in Narim's statement that Jack would have preferred another Stryga to rip out his liver than discuss it further. He didn't have time or clarity to assess the man who'd left him for dead—or so he'd thought.

"I know." His tone implied that Jack's refusal was what made Jack appealing—the chase, the wanting something Narim couldn't have; it was a fine line between desire and enmity.

Jack downed the elixir in a swallow. Warmth spread through his muscles, and his head started to clear. The drain from using so much magic was a dull ache now instead of a vacuum sucking the life from him. He slowly got to his feet again and attempted to focus despite the pounding in his head. No broken bones or fractures that he could feel. Bruises, lacerations, all things that would heal faster now.

Narim didn't seem to mind his silence. "I was only making an observation. Now, you can finish the mission with me, or you can die here. I'll be sure to record your heroic death. The last Scriver and all. Sounds like a great tale."

Jack glared.

"Runvir was an idiot, and Modon refused to see past his ego. Cozael, ah, she was a feisty thing—unfortunate she died to a centaur spear. What was that redhead's name? The Drannit elf. No wonder she won," Narim said, lost in memories that Jack would rather not indulge.

He recalled the elf had given up her gifts and competed fairly. She'd received the mark, so he considered her a Scriver whether others did or not. When he didn't respond, Narim changed tactics.

"You don't have a lot of options at the moment."

Jack blinked. From anyone else it was a threat, but from Narim ... "Sounds a lot like you're asking for help." He spat blood and mud at the man's feet. *Is he going to kill me, or does he truly want help?*

"I don't. But the Milytor needs a win here. If we can stop this, Asnor will be supreme among all the continents. The king won't be under a Stryga's curse. The Volg are inciting riots every night; the death toll is climbing."

Jack cursed his existence. This was exactly why he worked alone. This was exactly why he didn't want anyone in his life who could be used as leverage against him. He had no reason to trust Narim's word on the events happening in the outside world. It was also true he didn't have many options—Franziska could not be allowed to live. His mission wasn't finished. And if he were lucky, Narim might take a spell in the gut along the way. Trying to decipher the captain's emotions wasn't something Jack had the capacity or inclination to do. He thought that was already done in the past, but it seemed like all his ghosts were on the rise.

"Lead the way," Jack said.

Narim smiled. He plucked a different vial from his pack, a healing elixir that worked twice as fast as the ones Jack had. The Magenta fly wings that made up the elixir came from a rare cave in the Aura mountains. The unique, ethereal insects had properties that worked differently for each person. They were tricky to make because of the delicacy of the ingredients. Only the Milytor had the equipment to make it—and make it last for an extended period of time.

"I need you to be able to walk until we can treat that leg. I don't want to lose the time you've given us with Franziska being forced to recover."

Jack swallowed the second liquid, sweet with a hint of mint, and it spread warmly through his system. His muscle repaired itself, and the open wounds scabbed over. The cut on his leg wouldn't heal that quickly, but the tissue restored enough that he could walk with a minor limp. The potion probably would have worked more effectively on Narim, since it was formulated for him, but it did the job well enough.

A few minutes later, he realized Narim knew the Stryga's name. A name Jack had never told him. His mistrust grew by the second.

Chapter Twenty-Seven

Varen is considered the best gunsmith and weapons-crafter in all of Elgar. His secrets are guarded but he takes on apprentices occasionally. He is of the Dothspine dwarven clan but doesn't discriminate by race—if the pupil is talented enough, Varen will teach.
~ Scryptus, the Scriver Archives,
as recounted by Scriver #5 Jack Serpent, Tome 16

"Contact left!" Dean shouted. His black plaid shirt billowed in the wind, and tattoos covered his tanned skin. His hands glittered with a few rings, and he wore a bandana to keep his long hair out of his eyes.

Aylla set the baby girl down in a basket lined with blankets and placed the basket in a secure pit on the flyer's deck. It wasn't as big as the Milytor ships, but it had a full deck and three billowing sails. Ash and Hugo whined and cowered in a corner underneath. She was glad they were too scared to do anything. She didn't need them underfoot or tripping Dean as he ran about the flyer, preparing guns and checking wards.

When Aylla glanced to the left, her breath hitched. "I thought we lost them when Jack cast that spell," she said, whipping her hair out of her face.

"The Underworld Wheel and Infentessum only work for at most ten minutes. I thought she'd go after Jack, and he'll be pissed she didn't," Dean said, cursing as the Peryton's shadow chased them.

The creature's outstretched golden wings hurtled toward them, the Stryga on his back. She looked a lot worse for wear, but that didn't stop her from cackling. The Peryton dove, and his antlers caught the flyer's sail. Hissing erupted as the ship lost altitude and started to sink. The sails functioned not only to steer it, but also to keep it in the air.

Dean scrambled over the deck and grabbed a long-barreled Piat scattershot. The booms rattled the air, and the Peryton squealed as the bullets grazed his side. The Stryga screamed down curses, but nothing happened to them or the ship. Aylla expected to blow up, but Jack's spell must have still been working. She gave the Stryga a rude finger sign for Hecaya, the goddess of death, and picked up another scattershot.

"She's still weakened," Dean said. "Shoot any part of her you can."

Aylla had hunted with a scattershot before, but this gun was well above the quality of her old Piat. The rack was smooth, the barrel straight and an inch longer, and the blast had very little recoil. She fired, racked, and fired until the gun was out. The wolves whimpered. They hated the sound of scattershots. The Peryton vanished into the setting sun with a flash of white tail and an angry bellow.

"Who taught you to shoot?" Dean turned off the gas that powered the ship, and it went silent. The engines ceased, and the fires that propelled it stopped.

"My father." Aylla eyed his movements, which were hurried but controlled. "Are we going to crash?"

Dean half shrugged and half shook his head. "I think I can land her in that clearing. I have a repair kit on board, but it'll take a while to find where the blasted beast punctured the sail. I'd hold on to something."

Aylla grabbed the baby basket and hunkered down in the hold. The wolves were happy she was with them. She swatted their noses away after a few minutes of incessant licking. The flyer slowed, and she poked her head up to see trees now at eye level. The ship floated through branches and leaves scattered all over the deck. With a crunch, they plunged through a thicket of trees and into a small space of grass. A few scum-covered ponds fed by the streams of the swamp sat nearby. Aylla glimpsed a couple of crocodile eyes lingering at the surface, but they disappeared at the sudden arrival of the blimp. *Normal crocs*, she told herself.

The flyer slid to a complete halt and shivered as it settled in the soft ground. Dean sighed as he gathered in the light red sail.

"Well, welcome to continued hell. We didn't have time for introductions, but I assume you know I'm Dokoran—Dean." He gave her a small smile. Earrings lined his left lobe, rune tattoos were visible on his forearms and up the right side of his neck, and his dark hair was pulled back into a tail, though disheveled strands curled out. He wore fashionable leather boots and pants, and a shirt that showed off lean muscle. Just the sort of friend she expected Jack to have.

Aylla smiled back and stuck her hand out. He shook it firmly. Then he glanced at the two wolves behind her, who crept out slowly with their tails between their legs.

"Ash and Hugo. *Vastita, ourtha vatia.*" She soothed them and they flicked their ears. She turned to Dean. "They won't bite unless provoked. Just go slow."

Dean nodded and motioned to the baby. He took out a small kit and opened it.

"You didn't give birth magically, did you?"

"No. We found her in a Strix's hut. What are you doing?" Aylla hugged the baby closer as Dean approached with a clear vial and a piece of charcoal.

"I won't hurt her. These are just a few tests to be sure she's not infested or spelled. Jack didn't do these before?" Dean raised a brow and sprinkled some of the contents of the vial on the baby's forehead. She wiggled her eyebrows and squirmed.

"No. I don't think he had whatever you have. We were also a bit distracted by the bodies and the High Stryga." Aylla wiped the clear liquid off. "Is this just water?"

"Holy water." Dean moved the blankets and gently took out the baby's left arm. He drew several runes on the smooth skin. "Yeah, Jack has a one-track mind sometimes, or he was just going to wait it out, and you can bet he'd have destroyed her the moment she showed any signs. The Scriver in him wants to know everything, doesn't he?"

Aylla frowned, but she couldn't really fault that line of logic.

"No burning, no adverse effects, no disappearing into her skin." Dean smiled. "All good signs. I think she's just lucky you found her."

"Good." Aylla breathed in relief and covered her with the blanket.

"We're on our own now, but I'll get you out of the swamp. Where's home?"

"Churk Forest." Aylla held up a bottle for the baby. She brought her up on deck and sat on a chair bolted to the wooden floor.

"Alone? I mean except for those two." Dean nodded at the wolves, who were circling the downed ship and marking everything around it.

"Yeah, just them." Aylla paused in thought. "Do you have friends in the Milytor to call for aid?"

"I used to. I'm sure Grimarr remembers me as the shyf who stole half his arsenal and then replicated it and sold it for profit." Dean lifted a huge metal box and opened it. Tools of all shapes and sorts lay neatly arranged inside. "I think I can get her airborne, at least enough to get us out."

"Can I help?"

"I think you've got your hands full," Dean said with a smile and looked at the baby in her arms.

"I could help after she's asleep." Aylla didn't fully trust him, but she trusted Jack. It was a startling thought.

"All right." Dean checked the sail inch by inch. He glanced up at the fading light and lit some lanterns.

"Light in the swamp is a dangerous thing," Aylla said and glanced around. Counting her blessings, she spied a few yarba trees. "We need to use those seed pods. It'll change the color of the flames, so we don't attract huge insects."

Dean nodded, and a shot of warm surprise flooded through Aylla. She'd thought he'd brush her off or tell her to prove it, but he just took her word and went to gather the pods.

When he returned, he fed them bit by bit into the lanterns, and the light took on the blue-white color. Maybe if she ventured out more among people, she'd find there were decent ones. Aylla didn't want to think *that* positively, but it was time to stop hiding in the forest. Did she want to die without having had any more adventure than hunting with Ash and Hugo?

Aylla chuckled. She imagined taking them across the country or perhaps even to Muran someday to see the pirates, the beaches.

The baby dropped off to sleep after she was full, and Aylla set her down in the basket with a blanket tucked tightly around her. She couldn't roll too much in it, not that she seemed strong enough to even do that, and Aylla checked her often. Aylla worked with Dean as they checked the sail, found the holes, and started to patch them. Dean's presence was similar to Jack's, but not nearly as comforting.

"Aren't there any women in weapons dealing?" Aylla sewed with a large needle to pull the fabric together, and then it would be sealed with a clear coat of some gloop that Dean called "monstrously fucking sticky shit."

He laughed. "There are a few. I know a lot of good female dwarves who craft better than any man."

Aylla thought about Bean. She'd never complained—she'd just wanted to prove herself. Aylla hadn't gotten to know much of her history, but her and Mykel's conversations would stay with her forever.

"It seems like a rough life. Bean and Mykel were good soldiers," she said.

"I hadn't met either one. What happened?"

Aylla gave him the details, and to pass the time they had a good hour's discussion on what they'd do to Narim if they ever saw him again. Dean explained why he'd stolen the Milytor's tier-one weapons and improved them. They wouldn't let him while he was enlisted, so he'd gone on his own. Aylla found it supremely interesting that he'd apprenticed under a dwarf master. So many people had lives she could only dream about.

The baby woke, and Aylla fed her again. Exhaustion crept through every muscle in her body. The girl squirmed and cried. It was a distraction from worrisome thoughts about Jack. She had no doubt he would be happy they'd escaped, but at what cost? Was he even still alive? Aylla soothed the baby as best she could, afraid the noise would attract unwanted attention.

Dean knelt by her and held out his arms. "I can try."

Aylla gratefully handed her over and leaned back as she watched Dean rock the girl. There was something surprisingly tender in the way he held her. The cries faded as she drifted to sleep. Ash and Hugo munched on a few hares they'd caught and brought back to the ship. The crunch of bones and slop of tongues was not exactly soothing, but it was familiar.

"Do you have children?" Aylla asked as sleep wrestled with her.

Dean shook his head. There was a certain sadness in his features. "I wasn't meant to have any. But this is nice. I've always thought about fostering, but in my line of work, what's the point?" He glanced at her. "Why don't you get some sleep, and I'll watch her? The sail needs to dry before I can try to take off."

"Are we going back for Jack?"

Dean sat down with the baby cradled in a blanket in his arms and gazed at the moss-covered trees. "He wouldn't want me to take you back in there. It's bad enough we're stranded here for a few more hours."

"Do you think he's alive?" Aylla couldn't help asking.

He peered at her closely, as if trying to read something in her. "I'm sure he's fine. He's been a loner even before he was a Scriver. It takes a lot of skill to survive as long as he has, doing what he does."

"Have you known him a long time?" Aylla clapped her lips shut. *Stop asking questions and leave him alone. Don't let the anxiety control the conversation.* She didn't want him to get the wrong idea about her and Jack either. Was this what the schoolgirls experienced? Aylla didn't think it was like the little affections they talked about. It felt a lot deeper than a superficial attraction. That was saying something, since from the first, she'd felt nothing but distrust and annoyance.

"About eleven years now." Dean reached for a canteen of water and sipped it. The baby sleepily moved her arms. "It's not my affair, but you should know Jack doesn't stick with people for long. He knows the life he chose doesn't allow for relationships—especially ones that could come back to hurt him." He gave her a significant look.

Aylla averted her gaze and played with her fingers. Lyra. She understood why Jack couldn't bring himself to visit the woman, and why he wouldn't want to encourage anything between them. When had her thoughts even turned in that direction? She chastised herself. He probably wasn't even thinking about her anymore. Nor should she be thinking about him like that. Not to mention it was foreign for her to have someone else occupy so much of her thoughts; like a swirl storm, it left her off kilter. Aylla didn't have a life that suited Jack, and she certainly didn't want to live a life traveling all over. She liked having a place to call home, a place to come back to after an adventure.

"I understand what you're saying. We're not— I mean, I just ... well, he helped me a lot in there. I want to be sure he'll be okay. Even if I know I'll never see him again." She stopped her word vomit, and Dean just stared at her as if he were deciding something. "I'll just go lie down, thanks. Wake me whenever you need me to take over."

Aylla slipped into the hold, her face heated and her body flushed. She hated that she talked a lot when she was nervous. She wasn't used to conversing with people in general. It was as if Dean could read her like all the books she had stacked in her small library. She'd never felt so openly studied before.

The pile of blankets felt heavenly. She closed her eyes, but all she could see was Jack's face. Jack's body covered in the Stryga's black magic, the Black Insidian. Aylla reached into her pack and found the wooden rocking horse. She clutched it as she drifted to sleep.

After what seemed like only a couple of hours, Aylla woke to the sound of the baby crying. No, it wasn't a child, it was a shadow calling to her. A song like she'd heard before, though she was unable to recall when or where. The melody wrapped around her in delicate strands that burned her skin and made her feel restless. Longing, but for what?

"Jack?" Aylla whispered, stretching.

The ship was quiet. Dean and the baby were asleep, and lanterns flickered serenely. The shape moved among the trees.

"I need your help. Use the compass to find me," the shadow said in a deep, willowy voice.

Aylla rubbed her eyes, and the man disappeared. It sounded just like Jack. In her heart, she knew it wasn't him, but a deep compulsion forced her up. She found a compass on the flyer's railing. Had Dean left it there? Or had someone put it there for her?

The needle quivered and pointed west.

Aylla shivered as she followed the compass. Her legs moved of their own accord, and a haze drifted over her eyes. Something was pulling her back into the swamp. Back into the heart of darkness.

Chapter Twenty-Eight

Kyadem is a variation on a weapon a lot of Milytor use. Alaric had me sit with the metal for days, feeling it, absorbing it, speaking with it: one of the purest metals on the continents that retains old magic. Not indestructible but certainly deadlier than most swords, knives, axes, and even some older pistols. It took several months and a lot of accidents for me to wield her. I nearly lost an eye and other appendages.
~ Scryptus, the Scriver Archives,
as recounted by Scriver #5 Jack Serpent, Tome 15

Jack kept Narim in his sights. *Maybe he was there for the spell when I said her name.* But Jack hadn't stayed alive this long without maintaining some deep-seated mistrust of all beings. His instincts were to leave Narim and go alone, but something nagged at him. Better to keep his potential enemy in sight rather than at his back.

So, Jack stayed with the captain, and the slow pace was conducive to his wounds. His head was still foggy from the attacks, and even though he didn't trust Narim, he understood the other man needed something from him. That bought Jack a few hours to plan his next move.

They tracked Franziska for the better part of three hours, but the dark and constant sinkholes finally pinned them down. Jack didn't protest as they settled in for some rest. Narim lit a small fire—it was no secret they were here, so stealth wasn't a priority anymore. The Stryga wasn't running, and neither were they.

"How did you get here? This is your big plan—to come back alone and find the High Stryga?" Jack asked as he whittled a stick into a walking cane. His right calf still burned, and his body ached. He certainly intended to take the deaths of Mykel and Bean to Grimarr and have Narim punished but bringing that up was pointless until they got out of the swamp.

Narim turned to him and gulped water out of his canteen. The sun would rise soon, and they would have to move.

"I couldn't very well bring the entire Milytor out here without solid information. My plan, flawed as you think it was, did work. I had intended to aid sooner, but I got sidetracked." Narim side-eyed him in a way that prickled the back of Jack's neck.

"I went back to base," he continued, "and when the warding went down, I used a transport spell. I won't do that again." Narim grimaced. "I can see why no one does. Portals are more effective anyway but hard to come by." He held up his right arm, and the skin around his wrist was shriveled and discolored, one of the aftereffects of spelled travel. Jack was no stranger to both, since he was required to jump continents frequently. He preferred to use portals or portal gates over dodgy transport spells.

He had a rune tattoo that took a lot of those effects off him. He'd learned that lesson once when he'd portal-jumped into a gryphon's nest.

Dean's grenades must've taken out the last of the spell. Jack's thoughts turned to the flyer that he hoped was far away from the swamp.

"I wasn't surprised you were still alive. You weren't exactly hard to find," Narim said with a grin. He nodded to Kyadem. "That thing should be illegal."

"Why, because you can't wield it?" Jack grunted. He'd seen Narim trying to practice with other chained blades, and it wasn't a pretty sight.

Narim's face soured. "I can use one. I choose other, more efficient methods. You think you're something special because of Alaric, but the truth is he was a traitor."

Jack lay back and folded his hands over his stomach. "What are you accusing Alaric of?" He hadn't known all of Alaric's past, and the older man had been stingy on details, yet Jack had trusted him implicitly. If there was something he'd needed to know, Alaric would tell him.

"He was a warlock." Narim let that sink in for a moment. "Why do you think he knew so much about Strygan and how to kill them? Why do you think he picked you—whose parents were murdered by an organ-harvesting coven?"

Jack's fingers tightened against each other and his jaw set. *There's no way he wouldn't tell me that.* Narim was the last person he would discuss his parents with.

"He was no warlock—Grimarr would never have let him in the barracks or learn the weapons and train."

Narim snorted. "You think you know Grimarr. That old bastard was friends with Alaric and made secret alliances."

"You don't have any proof." Jack wished something, anything, would come out of the swamp to attack them. Talking to Narim grated on his already frayed nerves.

"I have records and memory gems—I'll show them to you when we get back. I could get over him being a warlock if he'd have trained the entire Milytor or given others more of a chance with his 'trials.' But then he stumbled across you. A poor orphan who made headlines when he burned down his foster home, escaped the mines. You have a thing for fire, eh?" Narim didn't bother to hide the delight he took in hammering Jack with these theories. There was nothing about Alaric that screamed warlock. Jack struggled to conjure a telltale smell or sign.

"There was a succubus in my closet," Jack said with more control than he felt. No one had believed him then, but the orphans had stopped harassing him for a good month after he'd eliminated that thing.

"You must have impressed Alaric, because he told me the next day I would be training with Harner."

"That can't be the real reason you have a Korykoa up your ass. Alaric chose me." Jack paused, not sure he was ready to go where this was heading. Then he plunged ahead. "I didn't save Jethen in time. It wasn't on purpose."

Narim flinched at the name. "You blocked me from that mission—it should have been me, and you know it. You knew Jeth was experimenting with alchemy. You and every other soldier wanted him dead, so he wouldn't jeopardize the precious integrity of the Milytor." He spat on the ground.

Jack squared his shoulders as he stood to stretch his uninjured leg. Kya hummed on his hip. "It's not my job to force you to believe what happened in that cave."

"Just like no one truly knows what happened at Ravenhell."

"You're welcome to speculate."

Narim sighed and seemed to check his rage. He paced in a small circle. "I've grieved Jeth's death. I was glad when you left the Milytor, but of course you got to walk a better path, full of glory and blood. You've never had the pressure of coming from a Milytor family. I was born into this. My father expects me to become a general someday, and my mother started obsessively teaching me folklore and spell work so I could become the first Scriver general."

"I'm sorry my parents were murdered before they could fuck me up," Jack said. He closed his eyes and tried to block out Narim's voice. And his lies. He was not swayed by the sob story. Alaric was not a warlock ... Jack had never smelled black magic on him except when the man had been teaching him to recognize the scent.

When he opened his eyes, Narim had closed the gap between them, his bulk shoving Jack against a tree. With his leg still healing, Jack was unbalanced enough to slam into it.

"You have no idea what it's like." Narim spoke softly, his eyes boring into Jack's. This close, Jack could make out silver flecks in those stormy depths. "Without the Milytor, without Jethen, I have no life. I failed the final trial, and now I'll never get the title."

Was I not clear that I don't need details? Jack sympathized with the man losing a partner, more than a partner, but he refused to take blame. He'd done the mission, and Jeth had done his part. But with someone like Narim, Jack didn't mind if the other man thought him heartless and cold.

"I cannot be a stand-in for Jethen," Jack whispered, shifting uncomfortably. Narim's hand on his shoulder burned as if he held ember magic.

Narim sighed. "I'm not trying to make you one. You never could be. He ... Jeth always told me you were never going to be mine." He stood back.

Jack cocked his head. "You thought there was any chance of that?" He shoved Narim back further. The captain didn't protest, but his face fell into shadow.

"It's funny how the line between jealousy and passion is blurred after a time. You knew they made jokes about how I always ended up being your sparring partner. How I lingered in the barrack showers. Only Jeth understood me, and for that we are soul crossed. Perhaps I'll see him again in the afterlife." Narim shrugged.

"I didn't make things worse for you back then," Jack said with a grunt. He hadn't reported Narim's behavior. And he wouldn't now, but the captain needed to back off.

"That's the only reason I saved your ass from the Stryga." Narim said it half-heartedly, but Jack knew he appreciated it. He could have made life very difficult for the young soldier in their training days.

A muscle worked in Jack's jaw. He felt every bruise, cut, wound in his body. This was the last thing he needed to handle. There was something deeply melancholy in Narim's expression, but Jack refused to feel sorry for him. He'd chosen his path, and he knew Jack did not return any feelings. He thought they'd shut that book a long time ago.

Narim nodded as his breached walls came back up. A cold smile once more crested his face. "I suppose some of the Milytor are prone to my tastes anyway. It's not as uncommon as you think."

Jack trudged onward with his makeshift cane. He turned back a moment. "The Milytor doesn't care what your preference of partner is. If anyone had issue with that, I might be inclined to actually side with you."

Narim's frown flickered into a small smile. He nodded at Jack.

For a few hours they rested, and then they each took their last vial of the thesal tracking potion. Jack's vision blurred and then tracks started to appear like viper-green signs. Jaguar, raccoon, hare, crocodile, and Stryga. Jack wasn't sure what warped their souls into body-thieving, blood-sucking, black-magic-thriving beings. The tracking was more of her scent than prints since the Peryton had carried her off the ground.

But the creature had touched down some time ago—cloven hoof tracks told him that. Its lavender blood spatters had dried or been licked away by other animals. It wasn't unusual for animals to care for each other by erasing tracks.

"She's smart, so I'll go around when we close in. You take point and I'll watch your six," Narim said as they tromped through mud and soggy ground. Insects buzzed in their ears and frogs splashed into reeds.

Jack gave him a look. *You're the less injured of the two of us—you should take point.* Plus, he didn't want Narim at his back; he wanted him in his sight. Despite their earlier understanding, Jack wasn't about to blindly trust the captain. He never had, and that wasn't going to change now.

Narim got his message. "All right, I'll flush her out and you come around the back. She knows there's two of us, but her power is draining. She'll need new sacrifices soon, and we can't give her that time."

Jack nodded and continued on a narrow trail through the trees to the northwest. Dean had said something about a totem in the distance. He kept his eyes peeled for it.

"Hold." Jack held out an arm.

A long, slimy, black, log-like appendage lay across the path, disappearing into the murky water on the other side. Jack peered into the water. Ghostly faces bobbed just beneath the surface. Their shriveled skin and lidless eyes stared up at him with desolation.

"A murcathis?" Narim whispered and crept up behind him.

Jack nodded. A tentacle lazily slid in and out of the water. Giant suckers the size of dinner plates squished around logs and rocks. The water hid its twelve other tentacles and the huge head filled with razorlike teeth. Jack stepped over the tentacle and walked as lightly as he could. Turtles lifted their heads as they basked on logs, and Jack hoped they remained still.

Narim slipped on the slime-covered ground and flailed as he slid. A turtle scuttled into the water and the ripples were like gunshots that alerted the beast. Jack cursed, grabbed Narim's vest, and tugged him forward. They sprinted into a run as tentacles flew out of the water and grasped anything it found. Trees cracked in half, bushes were plucked from the ground, and rocks were thrown like pellets. The murcathis bellowed as it launched from the pond. Waves of water crashed behind them, and Jack glanced back to see a giant, gaping maw of teeth hurtling toward him.

He didn't take the time to get Kyadem from his belt—he just ran. There was no sense in killing a monster that wasn't controlled by the Stryga. This was just an animal living in a swamp and doing what it had to do to survive.

Narim had no such qualms as he fired into the murcathis. Jack whipped around, grabbed his forearm, shoved it down, and gripped Narim's wrist with his other hand. He twisted so the man had to let go of the gun. Jack caught the pistol.

"What the Orcys are you doing?" Narim growled.

Jack didn't wait to answer as the murcathis was still charging after them. He broke into a pained run, his walking stick falling behind. Narim's pistol was a silver revolver, and Jack kept the piece out until they were out of the murcathis' reach. The beast gave up the chase and went back to its watery home.

Jack handed Narim back his weapon. He stumbled to a limping walk. The tracking potion still showed him Franziska's scent and the Peryton's blood trail.

"I could have taken a few fangs at least. They sell for quite a lot of san," Narim said with a roll of his eyes. "Oh right, you're above all that."

Jack shot back a withering glower. "I don't kill beasts for sport."

"Uh-huh. Fine, but let me tell you ..." Narim took the lead, shoving the revolver into a holster under his light jacket, and proceeding to start a story about some beast who'd tracked him for days.

Jack sighed. "I don't need backstory."

Narim regarded him for a moment, then burst out laughing. "Well, fine, I'll just talk, and you can listen if you want. This is going to be a long trek."

Jack sighed again. It was as if confessing had set Narim free, and he was treating this like they were of the same mind on a mission. Like their training days.

Jack fashioned another walking stick and took deep breaths. It would all be over soon. Just find the High Stryga and burn her, hex her, infuse her with silver, throw blood spells, anything. If it were up to him, he'd have retreated for a day to go over options or set traps.

Before he could banish the thought, Aylla jumped into his mind. She'd been a very patient listener as he'd gone over options on how to kill a Stryga. He hadn't realized how much he liked that. Her presence had snuck up on him like a comfortable jacket that he missed. He did intend to see her again, should he survive.

He also had other thoughts careening around. Alaric couldn't have been a warlock. Could he? Jack shook his head, hating that Narim had gotten to him. Jack would scour all the Milytor and Elgarian records and memory records he could when he got back. But flashes of old memories popped around like dancing beetles. Alaric teaching him how to disarm a wizard or Stryga, instructing him on the best ways to kill monsters with three heads or ones that exhaled poisonous gas. Alaric training him day and night to track and burn Strygan, insisting that Jack needed to always be vigilant and that nothing was as it seemed.

If—*if*—Alaric had been a warlock, why had he turned against his own kind? Jack could not recall a time when his mentor had spoken in a positive manner about Strygan or warlocks. He'd said he left a clan of warlocks but never included the fact that he'd been *one* of them. In fact, he'd seemed to have an unusually high candor for hating stolen magic.

Jack mentally swatted his thoughts away like the bloodsucking insects that pestered his neck. He had to focus. Just ahead, the scent faded away like smoke. That wasn't a good sign.

Chapter Twenty-Nine

Strygan apparently can only breed with warlocks. They mate, sometimes using force, and kill any child that isn't female. Only females inherit the Strygan magic. Warlock paternal rights is a raging debate.
~ Scryptus, the Scriver Archives,
as recounted by Scriver #5 Jack Serpent, Tome 4

Aylla woke to find herself standing alone in the middle of the swamp with just the clothes on her back, a compass in her hand, Jack's wooden horse carving, and a piece of parchment map Dean had given her. He'd been showing her the enchanted map before she'd drifted off. The map showed Asnor as he'd drawn it. He'd told her it could be used to communicate if they got separated when they landed.

The fog lifted as she blinked and whatever spell had lured her away from the baby and Dean wore off. Echoes of a song floated around her like smoke. The tune was both familiar and haunting. Aylla turned in circles, and tears flooded her eyes. Where was she? Her heart ached to hear the girl's cry and her wolves licking. Even Dean's off-tune humming would be welcome. She prayed he got them all out. She'd fallen for a Stryga trick, and it irritated her to no end. Aylla had vowed to never be under someone's power again, but it seemed magic was stronger.

"What in the Drannit fuck are you doing?" she shouted and kicked at some sticks. Aylla burned with madness. Jack had saved her life, and now she was going to repay that by dying in the same swamp. She cursed her weak will. She'd lived in such fear of being controlled by human will that she'd neglected to study the arcane. Aylla should have known better. Drace had always been fascinated with it—he'd thought her mother had possessed some sort of power. Aylla bitterly wondered if he had regretted the night he'd accidently killed her. What sort of power had her mother held that wouldn't allow her to protect herself or her daughter? None.

Aylla couldn't think about Lavynia too long without spiraling into a pit of self-loathing and loneliness that hurt like a permanent knife in her side.

The semi-dark, dappled swamp was filled with insects whirring, animals rustling through the brush, and moss swaying on the trees. There was no way Jack would have lured her back. Aylla cracked a stick against a tree trunk, but the splinters were not satisfying.

"You've come a long way for an awful lot of trouble," a female voice said to her right. "Right back into the place you shouldn't be."

Aylla spun, but there was nothing there. "No thanks to you. Why go through all this to get me back here?"

"I see potential—I've felt something odd inside you. I wish to know what it is before I kill you."

A pause. Again, Aylla thought about her mother. Had Lavynia possessed something she never told her daughter about? Maybe Drace had killed her before she'd gotten the chance.

"I am what you wish you could be. I can even stop death."

"No one can stop death." Aylla kept her talking. If she could just see what she was dealing with, she'd feel like she could form a plan.

"We can. We know some of the Malecanta secrets. But it comes with a price. I think you'd pay it—what would you give to bring your mother back? To ruin the entire van Hyde family for letting that troll of an uncle defile your mother like that and strike you?" The female laughed, tinkly and savage.

Aylla gulped and shook her head. She didn't want to know how this woman knew that. The little memories she had of her father were warm, like a summer afternoon spent swimming and drying by running in a meadow of wildflowers. She remembered his low voice, which didn't often rise to anger. He didn't say a whole lot, really. A young man who was just starting out his life and family when it had been ripped from him. Aylla's breath staggered.

Focus. Focus on something that doesn't hurt. That's what she wants. She wants your pain. Aylla wasn't sure if it was her own voice or Jack's.

If she were conversing with the High Stryga, was she near her hut? She glanced down at the compass. It pointed northeast, and the voice was coming from the south.

"You could join us, my dear, and give your life purpose. Living alone until the earth claims you? Chasing after a Scriver who will never want you doesn't seem like a worthy cause to die for, does it?"

Aylla's mind stumbled with her pretty words. They made sense, and yet she knew what she wanted. She refused to do black magic and become like the Stryga. And she wasn't chasing Jack ... he simply intrigued her.

He'd protected her despite all his ire at her very presence. There was so much under his cold exterior that drove him.

"I don't chase anyone. I owe him, and I don't let debts go unpaid." And yet somewhere deep inside, Aylla realized she had begun to feel something more than a camaraderie with the Scriver. She wanted to know his fears, his secrets, his wishes. Why? She chastised herself with a sigh. Jack was like mist—present in the moment but by sunrise gone. There wasn't really any hope that they could remain together.

"You can tell yourself that lie. But at your deepest, you desire a connection with someone, and he seems to have fooled you into thinking he could fill that. Men will always take power over us. Why do you think kingdoms fall under a man's rule? It's time for a queen," the Stryga said with a sneering cackle.

Aylla's hand shook. "Agreed, but not a Strygan queen." She spat.

A sigh. Ghostly moans rose around her, and the swamp shivered.

"I guess we're going to do this the hard way then."

Aylla didn't have time to react as a song began to thrum on the wind. The effect was like something hitting her on the head. She fell before she could get her bearings. Her eyes struggled to stay open, but a black shroud obscured her vision, and everything went dark.

Chapter Thirty

Travel by portal is complicated if one does not know the proper gates. One can portal without them, but it's possible they will lose limbs or end up in an undesirable place unless they have good control over the portal magic. And there are nasty side effects some people experience such as nausea, headache, diarrhea, sleeping sickness for days, greenish tint to their skin, new warts. I can't explain how the magic effects different people.
~ Scryptus, the Scriver Archives,
as recounted by Scriver #5 Jack Serpent, Tome 12

Narim turned in a circle. "Did your potion wear off?"

"No, but the track is gone." Jack took a few steps forward in hopes of finding the green scent again. The trees blocked his way, and rain started to fall on them. He shook his hair from his eyes.

"We're losing the light; let's stop." Narim sighed and sat on a log.

"Catch up when you're ready then," Jack said and continued on. He had no intention of stopping until he found the Stryga.

"Oh, all right." Narim grumbled something more about not being left behind.

Even without the potion, Jack's instincts were tingling. He took a deep breath—the smell was there, even if it was faint. Something was masking it. Wood smoke, decay, algae water. Where there was smoke, there would be a hut. He shoved moss out of his way, stepped over sharp rocks, and wiped rain from his face.

They sloshed up a small hill, and Jack grabbed a tree trunk to keep pressure off his right leg. But there it was: the Stryga's cabin. The totem rose about fifty yards away in the trees, a monstrously tall, thick wooden carving with bones and sigils written in blood all the way to the top. Black magic swirled around Jack like flies on feces. His stomach churned, and a cold sweat broke out on his forehead.

"Maybe I should call in a few units," Narim said, standing beside him.

They found a log to sit on and observed the hut.

You probably should have done that about three hours ago, but this isn't my circus is it? Jack thought with a grimace. Being with Narim was like waiting for a Chimera to finally get hungry enough to try human flesh. The man's pride overrode his common sense. He'd set a trap, and he thought he was going to take the glory when it sprang shut to catch the biggest prize in centuries.

"Do whatever you're going to do." Jack put all his attention on the hut and tried to determine the danger of attacking the Stryga at home. If she was home. He ran through all the various tactics and weapons he had available. It might be smart to wait for a strong force, but by then Franziska would have fled.

He pulled out an old ale bottle from his pack. Inside, nine bent nails rattled, along with a piece of flammable hearth stone. Narim eyed the bottle as Jack got out the rune quill and drew a hex rune on it before stuffing it into his jacket pocket.

"Strygan bottle," Jack said with a shrug. It was worth a shot. He needed a bit of the Stryga herself for it to properly work. To get any hair or nails, he'd have to get close to her. The bottle would suck her magic, and then he could kill her if he was lucky. Infentessum had worked the first time, but he doubted he could use it again both from a strength standpoint and he had to assume Franziska was skilled. She'd have warded against such an attack again.

Narim sat silently next to him, grumbling about the heat and bugs, but also observing and waiting.

Smoke rose from the chimney. It wasn't a terribly large hut, though made of sturdy logs. It had a thatched roof and half a wraparound porch. Trees and shrubs had been cleared around it in an expansive hundred-foot area. The wards were invisible, but Jack had figured they were there. It was just a matter of disarming them or blasting through them. He eyed Narim. Firepower and bullets were what the Milytor trained with from day one, but they didn't often break wards.

"Shall we do the old triggerman and slider trick?" Narim whispered with a humorless laugh.

One person would trigger the wards and the other would try to slip past them to the goal. It was an often-fatal training exercise the Milytor used. Jack wasn't sure Franziska knew there were two of them, so it might work. The question was, which did he want to deal with—unknown protection wards or the High Stryga herself?

"You take the wards," Jack said as he dropped his pack and opened it.

"I knew you'd say that. But there might be more than one, so wait until I've tripped them all," Narim replied as he took out his pistols.

The rain made everything slick, but it was slackening. Jack checked to make sure each pistol was loaded and tapped Kyadem on his belt. The two swords he usually carried on his back were stowed in the pack. They were too long to wield in such close quarters. He slid a knife in both boots and two on his back by his belt. He took out a vial for speed and downed it in one gulp.

"Oh, we're going now?" Narim observed him taking the potion and hastily pulled out his own. A blue glow washed over them both and then settled into their skin.

Jack's muscles twitched with energy; his right leg's pain masked by the potion's adrenaline-like effect. His heart thudded with the strength of a bull.

"Do I get a countdown ..."

Jack glared at the captain in an effort to get him to move, and Narim flipped him two fingers in a bent angle. The man stood and stretched, then marched down toward the cabin. He slipped a few times in the mud, and when he hit the wards a pulse of dark energy washed over them like a wave. Jack held his position.

Groans filled the air, sounding like wagon wheels stuck in a ditch. The swamp went quiet as soft cracks echoed in the clearing. Hands appeared out of the ground, fingers clawing for the sky. Pale blue shapes pulled themselves up, taking the form of ethereal humans. Skin sagged off their bones. Some of them limped, and others' necks appeared broken. They didn't seem to notice their injuries. They walked toward Narim with lips moving in incoherent moans.

"Bogles," Narim shouted, and held out his hands like he was conducting a dead orchestra. "You're dead, all of you; I've come to put you at peace."

Bogles aren't entirely human, and they don't always desire peace, Jack thought with a roll of his eyes. Narim was trying the old tales that would have everyone believe spirits were able to be reasoned with or that they wanted something left behind. Some violent echoes were just mean. The ghosts were the echoes of dead people, and they could be exceedingly vicious because they didn't understand what they were or where they were. They had one goal—devour anyone in their path, thinking it would get them home.

The Bogles rose, one by one, until over two dozen stood between Narim and the house. They paused at his voice, tilted on boney legs. Scraps of clothing floated around their bodies in an invisible wind.

A male Bogle stepped forward, and his mouth stretched in a scream that hurt worse than a banshee's. Jack winced and cursed. The Bogles lurched, and their hands turned into claws.

Narim fired. A few went down, but the majority pressed forward and attacked. Jack ran around to the left to get closer to the hut and the back door. Another wave of black magic hit, and Jack staggered.

"Serpent, get over here! I need ..." Narim's scream was drowned out by a howl.

Jack froze. Growls rose in front of him, vicious and sonorous.

Six large, black dogs with yellow eyes stood staring at him from the brush. They were larger than Ash and Hugo. Their panting jaws dripped ropes of saliva, and fangs the size of knives glinted in the rainy moonlight. Orcyshounds. Jack shook his head. He gathered his legs and then sprinted as hard as he could toward Narim's increasingly frantic gunshots.

Jack fired behind him, and a yip told him he'd clipped a hound. The dogs raced after him as he leaped over huge roots and flew down the hill. Sharp brambles cut Jack's legs as he burst into the clearing.

Narim was grappling with a Bogle. He snapped its arm and threw it to the ground, then knifed it in the chest, and it turned into a pile of bones. The blond man turned at the sound of the hounds, and his eyes widened. His scar stood out against his pale skin. Jack didn't have time to shout a plan. He just went back-to-back with Narim and started firing. Most of the Bogle's were down, but a few walked between the hounds with their arms outstretched, mouths gaping like hungry fish.

Jack fired his last five rounds, and a hound vanished in a pile of smoke. He dodged the grip of a Bogle and slid on his knees. He whipped a leg out and tripped it; yanking a knife from his boot, he plunged it into the shade's eye. Taking the same blade, he turned just in time to shove it into a hound's shoulder as it launched at him. The hound growled and clamped down on the wrist that held the knife.

Pain exploded as fangs ripped the bracer on his forearm. He thrashed as the hound pivoted with a renewed attack. Using his already battered wrist, he managed to catch the hound's leg. He yanked it and rolled, taking the hound under his body's weight.

He couldn't reach Kya, so he pulled the other knife from his boot and jabbed it into the hound's eye. The animal shrieked as it flailed, and Jack moved with it, pushing the blade as deep as it would go. It disappeared in a wash of smoke.

A Bogle came right behind the hound, and cold hands gripped his arm. Jack kicked up and swept the Bogle's feet from under him. He unfurled Kyadem and used the short blade to slice the hands right off his arm. The Bogle groaned but kept coming. It flickered in and out of substance, so Jack had to time Kya's swing.

Bogles and Orcyshounds circled them like a pack of wolves. He tapped a rune on Kya's hilt on the long blade, and it split into two. He didn't like to separate the weapon, but there were too many foes not to.

Jack swept the now three chained blades in dual arcs, and the Bogles shrieked as their corporeal bodies fell into pieces. The hounds were smarter and dodged the flying blades.

"I'll lead them away! Go," Narim said, out of breath. "Do you have an extra knife?"

Flipping his knife hilt first, Jack thrust it toward him. Narim took it with a nod of thanks and huffed out several breaths.

"We can fight them together," Jack said, but in truth, he didn't care if he stayed or not. Either way, he was getting into that hut.

"Just get the Stryga before my potion runs out." Narim broke through the circle of Bogles, and the hounds snapped at his ankles. He jumped high, and a set of teeth just missed his boot. As he sped off into the dark, the hounds raced after him.

Jack swung Kyadem and took the remaining Bogles down. He slashed and caught one of the hilts as another blade decapitated a Bogle. Catching, releasing, and swinging the chains in smooth arcs, he took out the Bogles as they flickered in and out between physical and ghostly forms. Piles of bones and ash lay on the Stryga's front yard when he was done. His wrist throbbed, and his leg gave out for a moment. Jack knelt, leaning on Kya's blade. He caught his breath and stood slowly.

The hut's windows glowed with firelight, and a soft song floated in the air. Eerie and haunting, it was oddly familiar. Where had he heard that melody before? Jack moved into the darker shadows just beyond the hut. He crouched and went over the next options. There wasn't much time before Narim was either killed by the hounds or they returned.

He didn't have any grenades, and putting rune bombs on the hut didn't seem like a good idea. There could be information inside, and Franziska wasn't likely to die from a simple bomb. Realization began to form in his mind. Franziska was not altogether a true Stryga—she'd shaken off his spells and bullets in less time than most. Something in the air shimmered, a long-forgotten secret, a humming tune that coaxed memories like a draining sieve.

Jack crept closer to the hut.

He was huddled under a blanket in the closet with a boot clutched to his chest. He'd woken again to boys staring down at him. Their eyes terrified him, like looking into the goblins' crimson ones as they slaughtered his parents. The lead boy, the one with red curls, jeered and taunted him. He instructed several others to hold Jack down as they drew obscene runes and pictures on his face.

At the first opportunity, Jack leaped out of bed and attacked the closest boy. They screeched, and chaos erupted. But this time, they were ready for his strength. This time, they hit him with pillowcases filled with books and shoes.

Jack fell and hit his forehead on the corner of the wooden bedpost. His vision went fuzzy, and rage took over his muscles. His hands curled into fists as he took on seven orphan boys. His knuckles were bloodied as they connected with hard tissue, muscles cramped from exertion, but his senses didn't allow pain to register. Not until he was safe.

They clamored together to fight him off before Jack got a hold of his senses. It wasn't a long fight, and at the end, two of them lay bleeding and unconscious on the floor as Jack retreated to the closet and shut himself in. The other five shouted an alarm and pounded on the locked door of their dorm. Jack's hands shook, and blood dripped from the sole of the boot like macabre paint. He shoved it away and hid it under a fallen sweater.

He hadn't meant to hurt them. He wasn't what they called him. Jack squeezed his eyes shut, and his body trembled. Was this preferable to cutting out the crystals in the mine?

Freakishly strong. Doesn't listen well. Odd. Talks to trees.

The Servun house manager barged through the door, and the boy's voices collided into a huge cacophony of complaints and fearful explaining.

"One at a time!" the man shouted over the noise. Jack could picture his big belly hanging over his pants, beard crusted with food and bushy eyebrows furrowed.

Jack was never picked in the small cliques that formed with the children in the mines. They thought he was cursed because of how his parents had died. And also how sometimes the crystals or a rare mushroom in the forest would react in his presence. No amount of goodwill or good behavior changed their minds. So, Jack fought. For survival. But he was finding fewer and fewer reasons to live.

And then a song. Someone was humming a song down the hallway. Calm, deliberate, and accompanied by heavy footfalls. Jack swallowed as the closet door opened. He tried to will himself into the back of the closet—if there was one magical power he longed for, it was to disappear.

But he didn't fall through the floor or walls of the closet. Instead, when the door opened, he sat facing a man who smiled at him. Broad shoulders, brown hair speckled with silver. A pair of light green eyes assessed him. The man continued to hum as he gathered Jack's clothes from the closet and stuffed them into a large carpet bag. He wore dark clothing and a long, expensive overcoat. A black hat with a gold lion and sword told Jack he was probably wealthy. A gentleman? The man eventually finished packing and held out a hand to him.

"Shall we?"

"Where would we be going, sir?" Jack remained in his corner like a scolded dog.

"And they said you didn't have manners." The man tsked. His graying stubble creased when he smiled. "I'm going to give you an opportunity. You have natural talent, but without guidance, I'm afraid you'll spend most of your life in a prison."

Jack took his hand, and from that night on, Alaric became his guardian, his mentor. Never a father, because Jack had already had a father. And in Alaric's words, he needed a purpose now, not a family.

Jack shook his head as the memory faded. It had to be another trick. How could Franziska know Alaric's song? It was as if he had no control over his will. The power this close to the Stryga was stronger than when they'd camped in the swamp.

"Are you going to stay out there all night, or do I have to drag you in?" The Stryga's airy voice called out to him.

The front door opened. Franziska, most of her youth restored with gleaming golden skin, leaned against the wooden frame. A few dark scars crossed her left cheek and right forearm. Her hair flowed in intricate braids, shimmering gold, and long waves of raven hues. The firelight behind her lit her white dress so that he could see almost every part of her.

"That was a naughty spell you used. I underestimated you." Franziska's laugh was like porcelain breaking.

Jack tightened his grip on Kya and stepped forward. His senses tingled, but there were no other wards. Just them.

He understood now what made her different than any other Stryga he'd tracked before. She was part siren.

Chapter Thirty-One

Dragons haven't been sighted for nearly fifty years. Partial skeletons have been found in the Corvea and Aura Mountains. I tracked a large lizard-like beast for a month only to discover it was an abnormally large wyvern. I am rather glad we don't have dragon issues to sort out—the amount they eat and then the waste they produce is something most people forget in their awe of the flying, fire-breathing serpents.
~ Scryptus, the Scriver Archives,
as recounted by Scriver #5 Jack Serpent, Tome 17

Jack stepped into the hut with every muscle tensed, waiting for a surprise. Her song floated on the air. He tapped a rune on his left forearm, it pulsed green, and the song shut off. Blocked. Who knew his time being held captive by a siren for months would pay off? That was a tale he'd written down, and the scribes that organized his information had gotten months of laughter and grimaces from it. Jack briefly thought about Scryptus, the monk in charge of the Book of Ryquera, and how he'd never let Jack forget he'd been captured by a school of fish.

Grimarr must have known there was something unusual about this High Stryga. He knew Jack had had experience with sirens. Jack had learned more in those months than anyone had in years and somehow come out alive. He didn't let thoughts of those months get in—those two months were the strangest he'd encountered. Perhaps Grim had suspected she was a hybrid, but what sort of mix, he couldn't answer. Jack recalled their previous conversation, when Grim had alluded to new monsters emerging from the dark.

They were breeding hybrids now? Jack's skin tingled. This changed everything he'd thought he could use against her. The Stryga bottle in his jacket might only piss her off. Kyadem might do more damage at this rate. Jack tapped two more runes on his forearms: protection and speed.

The cabin consisted of an open kitchen area with a large hearth and several back rooms with shut doors. Bookshelves filled with tomes and jars of body parts lined the left wall. Earthy wood, smoke, and citrus did not mask the sulfurous, decaying smell of black magic. Kyadem thrummed in his hands like a growling dog. He let the blades swing free. Franziska held up a hand and frowned.

"I see you've figured out my secret," she said.

Jack started to shift the weapon. "I don't want a history on how you were mutated or damaged," he said, and the air crackled with magic.

"No, I don't suppose a sad story about a girl who was abused and mutilated to become a symbol for those too weak to do it themselves would interest you," Franziska said with a forlorn smile. "A siren Stryga is immune to so much. I know how you lot love to study and record. I almost want to leave you alive enough to transcribe my story. You'd make a beautiful addition to my dungeon while we record my history, and we have more in common than you'd like."

She winked, and Jack ground his teeth. She was correct; sirens were notorious for being immune to most types of magic. They had their own magic that not even Malecanta usually touched. It behaved differently. Sirens were also rare. Jack couldn't imagine how they'd merged siren magic with Stryga magic. His curiosity must have shown on his face. He couldn't help it.

"They ripped out my vocal cords over and over. They bound magic to me, and every time it killed me, they were able to bring me back, until I could learn to control it," she said in a low tone. The hum washed over him, almost freezing him in place for a moment, the siren song like a mist in the air.

"Who's they?" Jack hated that she was baiting him, but he had to admit the more he knew the better he could fight.

"The High Council and Volg directors. They wanted a bloodhound to find Malecanta magic, but what they created was a lure. Any sorcerers and sorceresses left will come to me; they will be bound to me and give up their secrets," she said, and her eyes flickered cerulean. For a moment, Jack thought he heard the wash of waves and an echoing song.

"You won't overpower the Malecanta. This is a foolish plan. Are you ready to die for them?" Jack fixed her with a stare. "Haven't they taken enough from you?" The barb was hollow, but he would first try to appeal to the emotion she was showing.

Franziska wiped a tear from her cheek. He wasn't sure if it was for show, or if she was truly in pain.

"I will become the first queen to rule the five continents. I will unite them, and we will begin the era that the Malecanta were too scared to start. The age of combined, unified magic. Every monster will get a chance to live freely, no longer hunted and hated by humans and the damned Milytor."

"This *is* an age of magic. It's just not evenly dispersed. You can't change that," Jack said, and Kyadem warmed in his palms. The weapon's thrum overpowered the siren's.

"I know you must try to kill me. But I am not without a backup plan."

Franziska waved a hand, and the first door vanished like a mirage. In its place was a young woman bound in chains and kneeling in a pentagram on the floor, a cloth tied around her mouth. She appeared otherwise unharmed. In fact, it looked as if she'd bathed and been dressed in new clothing—a fitted cobalt dress with a gold belt, long sleeves, and a deep-V neckline.

Aylla.

Jack hoped he covered his surprise as he glanced at the Stryga. She watched the girl with delighted eyes, then turned to him.

"I believe you know this young lady?" Franziska smiled and tossed her long, braided locks over her shoulder. "I believe I could have lured her back even without a spellsong."

Aylla glared fiercely. Her anger was not at him but at being caught, or so he assumed by the looks she shot the High Stryga. Her wrists were red from where the chains chafed. Clearly, she was distraught at not having been able to resist the Stryga's lure. Jack prepared for what he had to do to her.

"She was dragged into Narim's path as a toy, that's all," he said dismissively.

Aylla's gaze bore into his. Jack glanced at her but knew she only saw a cold exterior—harder than the first face he'd shown her when they met.

"Has the infamous Scriver, the Razer of Ravenhell, found a lover?" the siren Stryga asked.

Jack scowled at her. Franziska waved a finger, and Aylla's gag disappeared. She coughed and licked at dry lips.

"Don't let her use me against you," she said and coughed again.

How long had it been since she'd had water? Why did the thought bother him so much?

He ignored Aylla and started to swing Kyadem; the deadly weapon would devastate anyone in a five- to twelve-foot radius. And that was the problem. He couldn't take Aylla's head along with the Stryga's.

Franziska arched a brow at him. "I've heard rumors you didn't have any misgivings about collateral damage. Let's find out."

Jack slowed the swing; it was apparent the Stryga was ready to die with Aylla. He'd been banking on her own desire for self-preservation.

"You've overestimated my attachment and guessed wrong," Jack said. He couldn't look at Aylla, or his resolve would break.

"Well, it was worth a try. I can entertain myself with her then," Franziska said. She laughed and waved her hand at Aylla.

She slammed a spell into Aylla, and it reverberated in the hut.

Jack forced his face to remain neutral as Aylla writhed in pain. Tears streaked down her cheeks, and her eyes avoided his. She sank lower, her chest heaving in. *It's just pain, it's temporary,* he willed her.

"Torturing innocents does nothing to get revenge on me." Jack ground out each word to keep her talking while he weighed options. No spell would get Aylla out of the hut safely before the Stryga killed them both. Kya was fast, but magic was faster.

"It makes me feel better. Thirteen of my sisters died at your hands. I believe it took them days to perish while you experimented on them," she said with a sneer. "And then recorded their secrets."

Jack didn't deny it. Although, "experimented" was a stretch. "I prefer interrogated."

Franziska smiled. Her smooth skin glowed in the firelight. Dark waves of hair floated around her waist in an invisible wind. She put a finger to her plump, crimson lips. She didn't have to say the obvious—the Strygan had probably promised her something incredible for her sacrifice. Jack didn't care what it was, since he was going to kill her.

"I told them not killing you the instant they found out they'd missed the child was a mistake. They've since learned to respect my opinion."

Jack didn't blink.

"You think there's a war coming, but we are bringing a new peace."

He pursed his lips. "Cursing an entire lineage and using babies to fuel your magic? Good start."

She tilted her head. "Sacrifices for the future."

It was what separated Strygan and sorceresses: one stole magic, and the other was born with it. The Malecanta had never resorted to stealing and murdering children. Or at least precious few had. Some that sided with the Strygan certainly were guilty of dark crimes.

"The Malecanta are gone. No one will answer your siren song," Jack pointed out instead. He'd met a few that still lived, but he swore he'd go to his grave before he revealed them. And he was starting to suspect what was off about Aylla had everything to do with why the Stryga wanted her and why his magic was drawn to her.

"More lies." Franziska blew him a kiss and tossed her hair over her shoulder.

Jack paused. If she was right and the Malecanta were still in existence, where had they been hiding? Why were they still hiding with the Strygan on the rise?

"You won't mind if I take the edge off—I'm so excited. I never have unwanted visitors, and the cabin is just a mess."

Franziska flounced around like a giddy housewife getting ready for guests. Plates flew back into a cabinet, shoes moved, a broom started to sweep, and her clock chimed midnight. In between her spells, she took up an iron from the hearth and poked Aylla with it.

Aylla's flesh sizzled, and she screamed as the poker pierced her right forearm, then her left thigh.

"Scars give you character, love," the siren Stryga sang, and Aylla's body convulsed with the compulsion. She couldn't move, but she could still scream.

Jack's patience snapped, and he swung Kyadem. The blades arced gracefully toward Franziska. She flicked her wrist, and the weapon was seized in the air, just as it nicked her arm. Kya thrummed angrily as the Stryga's magic flung it to the ground. Jack flipped the weapon back to him and dropped to a roll. A spell shot over his head. How fortuitous. He slid the blade with her blood on it down the side of the Stryga bottle to activate it. He didn't have time to throw it before he had to dodge another spell that nearly took his head off. Reaching into his left boot, he plucked out the knife and ran behind a table, throwing it on its side.

Black magic suffocated him in the small space, and Jack's nose wrinkled. He picked up a cast iron pan to use as a shield. He breathed on his runed finger and drew a protection symbol on the pan. Breath was often more than a fair exchange for protection magic for a human. What was more precious than air? Spells bounced off the hard metal as he ducked into different positions around the hut. Franziska waved her arms like she was conducting an orchestra, and the entire space became a warzone.

Knives flew at his head, and he deflected them with his armored forearm. The injured arm protested fiercely, but Jack ignored the pain. Embers from the fire leaped from the hearth and scalded his pants. He hopped over the coals and patted out the tiny fires on his legs.

"Herisan," he said, and ropes materialized, shot toward her, and wrapped around her limbs. The Stryga cursed.

"Incine." Jack ran to Kya as it burst into white fire. He picked it up and whirled it in a fiery tornado. Chains enforced the ropes that bound Franziska, and she tripped on a broken plate. She toppled over, her skirts flaring.

She glared at him with yellow eyes as her hair started to smoke. Black tendrils of magic leeched from her head and burned through the ropes. Kyadem's chains held, but within a few seconds, the links started to split apart. The chains shivered. Jack threw the Stryga bottle at her feet, and it exploded.

Franziska screamed. She contorted and writhed as gray smoke wrapped around her from the bottle's magic. She choked, and for a moment Jack wondered if the bottle had done its job. Then, in a flash of white light, the smoke vanished. Franziska stood with burns on her arms and neck, but she was very much alive.

Pain exploded in Jack's skull.

It was unlike anything he'd experienced before. A blinding ache numbed his entire body. His legs folded against his will, and the knife clattered to the floor. Another flash of white and he was staring up at the ceiling of the hut, the thick brush thatching interwoven in tight patterns.

Drannit, that worked in Reggate. Jack had hoped it would weaken the Stryga part of her so that he could fight the siren part. Apparently, he'd have to fight both at the same time.

A slow chuckle crested like a rogue wave in his ear. His body dragged and then levitated onto a table, where cold metal encased his wrists and ankles. Jack blinked and cleared his mind.

Push the spells out of you—you shouldn't need a sacrifice for each one, you're beyond that, Alaric's voice urged.

Some talented people practiced so much that they didn't always have to sacrifice something like blood, hair, or breath. He had always been drawn to magic or vice versa and never questioned why it came so easily.

Jack blocked and purged her spells, but others poured in so fast it made his head spin. It felt like fighting bog monsters that kept coming out of the muck.

The table flipped up so that he was upright. His arms protested as they snagged in the chains. Aylla sat in the pentagram with blood running from her wounds and angry tears in her eyes. The hut was a mess of debris. Franziska stood with her hair like black shadows, roiling with power. The ancient magic of the sea and the darkness of demons leeched from her. Kyadem lay in pieces at her feet. *Dean won't be happy,* Jack thought, and it grounded his pain, took the focus off it.

Franziska's eyes lit up yellow and her hands crackled with pale light. She raised a finger, and her pointer nail turned into a long talon. She strode towards him with the predatory pace of a feline.

"Your mentor was right about you ... you are unique. Alaric chose you for a reason, and now I realize what it is. I need something in your head," she said, and ripped his armored jacket down the middle. The black shirt split open, and his bare chest heaved as he fought through the pain.

You've gotten through worse. Breathe. She's giving you extra minutes—use them.

Jack shook his head and bared his teeth. White-hot pain clawed down his sides and fogged his brain. He forced spell after spell, trying all of them to protect his skin from her touch. The High Stryga's finger quivered as she tried to breach the invisible barrier. Her hand lay hot on his cheek, then his shoulder, then his chest. Jack's muscles tremored. His chest swelled, and the muscles ached with effort as the protective rune barriers were breached.

The High Stryga peered closely at his tattoos and ran a light nail over them. She dug in harder when she crossed the tattoo that barred her from his mind, the rune that sat on his left side. With a smile, she drove her talon into his skin and dragged it down. Jack bit back a scream as the rune was damaged. He jerked in the restraints, but they held. He swallowed hard against the acrid taste of vomit.

"You could be a great asset to us, and in fact, my matron wants me to bring you to her alive," Franziska said. "I don't know if I have that kind of restraint. You don't know how special you are, and that just makes me hate you even more. Wasted talent. Alaric turned you from your true path. He was one of us, you know—or as much as warlocks can be part of us."

Jack reeled. Narim hadn't been lying then—Alaric *had* been a warlock. Had he chosen Jack for a reason beyond that he felt sorry for an orphaned boy? Had he given the Strygan information?

"You all think you know what happened during the Covering. It's believed that warlocks hate Strygan almost as much as your kind and Dolfar elves. But in truth, a secret alliance was formed years ago." Franziska licked her upturned lips, and sharp canines flashed at him. "Let's see what Alaric hid inside your head."

Heat like a scorching sun washed over Jack. Jack blinked blood from his eyes, and his sweat stung the cuts on his face.

"What?" he asked hoarsely.

"I'm very interested in what was so important that he gave up his life to use such deep magic. Why are you so important?"

Jack had no clue what she was speaking of. Alaric was clearly involved in a lot more than he'd ever let on. Was he simply an orphan who had been trainable?

No. Alaric's voice was faint, as if he had to fight to get through.

Franziska pressed against him, her lips inches from his. One hand caressed his cheek and the other gutted his side to break another rune. Jack couldn't muffle the cry of pain as the tattoo shattered. His head slammed against the hard wooden table as his body convulsed.

"I've had ..." Jack gasped as her claw dug into another rune and stole his breath.

Don't do it, Jack, Alaric's voice warned in his head. *Don't provoke her. Find her weakness first.*

Jack grimaced and shook his head to clear it. Perhaps this was why he'd survived so long—he had nothing to lose.

"Nymphs bite harder than that," he said, voice cracking, but the words shot out.

Franziska frowned and traced a gentle finger over his cheek and down his throat. Sweat beaded on his skin. Her breasts pressed against his chest as she leaned over him. There was a blessed minute of relief, and Jack used it to just breathe. The tickle of her hair was like ensnaring seaweed, smelling of salt and sulfur. Then she chuckled lightly, licked his neck, and stabbed his side with her clawed finger. He tried to headbutt her, but the agony only allowed his muscles to spasm while he remained conscious.

The runes tried to reform the spell wards, but she repeatedly tore through them until they wore out. Her power shattered over him like battering rams until his skin felt raw and his muscles couldn't hold him up anymore. He sagged against the chains, and his vision blurred.

She hummed softly as Jack's eyes closed. It was as if she needed an audience worthy of her talents.

"I do wish we had time for leisure," she murmured. "But time is not on our side, Scriver. Don't you want to know the truth before you die?"

"Truth is often ... twisted. You just want someone to share your pain." Jack panted. "We don't come from the same darkness."

He lurched and fought against the torture in his limbs, side, and head. But it was the lie that hurt him the most. A secret alliance? Alaric had never mentioned this history. Jack had thought his mentor shared every pertinent detail, but it seemed the man had kept more than a closet full of secrets. Had he died for them? Had Alaric truly sacrificed himself against a coven of Strygan and warlocks for Jack's benefit? Or had that been all a ruse?

Alaric's face popped into his head with an apologetic expression. Franziska grabbed hold of that image and used it to break further into his mind. Jack contorted with the effort to fight her off. Whatever Alaric had hidden there, he would be the first to discover it. His eyes snapped open, and he spat blood at her.

Franziska snarled.

"You could live among a new order—or die among cowards." Franziska wiped her face. The bloody fingers of her right hand ran down his lips and over his abdomen. Her nails stopped just under his pant line. Trails of fire scorched his thighs.

"Fuck off," Jack rasped.

"Alaric knew your parents would be killed. He never told that coven about their son because he wanted you for himself. He disrupted Lyra's spell so she'd go mad. He didn't want her messing up the plan he had for you. He's shaped your whole life, and you don't even know it," she whispered darkly. Her words dripped poison as they seethed through his psyche.

Jack's mind reeled. He'd always been told the Strygan rituals were not targeted, that his parents were simply in the wrong place at the wrong time. By Alaric. She was lying. There was no way Alaric had sabotaged a child and ripped his family away. There was no way Alaric would let him be sold into the mines for years.

Would he? What for? The Stryga's words came back to him ... why was he so different?

"Your lust for vengeance worked to his advantage. I don't think even he realized what you'd become." Franziska grinned and licked her finger. "There *is* something off about you."

Jack spat a spell at her and thought he felt the chains slacken slightly. Silently, he kept pushing blasting spells at their hinges. No matter how he felt about Alaric at the moment, he'd use everything the man had taught him. Alaric had constantly forced him to try silent spells, an art that few could master. At the time, Jack had been proud of the acquired skill. Now, he realized perhaps he'd only been successful because Alaric was a warlock—he would have known how to do it properly.

His muscles screamed as they were stretched to the limit.

"I am many things, Jack Serpent, but I am not a liar. See for yourself," she said, and thrust a wave of magic at him. The use of his name empowered it.

Jack gulped as he flew into her memory. Her mind filled his like a venomous gas.

Six Strygan stood in a circle outside his home. Four half-elves that served them stood behind, heads bowed, hoods lowered to reveal their pointed ears. The Strygan wore red robes, also with hoods, and their white hands stretched out like those of hungry ghosts. Octagrams and runes burned into the grass. The huge oak tree he'd climbed several times a day was now decorated by several hanging bodies. Goblins strung them up like bags of flour.

Six warlocks assisted them. Jack gasped. *Alaric stood in black robes with a grim face, youthful and covered in a light stubble. He must have been thirty years younger in her memory. Alaric stopped a goblin who was struggling under the weight of Jack's father.*

"Are all the Serpents here?" Alaric asked.

The goblin shrugged and threw a rope around his father's neck, then flung the rope over a branch. "You said it was just these two—are there more?"

"No." Alaric was silent for a beat. "And after this, we're done with Orcys shyf." He turned to a tall, broad-shouldered warlock on his left. His face was shadowed by a hood, but his bearing was that of a leader.

The warlock nodded. "They will release two of our own and the two female infants."

Alaric inclined his head.

Jack swore and attempted to fling himself out of the Stryga's mind, but she kept him firmly in place. He had no choice but to relive the night.

His mother's mangled body followed his father's. The Strygan whispered incantations, and the bodies danced as if they were alive. Their skin split open, bones cracked, organs unwound. Alaric turned his dark eyes to his house but didn't mention there being a third, a child. He chanted with his brethren but kept glancing at the house.

Jack recalled escaping, wandering in the forest for days with a wild mind, hunger and thirst depriving him of rational thought. Alaric must not have expected him to escape the warded closet.

"He wasn't ever one of you," Jack said as pain stabbed him all over like needles. He had always thought he'd been a coward, but now he realized his parents had known what was coming. They'd spelled a closet to conceal him.

Franziska plunged them back to the present.

"He was a traitor to everyone, even his warlock brethren. He never told any of us there was a child. And thus, our power harvest wasn't quite as fruitful. The warlocks attacked our enclave that night, but they cannot wipe us out. Alaric was a powerful warlock. He was also manipulative—and even more so to you, handsome."

How had he gotten out, then? Jack only recalled feeling a tingling all over his skin as panic overtook his senses.

"You can siphon magic, reap it, can't you? Hold it. I feel it now when I'm so close," she murmured. "I've never met a human who can hold such power without dire consequences. He wanted to use you."

Jack couldn't feel the fingers on his right hand. The blasting spells resumed now that he was out of the Stryga's mind. Jack concentrated on his breath and cleared his own mind. Perhaps Alaric had chosen him for this unknown gift, so he'd use it to his advantage. Jack had always assumed it was the training that allowed him to wield magic more easily than most men. He didn't have time to figure out what was different about him.

"And your sweet Lyra ... just when you thought you'd found happiness, it's taken away like melting snow in the sun."

She leaned in closer again, and a sweet, heady aroma of nightshade and burnt sugar enveloped him.

"Alaric cursed her." Franziska giggled, and her plush red lips brushed his ear. "He made sure she would never return to you."

Jack stilled, though his chest heaved. For a moment, all pain was forgotten. There was one reason he didn't think Alaric had betrayed him so fully ... but it was starting to unravel.

"He wouldn't do that. He died protecting me," Jack said in a hoarse voice. He closed his eyes, and Alaric's pale face pleaded with him to go. He'd saved Jack from a surprise attack by a band of Strygan who'd sought revenge after Ravenhell, and three warlocks who did not agree with his decision to help Grimarr and leave the brethren. Their attacks were not coordinated, but they'd happened to land on the same night. Perhaps Alaric's guilt had finally caught up with him and that was the only reason Jack was alive now. Or perhaps Jack was a pawn in a game he didn't know the rules for.

"Grimarr Fox thought he understood Alaric's plight and offered him sanctuary and a new start." Franziska scoffed and kicked a pot. Sparks flew from the hearth.

"The Milytor have killed your kind for centuries," Jack said with a sneer. He should have been focused on tricking Franziska to escape or kill her, but his mind was stuck on his mentor. All the training with Alaric, and he'd never bothered to mention he knew Jack's parents or that he'd hidden something inside his head. When had he done that?

"I suppose the Milytor have their purpose—we shall use them as our war dogs until they're all dead."

Jack swallowed.

"I have not mastered resurrection, but here's my gift to you." Franziska took a deep breath and hummed Alaric's song. She took a lock of hair from her pocket that looked suspiciously like Alaric's shade of brown. She held it and chanted; the hair glowed, and magic blossomed around it.

Jack's eyes widened as Alaric's ghost appeared. He wore the clothes he'd died in: black armor and a light gray overcoat. His skin was pale, and he wasn't quite solid. Alaric glanced around and then rested his eyes on Jack. The older man's shoulders sagged, and he stepped forward with wide hands.

"Jack," he whispered.

The sorrow and regret in Alaric's eyes was all the proof Jack needed.

His lips twisted into a snarl, and Alaric fell to his knees. Alaric never apologized, never made excuses for himself. The shame on his face cut Jack worse than a Manticore's claw. The damn Stryga spoke the truth. For one terrifying moment, all Jack's resolve to live left him.

Alone, cold, no way out—and his entire past was a lie.

A warm hand lifting him up. A kind voice that eventually began to take the place of his own father's.

Choking panic when he was locked in any sort of room alone.
Alaric telling him it was counterconditioning.
Jack lost inside his head, in the dark.

"You bastard." Aylla's voice interrupted his spiral. Something icy licked at the air and prickled his bare skin. Her voice brought him out of the haze of rage and betrayal that had no depth.

Jack opened his eyes at her fierce whisper. His gaze found hers. She had stood up with a defiant glare aimed at Alaric and the Stryga. Something tightened in his gut. He'd never had much reason to live, but maybe he didn't want to die yet.

"Why would you do that to him?" she spat, and Alaric turned to her with a sad smile. Then he looked at Jack again, with such understanding that it hurt. Here was another girl, another Lyra, and Jack was going to get her killed. No, Alaric was going to get her killed. And for one stupid second, he let himself entertain the thought that she cared that much despite the situation.

"So that she didn't end up as you are now," Alaric said. "It was the only way I could protect them both. I did not curse Lyra out of spite or some grand plan—it backfired on me. It was supposed to be a protection charm."

"Shyf and fuckery." Aylla strained against the chains, and they rattled.

Jack's thoughts echoed her sentiment. It might have started out as a protection spell, but he'd bet Alaric knew what would happen should it go wrong. He'd driven Lyra from their lives like a plague that needed to be quarantined. All so Jack would focus on the Scriver Trials.

Franziska smiled as if she were watching a delightful play. Alaric walked closer to him, and Jack couldn't have moved even if he'd wanted to.

"I don't have time to explain," he said in a near whisper. "I did what I did for a reason. I'd apologize, but it wouldn't come close to making it right. You're stronger and more gifted than I ever imagined you would be. People need Scrivers to give light to the dark. Elgar needs you. Despite what you may think I did want to save lives. I wanted you to help discover mysteries that would prevent loss of life."

Jack had a hundred questions he wanted to shoot at him. Why had he left the warlocks? How did he *really* know Grimarr? How was he supposed to get them out of this now? Jack was fairly confident at planning on the fly, but his entire mental state was caterwauling in a freefall. Alaric was right; he'd never been good at silent spells. Some people gave up bits of soul for magic, but Jack had never paid that price. There were always other ways. Alaric put a hand on his shoulder; it was more of a cold spot than an actual hand. He leaned in as if to hug him.

"You are the Razer, my Scriver, whether you chose it or not. Your destiny is greater than you want to see. But you must choose it." Alaric's light green eyes drilled into his, and Jack channeled his rage into the situation. His mentor's bold words did nothing to sway him. "You have the ability to hold and harness more magic than any human I've met. Use it."

"If you weren't dead already, I'd kill you," Jack said, his fists clenched, jaw tight with tension. Anger radiated like waves of heat off him.

Franziska clapped her hands. "What a charming end to a long tale." She raised her hands, and Alaric's face crumpled in pain as he disappeared.

Jack looked at Aylla, and she swallowed. His chest constricted. He leveled the Stryga with a glower.

"You like to play with your food too much," Jack said.

His mouth turned down in a frown. His concentration slowed time—he sensed the drip of sweat down his cheek, Aylla's shallow breathing, the smell of old wood and mold, the acrid tang of black magic. He blasted the chains one more time with a mental spell. They shattered.

He rolled off the table and onto the floor to land in a crouch. He had energy for one last spell, and it might weaken her enough for him to kill her. He'd never used it on a siren, but perhaps the Stryga half would be destroyed. Jack offered the blood that already stained his side for the sacrifice and some of his breath to use the magic for his next spell; Alaric was right, Jack could harness all the magic hanging in the air like ripe fruit. He'd never paid it much attention, but the Stryga and most any practitioner left traces of power like spiderwebs. Jack gathered them to himself, and they came like gossamer threads, settling on his skin and simmering with power.

He'd only used this once before, and it was with Alaric's help. Yet the exchange was accepted, and the Stryga's own magic became his. "*Excindano.*"

The destroyer spell detonated in a flood of rippling blue light that cracked two of his ribs and sent him flying against the wall. Franziska gaped for a moment before a high, keening shriek exploded from her. She started to burn as the spell encased her and immobilized her magic. Blue flames ignited her dress and hair. He knelt on one knee, trying to breathe. Every fiber ached from fatigue, and he struggled to remain conscious.

He crawled toward Aylla just as the front door blasted open. A jet of red light stopped Franziska's burning, and her half-melted body sagged to the floor. Jack twisted around.

Narim stood in the frame of the door with two black Orcyshounds flanking him. Their upright ears pricked forward, and their mouths panted, showing long fangs.

Chapter Thirty-Two

Imprisonment in Barassus is a death sentence. Unless you're already insane, then your life expectancy extends a few more years.
~ Scryptus, the Scriver Archives,
as recounted by Scriver #5 Jack Serpent, Tome 8

Aylla tugged on her chains. Her heart was so heavy for Jack. The last person she'd expected to save them was Narim. Or was he more of an interruption than a savior? The black hounds at his side looked neither alive nor friendly. Muscle flexed under coats flecked with fiery gold, yellow eyes glanced in every corner, and Aylla had no doubt that they could tear everyone in the cabin apart in an instant.

"Narim!" she shouted. He didn't deserve the title captain. He hardly looked scathed at all, just a few flecks of mud on his boots. Where had he been? Was he connected to Franziska? The High Stryga lay on the floor in a half-burned state. Her chest moved shallowly, and her eyes tracked both men, but she seemed unable to do magic. From the conversation, Aylla had gathered that this was no ordinary High Stryga, but some sort of hybrid. Had Jack managed to kill at least one side of her?

Despite Jack's cold words earlier, he was trying very hard to get to her. Aylla told herself he'd been lying, but a small part of her wondered if it was truth. Truth in lies was far easier to get someone else to believe.

Her skin prickled at all the magic that hung in the air like a toxic gas.

Jack grabbed an iron poker from the hearth near her and slammed it in between the links. He jerked hard, and the chains snapped. His bloodied shirt hung in tatters around his broad shoulders, and rune tattoos left black scars along his chest.

"Do you know where the key is?" he asked, his voice hoarse.

Aylla nodded—she'd seen the Stryga put it in a jar on the mantel.

Narim stepped into the hut and surveyed the damage.

"You've only finished half the job, Serpent," he said with a grunt. He drew a small rune and muttered a spell word that encased the Stryga in a clear, liquid substance that lifted her off the floor. She hung suspended in the air. Her eyes frantically moved back and forth, and her mouth tried to form words, but her seared lips didn't allow it.

"Burn her, then." Jack struggled to stand.

Narim shook his head. "And let you have the win? I'd rather not. I get to prove to Grimarr we don't need Scrivers in our ranks. I bring in this mutated piece of bog shyf and the king will give me Asnor." He chuckled. "I never thought of mixing magics like this—she's a right horrendous sight."

"Grimarr doesn't even trust you to wipe your own ass," Jack said with a raspy laugh.

Aylla retrieved the key from the jar on the mantel as she kept an eye on Narim. He didn't seem to care where she was. The chain cuffs clinked open, and she set them down, keeping one in her hand to use as a weapon. Narim advanced on Jack with menace. Jack half blocked a gut punch and staggered into a wall. He rallied to a stand, blood dripping from his lips.

"You drew the hounds and Bogles away as a ruse." Jack shook his head and spat blood. "Couldn't handle one Stryga because you need someone to do your work for you—maybe you're even working with the Strygan. You'll lie to everyone, and even if they don't swallow it all, they'll be dead before they realize it's poison."

The two Orcyshounds growled and bared their teeth. Narim fixed him with a dismissive sneer. "It's better to know which side of history you should be on than to die ingloriously. My name will be remembered for eternity as the founder of a new world order. How could you possibly think I'd side with the Strygan? Do you think I'd let my father's death go unavenged? I am using them. I will bring new information to the Milytor, and we will find the Malecanta magic before they do—we will rule a united five continents. I shall be the general Asnor needs."

The Stryga screamed, and Narim inclined his head toward her. "I see I'm the only one who has not failed. I brought you the Scriver. Didn't find what the coven wanted, did you? I told you, his head is as empty as his legend."

The siren Stryga's eyes narrowed and flared cerulean.

Aylla looked at Jack. His expression didn't change except for a tightening around his mouth.

"You're just an iron cog in a rusting wheel. Grim's time is up—it's time this continent understood true power like old times. You've played a good hand, and I was hopeful I could persuade you at some point to see my point of view." Narim smiled. He stepped closer to Jack, whispering in his ear, one hand gently cupping his cheek. He wiped away rivulets of blood and sweat in an oddly tender gesture that Aylla found highly discordant. What was his play? Was all that hate just a cover for something deeper?

Jack shoved him back with a grunt. Narim glanced at Aylla, and she froze.

She didn't have a plan beyond survival. She had no weapons, no way of outrunning those black hounds, and no way to help Jack.

"I haven't forgotten you, sweetheart. I'm not surprised you survived with him watching your back. I'm afraid we didn't get to spend as much time together as I wanted."

Aylla grimaced. Narim swept a finger at her, and the black hound barked viciously. Saliva dripped from his mouth, and his claws scrabbled on the wooden floor, leaving marks, in his rush to get to her.

"She's what they wanted from me—don't kill her yet," Jack said and kicked at the hound. The dog yipped and turned on him as Jack's boot connected with his muzzle.

Narim snapped his fingers, and the hound halted with a growl. "What?" He looked her up and down as if she were a horse at market.

Aylla wasn't sure if Jack was lying or not. The look on his face was calm, calculated. Did he truly know something that would save them both? She wasn't going to let him save her and not himself. From what she knew, there *was* something in Jack they wanted, and it wasn't her.

"She's Malecanta," Jack said with a pained look. "Sorceress blood flows in her veins. You kill her and you'll lose your leverage, your path to gain glory. Everyone will want her talents."

"Dranakar shyf. You can't know that. She's nothing; look at her," Narim said, pointing. Aylla recoiled as if he'd slapped her.

It was a good bluff, though. Aylla was sure Jack was playing on Narim's doubt—he wouldn't kill her yet.

"Alaric hid his sight, a piece of his soul, inside my head. That's what they wanted. His sight. And he's given it to me now—I can see Malecanta magic inside her." Jack sighed.

The siren Stryga's muffled laugh sent chills down Aylla's spine.

Aylla ran her tongue over her cracked lips. She wished she did have some sort of magic she could wield. The bluff wouldn't hold for long.

No, we're both getting out of here.

She took a breath and swung the metal cuffs into Narim's face. The man howled as they caught his right eye, and he staggered to the left. She jumped on him and pounded the cuff into his temple and neck, trying for the carotid artery with the sharp edge of the restraint. Narim's elbow whipped up and caught her under her chin. Aylla's vision went spotty for a second—long enough for a hound to latch on to her leg.

She screamed as the hound tore her left calf. Narim's boot caught her in the abdomen as she tumbled. He cursed at her, blood streaming down his face. Aylla tracked Jack as he moved like a shadow. He had taken the poker and thrust it into the fire. It glowed red as he flung it like a spear into the High Stryga. She screamed, then grinned like a demon. The air leeched energy.

The red-hot poker had impaled her through her heart, and she pulsed with black magic; energy exploded out of her like a bomb.

Aylla flew backward. She grabbed an overturned chair to steady herself. The black hounds whimpered at the blast, and they scrabbled behind Narim. As Jack brushed past her, his hand slid something into her boot.

Jack grabbed a burning log and jammed it under the floating body of the Stryga. The spell Narim had bound her with broke, and she tumbled to the floor. Jack gave Narim a cursory glance before he tapped a rune on his forearm and flames exploded from his palm onto the Stryga. Her magic pulsed in murky waves that resembled crows' wings. A cackle rose into the air that chilled Aylla's bones. It was the sound of someone who'd gotten just what they wanted.

"Combus ipsa mala," Jack whispered.

Narim punched him with a fierce right hook, sending Jack to his hands and knees. The blond soldier threw fist after fist until his knuckles were bloody. Jack crumpled, protecting his head, but he didn't move. Aylla scrambled to her feet. He lay on the ground in a pool of blood, and his forearms limply slid down to reveal a semiconscious face.

She took a step toward Narim, but the hounds blocked her path, their fangs glistening in the firelight. Narim panted, and flecks of saliva speckled his chin. He wiped the mess with his sleeve. Jack's chest moved, but he didn't get up. Aylla barely felt the throbbing in her left leg or the heat rash from the fire on her arm. She only saw him and willed him to fight. Her stomach coiled in vicious knots, and her skin tingled with an itch she couldn't scratch.

I wish your lie was true. If I had any sort of magic, now would be the time. I'm sorry, Jack.

Narim grabbed her arm, and she cried out as his fingers dug into her flesh. He yanked her towards the door. Aylla struggled against him using all the dirty tricks she knew. But he countered her moves, and a fist wound into her hair to drag her head around more easily.

"I'll settle for you." His hand brushed her breasts, and Aylla jerked her elbow back as far as she could. It made a dull thud against his armor. Rage coursed through her as she thought of her mother in the same position. A chill spiraled down her arms.

"You'll get about ten paces before you're shot," Jack said in a hoarse voice.

Narim cocked his head. "By whom?"

"The transmitter I put in your pocket has broadcasted to the Milytor channel. Every soldier with their comms turned on will know you for the traitor you are. Kill an innocent woman with sorceress blood and you'll be tortured for years in Barassus."

Narim ground his teeth and let out a curse. He found the transmitter in his pocket and crushed it under a boot. Aylla struggled to get her arm out of his grip. Narim gave Jack a short salute.

"Then it's a good thing I have a bargaining chip." He paused and motioned to the black hounds. "Dinner time, boys."

Aylla screamed in protest, but her cries were drowned out by the thrilled snarling and scraping of nails as the hounds charged toward Jack. An icy lick of sheer panic and fear blasted from her like the venomous spit of an Orbvi spider. Her spine snapped straight, and her fingers splayed as if she were gripping her weight above a sheet of thin ice. Muscles spasmed, and her entire being seemed to ripple with an exaltation of freedom.

Something came unleashed. A ring of blue light exploded from her, and both of the orcyshounds yelped as they vanished into ash.

Aylla couldn't control her body as she collapsed. Pulses of faint blue light faded like embers. She lay with her eyes locked on Jack's. He winked at her.

He hadn't been lying. She didn't know what had happened, but her body vibrated with a different energy. Yet she couldn't move, even if she'd wanted to.

Narim regarded her as she began to dry heave.

What the Orcystars was that, and why now?

"Well, guess he wasn't lying. I don't know if that's sorceress magic, but we'll find out," Narim said with a thoughtful expression. "Guess it's the old-fashioned way to die."

He thrust Aylla into a chair and stomped over to where Jack struggled to stand. He took out a vial from his breast pocket, fending off Jack's weak attempts to block him. Narim grabbed his hair, twisted his head, and poured the clear liquid carelessly over his lips. Then he gut-punched Jack so his mouth opened in a silent grunt.

"Just takes a drop. Give my regards to Hecaya should you see her," Narim said, and shoved Jack into the wall. The Scriver swallowed and convulsed.

Aylla thrashed as Narim picked her up and carried her out of the hut. It burned like a torch, with purple smoke belching from the roof. Her mind reeled, and her body had no more fight left. She was numb with the fear that she'd saved herself but not Jack and paralyzed with the realization that her mother had kept a secret from her. Uncle Drace had been correct about Lavynia's magic, and it was clear now that he'd tried to get it and failed.

She had to hope Jack had one more fight left. He had to know how to counter whatever poison Narim had given him, right? Her head spun as she tried to gather more of whatever was inside her that she'd never known. It pooled and flowed like water, but she couldn't harness it again for the moment. Aylla refused to let him die ... but the magic did not respond, despite her panic.

Narim's transmitter glowed in the dark. "Tessel, come in. Ready for extraction." They both waited to see if Jack's message had been transmitted yet.

A clear voice responded loud enough for her to hear. "Two minutes out. See the smoke, Uncle Gunner."

Aylla's chest sank. They hadn't heard yet. Perhaps there was a delay, or more likely they were tuned to Narim's personal channel and not the general Milytor.

She had no choice but to let herself be carried into the swamp and up a small hill. The clearing was bathed in moonlight, and a whirring engine whined in the distance. A dark sail of a flyer with the Milytor on it approached. *No more flying*, she thought with a grimace.

Her body started to get feeling back, and her heart rate slowed enough that she could breathe easily again. Narim set her on the ground with a hand on her wrist. She wiggled on her feet, and something jabbed her uninjured calf in her right boot. Aylla recalled that Jack had shoved something in it—it must have been a knife. Her heart clenched.

She had to wait for the right moment; she couldn't waste the chance he'd given her. The flyer drew closer, and a ladder cascaded down. Narim wrapped a rope around her waist and climbed up behind her.

Aylla didn't even try to use her hands to help. She tilted her head at a sudden blaze of white light that rose in the distance like a shard of lightning.

"What …" Narim stopped too as he turned to gaze to the north.

Sparks shot into the air, and flames licked the black sky. Even farther north, another blaze erupted like a volcano. The line of white fires continued for miles until they disappeared. Was it a warning or an awakening of something?

"A beacon, sir—not one of ours. Get up, quickly!" a soldier shouted down to them.

Narim pushed her. She reached into her right boot and plucked the dagger from it. Turning, she struck like a viper, plunging the blade into Narim's shoulder joint. Aylla cursed herself—she'd been aiming for his neck, but her muscles were weak with fatigue. The swaying on the rope ladder hadn't helped.

Still, Narim bellowed. "Fuck Corvynia!" His fist hit her hard in her left calf, and Aylla cried out. She kept her grip on the rung and kicked out with her right leg. Her boot caught him in the face, and she stomped down on his already injured shoulder.

"Sir?"

"What's happening?"

"Pull the damn ladder up!"

Aylla kicked again, and Narim grunted as his grip failed. She heard his intake of breath as he fell from the ladder and into darkness.

"Don't shoot—I'm unarmed and have important information!" she shouted, waiting for the barrage of bullets. "Check your transmitters!"

Hands grabbed her and flung her over the side of the deck. Milytor soldiers trained rifles on her, and she put her hands up. She sat awkwardly since her leg couldn't support her weight anymore.

"What the hell did you do? Assaulting a captain in the Milytor is a death by beheading." A tall, thin agent came forward. His eyes were dark, and his uniform stretched across his broad shoulders. He paused as a voice spoke into his ear, and then he frowned.

All the soldiers froze as someone spoke into their coms.

"Narim is a traitor—he poisoned Jack in the Stryga's hut!" Aylla shouted, not caring who they were listening to. "You *have* to go back and help him. The whole thing is burning up."

The captain regarded her now with less suspicion and more urgency. A muscle above his right eye twitched. He pulled another soldier aside, and they conversed quietly away from the others. Aylla put her hands down, wishing they'd hurry up. Jack could already be dead. However, he was a Scriver, right? She had to believe he had plans upon plans. She had to believe he was too stubborn to die.

The captain approached her with a frown. "I'm Captain Halstead. I'm presuming you're Aylla."

Aylla nodded.

"You are to be escorted to back to Ghoul Base—Grimarr needs a word."

She narrowed her eyes. "And you know Narim is a traitor, right?"

"That has been passed down as classified information, but in so many words, yes." Relief flooded through Aylla and made her bones weak. "A team will go after Jack as well."

Captain Halstead called out orders, and several soldiers climbed down the ship on rope ladders, heading into the swamp. Torches ignited below the flyer as Aylla peered over the side.

A soldier walked up to her with metal-chained cuffs in his hands. He was young, like Bean and Mykel, with sun-streaked hair and smooth skin. She tried not to flinch but couldn't help it. The soldier's brown eyes softened enough that she realized the Milytor was as divided as Jack and Narim had alluded. Perhaps the power structure was shifting.

The soldier held up the restraints. "It's just protocol. We'll get this sorted out."

Aylla let him put the metal cuffs on her. She didn't care as long as they were sending someone after Jack. The metal-barred room at least had cushions on the benches. She took a seat as the soldier tossed some bandages, a canteen of water, and a liquid salve in. "We can get that leg looked at when we arrive."

"Thanks."

Aylla busied herself cleaning the bite wound and dressing it. If her hands were occupied, her mind didn't wander too far into dark territory. If Jack— No, *when* Jack survived, would she see him again? Would he even want to? Slipping a knife to her was just a survival tactic, not a declaration of love.

She snorted. *Well, what would I know about any of that? Love is not a part of this equation at all.* Yet the knife in her boot spoke volumes more than any words he could have uttered to her.

You need to figure out what the blighted Orcys just happened. No one is going to allow you to have this kind of magic and leave you alone now. She bit her lip. Like it or not, she was headed back to a city full of people who either hated magic or loved it.

What were you hiding from me, Mother? Aylla was certain she had been a sorceress now. The question was why she hadn't told her daughter.

Chapter Thirty-Three

Ardis. Thought to be a mineral but has so many magical abilities it's hard to say what it is exactly. Extremely rare. Appears pearlescent in the light. Malecanta used it to enhance their powers (a well-kept secret until one of their own betrayed them). Ardis could change the balance of magic if larger sources were found.
~ Scryptus, the Scriver Archives,
as recounted by Scriver #5 Jack Serpent, Tome 12

The Stryga hadn't interrupted all his wards—Jack's immunity to poisons was both a result of runes and years of his mentor injecting or exposing him to every known toxin.

And he hadn't been lying to Aylla when he said he saw her magic. It was like the shimmer of new snow around her, lighting her features and changing the energy.

Alaric had let him see what he'd hidden—the gift of sight. A trait that few warlocks possessed. Jack hadn't wanted to accept, but the old warlock had said it could save Aylla's life. Going with Narim was better than dying in a fiery hut. Maybe he'd saved her life, or maybe she was doomed to be like Franziska: hunted, experimented on, studied, turned into a beacon for something else. The power of Aylla's magic killing the Orcyshounds still shimmered in the air like fairy dust. It was as different from the Stryga's magic as a volcanic mountain was to an ocean sunset.

She was a Drannit-cursed sorceress. That changed quite a lot.

Jack clamped a hand to his gushing side as the poison thrummed through him. Strynine, if he was correct. It had tasted like raw sugar with notes of earthy dirt. Widely used by wives who wanted to get rid of their husbands slowly without detection. The amount Narim had forced into his mouth had been more than enough to kill him.

His stomach lurched from nausea, and his head spun. Jack's sides ached with agony, and the smoke in the hut clogged his lungs. He tried to draw a blood spell that would conjure more healing. His fingers were exhausted, and he settled for crawling through embers as the hut burned. He wouldn't make it much longer, so he resolved to search for arrunroot. Once again, the foreign pull to survive for more than himself surfaced like a breaching whale. It was only because he needed to see the end of the tale, he told himself. Narim couldn't be allowed to kill him like this—not after everything.

Crawling was getting him nowhere. Franziska had to have some arrunroot somewhere. Gathering magic to himself was useless now since he had no energy to use it. Jack might learn more stamina if he survived, but that was a pretty big "if" at the moment.

"What in the seven underworlds is that?"

Distorted voices came over his transmitter, and Jack used them to ground his spinning head.

"Fire, sir. In the distance!"

"Sir?"

"Narim is a traitor!"

"Girl attacked him with a knife ..."

"He fell ... can't see a thing down there."

"Get to the cabin and find Narim."

Good girl. Jack would have laughed, but it hurt too much.

The voices jumbled together. He smiled faintly, hoping if he didn't make it that Aylla would exact some sort of vengeance. Or maybe she'd forget all about him—it sounded like they were taking her to Grimarr first. The general would definitely have ideas for the first sorceress found in years.

Of all the Drannit-fucking places to die, Jack thought as he hauled himself across the floor. Blood loss made his head dizzy, strynine pulsed inside him like a drum, slowing his heartbeat, and he ached in so many places he'd lost track. Narim's punches had improved since the last time he'd sparred with him years ago in training. All the captain's roiling emotions left Jack drained. At least the goat-fucker had finally decided Jack wasn't worth his time anymore.

He ripped doors open and threw drawers to the floor. Their contents ranged from torture instruments to dried jerky. He jammed his hand on something hard and sharp.

The wooden rocking horse he'd carved lay on the ground. Jack picked it up and sighed. Aylla must have had it with her when she was captured. He pocketed the charred piece of wood and continued his search.

The arrunroot's distinct beet-like, earthy aroma hit his nose, and Jack groped through the smoke to clutch a sprig. He didn't have time to make it into a potion, so he chewed it dry. The plant worked quickly, but not enough to get him to his feet. Jack listed in the corner of the hut and watched it burn. He couldn't conjure a water spell. Flames licked up the walls and ate the thatched roof. He covered his mouth with a sleeve of his torn shirt and breathed as shallowly as he could. Soon it wouldn't matter, because the poison was making his vision fuzzy and the blood slow in his veins.

Could these men take any longer to kick something in? A door, a window?

Jack reached a shaking hand into his pants pocket and plucked out a mangled cigar. His father had liked to keep one in his uniform, saying it felt like carrying home with him. Jack always had one in a pocket somewhere. He didn't remember home too well, but the earthy, woodsy scent was comforting. There was also some arrunroot in it—he liked to be prepared for anything. The wrap had come undone, but it still held its shape reasonably well. He chuckled. He'd burned so many monsters that perhaps it was fitting he should perish the same way.

Guess your secrets die with me, Alaric, Jack thought. For the best, really, as the ability to attract and use another's magic was a secret he wasn't going to be bragging about.

You are meant for far more, Jack. You will not perish here ... you cannot. Along with my sight I give you, I have a piece of my soul in you. You can resurrect me. Alaric's whisper floated to him. Or perhaps it was the whooshing of the flames.

"That's what she was searching for. Your gift and your soul."

The Strygan want to be able to see Malecanta magic like some of us can. They think capturing and creating with enough warlocks will produce offspring more powerful than we've seen in decades. I couldn't let them have me ... either side.

"No loyalty to warlocks, humans, or Strygan. You're a hero," Jack whispered hoarsely, sarcastically. He rested his head against the wall of the hut in exhaustion. He was just another back up plan for Alaric, and the thought burned him more than the poison.

No, Jasyth ...

Jack forced Alaric from his mind with a growled curse.

A blast, and the flames parted as several figures in black armor crashed through the wall. Jack coughed harshly as five Milytor soldiers burst inside. They had their scattershots out and silver knives in hand. Some wore helmets and others held lanterns. Two of them shot water spells at the fire, and it sputtered.

"Over there," one soldier said, and pointed at him. "Give him the antidote."

Jack regarded the soldiers warily as they approached him with caution. He couldn't know which ones were in Narim's pocket, and therefore all Milytor were on his hit list. But he also couldn't do more than roll his eyes at them. His injured right eye threatened to close permanently. And from the sound of it, Aylla had told them he'd been poisoned.

"Thank the Drannit, I need a light," he said.

The soldiers exchanged confused glances.

"Do you know what Narim gave you?"

"Strynine."

Jack's body shuddered. The soldier lifted a vial to his lips and the cooling antidote to strynine slipped down his throat. The effect was not immediate, and Jack expected it would take a few days to fully get the poison out. His heartbeat lifted though, pumping normally again. They helped him up out of the hut into the cooler night air. As he was transported up a ladder to a waiting flyer, he glimpsed fire.

Raging beacon fires on the mountaintops ran farther than he could see. Was this the fire the soldiers had talked about? He figured if these soldiers were in Narim's pocket, he'd have been left for dead. The fact that he was safely on a flyer heading out of the swamp was probably a good indicator that they were on Grimarr's side.

"What's happening?" he asked the nearest soldier. His normal deep rasp sounded more like a dying frog. The effort it took to ask a simple question annoyed him.

"I wish we knew. We'll take you to base and let Grimarr sort this out," the young soldier replied, trying to peer at Jack's wounds in the dim light. "The fires started about twenty minutes ago—no idea what those are about."

Jack sighed and leaned his head back down on the pillow on the stretcher. That was something to deal with later. He tried to think through the possibilities, and how to keep Alaric out of his mind, but his body gave out. Everything went dark.

Chapter Thirty-Four

Advice from a fellow Scriver: Don't make assumptions.
Seems a tad obvious to me but said Scriver fell in love with a woman
who, of course, was not human. Turned out she was an Echo looking for
someone to perform a release ritual. Her spirit form ascended and moved
on. If I may make another obvious observation, don't become attached to
anything—nothing is eternal. Several have argued that with me, but I am
not swayed by any argument thus far.
*Archivers note: for more on Echoes see Scriver #3's journals
~ Scryptus, the Scriver Archives,
as recounted by Scriver #5 Jack Serpent, Tome 6

Rinsed off, dried, and in a set of new clothes, Aylla sat in a holding cell at the Ghoul Base barracks. A medicus had looked at her bite wound, sewed a few sutures in, and told her to keep the bandage clean for a few weeks until they could be removed. She was surprised she wasn't in the royal prison, but she also wasn't sure who Narim paid and who he didn't. She kept her mouth shut.

Ghoul Base. From the little she'd seen of the outside and interior, it operated like any other military force, with low log cabins, tents, a mess hall, training grounds, a stable, and farm plots. A clear stream ran right down the middle. The Milytor soldiers hadn't given her much time to look around, though, as she was hurried into the largest cabin.

She stretched her neck muscles. In her pocket, she'd found Dean's map, the only thing that reminded her it hadn't all been just a nightmare. She'd lost the wooden rocking horse, and the resulting hole in her heart wasn't easy to explain. She'd probably never see Jack or the baby again.

Aylla wasn't sure she should tell them about Dean. She certainly wasn't going to give them the map that led directly to him. She'd have to find him once she was out and make sure the little girl was taken to a good home. Dean might have already done that by now. Or maybe they'd died in the swamp, and she'd never know. She hated herself for being lured away from them.

Why hadn't her magic surfaced until now? Questions flooded her brain until she started to spiral. One thing at a time.

The bare walls were clean and boring, the bench was covered in a thin layer of cushion, and a huge fireplace blazed warmth. The soldier had removed her restraints, at least, but there was no way out. Aylla could feel the wards near the windows as she strayed toward them. The iron bars obscured her view of the sprawling gardens and forests beyond. The normal din of Asnor floated through the windowpanes. People going about their lives as if they had all the time in the world. As if their world wasn't about to change. As if her world hadn't just imploded.

What were Ash and Hugo doing? Had Dean been able to get them back into Churk Forest? Aylla hoped that, if she didn't return, they'd rejoin a pack or go find new territory together. They wouldn't stay around the cabin forever. She'd tried to cast spells again, to feel the Malecanta magic, but nothing came. Perhaps it was just a freak accident when she'd killed those hounds.

Aylla didn't have a good feeling about anything, but she was sure Jack was alive. For whatever reason, she had to believe the soldiers had found him in time to administer an antidote. She couldn't be sure what Narim had given Jack, but surely the Milytor had counters for all kinds of poisons.

The door opened, and she started upright. A tall, aristocratic man in a black Milytor uniform walked inside. His hair was dark but graying, and he held a shiny onyx cane with a silver fox head at the handle. Medals and sigil coins adorned his shoulders and chest. He smiled softly, assessing her.

"Aylla van Hyde, I hope our medical team has treated you well?" he asked in a low timbre.

Aylla nodded. Power radiated from the man like a light. He wasn't terribly large nor bulky with muscle, but she had an inkling that he was a lot stronger than he looked.

"Grimarr Fox?" she asked. "Sir," she added, not sure if the address was even appropriate for a man of his position.

Grimarr nodded a and motioned for her to follow him. He led her through a previously locked door. The room was lavishly decorated with a fire that sparked cheerfully, tea out on a table, and sandwiches piled five high on white plates. Aylla's stomach grumbled as she sat. The room boasted several floor-to-ceiling bookshelves and huge picture windows. Asnor's bustle carried on outside the windows, but it seemed a world away. She wished she were in something finer than the too-loose, blush-colored gown that she assumed had been left behind by another woman. Her own clothes would have made her much more comfortable. She supposed it was better than being in that silken dress the Stryga had put her in.

Grimarr sat and poured her tea with weathered hands. Aylla couldn't stand the silence, and she shifted on the plush seat.

"How much do you know about what happened? Is Jack alive?" she burst out and then bit her lip. The not knowing always bothered her. "And you should know the soldiers that died ... it was Narim's fault." Aylla was fairly certain the general wasn't on Narim's side, but—she cursed herself—she should have waited to see what he knew first. Jack had said he was a good general and old friend, but she didn't want to assume anything.

Grimarr nudged a plate of cookies toward her. "I know it all. Unfortunately. I didn't knowingly send Jack and the team into the swamp to their deaths. I had no way of knowing you'd cross their path, but I'm glad you did."

Aylla couldn't resist—she grabbed two cookies and shoved them in her mouth. The buttery softness that melted on her tongue was enough to keep her silent as he spoke.

"Let me speak freely and allow you to do the same. We are all quite surprised by the level of Captain Gunneran's betrayal. He has been a great help in eradicating Strygan, but I believe he was unable to resist a deal when it was offered. He did always feel he was meant for greater things than what I provided him." Grimarr's eyes fell to the table, and the lines around his mouth sagged. "I'm deeply saddened by what happened to Benjamina and Mykel."

Aylla blinked away the fresh grief in her eyes. "Did they have family?"

"Benjamina did not—orphaned at five years old. I've already paid a visit to Mykel's parents in the outer fields of Rimmon. They knew the risks, but I hate delivering that kind of news. They will both be given burial rites here, even with no bodies to bury and their names carved into the Infinity Tree." Grimarr sighed.

Aylla distrusted everyone she met, but she had a warm feeling about Grimarr. It was unlikely most men of his status would deliver news of a lesser recruit to a family in person. He didn't seem to want the chaos and war that Narim did. Perhaps there were too many moving parts for him to oversee. He'd said she could speak freely ... did that mean he knew about her newly discovered ability? Whatever that was exactly. She didn't have a clue how sorceress magic worked.

"I'm glad to hear it. They were brave, and they looked out for me even though they knew nothing about me." Aylla drank the tea, and a wash of berries and bark sweetened her taste buds.

"I must confess I do not know what happened in the Stryga's hut, but I'd like to hear your account. I have a special talent for scrying—seeing the future—and something disturbed my vision, but I couldn't see it clearly. I felt a resurgence of something," Grimarr said. He watched her with careful eyes, and Aylla squirmed under their scrutiny. It was like being back in school again, with the teacher expecting the correct answer. He folded his hands in his lap and continued, "I am no Scriver, nor warlock. I am just a soldier, but I have always had a talent for magic. Don't tell any of my men that." He winked.

Aylla laughed. If he was evil, he was doing a good job of covering it up. Something told her he wasn't lying. She gave him a quick explanation of what had happened, including her sudden ability to use magic. Grimarr's brows knit together for a moment, but he did not interrupt.

"Did they get to Jack in time?" she asked at the end. She had to know.

Grimarr gazed at her with an unreadable expression. "They did. He will live, and I'm sure I'll live to regret it." He chuckled.

Aylla was happy he didn't seem inclined to press her about why she was so invested in Jack's wellbeing. Plus, a bigger question nagged at her. He wasn't a mage or a Scriver, but he had some experience.

"I assure you, this is a secure room. There are wards that will not allow anyone else to hear," Grimarr said as if reading her mind. He took a sip from the teacup, which looked absurdly dainty in his large hand.

"Why hasn't the magic surfaced before? Why couldn't I save ... anyone else before?" she asked. If she'd been able to save her mother—how different her life would be. If she'd been able to save Bean or Mykel ...

Grimarr put the cup down and held out a hand for her. "May I? Sometimes, through touch, I can better see into people's pasts and futures."

Aylla nodded and placed her hands in his. They were calloused and rough. Warmth like sunlight after a cloud parted filled her palms. She took a deep, steadying breath as he half closed his eyes. He searched for a few minutes until he sighed.

"Magic does not save us like a miracle—there is usually an exchange—but for those with Malecanta blood, magic is like breathing. It's been buried inside you so long that it's nearly forgotten itself. Your mother didn't want you to know there were sorceresses in your lineage—I saw her cast a protective charm so you wouldn't feel your power. Not until you found a way, a worthy cause, to break its hold over you."

They didn't discuss what that moment had been; they both knew, both saw it in her mind's eye. Aylla's cheeks heated, and she withdrew her hands.

"Your mother concealed her own power as well. She wanted to leave the Malecanta and live normally. As was her wish for you," Grimarr said softly. "The only way to keep the enchantment alive around you was for her to sacrifice herself. Beyond that I cannot discern ... there is quite a bit of unknown."

Aylla didn't need him to continue. Through their connected hands, memories had flooded her mind. Things she couldn't have seen as a child: her mother giving up bits of magic to keep Drace's hands off her daughter, her mother proving to him Aylla had been tested, and her blood was clean. Lavynia had died denying she had Malecanta magic. The last memory of her mother murmuring the spell words as Drace threw dishes across the room, which shattered against the walls, windows, and finally lodged in her mother's neck. Shielding Aylla from his wrath. Making him unable to truly harm her.

"She should have told me." Aylla was torn between the relief of knowing the truth and annoyance that her mother was not here to help her now. No wonder with Lavynia's death, Drace had stopped hitting her. All he'd been able to do was throw dishes and yell.

The sorceress magic was why her uncle had wanted Lavynia so badly he'd killed his own brother. Aylla shuddered. She could only imagine what Drace had intended to do with her mother to get her power. Lock her away in a room and use spell after spell to drain her? Aylla had heard of husbands who forced their gifted wives to give them money, prestige, estates. She'd even heard of legends where Malecanta were imprisoned in iron boxes, their magic-infused blood used without consent. Tears burned her eyes as she blinked. Her mother had weathered so much for her that Aylla couldn't have even known. It hurt like a festering wound cut open again and again.

"Malecanta magic can skip generations, sometimes even two or three. It's not well known. If you wish to be trained in sorcery, we will have to proceed carefully. I haven't been in contact with old Kylen Vassen in years—he may even be dead in his library with seven thousand golden cats." Grimarr rolled his eyes, and Aylla couldn't help the laugh that escaped.

"I assume you have to report me to the king," she said, sobering.

The general looked around the room. "The king is dead."

Aylla gasped. "What?"

"Taken by a curse, we think. Another reason I couldn't personally come find your team or send more backup—although we were also operating on the news from Narim that all of you except Jack were dead." Grimarr grunted. "I will keep your secret as long as you desire, but you know others have witnessed it, and if Narim is alive, he did too."

Aylla blinked back the stinging in her eyes for the hundredth time. She'd never had secrets that mattered to anyone. She didn't know what to do about her gift, but if he could give her time, that was all she could ask.

"Thank you."

The older man cleared his throat, and his hard, steel-blue eyes snapped to hers. "And to the next question I think is coming—Jack is being treated at our medic's facility just north of the base. He needed more care than we can provide here."

Aylla nodded and stuffed her mouth with a sandwich of peanut butter and cherry jam. Relief flooded through her like sunlight breaking through the clouds after a storm. She tried not to let it show but was sure she'd utterly failed. Would he even want to see her? The absurd thing was she wanted to see him. Aylla admitted it to herself, and it felt like relief.

"All right."

Grimarr's eyes twinkled. "I can provide a horse or carriage if you wish to visit."

Aylla gave him a withering stare even as her cheeks burned. "I think I've inconvenienced Jack enough. I'm just glad he'll recover. And I hope you find Narim—he fell twenty or so feet from the flyer when I stabbed him. He would be lucky if you found him before Jack did. If he's still alive."

Grimarr inclined his head with a grim smile. "Indeed."

After a few more hours of both light and heavy conversation, Aylla was free to leave the base and return home. They spoke of Malecanta mostly—even Grimarr wasn't entirely sure where they existed or how many were left. But one thing was certain: at least one was still alive, Kylen Vassen. That was as good a starting place as any.

She thought about borrowing a horse but then decided walking would give her time to think. Her boots were strong, her legs ached to move, and she headed out of the base with a warm cloak. Aylla squared her shoulders and made a deal with herself. She needed to heal and sort herself out before she tried to find Dean and the baby, if he still had her. There would be time for finding what had been lost.

Chapter Thirty-Five

All of us in this life only ever have the illusion of choice.
~ Scryptus, the Scriver Archives,
as recounted by Scriver #5 Jack Serpent, Tome 6

Jack lay his head back in a steaming bath full of lemon essence and salves that helped heal his broken ribs, deep tissue wounds, and mangled wrist. A black eye patch obscured his right eye as it healed from the cut from the Orcyshound's claw. There was nothing to heal his mind, however. He went over and over the events. The walls of the Milytor recovery quarters were sterile and made of blank stones, with small, barred windows that let in weak sunlight. A medic came around the privacy curtain with a notebook and quill in hand.

"Well, a dozen healing elixirs, poultices changed every three hours, unicorn blood transfusion, and you're healing remarkably well. I'm surprised you survived the journey here," he said with a chipper smile.

Jack arched a brow. "Do I want to know how you procured unicorn blood?" The beasts were so shy they earned their mythical status. Hardly anyone had ever seen one, let alone a herd, let alone gotten close enough to draw blood.

The medic stopped scratching with his quill for a moment. "Let's just say you have friends in high places."

Jack left the subject alone. He didn't care where they'd gotten the blood. However, he could now report that it did have healing properties. His body was in far better condition than it had a right to be at this stage.

"Is a woman named Aylla here?"

The medical barracks wasn't just for soldiers. Sometimes families would get treatment as well, so it wasn't impossible that Aylla would have come here. However, he would be glad if she wasn't, because only the most severe soldiers were treated here rather than at Ghoul Base.

"I'm not allowed to give out information, sir—you know that." The medic pushed his glasses up his nose toward his bushy gray brows and surveyed Jack's body as he motioned for him to stand. Jack winced. His ribs protested, and the water ran off him.

"Mmhmm, still broken—" He broke off as Jack stepped toward him and pressed a hard forearm at his throat. The medic glared but wasn't foolish enough to fight back.

"Any news of a woman named Aylla?" Jack dripped water all over the man's brown coat and Milytor badge.

The medic coughed. "Yes, a woman by that name was being treated at Ghoul Base."

"Narim Gunneran as well?" Jack stepped back, and the medic cleared his throat. He grabbed a towel and wound it around his waist.

"Narim was never brought here. I hear they're searching for a body, though."

"Body?" Jack pressed, and the medic spat out the short story of how they believed Narim had been killed in action.

"I heard you fought off Orcyshounds—there were bits of everything all over you when you came in. How the devil did you do that?" The man tapped his quill against his knuckle.

Jack turned his left arm so the medic could see the twisted rune tattoo in the shape of a triangle over a sigil on his middle knuckle.

The medic shook his head. "An underworld ward. You paid a pretty price to get that."

Jack would have shrugged, but it hurt too much. He stood gingerly. He certainly wasn't going to set the medic straight that a sorceress had saved him.

"Where are you going? You need to rest, and General Fox will speak with you tonight."

Jack dried himself and tugged on fresh clothes, black pants, a dark shirt, gray vest, and leather boots. His tattered, spelled coat hung on a peg. Jack slipped it on even though there were slashed holes all over it. The buttons sparked with spells interrupted. Jack would have to fashion it again. He tapped the topmost button, and the coat transformed into a calf-length, light black coat that would blend him in with most any crowd. The holes weren't so noticeable in this form.

He limped into the other room, where a bed and basic desk stood. The door to the rest of the recovery ward was locked, and he sighed.

"I'm authorized to use force, Mr. Serpent. Please don't make me." The medic walked around him to the door and stood his ground. A golden light flickered at his fingertips.

If he hadn't felt like so much shyf, Jack might have tried to get past him. As it was, his entire body ached as if he'd been hit by a Manticore. Jack stumbled to the bed and sat. "Tell Grimarr he has—"

He was cut short as the door opened and Grimarr Fox himself stood in the frame. "Always in a hurry to leave, Jack." He laughed and waved the doctor out.

Grimarr tapped the floor with his silver-headed fox cane and took a seat across from Jack in a wooden chair. He grimaced. "We need to reupholster the chairs in here." He noted Jack's eye patch with an amused smile. "I must say I don't mind the new look."

Jack smiled. He'd glimpsed himself in a mirror, and to say he'd fit in with Muran pirates would have been an understatement.

"Now, time is a matter of concern, and for once I'm glad to see you are eager to get out of here. First, Aylla is well. She returned home, I imagine, but should you want to find her, I leave that to you. Two, the king is dead. Three, Narim is missing, and until otherwise I will presume alive."

"The king is dead?" Jack interrupted. That wasn't good news. It was also quickly followed by an intense relief that Aylla was alive. He wasn't sure what to make of the foreign emotion, but he let it sit in the back of his mind.

Grimarr sighed. "Narim has had no small part in that. The beacons of the covens have been lit, and they remain so despite our efforts to put them out. Hours before this, the king was struck with a black illness and succumbed. The High Stryga might have not succeeded, but she got the Strygan a foothold in what I predict will be war."

"You knew she was a hybrid." Jack leveled him with a glare.

"I heard rumors the Strygan were experimenting with breeding and magic fusions of sirens or hydras. We weren't sure what they were breeding with. I take full responsibility for what I sent you into. I apologize that my information was not exact," Grimarr said with a shake of his head.

"Narim played all of you. And the Volg kept you busy, I heard." Jack would have gone after the Stryga even if he'd known what she was. He gave Grimarr the short version and paused when he got to Alaric. The warlock had been silent of late—whether that was from Jack's constant push to keep him that way or Alaric's own guilt. It was like carrying a disease inside him—always present and feeling disgusting.

"Did you know he successfully performed a resurrection fracture?" Jack accused him with a look. He tapped his head where a piece of Alaric's soul resided and could be used. Jack didn't bother to explain that piece. Grim knew.

"No. I did know he was a warlock, but he turned against his own when they began murdering humans." Grimarr sighed. "He lied to you and betrayed you, but it was for a greater destiny. I know you can't see that right now."

"I can't see it because Lyra is rotting in an asylum!" Jack slammed a fist on the wall, and the resulting pain didn't do anything to numb his anger. "Aylla was nearly killed for this destiny too."

"You do your job too well, Jasyth. I can't apologize for Alaric's choices, but I'm asking you to help me. Help Ocrana."

Jack exhaled, and his ribs throbbed. It was rare he lost his temper, but this time he couldn't resist the rage, the confusing truths converging on him like sharks. What was done was done. The only thing he could do now was make sure it didn't continue.

Grimarr kept an eye on the door, and his hand tightened around the black cane. "Aylla has chosen to go home, but she'll need protection. She told me her secret. I can send soldiers, or I can send you."

Jack realized he was being played, but he didn't mind this time. If Aylla had told Grimarr willingly about her Malecanta power, then she must have developed the same trust in him that Jack had. Jack's trust might waver slightly in the wake of Alaric's betrayal, but Grimarr wasn't Alaric.

"I still want a Scriver in the Milytor. Possibly even a militia of Scrivers, if there are worthy men and women. With Alaric gone, I'd have to rely on you to train them." Jack didn't say anything. "There's a lot of chaos coming our way with the monarchy in graves. Cousins, long lost and real, are emerging from every continent to vie for the throne." Grimarr stood and checked his pocket watch.

Jack scratched his head, and even that motion sent his injuries into a chorus of pain. He chuckled derisively. "You're giving me a choice, unlike Alaric."

"I am. And Alaric has much to answer for, but his love for you I never questioned." Grimarr's eyes softened. "We could begin a new chapter of the Milytor. Perhaps the trials will be reinstated but open to all races. With the monarchy in disarray, Ocrana will be in distress until an heir is found."

Jack left out some of the details about Alaric and his suspicions. There was no need to get Grim on alert until he'd sorted some things out first.

"You know I'll not refuse your request for aid." It was the best Jack could offer at the moment. He couldn't commit to training soldiers or reviving the Scriver Trials. He stood on shaky legs but held himself together as he limped to the door.

"I'll check on Aylla, but she lives with two wolves. I'm sure she's safe for the time being."

"Nonetheless, I'd feel better," Grimarr said with a slight roll of his eyes. "She seemed to be under the impression you wouldn't want to receive her here." He opened the ward door, and weak autumn sunlight warmed Jack's face. The air was so much better here than in the swamp.

Jack tilted his head. Aylla didn't think he'd want to see her? To be sure she was well? Did that also mean she didn't want him to come to her ... and why was he so preoccupied with these thoughts? He groaned inwardly. The truth was that he wanted to make sure she was in good health, so that was where he was going next. Everything else could wait.

"One more thing. I was supposed to give this to you years ago, but you disappeared before I could." Grimarr handed him a small flint. Its casing was etched with sigils, most noticeably a hydra with fang-baring heads elegantly curled. It had been Alaric's flint—it held an eternal flame supposedly taken from Mount Illendium's lava pit. Only one human had ever succeeded in finding a way in, and he stood beside Jack.

"Can this burn hybrids too? That would have been helpful."

"That's your job to find out." Grimarr smirked. "I apologize for forgetting."

They headed toward the small stable. A clash of a hoof on wood resounded. Jack raised a brow.

Grimarr winced. "We found Shertan wandering the market streets eating pie—a habit you taught him, I wager. He has not been happy with his confinement."

Jack grinned.

Chapter Thirty-Six

To get to uncharted territory is an exercise in chaos and usually death. Mode of transportation being the first problem. Most unknown land is beyond the oceans and many ships (both flying and nautical) have disappeared searching for better lands, fertile valleys, new lives. Who knows how many crossroads of magic are covered by the seas?
~ Scryptus, the Scriver Archives,
as recounted by Scriver #5 Jack Serpent, Tome 5

Shertan's smooth gallop took Jack out of the frantic city and into Churk Forest. The people were manic about protection charms and spells. Their fear invaded every corner of the markets. Even the pickpocket gangs were cautious. Whispers of darkness coming and mutant monsters were rampant. The death of the queen and now king was stirring up all sorts of unrest, and cockroaches emerged from the cracks in the continent.

Low, gray clouds sat in the sky. The smell of snow carried on the wind. The leaves weren't yet off the trees, but snow wasn't uncommon this time of year. Jack inhaled the crisp cold, and on the exhale it was white. He slowed Shertan and hopped off. The saddle, blanket, and bridle, he stowed in his spelled pack. He tapped the horse on the hindquarters. Shertan turned his head to gaze at him.

"I swear I'll be back sooner than last time," he said. Shertan snorted, and Jack was inclined to agree. He should leave Aylla to her own path. He had already gotten her into a lifetime's amount of trouble. The horse trotted off to graze on the last of the grass before it froze.

Jack picked up Aylla's trail by tracking the wolves. He heightened his sense of smell by drinking a potion, and though she had covered her tracks well, he did find her after a few hours. The modest cabin sat peacefully by a small stream with the water wheel churning. Lanterns in the window blazed light into the darkening forest.

He wavered for a moment. Something foreign stirred in his chest and caused his stomach to tighten. He should just circle the cabin until he saw she was fine. There was no need for conversation. No need to return the little rocking horse or see how their connection felt when they weren't in imminent danger. Perhaps their bond had only existed due to circumstance.

"You can't sneak up on a woman who lives with wolves," Aylla said from behind him.

Jack turned with a guilty smile. He held his hands up as Ash and Hugo ran over to sniff and lick him.

"You made it out." He looked her over. In the twilight, it appeared as though she was all right—no obvious bruises on her face or neck. She walked stealthily enough despite the injury to her right calf. He hadn't seen smashed foliage or broken brush. Her tanned skin and dark hair glowed in the twilight. She wore a long-sleeved, dark purple dress with a wide belt that held several knives. The darker black skirt had a slit that went up to her thigh to let her walk freely. A light coat, knee length and trimmed in fur, kept her warm.

"I like the eye patch." She grinned.

Jack laughed roguishly. "I'm ready to join the Muran pirates. But I must confess, sailing ships appeal to me about as much as flying ones."

Aylla chuckled. "Agreed. I like solid earth under my feet."

She brushed a strand of hair behind her ear. She adjusted the string of bush fowl over her shoulder, and the wolves licked their lips.

"Thanks for the knife." She reached for it on her side holster, but Jack motioned for her to keep it. The meaning hung in the air between them like a hungry plains cat, waiting.

"The knife was the only thing I could think of to give you that would be useful." He laughed with a little shrug. "I was running out of ideas." He didn't like to admit that but saying it out loud made the tension dissipate.

Aylla laughed. "Is Narim alive?" she asked.

"No body found yet." Jack shrugged. "But I'm betting he's waiting, healing. He'd be a fool to come within ten miles of Asnor."

Aylla nodded and tucked a strand of hair behind her ear. It was so familiar, and yet Jack felt like he was intruding. He cleared his throat to make some excuse for leaving.

"Can I interest you in dinner?" She headed back down the slight hill to the cabin. Jack took her invitation without pause and walked with her. He admired her handiwork in crafting the cabin. The structure was solid, the door had a big lock, and he sensed wards.

"These are good," he said as they passed by an almost invisible ring of stones with an offering of mushrooms and blood. It was an alert ward—she'd know if someone came close to the cabin.

"I learned from the best." Aylla smiled at him, and a once dormant longing for company other than Alaric or his own thoughts overcame him. She must have seen it on his face, because she started plucking feathers perhaps a little harder than necessary.

Jack held out a hand to help, but she brushed it off. Alaric was good at social situations, and he'd had more than his fair share of ladies. The thought of his mentor burned him. On the journey to Aylla, Jack had blocked the man's voice completely from his mind with painstaking rune work. Until he decided what to do with his mentor, he wanted him silent.

"I had Dean's map, but one day it was simply blank. Spelled, as I imagine he would have done—have you heard from him?" she asked.

"It's on my list. His maps don't last forever, you're correct—just in case it should fall into the wrong hands." Jack hesitated but plunged on before the words left. "You're welcome to come with me."

Aylla nodded and dusted her hands of feathers. "Thank you." She got out a large knife from the leather pouch that held a variety of sharp cutting knives.

Normally, he'd be on alert with anyone wielding a knife in his presence, but with Aylla he settled for comfortable awareness. If she turned it on him, he had a dozen ways to disarm her, but more to the point was he couldn't imagine any scenario where she would use it against him. Instead, the awkwardness filled his head with things he wanted to say but had a hard time speaking.

"I ... I'm glad you're safe. Grimarr certainly is interested in keeping you that way."

"Then why didn't he just send a few soldiers?" Aylla arched a brow and cut the head off the fowl.

"You know why," he said in a low voice. There was no sense in dragging it out. Lyra was lost to him, and he wasn't going to allow Alaric or anyone else to curse this relationship. Or whatever it was.

"I don't want to complicate your life any more than you want," Aylla said, but her eyes sparkled.

Jack swallowed. "I think it's me who's complicating your life. I told Narim your secret because I knew he'd save you. I didn't think I'd see you again."

"Neither did I. I wasn't sure what poison he gave you ..." Aylla bit her lip and turned away. "I'm glad the Milytor heard the transmitter you put in his pocket."

"I heard you over the comms," Jack said with a dip of his head in thanks.

Aylla smiled at the compliment. She put the birds on spits, sprinkled them with salt, and they sizzled in the hearth over the fire. She turned to him with an open gaze.

"Maybe we're even then. And if it weren't for you, I'd never know my mother had put a charm on my gift to suppress it. She never mentioned anything about sorceress magic. Grimarr said she was trying to protect me from Malecanta magic." She blew out a breath. "I just have to deal with it now. I can't summon it—barely feel it, really."

Jack's interest flared. He'd never had the chance to ask the Malecanta all the questions he had. He quelled his natural curiosity out of respect.

"I can see you want to study me," Aylla teased and sat on a large chair with pillows. She motioned for him to sit.

Jack couldn't remember the last time he'd been so comfortable in someone else's home. Ash and Hugo lay on stuffed beds, their yellow eyes alert and relaxed. If they noticed Aylla was different, they didn't act like it.

"I want to more than study you," he said, and she stumbled a step toward the jars of bourbon. Jack didn't try to hide his smirk. Aylla's brow rose, but she didn't say anything, just motioned for him to sit again.

He took a seat as the birds cooked, and Aylla poured him a Cafferian bourbon. He sniffed it and sighed.

"How did you know?" He sipped the drink, and the smooth, rich flavor soothed his senses even more.

"I wish I could take the credit, but I love it too, and I got a jug on my way out of Asnor," Aylla said with a chuckle.

Jack shifted as the swords on his back made it difficult to sit. He unstrapped them and the pistol holsters. The wolves pricked their ears at the thump. His spelled coat, now fixed, was a short hunting type of armor, dark with brown patches on the arms and pockets.

"Planning on staying a while?" Aylla asked with a playful smile.

Jack tilted his head at her. "Do you want me to?" He put the question to her in jest, but he needed to hear her answer.

Aylla stood and bent over him in the chair. Her hair brushed his hands and sent whorls of heat up his arms.

"If there's one thing I've learned from surviving this, it's that I don't want to live in fear. I don't want to live alone, but mistrust has kept me alive," she said, and the ties of her blouse dangled. Jack kept his eyes on hers, but he wanted to be distracted now. He wanted to feel her skin and the weight of someone who wasn't trying to kill him.

"You're not going to turn me into a toad if I don't give you the answer you want, right?" Jack asked with a grin and slid an arm around her waist. He tugged her on top of him, and her lips stopped inches from his.

Aylla laughed and traced a finger down his jaw, over the bruises and cuts. "I'd say you're safe for now."

Jack captured her mouth with his, and everything ceased to exist. He chased the lightning heat that cascaded down his chest. The softness of her lips teased him until every sense spiraled to the edge of control. He grabbed her hair to pull her in closer and grind into his hips. His ribs protested, and his injuries screamed. He shifted and groaned as she pulled back in alarm.

"I'm fine," he said, but she smacked him lightly on the arm and he winced.

"It's better that I don't let our dinner burn anyway. Eventually we'll have dessert, no?" She gazed at him in a way no one ever had. Not even Lyra. Lyra had been a woman trying to prove she was just as good as men, and she was, but that chip on her shoulder had never let Jack get too close. Aylla might have her baggage, but he could tell her heart wanted something fiercely passionate. The kind of love her mother had been deprived of too soon. Jack didn't know if he was worthy of the chance she was taking on him.

"You lost this. I didn't know if you wanted it back." He pulled out the charred carving of the rocking horse.

Aylla's eyes lit up as she took it. "Of course I do. I didn't want to tell you I'd lost it." She reached to place it on top of the fireplace mantel. Her tunic rode up over her waist, and the skintight pants molded to her backside.

Jack took out the only vial of healing elixir he had. It wouldn't heal everything, but it would numb the pain. It was for emergencies. Jack figured this counted as one.

Chapter Thirty-Seven

It is unusual for Malecanta to possess all three traits of magic; elemental, transfiguration, ancient magics. Most Malecanta perfect one.
~ Scryptus, the Scriver Archives,
as recounted by Scriver #5 Jack Serpent, Tome 11

Aylla listened as Jack explained Dean's stone locator trick. She couldn't help the smile that crested her face. Jack kept pace but scanned their surroundings to be sure they weren't being followed.

They were back in Asnor but on the eastern Thura River side of the city, where the trade ships docked. He wore simple black, no armor, the coat spelled to blend in as a long, light duster. Twin swords crossed his back, and a pack strap slung across his chest. He'd shaved to stubble, and the eye patch was gone.

She'd never thought he'd stay. She'd expected to wake up and find a note or another carving. But Jack had lingered for three days with her in the forest. They'd hunted together—she'd taught him wolf behavior, and he'd taught her basic spells. She still couldn't summon the Malecanta magic easily, but it did come. Jack assured her that with practice, she could learn to use it—not control it entirely but utilize it. Magic seemed to like it if the host was willing to work with it, not demand from it.

And they'd spent a lot of evenings naked by a fire. Aylla bent her head at the thought so he couldn't read her face. She'd only been with one other man, and that was a distant, unsatisfying memory. She kept reminding herself that the past few days were no guarantee they could remain together—their paths were going to take them on separate courses.

Jack had let her in more than she'd expected. He told of his past with Lyra and Alaric. From his tone and manner, Aylla only felt sorry for the other woman. She'd tried so hard to prove herself that Alaric had thought her a threat to Jack's destiny. It was apparent that Jack carried that guilt, but the love they'd shared was a thing of the past.

They treated those three days like they might be their last. Aylla had to find any Malecanta left, and she understood Jack needed to keep fighting, to find out what the Strygan were up to. Her chest tightened at the truth and what it might mean to leave him. To never see him again. Would she only hear of his untimely death sometime in a tavern? Or would Grimarr himself deliver the news? Jack had said as much—he accepted that his path was just another road to the underworld. But he was determined to take as many dark creatures as he could with him.

"Do we need to find a tavern?" Jack asked as he came up beside her and kissed her neck. Aylla groaned into him. His hands ran up her arms and cupped her face.

"We need to focus. We don't have time for a tavern," she said with a swat at his hands after his kiss. "Don't your lot crave being alone?"

Jack rolled his eyes. "While I've been a loner for a decade, I do enjoy companionship some of the time. You happen to be in the right place, at the right time." He dodged her slow punch.

They walked down the ever-changing streets. The market vendors liked to make things difficult if they didn't get their way.

"Dean likes to hide in plain sight," Jack said with a grunt. He led them down several alleys and to a nondescript building with a worn, faded sign: *The Wraith*. It smelled like an old apothecary shop. The windows were adorned with charms and dried herbs, and a few people milled around inside.

Jack gestured to a built-in ladder on the side of the building.

"Is he living on the roof?" Aylla asked as she climbed. The building's roof was a flat structure with several chimneys protruding out and, oddly enough, five different doors. She stood with her hands on her hips.

"Tell me which door. Use your magic," Jack said, as if that were an answer. He folded the map and stuck it in the pack.

Aylla took a breath to calm her nerves. The Malecanta power flooded through like mist, ever changing and light. It didn't listen to her most of the time. She asked it to search, to feel for Dean. Was he close?

She gasped when the magic warmed to her, and the third door to her right glowed faintly with an X. Aylla pointed.

Jack nodded. He tapped irregularly on the door and waited. A small hole opened, and a black device poked out. Jack leered at it, and the device popped back down. The door opened with a bang. He gestured for her to go first, and Aylla stifled a grin.

"Dean?" She climbed down into a room that was a lot more spacious than she'd expected. The muted sounds of the apothecary shop were still there, but the room was not connected to the shop.

"About time, you two. I was going to have to actually search, and I really don't have the time." Dean's voice floated to her from just ahead. "I couldn't get within fifty paces of the barracks."

Aylla strode forward into the light of two hearths and lanterns blazing in the room's corners. A kitchen bubbled and hissed with cooking food, a long table was laid out with plates and silverware, and a baby cooed in a bassinet by the fire. Aylla gasped and ran the last few steps to the baby girl.

She glanced at Dean with a wide smile. "You saved her."

Dean ran a hand covered in runed rings through his ebony-colored hair and shrugged. He wore a muted plaid shirt with black pants and boots. His brown eyes sparkled as he greeted them both. Aylla hugged him after she'd made a few faces at the baby. Onions and pine wafted around her.

"Jack," Dean said, with a knowing smile.

Jack just grunted. "Congratulations?"

The man pretended to be insulted. "She's orphaned. Who knows who her parents were, but it's safe to assume they're dead. I asked around. More families than I care to count have lost children to Strygan. Sometimes whole lineages just vanished." He stirred a steaming pot.

"A problem we can't ignore any longer," Jack said.

Aylla went to the bassinet, and her heart swelled. She might never have children of her own, but she was incredibly happy that Dean had kept her.

"Did you name her?" she asked. Aylla knew they had to ask Dean for his help eventually, but she wanted to savor the moment while it lasted.

"Cahira. I don't know what it means, but it was my mother's name—that's all I remember of her," Dean said with a small smile. "I'm no good naming things, which is why I have no pets."

"Well, you've got more than a pet now," Aylla said, and picked the baby up. Cahira squirmed in her arms for a moment before grabbing her hair and ties of her shirt.

"I know it's mad that I kept her, but without me she'll just end up in an orphanage. Not that there's anything wrong with that," Dean said with a side-eye at Jack.

He grunted. "They build character." The sarcasm wasn't lost on any of them.

"I get the feeling she's not the only reason you're here." Dean took a kettle off the hearth and held it up in question. Tea? Aylla nodded, and Jack shook his head. Dean got out mismatched cups from the cupboard and poured the water into an herb-filled strainer that would steep it in a large pot.

Jack pulled Kyadem from his pack, and Dean groaned. He set the cups and pot in front of Aylla and rushed to the weapon. The chains were charred, the silver dull.

"That bloody Stryga was that powerful?" Dean ran his hands over the injured weapon. It wasn't completely broken, according to Jack. He'd told her how Kya whispered to him since the weapon was made partly of his own bone, blood, and tears.

Aylla hadn't pried into that story, sensing a lot of anger in it. She recalled Jack telling her, mildly, of the "training" he'd gone through with Alaric. The months of sickness from an unknown bite or poison just to see if he'd survive the experimental medicines and potions used. Aylla wasn't sure she would have survived what he had and still retained any sanity. That was before the trials had even begun.

"She had a good fight," Jack said with a sigh. "The High Stryga was a hybrid—mutated with siren blood. I'll have to modify her after you fix her."

Dean's eyes widened. "I'd heard rumors. There haven't been hybrids in a century. Too risky, too unstable." He took Kyadem to a makeshift worktable. Black cases lined the back, and he unlocked one, then placed the weapon into a velvet-lined box. The lid shut and locked. "Someone's been playing god. Isn't it your job to find out who?"

Jack shrugged. "Better me than some poor kid in a forest, eh."

"You're even luckier than I thought you could be," Dean said, and shook his head. "How the Drannit did you survive that?"

Jack gave him the quick version, and Dean was laughing by the end of it.

"If I'm ever at Hecaya's doorstep, I want you with me. I bet you could convince a dozen demons to kiss our asses."

Jack pursed his lips at the mention of the underworld. "I doubt that. I've spoken with demons, and I find them to be deplorable fucks." He glanced around the open room. "We also came for weapons—and your skills. Grimarr has convinced me a branch of the Milytor could be trained to do more than burn villages and Strygan."

Dean gazed at him expectantly. Aylla knew it was hard for Jack to say he was going along with someone else's plan for now. He wasn't sure he could or should lead soldiers in the training of hunting monsters, but he'd agreed to try at some point, if the time was right.

"A legion led by a Scriver would be formidable," Aylla said. She didn't want him to diminish his skill set.

"Ah, that would be ... interesting," Dean said with a nod at Jack. "You want to train stinky, unruly, defiant young men?"

"No." Jack rolled his eyes. "But there's war coming, and we'll need all of them. Grim's asked for my help. But I need to make a stop at Karnuhym first."

Dean tilted his head and shrugged in understanding. "Tell Scryptus to give my compass back."

Jack grinned. Memories of Dean and Scryptus verbally sparring were always amusing.

"You think the Strygan will retaliate hard and the Volg will certainly help. Does explain the timing of the beacons … started up a week ago and only now are dying out. Signaling something." Dean stirred his stew and tasted it. He took it off the fire and set it on a metal trivet on the table. Aylla poured tea and inhaled earthy aromas of vanilla, lavender, Churk leaf, and honey.

"No one's been able to get within a hundred yards of the beacons to inspect them, so I hear," Jack said, and a muscle in his jaw clenched.

"Just another thing in a long list for you to handle." Dean shook his head. "Don't they know you're just one man?"

Jack grunted.

Aylla sniffed the air appreciatively as the scent of baked pastry started to permeate. It was similar to the one at the Brown Shepherd, with hunks of beef, onions, potatoes, and a blend of spices that smelled like comfort.

"Do you have pie in that oven?" Jack asked, and the subject change made them all chuckle.

Dean tossed him an apple. "You want pie, you can start peeling."

Aylla covered a smile with a hand. "I didn't know you were so domestic, Dean." She caught the apple he tossed her as well. She picked up a small knife and started peeling.

The other man half bowed and spread his hands. "A skill much overlooked, my lady. A man who can cook wins just about any battle—on the field or with a woman." He grinned.

Aylla couldn't argue. She hadn't felt this comfortable in a long time. She might have to figure out what to do with the Malecanta blood running through her veins, but that could wait a day. If longing was like wings, hers would be stretched so far out she'd be carried off by them. She wanted to stay with Jack. She wanted him to come with her—and had almost tried to entice him by saying he could study her magic. If things went wrong, and with her luck they would, there was no one she'd rather have by her side to help.

That's a new one—me, wanting help, she thought with a grimace. She'd come to realize however that being with someone who could help wasn't a blight on her strength. It was rare to find people who would stick around that long.

For the next hours, though, there was good company—and pie. Aylla insisted Dean teach her how to bake one, and she enjoyed the quiet moment while it lasted.

Chapter Thirty-Eight

Why are crossroads portals for magic? Sounds like a bad joke. From my understanding in speaking with "roadies," it's because there are lines of old magic, perhaps even Ardis-infused rock, under mountains, buried deep in the earth. When they meet, their magic is enhanced tenfold. We don't know how far these lines reach or where all of them are. The ones we do know of have inexplicable happenings: sometimes a child who wasn't thought gifted is wakened when taken to a crossroad.
~ *Scryptus, the Scriver Archives,*
as recounted by Scriver #5 Jack Serpent, Tome 12

Jack stood outside Parathorn asylum, and his breath misted in the cold air. A light frost covered the dying grass and golden leaves on the ground.

The asylum's white stone walls and black iron fences were meant to keep the residents in more than anyone else out.

He remained under the giant Jarka trees with their skeletal branches. The trunks were thick enough to hide grown men, so he had no fear of being spotted. Shertan grazed behind him. Jack's left ribs still ached, as did his side from where Franziska Strain's claw had ruined the rune and glyph tattoos. He wouldn't be able to repair them until the skin healed.

A low, familiar voice spoke in his head. *If I may speak.*

Jack's lip curled at the unwanted intrusion, but he'd untapped the rune to let his mentor speak. He needed some answers, and the only way to get them was to talk with Alaric. All those "hypothetical" conversations had been real. At least he wasn't mad enough to belong in the same asylum, then.

"The first thing I'm doing after this is finding a way to get you out of my head permanently," Jack said. He kept an eye on the building. A few nurses walked the grounds. Alaric would understand that Jack didn't mean resurrecting him like his mentor wanted. There were other ways to get an unwanted spirit out of one's body or mind.

I don't deserve your forgiveness, so I won't ask. I thought I had a way to reverse the hex on her. I will do everything in my power to find a cure should you revive me.

"You won't do this to anyone else again." Jack knew he could close his mind and shut his mentor out. But it required more willpower than he had at the moment. All those years of training and learning were for what now? Had they even been real? Or was he just a vessel to keep Alaric alive? The piece of his mentor's soul lodged in his brain, so that one day Alaric could be resurrected.

Don't you want to know why? Why I interfered with Lyra, why I placed a piece of my soul inside your head?

"Fine," Jack said grudgingly. He didn't want to encourage this conversation. But there was so much history between them, it was hard to ignore.

You are unusual ... for a human. Magic has always been drawn to you. You learn at an incredible rate, and you can spell cast like a warlock.

"If you say I have warlock in my blood or we're related in any way, I will shut you out." Jack's jaw clenched. He liked using magic, and he was good at it. That didn't mean he wanted to be identified by it.

A chuckle, so familiar and reminiscent of better days that it cut. *No, nothing like that. You're something much greater. A conduit. Ancients had a word for it ... Reaper, if I recall. You can channel magic that most humans cannot. You can hold souls within you—as I forced mine. Recall the Stryga's magic in the cabin that you pulled from the air?*

Jack grunted. "I have no interest in holding any more souls than the one I have." He changed the subject before Alaric could become that steady, comforting presence again.

You can bring me back.

Jack stilled, and his skin prickled.

"Why would I do that?"

I think the real question is how. I know how your mind works. Alaric's knowing, chiding tone floated through the air. *You're curious. You want to know what a resurrection fracture looks like and how it works. I left a piece of my soul inside your head attached to the gift I gave—so the spell didn't recognize it as a resurrection fracture. The Strygan wouldn't figure it out even if they got into your head, nor my own kin—which she tried—and thanks to you, she's going to keep her secrets in Orcys.*

"You're a tricky bastard. I would've agreed had you just informed me." Jack shook his head. Or he would have before he'd realized Alaric's true sins.

I didn't tell you so no one could compel it from you. You can't give up what you don't know.

Jack shrugged. He supposed that was a good point.

"You suspected what I was because ..."

Alaric sighed. *The night your parents were murdered, and you escaped their warded closet. That wasn't supposed to happen ... I lost you, and luckily the slavers didn't know what they had. My scryer foresaw nine conduits or Reapers born within a blood moon. He's not often wrong, and I happened upon you. But finding you only proved what I knew. You have the uncanny ability to survive in a world of chaotic magic. It's been untamed since the Malecanta have stopped enforcing boundaries upon it.*

Jack didn't have any words left. The Scriver sigil tingled on his left bicep. He would figure it all out later. Whatever he was or was not didn't change the fact that there was war brewing. There were covens of Strygan convening, and it could mean the end of peace among the continents, the balance of magic, and free human life perhaps. And the fact that this path would take him far from Aylla—he wanted no part of preparing for battles or politics in the palace. She'd never asked him to change course or go with her to find Kylen Vassen, but he'd wanted her to. He'd almost offered, but it would be to everyone's detriment. Should war begin while she was still studying how to use her power, they'd likely be dead anyway. Jack needed to get to the root of the darkness. Someone like her could tip the balance, should she learn how to control magic like the ancient sorceresses.

If you bring me back, I can help you as I swore to. I will leave you until you wish to speak to me. The truth is, you're ready to surpass me. You're a better man than I ever could be.

Jack didn't think the former was true. He'd only ever read about resurrection fractures, never come close to attempting one. Alaric was lucky he hadn't been damned forever or lost in a corner of Jack's mind. Bringing someone like his mentor back was a risk.

He was distracted from speaking when residents of the asylum trickled out for their morning walk.

His breath stilled as Lyra appeared. Her long, light brown hair was braided, she wore a blue hat to match her dress, and her hands were kept warm in black gloves. She didn't appear malnourished, but her movements were jerky, and her eyes scanned every shadow, every dark corner. They were not the brown eyes he knew. Even at a distance, he could tell she was still damaged from the hex. Dean had not lied.

Lyra shied away from the others when they tried to speak to her. A nurse had to guide her down the path to follow the group. Jack took a step forward and then stopped. There was no use in trying to speak with Lyra. Her mind was gone. If he could find a cure, he would. Perhaps he'd have to release Alaric to do that. His mentor still knew things Jack couldn't even dream of.

A flare of light issued in the distance, high on a mountainside. Dark clouds gathered over it, swirling like an angry flock of vultures. Purple smoke rose from the beacon's fire. Jack hurried back to Shertan and swung up.

Was this Strygan doing or a monster long asleep now stirring? A deep, thunderous roar split the air, and the patients of the asylum screamed. The nurses ushered them all back inside. Jack had placed new wards around the asylum. It was the only thing he could do for Lyra until he could move her. An alarm clanged, and two horses and riders burst from the stables—messengers for help and to alert nearby villages of the danger.

The roar sounded again, and the mountain trembled. For the first time in a long time, Jack's inclination wasn't to study the monster but to get back to Aylla and the wolves—fuck their plan to go separate ways. The

Strygan would come for her soon. But he knew he had a target on his back as well. *All I can do is find a way to stop this first so she can focus on using her power.* Who knew how far the rumor went that there was a young sorceress again in Elgar?

"Tell me how to resurrect you, Alaric," Jack said, his tone laced with a threat that Alaric couldn't miss. Jack wasn't sure, if he resurrected his mentor, whether he'd kill him before the older warlock could be useful. He'd try not to.

Jack nudged Shertan into a gallop back to Asnor. He'd be damned if he wouldn't kiss Aylla one more time. The saddlebags rocked on either side. They'd agreed only hours ago that it was goodbye. Aylla had proven herself resilient, independent, but also willing to sacrifice for someone else. Jack refused to die without one more touch of her hand, one more rune he could draw on her smooth skin to protect her, one more embrace that erased the pain for just a little while.

Alaric's presence in his mind leaped at the words like a lit candle.

Go to the pools of Anasta in the northern most mountains of Elgar. Go slowly, form a plan, gather your weapons. We don't know what has been woken or remade.

Alaric was right about one thing, and that was to slow down. Jack glanced at the north mountain as it shivered. Nothing came out, but something was preparing inside. He still had time. Grimarr's brilliant plan to have him train soldiers would have to wait until he could bring Alaric back. Despite the hate boiling in his gut, they needed all the help they could get.

Jack glanced back one more time as a low roar rumbled up from the ground, making the forest shake and resounding over the mountain. This time he didn't have a death wish; the will to live was even stronger. He'd never had much to live for but all that changed with a soft smile and a listening ear. The chill wind whipped at his long black coat and through his hair. A flurry of snow swirled in the air. Magic called to magic. To him. He was not an iron cog in the wheel of destiny but the hammer that broke and reforged it. Alaric's thought echoed in his head.

This is what you were meant to do.

Acknowledgements

First, for you, the reader. Without readers there would be no reason to tell stories. I hope this book gives you the escape you need.

A writer is never an island, and I have my amazing, hardworking publisher, editors, and team of marketing experts to thank for giving me a chance: Alex, Tina, Natasha (Cover Desig), Abby. Tina and Alex, as always, thank you for believing in my books.

I would not get far without my critique partners and beta readers. You all make the writing process slightly less painful and more hopeful even as we nitpick. Andrea Benson, Mark LaMonica (KC Aegis), Kyle Robertson (thank you for reading multiple versions of the books with enthusiasm and helpful insights), Randi Garavaglia.

Of course, it's never a good idea to be alone with my thoughts too long, so thank you to my friends who keep me company even during the busiest times and share in the wonderful chaos of life: Randi Garavaglia, Andrea Benson, Rachel Acevedo Kedas, Sara Ferguson, Nicole Regan, Beth Valdez, Cathrine Hudon, Grace Prince, Joy Thomas, Kimberly Tanquary, Donna Trinko (and Ebony and Boone).

To fellow author Annie Cathryn for helping promote me and sharing all her writing/industry wisdom! We may not write in the same genres, but we share a creative spirit and support system that is invaluable on this career path.

I would be remiss in not thanking author Tom Wood as well for always being so open to talking about writing and the industry (and getting our nerdy memes). Your encouragement to "just write" came at just the right time.

To the booktok and cosplay community, thank you for supporting me and being ARC readers! I have made some very great friends over the past few years and the love I feel is extraordinary. Cosplayers make book characters into reality and that's something I never thought I'd experience. Thank you, Steph, for cosplaying Aylla down to the last detail! Your creativity and friendship as a fellow writer (Elemental Fae shout out) and cosplayer has meant a lot to me.

Particular gratitude goes out to Randi Garavaglia for making gorgeous jewelry for me and bringing the characters of The Scriver Archives to life. Some soul sisters you don't meet until the time is right. You're the Diana to my Anne!

Thank you Hannah Smith who introduced me to Chris who made a great map of the Scriver world. Thank you Chris for all the meetings and your patience as we changed mountains, rivers, and the names of towns.

Special shout out to Dan at Barnes and Noble as well for always being kind to me and open to doing events at the store! I appreciate the enthusiasm and welcome each time.

So much gratitude and love to my my family; my parents Scott and Lynda for wrangling the kids and being such great role models not only for them but me. My kids, who inspire and keep me young (and also age me so much faster somehow).

And last, but not ever least, to my husband who supported me from the beginning of the journey into Mordor and back again. The concept of Jack Serpent was your idea first and I am lucky to have a partner to adventure with, even if that means not being able to wear Liverpool jerseys to fantasy balls. Cheers to many more!

A SPECIAL THANK YOU

Thank you to Lindsay Dills who has composed music for Jack Serpent in a wonderful collaboration. You've brought to life a component of the story that words cannot describe. I'm immeasurably grateful and proud of our collaboration! You can find her music on Spotify and check out her website lindsaydills.com

Thank you to Ash, The Siren Witch, who also composed amazing music for this book! Your songs are truly inspiring and I'm so glad we became fast friends! You can find her music here: TikTok and Insta @Thesirenwitch, Spotify, and thesirenwitch.bandzoogle.com

Thank you to Heather Cavill for being so open to a collaboration for an unknown author and enlisting Charles' help as well. You're not only a business collaborator but a friend. You've brought scents to life for the Scriver Archives series, and I am forever grateful for all the samples we went through, the zoom meetings, and creation of a line of bookish candles! We hope you enjoy reading with these themed candles that capture the world of Jack Serpent, book one. You can order your own on the Cavill and Wicks website (Cavillandwicks.com) under Jack Serpent candles, or check links in my socials (@eafieldwrites on Instagram and Tiktok).

About the Author

Emily lives in the Midwest where she struggles to escape the humid summers every year. While there are no official credentials to list for why she's an expert on fantasy worlds, she has gotten lost in so many, she assumes that experience will speak for itself. She is the author of *IRL: In Real Life* in which cursed zombies are hunted by an ancient archeological society and two gamers, and a short story in the *Through the Aftermath* anthology. She has been previously published, under pen name Anne Bourne, with the fantasy romance *Blue Moon*, and her next novel, *Moon Dark*, is releasing in March 2026. She loves to blend genres with science fiction and fantasy being her favorites. She's an avid cosplayer, animal rescuer, horseback rider, reader, and baker. *Jack Serpent* is her third novel, the first of *The Scriver Archives* series.